UNKINDNESS OF RAVENS

E.D. Degenfelder

Unkindness of Ravens

Copyright © 2016 E.D. Degenfelder

All rights reserved.

ISBN-13: 978-0-9972422-2-5

To John, Levi and Kayla
All My Love

Unkindness of Ravens

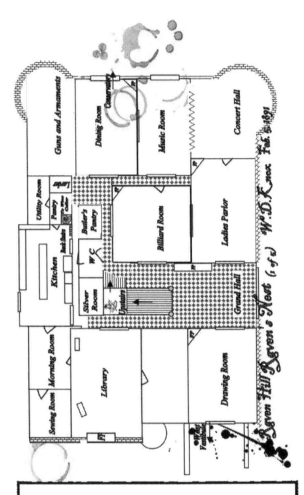

Floor Plan. Ground level sketch by William Knox. Found in the library by Clay and Eleanor Abbott during restoration of Raven's Nest, April, 1990.

Unkindness of Ravens

CHAPTER ONE
18 months ago

California's Highway 17 is a dangerous road. Hilly, curvy, and often windy and foggy. Located in the Santa Cruz mountains, it's the link between Santa Cruz and Los Gatos, continuing on to San Jose. It was the road that took Clayton Abbott to his death, late on a Saturday night in October. As he drove, foggy, wet night air blew against his face from the open window. It helped sober him as he pushed his small car up the hill from Santa Cruz.

Clay was tired. He had put in a full working day, then spent the last several hours in Santa Cruz at an award banquet in his honor. The Chamber of Commerce fêted their company for investing in their community with multi-millions of dollars in new construction. Construction naturally meant jobs. Nothing like a few hundred new jobs for someone to become suddenly popular. The projects, a huge shopping plaza, and a couple of large condominiums, were another brick in the building of an empire. The town loved him, Clay thought with self-satisfaction. He belched and peered out the windshield trying to make out the edge of the road. Fog didn't bother him, but it was dark and the marine layer so dense, he could barely see the fog line. It'll clear up when I get on the other side of the hill. Highway 17 is always a bitch.

Clayton Henry Abbott, a true self made man, thought of himself like Rockefeller, Carnegie, the Morgans or Vanderbilts. Like all the industrialists of the nineteenth century. No one handed them their start and no one handed him his. He built his business with hard work and calculated risks. He started his company with his savings of ten thousand dollars. When he and Eleanor married, she became his equal partner, with an investment of her ten thousand, nearly forty years ago. God, what a fortune that had seemed in 1971.

By the time they had been in business for five years the company's value stood at over twelve million. Ten years later they met James Edgerton. Edgerton had the money to allow the business to leap to the big time. What a fucking disaster *that* was. Clay shook his head. There had to be a way to get him out. I'll just have to get creative. Ellie's smart and resourceful, together we'll come up with something. Too bad she didn't come tonight. Not surprising though, after so many years she can't stand this kind of schmoozing and politicking. She was a great business woman and lent many hours to her charities and other philanthropic ventures. But Eleanor was completely uninterested in anything she viewed as a waste of her time.

Clay shifted, marveling at the great response of his sleek little car. He'd found the 1960 Austin Healey 3000 several years ago in Santa Maria, California, of all places. Some guy had bought it off the sales lot in England in 1960, and had it shipped to California for his wife. The wife ended up unable to drive. It had been garaged, un-driven for the intervening forty-five years. Twenty-four thousand original miles. Rare Florida Green over Ivory, in perfect condition. Clay fell head over heels.

He and the guy had a couple dozen beers while they bargained and dickered. In the end Clay agreed on forty-two thousand, cash. Although he rarely drove it, when he did, he felt like a fourteen year old kid on a joy ride. He loved this car. It spoke of class and sophistication, the elusive things he'd struggled to achieve all his life. Lately he had begun to wonder if the things he had were truly important. He adored his daughter. Madeline was his angel. He loved his home, his wines and his art collection, and he loved Eleanor. But what did it all mean? If Clay were to be honest with himself, the only thing that still excited him was work. It's always been about work…and winning.

A sharp curve appeared suddenly out of the fog. He jerked the wheel, over correcting. The small car swerved violently then swerved back. Clay regained control and belched loudly again, this time re-sampling both the Cristal champagne and the shrimp hors d'oeuvres he had earlier. Jesus! He grimaced and loosened his belt and undid the button on his slacks. Suddenly he felt claustrophobic, like every piece of clothing he had on was too small, too tight. Oh thank God, finally, the summit of Highway 17. He glimpsed the crest elevation sign in a split second. It was there and in a blink, vanished into the fog. Shifting the Healey as he headed down the hill, he started thinking how good his bed was going to feel. When he realized what he was thinking, he laughed out loud. Jesus Christ, I *am* getting old, it's only midnight. Only a few years ago I would still be raring to go, out at a club till two. He sighed. I'm closing in on seventy. When I met Ellie I was only twenty-eight. Twenty-eight! At that age, I couldn't imagine being fifty much less seventy.

At the next curve he braked to slow. The brakes were a bit mushy. Thinking they were wet, he released it and braked again but they were, if anything, worse. Clay tried once more but this time there was nothing, not even mush, and his foot took the pedal all the way to the floor. Idiotically, the phrase *pedal to the metal,* jumped into his mind. Clay pumped the brake frantically again and again. Nothing. A tidal wave of adrenaline poured through his body as the Healey gained speed. At once, he was stone cold sober.

The next few seconds for Clay were just that—mere seconds. But in the surreal, frightening experience, they seemed to last hours. Nausea erupted suddenly in his stomach and sweat poured from his body. He jerked violently on the emergency hand brake. Nothing. He pulled at the useless hand brake repeatedly. His thoughts crystallized as he realized there was no way to stop the car. He would never be able take another curve without losing control.

Thoughts crowded his mind, options came and were discarded. The speedometer was now pushing fifty-five. Darkness and fog pressing in on the windshield increased his claustrophobia as he strained to see. He couldn't even make out the end of the car hood. Terror uncurled in him, making Clay want to scream. *If I can keep control until the road straightens out I might be able—*
His conscious thoughts stopped abruptly as a tight curve to the right was suddenly upon him. In panic Clay reflexively stomped again and again on the useless brake pedal and instinctively wrenched the steering wheel hard to the right. He felt resistance in the steering wheel snap, and it spun uselessly in his hand. The tires screamed as the car leaned up onto the two left side wheels and the little Healey raced through the curve. A split second later the car was airborne. Clay felt his body become weightless and rise from the seat, straining against the lap belt. The car rocketed over the guard rail and the mountain side. The lap belt held him in. Now Clay did scream as the realization of what was happening bore into his brain. Two hundred feet down Clay and his beloved vintage roadster were stopped abruptly by impact with a stand of live oaks and Manzanita. His sweet little car crumpled as though made of tissue.

CHAPTER TWO
Wednesday

Madeline Dean examined the oak floor under her feet. Damn it, damn it, damn it. Those effing Carsons. This is the third time in two months. If they don't start taking the work seriously, I'll...I'll effing fire their asses, she fumed to herself.

"Just look at those bubbles," Mildred Stanley said. "And there. The streaks...and more bubbles. Frankly, I don't think the floor has been sanded properly, either." Her bony, gnarled finger pointed to an area by the bank of windows in the dining room of her late Victorian home. Early morning light streamed in. The two platinum rings she wore supported enormous diamonds that caught the light, their brilliant facets flashing as if she were sending out distress signals. Mrs. Stanley was one of those widow women who had been left well off when her husband died and could easily afford just about anything she wanted. Still, she acted as though each and every cent was an effort to part with and when parted with, it was done grudgingly.

"Yes, of course. I can see what you mean," Madeline said, striving to maintain a calm professional tone.

Madeline towered over Mildred Stanley who was petite, at barely over five feet tall. Mrs. Stanley wore a beautifully made and expensive suit that had probably been perfectly in fashion forty years earlier. It was coal black, as if she were still in mourning for her husband, dead now more than eight years.

"I will not accept shabby work, Mrs. Dean. No," Mrs. Stanley said stiffly. "When I hired you I did so expecting to have an excellent result. Mrs. Jameson is a personal friend of mine, and she gave me a very good reference as to you and your company's qualifications. I expect high quality work for what I'm paying. Not this......rubbish." She waved her hand in a vague sweeping gesture to encompass the whole room. Madeline winced at that word, turned and looked down at the tiny old woman.

"Of course. I completely understand. I apologize for this. As you know, we do guarantee our work to your satisfaction." Now she carefully segued to a soothing and conciliatory tone. "I'll have my crew back in here as soon as possible, to completely strip and refinish the floor. It will likely be tomorrow morning. And they will have it done in forty-eight hours. You have my personal guarantee that it will meet your expectations."

Mrs. Stanley pulled her silk suit jacket closed over a flat bosom. "Well I certainly hope so." She sniffed. "Must I wait another day? This has already been such a waste of my time, and so inconvenient. I have guests coming on Sunday."

Madeline stifled the urge to run out the door. Instead she said, "I sincerely apologize for the inconvenience. I realize how important your time is, but, I regret that we will have to wait until tomorrow due to a scheduling conflict with the crew. However, we will be back tomorrow morning early to begin again. I'll let myself out."

Madeline needed chocolate, not just a latté after going two rounds with Mrs. Stanley. She ordered a mocha at a drive through espresso place she frequented on Willamette street. She took a sip and silently thanked the coffee gods before slotting it into the drink holder. Driving in Eugene, Oregon, was a two handed operation if you liked to keep your car in reasonable shape and maintain your insurance. She caught a break in the traffic and bolted out. Not fast enough though——she received a horn blast from the car racing up behind. She rolled her eyes and punched it to get up to speed. She loved this town, but damn, the traffic.

Mid week and Willamette Street was busy as usual, everyone scurrying to get to work. Or to the gym, yoga or Pilates classes or shopping, not that any of those past-times are a part of *my* life, she thought. A couple minutes later she pulled into the parking lot and her private parking space. *Pacific Northwest Design,* gleamed in a matte stainless steel modern font along the side of the low slung building. Madeline stared at the sign. Her building. Her business. She sipped the mocha. With a sigh, she gathered her bag, tote and coffee and trudged inside.

Office manager, Nadine Coleridge, was on the phone, and in the corner behind her desk the largest copy machine was cranking. Madeline saw Jamie Bradley through the open door of the conference room, perched on a table, thumbing through a magazine.

"Hey, Mrs. Dean," he called out with a wave, a wide grin on his face.

She nodded at Nadine, waved to Jamie and walked on, slipping into her office. With a glance she took in the stacks of product samples that teetered on one side of her desk, the IN box piled high and the stack of pink message slips waiting for her. Madeline kicked the door shut and dropped her handbag and tote on the table by the door. She sank into the desk chair with her coffee and eyed the piles. Looks exactly like it did yesterday, she thought. And the day before.

Next to the pink message slips were a few hand written notes from Nadine, about one bill or another. She glanced through them wondering just how she would juggle those that were over-due and with payroll coming up on Friday. Wasn't a company supposed to be profitable by its third or fourth year? PND was struggling and was in its fifth year. Too many more screw ups like

Mrs. Stanley's floor, and Madeline thought she might have to close the doors. She sighed mightily. Would that be so bad? She had wondered this a couple dozen times in the last six months.

Madeline, a California native, was raised by two very successful parents to whose image she strove to measure up. Educated and smart, yet in her heart, she believed she had fallen quite a bit short. A failure of PND when her parent's own business success all these years had been so good? Maybe I'm just not cut out for it, she thought. Frowning, she dug into the piles on her desk.

A few minutes later a tap on the door preceded Nadine's lanky body.

"David called, just before you got here," she said.

Madeline closed her eyes for a few seconds and sighed deeply. "Did he say what he wanted?"

"Just said he needed to talk to you."

"Uh huh."

"Also, Bruce called to say his crew would be finishing the Brandt's paneling by Friday," Nadine said.

"Oh, thank God, for one bit of good news," Madeline said with a relieved smile. "Before I forget, please call the Carson boys, immediately. I stopped by and saw Mrs. Stanley's floor. It's a freaking disaster. They have to go back and do it over, completely. Tell them they have to be there tomorrow morning at eight sharp, and no screw ups." Madeline looked up at her. "By the time we satisfy Mrs. Stanley if we ever do, we'll be lucky if that job is a break-even, if not a loss."

"I'll call the Carsons," Nadine said. "It will be my pleasure." Nadine disliked both Ted and Will Carson, almost virulently, and it was hardly surprising. Any time they were in the office they badgered and picked on her with sly innuendos, comments about certain aspects of her figure and other sexist remarks. The fact that they were each old enough to be her father made it even more revolting. Nadine paused. "Are you going to call David back?"

"And say what? No, I won't have lunch with you, no I won't have dinner with you? Or, no, you can't move in?"

"Okay, okay." Nadine raised her palm.

She started for the door then turned back. "He'll just keep callin', that's all I'm sayin'."

Madeline cradled her head in her hands. "I know." *My God, and the day has just started.*

Nadine was about to pull the door closed when Madeline called out, "Nadine, wait a sec. What is Jamie doing here?" The twenty year old architecture student had come to PND, when the company partnered with University of Oregon to provide an intern training program for one student. The program ended last term, but somehow Jamie Bradley hadn't quite gotten the message.

Nadine scowled. "I don't know. Maddie, that kid is harder to get rid of than bed bugs. He said he came to run errands, deliver stuff to job sites, whatever we needed. But I couldn't come up with anything for him to do, so he's just been hanging out. Again. I mean, I like him and everything, but, jeez, you'd think he'd get a clue."

Madeline shook her head. "You tell him I said thanks, but we have it all covered. He can go on home."

Nadine pulled the door closed with a drawn out, "Umm-hmmmm…"

Madeline worked through the day without stopping. She was determined to reduce the enormous stacks on her desk to something more manageable. She returned phone calls, did a bit of organizing, contacted suppliers for materials quotes and made some decisions on a 1930s bungalow kitchen remodel they were bidding on.

The owners were interested in bringing the kitchen into the twenty-first century but wanted to keep the look as vintage as possible. This was the kind of project Madeline really liked. It gave her a chance to research all the new 'old' appliances that were now available, new period color schemes and new surface products. It was the most fun part of her job. She glanced at her watch and was astonished to see it was past six-thirty. She vaguely remembered hearing Nadine call out goodbye, but that had to have been an hour ago. When she got involved with a fascinating project the world slipped away. Time to head home, and she was starving.

* * *

Madeline unlocked the door to her small craftsman bungalow just after 7:00 P.M. She had hurriedly closed the office and made a quick stop at the market for a bottle of wine. By the time she kicked off her shoes at home she was exhausted and famished.

The land line's red message light blinked like an evil eye from a horror flick. It was the only light in the darkness of the living room. Five messages. She knew that two were from the previous night when she had had no inclination to listen to, much less return, any phone calls. Introverted and shy, Madeline could always find a reason not to answer a phone call or return a message.

She poured a glass of Cabernet and sank into her favorite arm chair. She punched play.

"Madeline, it's your mother." Madeline's stomach clenched. Guilt, her nearly constant companion, reared its head. "I called last weekend and of course haven't heard back from you. We must talk Maddie, it's very important. There are things happening here... I don't want to discuss it over the phone. Please say you'll come down. This is really important. I know what you're thinking, but there are some things going on that we must discuss! I expect to get a call back from you by tomorrow."

Madeline pondered the message. Her mother sounded almost desperate. As desperate as Eleanor, with her preternaturally calm demeanor, ever sounded anyway. Something wrong with the company? That's unlikely. Maybe it was something having to do with the house? The staff? With another swallow of wine, she started the next message.

"Hi, it's me. I, uh, called your office this morning, Nadine said you weren't in yet. I was hoping to take you to lunch today. Never mind, we can do it another day. Maybe we can go to the Willamette Street Brewery, for dinner one night? I'm kinda in the mood for some of their chow and porter. That'd be fun, wouldn't it?"

I'll just bet it would be, but only you would think so.

"Look, Maddie, I really want to talk to you about things, you know, about us. See, the thing is, this separation has been dragging on a long time now. We need to talk about getting back—"
......*BEEP!*

Madeline burst out laughing at the machine cutting him off. Of course now she had to think about the idea of actually calling him back. She punched play on the next call, but it was a hang-up. As was the next. She gnawed at her thumb nail for a few moments while trying to decide the best way to deal with David. It was not an easy thing, calling him. In fact, there was nothing she wanted to do less. Should I call him now? Put it off? When I do put it off (nearly all the time) it only makes things worse when we do finally talk. Thinking of calling David almost made her physically ill.

"Oh *hell,*" she cursed to the empty room. She was too tired. Why him, why now. She dialed. David answered on the second ring.

"Maddie, I'm glad you finally called."

She replied, "Yeah, well, sorry, but I've just been really busy at work. What's up?" Before he could speak she hurried on. "Actually, let me go first. I've been thinking we really need to move forward, don't you? It's time—really it's past time—to finalize things. I know you've received the papers, now you just need to sign them and send them back."

"Maddie, wait a minute. Wait just a minute." David sounded odd. "You don't mean that. You can't mean that. We've had a breather, you know? The separation, just like you wanted. It's time now to put our lives back together."

Breather? Madeline was incredulous. She didn't respond. She knew she had to be careful not to say anything that David would only misinterpret. They had separated a year ago. After limping unhappily through a volatile marriage for four years Madeline had finally had enough, and moved out. Terrified of David's anger, she had a cadre of friends help her move over the course of one day while David was at work.

David had been furious. He raged at her verbally over the phone until Madeline finally stopped taking his calls. Terrified of his anger, she made sure she never went anywhere alone, for more than a month. She was so relieved and happy to be on her own again she threw a party. Possibly in retrospect, not the best thing to do. David, unable to deal with his fury, went on a two week drinking and drugging binge. He promptly lost another job.

"No, David," she replied in a firm, unemotional tone. "I've done a lot of thinking in the last several months. A lot. Look, it's pretty clear to me that there's nothing left between us, nothing that——"

"Goddamn it, Madeline!" he roared in her ear. Madeline winced. Her immediate conditioned response: her body began to tremble. He lowered his voice. "If you would just *listen*. We need to give ourselves a chance to work out our problems. Don't we owe ourselves that? I think I've been really patient, Maddie. Maybe we could try some counseling. I talked to Jeff about it and well, he understands. He gave me the name of a guy, says he's really good. We could go together and talk to him. I still love you—I miss—"

"Stop it, David." Madeline interrupted, her voice low and quiet. "Stop. I don't want you to start that same old shit again." She heard the beep of an incoming call. "I have to go."

"Maddie, wait."

"No, I have to go. Just sign the papers. Don't make this any harder than it needs to be."

"Listen to me, will you? Let's talk. There's no reason to throw away five years."

Madeline steeled herself. She took a huge breath. "Would *you* listen? I'm tired. I'm tired of the struggle and the fights. I'm tired of you never keeping a job. Your lying, drinking……the goddamn drugs. There's no saving this. Counseling will not solve our problems. Just let it go, for God's sake. Let it go. Sign the papers." The beeping started again. "Okay, I have to go, I have another call coming in."

"Sure, I'll let you go," David snarled. "Let you take your call—from who? Your—your boyfriend, the little stud college boy I see hanging around your office?"

"Excuse me?" Madeline said, dumbfounded.

"It's so easy for you isn't it? You have your friends, your precious business," he whined, his voice nasty and petulant.

"Now, you hold on a minute David. It is not easy for me. But I can recognize the truth when it's staring me in the face. I'm not having this argument with you, ever again. Are you listening? *Never* again." She slammed the phone down.

Madeline sat still, her hands and insides shaking as she tried to slow her breathing and calm her racing heart. How did he dare talk about their problems with good ol' boy Jeff? *His* version of their problems. She didn't know what infuriated her more, that he kept wheedling with the idea of getting back together, or that he had told personal things about her to one of his ignorant, beer drinking, dope taking buddies.

She sipped her wine. After several minutes of deep breaths her heart rate came down. Eventually more calm, she realized she felt lighter than she had in months. It was as if something in her chest, in her heart had broken open and had released its grip on her soul. It had been hard, but not impossible, she thought. Facing it head on and saying what had to be said to David. I've actually been afraid, she thought. Afraid of him. I've been afraid of David and his temper, his ugliness and violent moods. His refusal to accept that the marriage is over. Madeline saw that her method of handling David by attempting to soothe his ego, never making a concrete declaration of intent to split from him, had been a mistake. It allowed him to continue to believe there was a possibility, even if remote, of reconciliation.

In my heart I knew from the moment I moved out that this was no trial separation. I was no longer in love with David, if I ever had been. Madeline laughed out loud, a shaky, warbling sound. No more ambiguity, she thought. I told him directly and clearly. Huh. And I didn't die or fall apart. Getting his cooperation still may not come easily, but it feels like, for the first time, I've actually stood up to him. The effing bully.

Her stomach reminded her that she had not eaten since early that morning. She made a grilled cheese and sliced an apple. It tasted like heaven.

CHAPTER THREE
Thursday

Madeline rushed through her morning routine and raced to pick up her coffee. She was truly eager to get to the office for the first time in weeks. She had received a cell phone call just twenty minutes before from the Litchfields. Doctor and Doctor. Together they were a true power couple in the medical community of Eugene. They had been in the market for an older home to purchase that had a bit of land. When they toured the Barron estate it was a case of love at first sight.

The Barron estate, a twenty thousand plus square foot mansion in the hills of southwest Eugene, was built around 1920 in the Spanish Revival style. It sat on several acres, with many additional buildings: multi car garage, cottage and caretaker's quarters. The only problem was the fact that the historic estate had been neglected for years. It would require a massive effort and a great deal of money to bring it back to its former glory.

The Litchfields had been introduced to Madeline Dean at a fund raising event and had taken an immediate liking to the young woman. Hers was one of the first companies they called for a restoration proposal. To Madeline, it was time to spread the—tentative—good news.

Juggling her coffee, purse and tote she opened the office door to barely controlled chaos. Nadine was on the phone, part time office assistant, Aiden, had the phone wedged between his ear and shoulder, while fiddling on the computer. He looked up and waved. The third line began ringing, and like a magic trick Jamie Bradley popped around the corner from the conference room (why was *he* here?) to pick it up. Madeline made a bee line for her office.

Fifteen minutes later, with a short agenda in hand, she called a meeting to order in the small conference room. Nadine, Aiden, Jamie, main contractor, Charles Wilbur, his assistant, Cally Jacobs, and a few others packed in around the table.

She simply hated doing this kind of thing. Speaking in front of a group, even a small one like this, even with people she saw every day, made her feel queasy and even faint sometimes. She made an enormous effort to compose herself. With her coffee as a prop, giving her hands could do something besides tremble, she looked around the room. "I have some interesting news. I got a call just this morning from the Litchfields."

Nadine nodded. "They called here. There was a message on the machine. They wanted to speak to you right away, so I called them back and gave them your cell. I hope that was okay?"

"Perfectly okay, in this instance, Nadine," she said with a huge smile.

Madeline explained: "For those of you who may not know their name, Dr. Max Litchfield, and his wife, Pauline, are both highly accomplished surgeons. After a couple months of thinking it over, it looks like they've decided to purchase the old Barron estate. They're now looking for a firm to handle its restoration." She took a deep breath and raised her eyebrows. "Do you all know what this means?"

"It means work, and lots of it, months of it," Charles said with a grin.

"It means, the *possibility* of work. It means that we've been asked this morning to submit a proposal. The purchase is closing in about forty-five days. You and I need to coordinate our schedules,

Charles. We'll assess the scope of the job, get with the subs, electrical, plumbing, and so forth. Let's call Randy for landscaping design." Charles and Cally nodded.

"Listen everybody. We aren't the only firm they'll be receiving proposals from. There will be a lot of interest in this job, you can bet on that." Madeline looked at her notes. "But, they said they had heard 'good things' about us." She paused. "Let's hope they haven't heard about the Stanley floor." She gave a wry smile, and continued, "They were particularly interested in seeing what our vision would be for the estate."

Madeline paused again then said, "I expect our assessment and bid prep will take a solid month, if we can get all our people in line in time. Obviously, that has to take into consideration that we keep up on prior commitments too." There was a rising buzz of chatter. Madeline held up her hands. "But, listen, we need to move quickly on it. After our initial look, Charles and I will be making assignments. Everyone will be helping with research, materials quotes and other jobs."

"*Yes!*" Nadine's slender brown arms shot into the air in celebration. The room filled with clapping and cheering. "Okay, okay, hold it down…" Madeline said smiling. "Lots of work to do, so let's get on it."

"Oh by the way, Charles," Madeline pulled him aside, as he and Cally were heading toward the door. "On a less happy note, you already heard about Mrs. Stanley's floor?"

Charles nodded. "Oh, yeah."

"Well I saw it up close, and it is a disaster. I would appreciate it, if you could you go over to the Stanley place right now and stay on those Carson boys like a hawk. They go no where and do nothing until that refinish is done correctly. It's only the one room, you'd think they could have managed it. Anyway, We have till close of business tomorrow or it's curtains for us." She drew a finger across her throat.

Charles' leather like face broke into a wide grin. "I'd be pleased to do that, Miz Dean."

* * *

Nadine Coleridge closed Madeline's office door behind her.

"The Barron estate? Are you freakin' kidding me?" Nadine's pretty smile lit the room. "I've heard stories about the place. I heard whoever owned it used to run hooch during prohibition and had a secret speakeasy. People from all around Eugene, Springfield, even as far as Cottage Grove and Corvallis came to party there. Some say they were making bathtub gin and made tons of money selling booze to all the counties around. Sort of romantic." She sighed.

"Yeah, I've heard some of that stuff too," Madeline scoffed, "but who knows if it's true? I guess we may find some evidence of it......if we get the job. Oh my God, I'm so excited!" Madeline couldn't suppress her enthusiasm. "I wouldn't want to guess what they're paying for it, but you have to know it wasn't cheap. What a *coup* this would be. This is one project that could bring in enough cash flow to take the pressure off. My guess is, it would be a eighteen month project. Plus, just think of the media attention," Madeline chortled.

"Do you think there's a chance? Would they really hire a little bitty firm like this—Oh God, Maddie, I'm sorry, that sounded awful." Nadine clapped her hand over her mouth. "I just meant well, they're so rich and hoity-toity." She grinned sarcastically and shimmied her narrow hips.

"Oh for heaven's sake, Nadine......they're not hoity-toity," she said with a laugh. "I've met them. They're really nice, regular people."

Madeline propped her chin on her hands. "We have as good a chance as anyone, right? Yeah, they're rich and well connected. And I think they're going to do it right. They know it'll be millions to restore it properly. I just have a good feeling about them and the project." Madeline scooped her dark hair up into a curly mass on the top of her head and leaned back in her chair.

"Besides, I think things are about to really change for me. I'm finally getting rid of my good for nothing husband—" At that her friend's head tilted sideways and her eyebrows rose. "I know what you're thinking, you've heard it before." Madeline continued, "This time I'm going to make it happen. I won't go into that right now, it's too complicated and way too much of a downer. Anyway, I'm going to draft the best bid the Litchfields will see. We're going to land that job, or die trying."

The rest of the day went by in a blur. Just before two o'clock, she realized she hadn't set an appointment with Charles for Saturday, at the Barron estate. She called his cell phone and told him she wanted to begin at the estate this weekend, and he agreed to meet her there at eight. "I'll bring Cally. I'll start making a few calls to the subs and get as many of them as I can to meet us there too."

"Good. How's it going there. Be honest."

She heard Charles sigh. "Shee-it, 'scuse my language Maddie." In front of other employees, he always referred to her as Mrs. Dean, when they spoke privately, it was different and Madeline didn't mind. "You know these guys. I've never met two lazier individuals. Good thing I came over. When I'm breathing down their necks, they stay with it. What's too bad is, when they put out an effort, they can do good work. But, my advice is, that once this is finished, we lose their phone number."

"Once I saw that floor, I mentally tore up their business card. That was after I imagined myself strangling them both."

At that, Charles chuckled.

Madeline continued, "Okay, Charles keep at them. And thanks. Since you will be at the Stanley's for the rest of today and tomorrow, I guess I won't see you till Saturday. I'll meet you and Cally there, at eight."

Madeline pondered her good fortune at having found a contractor like Charles Wilbur.

Charles was highly skilled with twenty years' experience and a stellar reputation. He could have gone to work with any of a dozen fine companies.

Unbelievably, he had won a substantial state lottery a few years ago and retired at age forty. Charles was a confirmed bachelor though and by forty-one was bored and looking for something to do. His love of old and historic houses led him to Madeline's door. He didn't ask for a huge salary but was insistent that he manage all construction aspects of her business, as well as overseeing subcontractors and keeping them honest. Madeline agreed and granted him those responsibilities. She relied heavily on his judgment and trusted him implicitly.

Then Cally came along. When Charles asked for an assistant, Calinda Jacobs was one of the candidates. The first day Madeline saw Cally (as she preferred to be called) she was apprehensive. Cally was very smart, a bit of a tomboy, very young and slightly built. She came to her interview in a pair of well worn overalls, a men's plaid shirt and steel toed boots. Then Cally met Charles. Charles looked her over and stuck out his hand. They clicked immediately. She was only twenty but already had knowledge in many trades. He agreed to take her on as an apprentice, and soon was fiercely protective of her as if he were her father, and she were the son he never had. Cally literally became a jack of all the trades under Charles's tutelage. She was an ideal employee, that could help with nearly any task at any time.

Madeline smiled at the thought. I'm so blessed to have the people I have. If we can pull together this bid…this might just be the job to put us on an even keel——and even beyond that. She sighed. Don't count chickens. How many times have I heard that?

Have to quit dawdling. Madeline pulled out the list of calls to return and got busy.

* * *

Over time, four people determined that they had common interest in the subject of murder. Disparate reasons, but common interests. Eventually, a couple more joined the group. How they got to the subject in real, tangible terms is anyone's guess. But when people speak about revenge and money, things change. Revenge is sweet they say. Money makes the world go around. Trite as the sayings are, they are often the first, best motivators for murder or conspiracy. Is *this* how these people begin talking about murder? Revenge and money fuel fascination with a morbid topic? Stories they've heard? What happens to make them go from hypothetical conversations to speaking in concrete terms? Terms that apply…to *them?* Where is that transition? How do people know whom to trust? Are they ever sure, absolutely sure, that secrets will be kept?

The death (actually the murder) of Clay Abbott eighteen months ago had not resolved the central issue for some. One person thought it might. However, that person had come to the conclusion that the death of Clay Abbott was not…enough. It served to open the subject of murder to further study, consideration and expansion of the original idea. More thought was given to what would satisfy and to what extreme would they be willing to go to achieve it. Ideas were considered. Meetings were held. Propositions discussed. Everyone's needs were voiced. The next step was developed with precision. Some balked. Some did not. But everyone stayed in the group. Birds of a feather.

The next step was assigned to one of the group. Everyone agreed on who the right person was for the job. Planning of this step was extensive. Timing was thoroughly examined. Information was gathered by using connections to others. Secrecy was paramount. They were ready to proceed. But, there was a hitch. The assigned person refused the job. This hiccup was almost enough to stop the plan. Almost.

The city of Los Gatos is nestled in the Santa Cruz mountains. It is part of the Pacific Coast range which spans virtually the entire west coast. The name, Los Gatos, is Spanish for 'the cats', referring to the indigenous bobcats and mountain lions that roam the hills.

It is a beautiful, small incorporated town within Santa Clara County, California. It is an enclave of wealth, privilege and power. In fact, at one time it was listed as the thirty-third wealthiest city in the United States. In the middle between Santa Cruz on the Pacific coast and San Jose inland, it exists like an island unto itself. A small but ritzy village outside the dangers of the big city of San Jose.

Beyond the city of Los Gatos proper there is little light, just beautiful, mostly forested mountainous land. On this particular early spring night, the sky above was velvety black. There was no moon, and not a star was visible. Swirling masses of fog clung to the ground. The fog was so dense, it was difficult to make out the mansion across the road. It sat near the top of the hill, and had done so for more than one hundred twenty-five years. In daylight it seemed a little menacing, but in the darkness it looked sinister. It was an enormous black shape with a few lights showing feebly through foggy darkness. She's still up. Good.

Two figures dressed in black stood under a huge cedar tree in a wooded area on the rural road that bordered the front of the property under surveillance. They didn't speak. All that needed to be said had already been said.

Mixed scents of cedar, pine and spicy eucalyptus filled the air. It was a clean, invigorating fragrance, that the figures might have appreciated had cigarettes not been more important. It was silent as the country or wilderness typically is except for the call of an owl close by. If one were the jittery type, the look of the place might have a person making a run for it. The watchers had no such jitters. The decision was made, the job was to be done. One person had backed out, but that in no way meant the task would not be completed.

Concentrating on the mansion up the hillside, they smoked cigarettes and watched. The burning coal ends were the only things visible. Rhythmically they rose, glowed brightly and fell. In their black clothing the two shapes melted into the surrounding darkness, and the burning cigarette ends looked a little like fireflies. When finished, they each lit another immediately, and once again the glowing ends rose in an arc then fell. Finally, a quick glance at a cell phone showed the time to be 12:45 A.M. Just like the first ones, the second cigarettes were scrubbed out against the tree bark, and the stub ends carefully deposited in the back pockets of the black nylon running pants they each wore. The figures began the half mile jog up to the mansion and the mission for the night.

* * *

Over the subdued crackle of the fading fire, she heard the faint whistle of the tea kettle from the kitchen. Eleanor Margaret Abbott rose from her wing back chair. She felt her age in every joint. Pain had to be coped with she supposed, but it was not easy. Sixty is the new forty, right? "Right. Tell that to my hips," she said caustically to the empty room.

Eleanor walked out of the library, her silk robe tied around a slender waist, slippers slap-slapping softly on the polished marble tile floor. She shut off the gas burner and dumped the pre-heating water from the paper thin Belleek tea pot. When the scent of chamomile enveloped her, Eleanor sighed with pleasure.

In recent months, she began to have trouble sleeping. Tea was nice, it was comforting, but it wasn't enough to help her sleep.

More often, because of the pain, it took tea and pain killers. Her doctor had given her a prescription for Ambien, but she was so tired of taking pills, the thought of one more......well, she rarely resorted to using it. She often woke by 5:00 A.M., sometimes earlier. Another fine attribute of being older, Eleanor thought. If I could just stop worrying about Maddie. I need to talk to her about so many things.

As she mused, a sound finally registered in Eleanor's mind. She paused, listening. With tea cup in hand, she rose up on her toes and peered out through the glass of the back door of the kitchen. The night was very dark. A pool of light from the lamp over the door reflected off thick clots of fog on the stoop, the stairs and the cobbled courtyard. Lamps were on, at each corner of the garage. The pools of light glowed an eerie, unearthly yellow, on her BMW, where she had left it this afternoon, parked outside the garage. She saw nothing else.

She smiled as she suddenly remembered the night last year when a mother raccoon, and her four cubs, had raided the galvanized trash cans. What a racket! Pancho had gone crazy, barking and leaping about. Eleanor didn't have the heart to let him out to give chase. What a mess they had left, she thought laughing softly. Eleanor checked to be certain the lock was engaged. She suddenly shivered. She'd be so glad to see Pancho again tomorrow. The huge old house was lonely when he wasn't here with her. She smiled at the thought of him. Pancho, a silver standard poodle, was large for the breed at almost seventy pounds. She got him as a puppy and loved him fiercely. In Eleanor's opinion Pancho was the perfect companion. He would listen to Eleanor if she needed to talk and rarely talked back. Pancho was obedient to her, Maddie and sometimes Mrs. Temple. He was intelligent, protective and was deceptively strong——although he looked like a large ball of dryer lint.

By the fire, in the library, with a blanket tucked around her legs, Eleanor sipped her tea. She stroked the fine Black Watch wool lap blanket she'd bought in Scotland, when she and Clay visited there…what, was it thirty-five years ago? When she used the blanket she was swept back to the trip, the scenery, the wonderful people they met and the fun that she and Clay had had. That was so long ago. Before everything changed. The thought made her throat thicken with sadness, and she coughed.

The slowing flames snapped in the silent room. With only the fire and one lamp on the side table lighted, the enormous room was mostly in shadow. Eleanor loved it that way. It was comforting and made her feel she was in a protective cocoon. She sat here in the evening, reading, writing, sometimes slipping into thoughts of the past. It was during those times that she missed Clay. She would think of their early years, building the business, the children. She had loved him once. But there was so much history, so much pain in the past. Loss and misery and regret. It hadn't completely erased love, but it did change it. Irrevocably.

Eleanor stared into the fluttering, hypnotic flames and glowing coals and absorbed the warmth. The fire felt good to her tired and aching body. The library was her favorite room in the entire mansion. There were many fireplaces throughout the great house, but this one was in her opinion, the most beautiful. Fantastic stonework and the Trent Company art tiles. The entire fireplace surround was handmade, dating from the late 1880s. She and Clay had discovered them during the restoration of the mansion. They had been ecstatic finding them intact. The hearth had been destroyed, but they found replacements for those. The huge fireplace was truly a one of a kind work of art.

As Eleanor sipped her tea, her mind drifted on to Madeline, as it did often now. What do I have to do to get Madeline to come home? I've got to get her here to talk. So much to discuss, so much to tell her and so little time. It must be done before, well, before it's too late. She's just like Clay, and she doesn't realize how true that is. And, that business of hers! Eleanor shook her head and sighed. She's struggling. She doesn't want to admit that she needs help. Why is she making her life harder than it needs to be? So she can say she did it without help, just like her father.

A stirring of chilly air around her ankles made Eleanor shiver again. Mrs. Temple must have gone and left a window open somewhere, the great nit, Eleanor thought crossly. Why can the woman not keep her mind on her duties? She's an excellent housekeeper, she can build a wonderful fire like the one burning now, but she's only a fair cook. So why do I keep her on? I guess, she's been here so long now the place wouldn't be the same without her. Eleanor smiled and sighed, which started the coughing again. The things we put up with just because we fear change.

As she drained her tea cup the grandfather clock chimed 1:00 A.M. Time to get started on the nightly battle, she thought wryly. With the cup and saucer in hand she pulled off the blanket and began to rise. At the last fraction of a second Eleanor sensed a presence. Before she could turn, the first blow fell, dropping her back into the wingback chair. The exquisite Belleek porcelain cup and saucer flew from her hands, like delicate ivory birds, and shattered into a dozen pieces on the Persian rug as the blows fell.

A small amount of yellowish light came through the window from a street lamp. Most of the room was in darkness. And silence. He sat in a richly upholstered leather chair which creaked as he occasionally shifted position. In his hand, was a crystal whiskey glass with an inch of Dewar's Signature, neat. He sipped and waited. At 1:30 a.m. the cell phone on the table next to him vibrated.

"It's done," a voice said.

"You're certain." He answered.

"Of course, I'm certain."

"I will contact you using the same email. Check periodically."

There was a pause. "Don't forget, there's the matter of payment."

"I said, I'll contact you." He answered, and turned off the phone. He swallowed the rest of the scotch, gathered his briefcase and coat and left, locking the door. He pulled the SIM card from the prepaid phone and ground it under his heel, disposing of it in a nearby public waste bin. He drove out of the parking lot, and after traveling a mile, he rolled down the window and threw the phone into an overgrown ditch and sped on.

CHAPTER FOUR
Friday

Nadine gritted her teeth. "Yes, Mrs. Stanley, yes. I assure you that the crew will be there again this morning. Any minute in fact, to finish the job. Yes, they will have it completed by the end of today."

Madeline Dean walked in the office door in time to hear, "Yes, Mrs. Stanley, we certainly do understand your position, and we absolutely will meet the agreed deadline of end of business today."

Madeline's brows rose, and she mouthed, "What?"

"Thank you, Mrs. Stanley…yes, yes, of course. Alright…Goodbye." Nadine slammed the phone down and exploded, "Dear *God!*"

"What was that about, or should I ask?"

"Mrs. Stanley thought it was necessary to call and remind us of our promised deadline." Nadine frowned. "The old bat. Jesus, if that's what money and old age do to you then I don't want either one."

At that comment, Madeline burst out laughing. "Charles was over-seeing them all day yesterday, and he'll be there again today." She wiped a tear from her eye. "It'll be finished, and properly this time. She's just being a gigantic pain in the ass."

"Yeah, well…"

Nadine filled Madeline in on calls that had come in and handed her the mail. She trailed Madeline into her office, and slumped into the chair next to the desk. Madeline sat down and sipped her coffee and glanced at Nadine. The silence stretched out.

Finally, she said, "What?"

Nadine's brown eyes slid to the window and gazed out. She gave a huge sigh. Her shoulders slumped.

Oh good, Madeline thought, something's wrong. She frowned, her dark brows pulled together. "Come on, give. What is it?"

Nadine finally looked at Madeline without answering. She sighed again.

Madeline took a stab. "Is it Jamal?" Nadine was raising her twelve year old nephew alone. She was only twenty-seven, and Madeline had often wondered sadly about the impact the responsibility was having on Nadine.

"Yeah, it's Jamal," Nadine replied.

"Okay, what's the problem?"

"The latest is, he got suspended."

Jamal was a sweet and funny boy. Madeline gave her a puzzled look. "For what?"

"Oh, let's see." Nadine began, with a scowl on her face. "Skipping almost half of his classes. Disrupting the classes he does go to. Oh, yeah, he tried to stuff some nine year old into his own locker."

Madeline clamped her lips together to hide a smile.

"Maybe the little guy asked for it. Fourth graders can be brutal," Madeline offered.

Nadine shook her head, and crossed her slender arms across her chest. The same defensive position she often took when the Carson boys were in the office.

"Yeah, well there's no excuse for that. Jamal needs a man in his life. He's getting to be too much for me. What am I sayin'… he's always been too much for me. I don't know what to do." She rubbed her upper arms, as if she were cold. "Of course, now I have *puberty* to deal with. He'll be *there* in about, oh," she made a show of looking at her watch, "fifteen minutes."

Madeline looked intently at Nadine. She felt such pity for her friend, and often didn't know what was the right thing to do to help. Suggesting picnics and going to the movies together only could help so much.

"Look, here's an idea. Have you thought of getting Jamal a 'Big Brother'? I understand they are really good with kids that have had difficulties. A Big Brother might give him someone to talk to. I mean a guy, you know? Maybe he doesn't feel he can really tell you things. Especially if puberty's getting to be an issue. He could take him to ball games, maybe out to play arcade games or paint ball once in a while. Besides, it would give you a bit of a break." Madeline then tried diverting her attention. "Are you still seeing that computer guy, Brad somebody?"

Nadine put one of her hands out and studied her fingertips, checking her manicure. "We see each other from time to time, nothin' regular." Her smooth skin took on a flush.

Madeline fussed about, straightening things on her over crowded desk top, before finally glancing at Nadine. "Something you're not telling me? Is there *someone* you haven't told me about?" She asked slyly, trying to inject a shot of humor into the conversation.

Nadine shot out of the chair. "Of course not. Just worried about Jamal."

Her sister's death in a car accident was still raw after two years. Nadine had been very close to her sister, and Madeline knew she felt a lot of pressure to do right by Jamal. They were both still grieving. Nadine stood by the desk, her face a solemn mask. Abruptly, she headed for the door then stopped and turned back.

"What? Something else?" Madeline asked.

She paused for a moment then said, "No. Nothin'." Her face was inscrutable.

"Look, Nadine, check up on the Big Brother group. It would be worth the time to at least find out what all they do, what kind of services they have. It might end up helping Jamal." Madeline paused. "Okay?"

"Okay. I will. I'll give 'em a call," Nadine answered. She remained by the door.

"Anything else?"

"No. That's it."

"We should get back to it then," Madeline suggested. "Lots to do to get that bid done."

"Right. Okay." Nadine left. Madeline had the feeling the whole conversation was about something else entirely. She gazed at her retreating back with a puzzled frown.

* * *

The first they saw of the Abbott estate was the pair of massive, dark stone columns that flanked the entrance to the drive. Standing at least twelve feet tall, each was topped by the huge figure of a large black bird. The birds appeared to be over three feet long in size, and each one exhibited a different pose. On one column was a bronze plaque bearing the name, Raven's Nest, with its build date, ca. 1893.

The mansion itself, was set back from the road nearly a half mile. Detective Scott Cooper gave a low whistle as they drove up the curving cobbled drive. They had broken through a dense forested area of cedar, pine, maples and oaks to glimpse the house. If house was the appropriate word. "Jesus H. Christ on a crutch," he muttered.

His partner, Detective Isabelle Morales nodded. "No kidding."

The old mansion known as Raven's Nest, occupied an area near the top of a hill, and looked like a massive sleeping beast. Curtains and blinds were closed. Several vehicles were already on the scene, lights flashing. Three police cruisers, an ambulance and an SUV, with the Santa Clara medical examiner emblem, were parked in a line. The police tape, already up, fluttered in the breeze.

Two uniformed officers milled around in the shade of the porte-cochere, over a west side entrance to the house. Cooper drove past the vehicles and to the courtyard beyond. He and Morales got out of the car and stared up. Stone walls soared three stories. The granite, or whatever it was made of, looked dark grey, nearly black, in the early afternoon light.

The detectives started for one of the uniformed officers, near the side entrance. Huge and hulking, he stood at least six-three and had a pair of aviator sunglasses perched on his gleaming shaved head.

"Oh, God, no." Morales said *sotto voce*, as they approached.

"Willis," Cooper said, when they reached him. "What's going on?"

Officer Del Willis, hooked his thumbs into his belt under his considerable gut and shifted a toothpick to the side of his mouth. "Deceased female. Little old lady. Looks like somebody brained her."

"Name?" Morales asked. Willis cocked his head and stared down at her for several beats before flipping open his notebook. "Abbott." His toothpick twitched and twirled while he continued to stare at Morales without blinking. Cooper saw himself reflected in the lenses of Willis' sunglasses. "Eleanor," Willis added.

"Okay!" Cooper said, breaking the tense atmosphere. "Let's go, Izzy."

They climbed a set of wide stone stairs, past a massive oak door that stood open and entered a large vestibule. Cooper stared at the door. The ornate hammered iron hinges straps were probably three feet long. Inside, Cooper turned to his partner and lowered his voice. He could feel the anger simmering out of her.

"Ignore him, Izzy."

"That's easy for you to say. He's a chauvinistic, misogynistic, racist, homophobic pig. And a bastard," She added. "I can't stand him."

Cooper stood, hands on hips, looking down into Izzy's huge brown eyes. Isabelle Morales worked hard coming up through the ranks. It had been difficult, but she bore it without complaint. When Izzy made detective, things got worse not better in Los Gatos' predominately male police force. Cooper sighed.

"We'll just have to stay out of his way."

"Scotty, that's no way to deal with his type. He needs to know I won't stand for his shit," Morales whispered as she glanced back out the door.

"You're right, but right now we have work to do. We'll figure out what to do with prince charming later. Besides," Cooper said with a grin, "he'd probably have to find a dictionary and look up what those words mean."

"Oh, stop it," Morales said as she punched his arm.

Another uniform, Officer Ginny Bell, appeared at the door across the room and motioned for them to follow. They went through an enormous sitting room or living room, full of sofas, deep chairs and a massive fireplace. The brocaded walls were covered with gilt framed oil paintings that Cooper felt certain were not reproductions.

Finally, they came to another huge space that looked to be the main foyer, with its broad expanse of polished black and white marble tiles. Cooper and Morales paused, open mouthed at the grand staircase, easily twelve feet wide, of polished mahogany with a deep red carpet. It curved gracefully up to a landing where the detective spied what looked like a medieval suit of armor. The stairs then turned, continued up to the second floor and disappeared into the gloom.

In the center of the space sat a marble topped round table which displayed a crystal vase of fresh flowers. The mixed floral scents permeated the room. They hurried to catch up to Officer

Bell who had headed down a long gallery to the left of the central stair. Through double doors on their left they glimpsed another room, this one a feminine collection of what Cooper thought was probably French, Louis the something (he couldn't remember which) gilt furniture. The walls and carpets were a pale robin's egg blue.

Bell turned to them and pointed into one room before she disappeared into a door further down. They stopped at the door opening of the library. This room was magnificent. Floor to ceiling built-in mahogany bookcases, mouldings and paneling. Thousands of leather bound books filled the shelves. Walls without bookcases were paneled up at least seven feet. The ceiling was criss crossed with heavy mahogany beams. On the far wall was a massive fireplace of stone and tile so huge Cooper was sure his six foot two inch frame would fit into it, with room to spare. Morning light filtered into the room from beautiful windows which flanked the chimney breast. They were large, multi-paned, and held a mix of beveled and stained glass. A police photographer was busy recording the scene.

Directly in front of the fireplace was a grouping of a leather Chesterfield sofa and two wing back chairs. A woman's body was slumped in the chair on the right. Near her feet was what looked like a blanket.

Kneeling beside her was the Santa Clara County Medical Examiner, Walter Simmons.

"Morning, Walt," Cooper said.

Simmons rocked back on his heels. "Detective Cooper, Detective Morales. How are you two doing this fine day?"

"Good. What have you got?"

"Eleanor Margaret Abbott, aged sixty years. Died from blows to the back of her head, likely that bookend," he said, motioning to an object a few feet away.

Cooper saw what looked like a marble and metal object lying about four feet behind the chair.

"So……when, do you think?" Cooper asked.

"About two decades early."

Cooper rolled his eyes. "Walt?"

"I'd guess sometime between 12:00 a.m. and oh, say, 2:00 a.m."

"Who found her?" Morales asked.

"The housekeeper. I think Bell's got her in the dining room."

Morales turned. "I'll find them."

Cooper stood over the object and snapped on latex gloves. In the shape of a cornucopia with fruits spilling out, it looked like bronze and had a substantial marble base. Quite a weapon, Cooper thought as he hefted it. Seven or eight pounds. Dried blood and a few strands of hair stuck to one end. He returned it to its marked location on the floor.

He scanned the large antique walnut desk that sat at an angle in one corner of the room. It was covered with several file folders, stacks of papers, and what appeared to be a handful of receipts paper-clipped together. The mate to the cornucopia bookend, rested on the front edge of the desk, with a cascade of slender leather volumes no longer supported. He picked up one volume. Shakespeare. A very thin laptop computer stood open on the left side. Several pens, pencils and an obviously expensive fountain pen rested on the calendar desk pad. Everything appeared to have been been gone through. Drawers were open. Between the edge of the desk and the bookcase, an ornately carved wooden trash can rested on its side. Next to that was a leather handbag, turned over and pilfered, items spilled out, including a leather wallet that looked emptied.

To the right in the opposite corner, was a small wooden desk with an oak chair on casters. Behind it sat a printer on a stand and a file cabinet. The desk had a land line. There was an assortment of pens and pencils in a ceramic mug, with a printed caption: *To Save Time, Let's Just Assume I Know Everything*.

Cooper went back to the victim and continued to look about the room trying to imagine the sequence of events. Simmons had bagged the victims hands and was about to zip her into a body bag. A pair of assistants stood by to load her on a gurney.

"I'm done here, Detective Cooper. If you need me I'll be at the morgue. I'll have the PM done first thing in the morning."

Willis entered the library, his deliberate plodding gait set Cooper's teeth on edge. Cooper strove to keep his expression neutral.

"What have you found?" he asked.

"Thought I'd show ya the kitchen. Looks like that's where he got in, through the door. There's a broken window." Willis used the toothpick from his mouth as a pointer. "In through the kitchen door, up the hallway... in the library he grabs the bookend thingy and—" he made a chopping motion.

"Maybe we'd better take a look."

* * *

Every room they had seen thus far was enormous in scale and the kitchen was no exception. It reminded Cooper of restaurant kitchens he'd seen. Miles of tile counters and wooden cupboards, six burner stove, a couple of ovens and a wooden table down the middle of the room that had to be twelve feet long. At the far end of the room Cooper saw a narrow hallway leading away from the kitchen off which he could see doors (service areas?) and on the opposite wall, a stairway going up through a door opening.

The back exterior wall was covered with a bank of large windows and a door which stood open. Through it he could see the brick paved courtyard, an eight bay garage and more terrace area extending the length of the mansion.

Cooper studied the back door. It was large and heavy with multiple panels of oak. There were several panes of beveled glass on the top third, designed in a arched shape, with a center panel of stained glass that depicted a coat of arms. Beveled and stained glass in a kitchen door, thought Cooper. Good Godalmighty.

Shards of glass lay on the floor on the inside, one of the panes apparently punched in.

"Have you touched the door, or moved it?" Cooper asked.

Willis looked at him sourly. "'Course not." He sucked at the toothpick like a pacifier.

"Okay, the photographer is probably done. Fingerprint, hair and fiber guys are done in the library. You and officer Bell go ahead and bag anything else in the library. Get it all, including the stuff from the trash can by the desk."

Willis turned and with his body language saying, 'I'll take my own sweet time', left the room. Cooper watched him go and shook his head. Dumb-ass.

The kitchen was tidy except what was out for making tea. Tea canister, strainer, sugar bowl, creamer and a spoon sat on the counter, next to the stove. On the near end of the table was a a folded newspaper and a handbag. So, the victim fixes tea, goes to the library for a sit down, then what? Someone breaks in the back door, comes up behind her without her hearing anything? The library is quite a distance, it's night, it's quiet, no television, no music. It didn't make sense. He eyeballed the broken window pane. He extended his hand to its widest and made an approximate measurement from the broken pane to the lock. Maybe, if you were a contortionist.... But how, without getting cut? No evidence of blood.

Cooper rubbed his neck, it was getting stiff. He knew one of his personal failings being a detective, was that he found it damned hard to avoid becoming too involved with certain cases. It already felt as if this might be one of those.

Scott Cooper was only thirty-one and had been a cop for the last six years. He got his degree in History and took a lot of ribbing about 'what in the hell do you do with a History degree'. The truth was he hadn't known *what* he wanted to do with his life. He taught high school history for one year before realizing he was not cut out for it. Trying to keep hormonal high school kids in line and teach them things they had no interest in, wore very thin.

He returned to school and got a degree in Criminal Justice. After toying briefly with the notion of law school, Cooper thought better of it and went to work for the Dallas PD. It took him only three years to make detective. Scott found to his astonishment, he had a knack for it.

The opportunity to transfer to Los Gatos came at an eerily coincidental time in his personal life. He had reluctantly insisted on a divorce from his wife, Angie, just as the job came open. Scott put in for it and was flabbergasted when he got called to come out for an interview. When he subsequently got an offer he took it as a sign.

Angie and Scott were married for three years. Scott blamed himself for the break up, because as Angie always told him, he was not communicative enough. But neither could he deal with Angie's intense attraction to gambling—and their budget couldn't survive it either. There was blame to go around.

With his divorce freshly minted, he took off for Los Gatos. He liked the area and so far he had enjoyed his time in the Los Gatos PD. Everything was so much more expensive. What he had first viewed as a serious increase in pay didn't seem like so much after finding an apartment he felt he could afford. He was in the department for a year before he ended up with a permanent partner, in Isabelle Morales. There was always talk, subtle and not so subtle comments about Izzy. But he was fine with the assignment, and by the time his first six months had passed he felt that his partnership with Izzy was a nearly perfect fit.

He looked up from his woolgathering to see Morales escorting an older woman and a large grey dog into the kitchen.

"Mrs. Temple, this is Detective Scott Cooper, he will also be working on this case. Detective, this is Mrs. Abbott's housekeeper and cook, Mrs. Alma Temple. Mrs. Temple found Mrs. Abbott this morning. Oh and this……is Pancho." Morales said formally, pointing with the flat of her hand to the curly haired dog as if introducing a game show contestant.

Mrs. Temple looked a tired seventy, with frizzy grey hair and a lined face, now swollen and red from crying. Pancho looked up at him with dark brown intelligent eyes along side a long, slender nose. His body was covered in a close clipped mass of tight silvery grey curls. He's not crying yet, but he looks like he could at any second, Cooper thought.

"Let's sit down why don't we, ma'am?" Cooper pulled out a stool from under the wooden table for Mrs. Temple and then sat across from her. Pancho padded to her side, and sat quietly erect, like a military man at attention.

"Can you take me through what happened today?" he asked.

"What happened? I don't know what happened. Mrs. Abbott is *dead*, that's what happened." Her eyes filled with tears again. She sobbed into a handful of soggy tissue. Morales grabbed a couple of paper towels from a holder on the counter and handed them to her.

"It's okay, Mrs. Temple, just take it slow and tell us what you did when you arrived."

She rubbed her nose hard and sniffed. "I got here just before noon today. Well that's the usual routine—every other Thursday night I take Pancho here with me when I leave. He's got a regular grooming appointment first thing Friday morning over at the Spa For Pets, in town." She looked down at Pancho and stroked his fluffy head. "It's a bit of a way into town, so I figure there's no need for Mrs. Abbott to have to make a special trip since that's where I live anyway. We've done it this way ever since Pancho was a puppy."

Cooper smiled at Mrs. Temple. "Sounds like a good plan."

"Everyday I'm at work at 9:00 AM.," she continued. "But every other week on Friday morning I take Pancho for his clip and bath then run errands for Mrs. Abbott—pick up dry cleaning, take the mail, pick up groceries if we need something, things like that."

"You take Pancho every other Thursday night and then are late every other Friday, regularly? Who knows about this schedule?" Morales asked.

Mrs. Temple looked up from the wad of paper. "Who knows about it? You mean me taking Pancho on Thursday nights?" She looked bewildered. "I…I don't know. I guess a few people do, people who are close to Mrs. Abbott. Her assistant does of course. Maybe Madeline…. I really don't know, I've never thought about it."

"Okay, Mrs. Temple. Go on." Morales said gently.

"Okay, like I said I'm late every other Friday, but I'm always here by eleven-thirty, eleven-forty-five. I take my job seriously, not like some I can mention. That assistant woman Mrs. Abbott has…had…" Tears welled in her eyes and she grimaced as if in pain. Cooper reached across the table and patted her arm and said kindly, "I'm sorry, ma'am, we wouldn't be asking this of you if it weren't important."

She nodded, blew her nose and continued. "Today, I got here about eleven-forty. I had my mind on what I'd be fixing for Mrs. Abbott's lunch. She had told me she would be in for lunch today. Well I wasn't even completely out of the car when Pancho jumped out and set to barking like he'd gone completely crazy. He ran into the house and disappeared."

"You saw the open door, the broken glass?" Cooper asked.

"I, I did I guess, but I mean, somehow it didn't hit me really. The door was standing open, and I heard the glass under my feet but all I could think of was what was the matter with Pancho? Going on like a banshee somewhere in the house." Her lips trembled. "I put my things down here on the table," she waved in the direction of the purse, "and I followed the sound down through the gallery to the library. That's when I saw her."

"You saw Mrs. Abbott in the chair?"

She nodded wordlessly. "Then what did you do?" Morales asked.

Mrs. Temple cleared her throat. "I tried to shush Pancho, he was making such a racket, barking and whining. All I could really see was her...her arm."

"Did you go over to her?" Cooper asked, glancing over to Morales.

Mrs. Temple shook her head jaggedly. "No, I called out to her, hello Mrs. Abbott, I said. But then I saw the b-blood...on the chair."

Izzy Morales put a hand on her shoulder and gave her a comforting pat.

Cooper paused giving Mrs. Temple a moment to recover, then started again.

"Do you know if Mrs. Abbott had any plans to meet with someone, an appointment, maybe? A business meeting?"

"I don't handle her schedule and such like that. That assistant, Diane, is responsible for that. But I don't *think* she had anything on her calendar for last night. She never mentioned it. She doesn't usually make appointments at night, I'm sure not business appointments."

"What happened next?" Cooper asked.

"I finally got Pancho to come to me. I caught him by the collar and came back here to the kitchen to use the phone. I didn't want to use the one on that assistant's desk. I called 911. They asked me some questions...I don't know, I don't know what I said. Oh, dear Lord..."

"You're doing fine, Mrs. Temple, just fine." Morales said, giving her shoulder a gentle squeeze.

"We have to begin contacting Mrs. Abbott's family, Mrs. Temple, relatives and friends. Can you help us with that?" Cooper asked.

Mrs. Temple sighed heavily. "Her daughter, Maddie, Madeline that is, lives up in Oregon, she needs to be called. This is going to kill her." The tears were starting again. "Their family attorney, Selwyn, Arthur Selwyn? He's a close friend of Mrs Abbott...Ian, all those phone numbers will be in her cell phone, I guess. She has an address book on her desk or in her purse somewhere I think. Oh God, I don't know." She shook her head in misery. "How are they going to bear it?"

"You've been a lot of help, ma'am." Cooper squeezed her hand. "Why don't you go on home now and take Pancho with you. Detective Morales or I will be in touch soon."

Mrs. Temple nodded. She rose unsteadily to her feet and gathered the purse and newspaper off the end of the table. "I'll be at home if you need me, I gave Detective Morales my number," she said quietly. She grabbed Pancho's collar and said, "Come on Pancho, you old dear." She trudged through the back door, trying but failing, to miss the broken glass. It crunched under her feet.

Cooper looked at Morales. "We need to get those names and numbers."

* * *

Eleanor Abbott's cell phone was on her desk in the library. Morales compiled a list of names and phone numbers by scrolling through Abbott's phone and thumbing through the old style address book she found in the center drawer of the desk. There were many dozens of numbers in the contact list, and it was impossible to determine how important each was. She looked through the cell phone and made a judgment based on how frequently calls had been made to those names and numbers and how recently.

She came up with a list of about twenty names that she and Cooper could use as a starting point, notifying people and setting up interviews. When she showed the list to Cooper she had put an asterisk by the attorney's name: Selwyn.

The dated memo book she found in the handbag had interesting entries which dated from the beginning of the year. There were some comments written in concerning James Edgerton. Several referencing Selwyn, some Madeline, even a few other names: David, Ian, Phoebe, Helen. Richard and Sydney? Tom, Rachel, Margaret? Who were all these people? Morales gathered up the phone, memo book and address book to show to Cooper. She suddenly wished mightily she had asked Mrs. Temple to make a pot of coffee before she left.

"I can't believe this." The voice of Arthur Selwyn was distant. It sounded as if his mouth was not near the phone, his breathing was audible, but sounded labored.

"Are you all right, sir?" Cooper could hear the strained breaths. "You are the first person I've called. Since you live in Los Gatos and with your close relationship to the family—I thought you should be notified first." Cooper said. "We have to get in touch with her daughter and Eleanor's friends, her business partner, uh, James Edgerton. We need to speak to those who were close to Mrs. Abbott."

"Eleanor......*dead?* She's been murdered? It can't be." He didn't seem to be hearing anything that Cooper was saying.

"I'm sorry, sir," Cooper paused, listening to be sure he could still hear breathing. "We are going to need to talk with you, as well as the others on our list."

"What? What did you say? Oh, of course, of course. Who do you need?"

"Why don't we start with James Edgerton. What's the best way to get a hold of him? We have his cell phone number from Mrs. Abbott's phone."

Cooper heard Selwyn blow his nose. "He's usually at their business office on a weekday I believe. It's just outside of the downtown area, on Winchester boulevard." Selwyn gave him Edgerton's address and office phone number. "I simply can't believe she's dead." His voice broke into a sob. "I've known Ellie for over forty years…"

"I'm very sorry for your loss, sir." Cooper said. With that trite comment he felt like a rube, inadequate in his handling of delicate matters, and was reminded once again how much he hated this part of his job.

"Detective......detective, wait." There was another hitching sob. "You haven't called Maddie yet?"

"Madeline Dean, her daughter?" Cooper read from his notes. "No, I haven't. We have a number for her, also from Mrs. Abbott's phone which we presume is the best way to get in touch. She was going to be my next call."

"Please, if you don't mind—please let me be the one to call her, Detective Cooper. This will be devastating for her. She's had so much heartache already. It might be easier coming from someone she knows."

Cooper pondered for a moment. What the hell kind of cop was he anyway, he thought. "Alright, you can make the call. But be sure to give her my name and number and tell her I need her to call me, as soon as she possibly can." He hung up, ashamed at the relief he felt.

By late afternoon Cooper and Morales had nearly finished their search of the huge house. The fingerprint, hair and fiber team had gone over all the rooms thoroughly and the photographer, having taken hundreds of digital images, had gone. There were two uniformed officers with their cruisers parked at the entrance to the estate, now holding back a large contingent from the local press and state media.

Morales found Cooper in Eleanor's bedroom still looking through drawers.

"Scotty, what do ya think of this house, huh? It's gigantic...and spooky. We haven't even been to the third floor." In her gloved hands she held out a small spiral book. "I found this in the purse Willis bagged up." She handed him the book. "Mrs. Abbott called the Selwyn guy three months ago if this date is right." The note read: 'Call Arthur re: changes, effective immediately.' There was another one more recently in fact, with the same notation, just last month. I mean she has other entries about him…you know, other notes to herself, but 'changes, effective immediately', sounds to me like something to do with a will."

Cooper continued to page through the book. "You know, this name……Abbott, it sounds so familiar. I know I've heard it somewhere."

Morales looked up at him and with her typical shrug and said, "Don't know, doesn't ring a bell."

"I wonder when was the last time she spoke to Selwyn. He didn't say anything about talking with her, when we called him earlier."

"He was in shock, Scotty," Morales answered. "If they were close, something like that was probably the last thing on his mind. This could be anything. It was a few months back."

"I got a call back from the daughter, a few minutes ago," Cooper looked at Morales and shook his head. "She didn't sound good. She's planning to catch a flight down tomorrow morning."

"Are one of us picking her up?"

"No. Said she'd rent a car. Thought she'd be here by noon, if the flight is on time. She seemed calm, but spacey, you know?"

Morales nodded and said, "I guess that's pretty much how I'd feel if someone called me up out of the blue, and told me my mamá had been murdered."

"Well, I'm going to meet her here and maybe get a brief interview, if she's up to it. Let's get started on the list. You get in touch with Abbott's PA, Diane Kenyon. When you get her line up an interview as soon possible."

At four-fifteen Madeline still had a lot of paperwork to do before she could think of going home. Not good for a Friday and she hadn't even started on payroll. Even though PND payroll was relatively small, only ten people, she preferred to do that chore herself, rather than hire it done. It seemed unlikely this would be an early evening. Still, it was Friday (TGIF! ran through her mind), and she remained high on the prospect of the Barron estate bid. She planned to devote the entire weekend to it. Madeline would spend all day Saturday with Charles and Cally at the estate, making sketches and notes. She was so excited. She had never been inside or even seen the place close up. She had seen photos, but this would be such a kick. She realized she was humming under her breath.

The intercom buzzed. Nadine's voice came through the machine, "Maddie, line three for you."

"Who is it? No, never mind. Just take a message. I'm too busy. I've got less than an hour to get payroll done."

"Sorry, it's some guy named Selwyn. He insists he speak to you, he says it's very important." Madeline's brows knitted as she stared at the blinking light on the phone. Arthur Selwyn? What could he possible want, and why call her here, at the office? Madeline's thoughts traveled quickly, the only way they could-her mother. The excitement of weekend plans evaporated like a wisp of steam from a tea kettle, and frisson of fear hit her stomach. Immediately an idea played through her mind. She just wouldn't answer. If she didn't answer then she might be able to put off whatever this was. Instead she punched the blinking button.

"Arthur, how are you?" she began, in a cheerful tone.

"Hello, Maddie, I'm fine. It's good to hear your voice." His voice was subdued.

"It's good of you to call, it's good to hear your voice. We haven't spoken in such a long time." Madeline's stomach fluttered unpleasantly. "Arthur, I hope all is well with you…" she trailed off, suddenly afraid to speak.

"I'm fine, but I'm afraid this isn't a social call, Maddie, I'm sorry." He cleared his throat, and Madeline could feel her palms become damp with sweat as another wave of nausea hit her stomach. She began to feel light headed and tightened her grip on the receiver.

"I'm calling with some bad news, Madeline. Very bad news, I'm afraid. I would like you to sit down please and try to be calm. Maybe you could call the woman who answered the phone to come into the room?" He paused, but Madeline didn't respond. "I hope you know I would rather do anything than call you like this."

She didn't move or speak. "Maddie, my dear. If there was any other way…" There was silence along the phone line as Madeline's world began to cartwheel.

"What is it," she whispered.

"It's your mother, Maddie. It's Eleanor", he said. Then he told her.

The receiver slipped from her hand and clattered to the desk.

CHAPTER FIVE
Saturday

Cooper and Morales met early at the office to continue their list of interviewees. It was easier to think at seven in the morning before the bulk of the day shift people came in. Their list was developed from the names Morales had gleaned from Eleanor Abbott's cell phone, her address book, and their first examination of the laptop that was found on her desk. There was a great deal of information in the laptop, and Cooper wanted it examined by the forensic team, but not before he had the opportunity to take a quick look. He got it back from the techs who had fingerprinted it. None except Eleanor Abbott.

Records of business dealings on her computer were extensive. She was an incredibly busy woman both in business, her charities and in her social life. Almost frenetic. Reading about all the events, hours spent in meetings, philanthropic activities, clubs and all charities she gave time to, made Cooper feel like a do-nothing layabout.

Eleanor had a memo area in the computer where she logged in notations, feelings about transactions and deals in general terms. It was written in a weirdly conversational tone, almost a blog. In this area Morales found several unpleasant comments about James Edgerton. Many of the comments were in regard to specific properties or projects, and the information made no sense to the detectives as they knew nothing about the details. Often though, the intent was clear.

Abbott's email contact list was lengthy. There were over five hundred email addresses. Morales wondered out loud how anyone could possibly know that many people. Cooper allowed as how he would be lucky to scrape up fifteen names, and half of those were back in Texas. Fortunately, the names on Eleanor's list were divided into a few categories. Most were business, many were friends. There were very few that resided in the family category.

They ranked the importance of interviews according to Morales's observation of the number of times each was called recently. Ian Andrews, Phoebe Deardon, Richard Kelsey and Sydney Poole, were the names most frequently called, they were also the names associated with some of Eleanor's charities. She seemed to be in touch with Arthur Selwyn more often than one would usually associate with an attorney, but it seemed reasonable given his status as a friend, not a business associate. Also there was a couple, Frank and Kathryn Van Gessler. Richard Kelsey, apparently coupled with Sydney Poole.

The family side was woefully small. Husband was dead. Daughter and her husband, Madeline and David Dean, lived in Eugene, Oregon. Elderly aunt Prudence (age 85), lived in Palm Springs, Florida. Morales had a good laugh at that one wondering out loud who would name a kid Prudence. Until Cooper told her that the name Prudence was the inspiration for one of John Lennon's songs, 'Dear Prudence'. That shut her up. One cousin on Clay's side, Jack Abbott (age 67), lived in Denver. Most communication with the living relatives was via email.

The detectives thought it was likely that most of the relatives, with the exception of her daughter and son-in-law, lived too far away to be included in the investigation. But they had to be notified. Cooper decided that he would get Morales to do it.

How lame, pushing this onto Izzy, but I just don't have much stomach for it. He viewed this tendency as a weakness but if there was an opportunity to delegate job of notification, he usually took advantage of it.

With the list complete they started with people closest to Eleanor. Morales got on the phone and the first person she called was Phoebe Deardon.

* * *

"I'm sorry, detective, you must forgive my abruptness, but I don't know what you think I can tell you," Phoebe Deardon said, hands on narrow hips. With a sigh, she had finally waved them into a large, light filled living room. She was dressed in a floor length embroidered silk caftan of bright coral, that accentuated the over tanned skin and the poufy, bleached coiffure. The info they had on her said she was fifty-six, and she looked every day of that age. That hair and that get-up, Morales thought, looks like she's trying out for *Mame*.

"I can't believe Ellie's been killed. How can you think I might have information concerning who murdered her? I've been in shock since you called." Mrs. Deardon began pacing the white shag rug that lay between the sofa and chairs. So large and white, it resembled an ice floe.

She strode nervously in front of the modern white leather sofa, a linen handkerchief pressed under a red nose. She looked emotionally drained, but composed. Cooper and Morales sat in a matching pair of leather chairs opposite the sofa that were so uncomfortable Cooper envied Mrs. Deardon's pacing.

"When did you last see her?" Cooper asked.

"Why just a few days ago. Wednesday, I think. I believe it was Wednesday. We met in town, she and Helen and I, we had lunch, did a bit of shopping." She abruptly stopped. "God, I need a drink," she said, heading to a chrome and glass table. Her low heeled satin slippers clacking noisily as she stepped from the rug and crossed the wood floor. "Can I get you anything?" She turned and raised a crystal decanter from a drinks tray at them. "Or perhaps you'd rather have coffee?"

Morales opened her mouth. "Nothing for us, thank you, ma'am," Cooper interjected smoothly. Morales closed her mouth with a scowl at Cooper.

Phoebe Deardon returned to the leather sofa opposite them, carrying a short crystal glass with a generous helping of whiskey and rocks. The lead crystal sparkled in the light. "This doesn't happen to people you know," she said, her eyes staring into the glass, swirling the whiskey. "It feels like I'm dreaming."

"Unfortunately it does happen, ma'am," Cooper said. "Where were you on Thursday night Mrs. Deardon?"

"Where was *I*? Well, I have to think. I believe I was here that evening. Yes, I was here watching a movie with my daughters. They were here Thursday to visit. They're here a couple of times a week to have dinner with me. Why?"

"We need to have an understanding of where everyone was the night of the murder. Can you think of anyone who might have a reason to hurt Mrs. Abbott? Anyone you know of that might be holding a grudge or be angry about a business deal maybe?"

She leaned back with a sigh and took a generous swallow of whiskey. She shuddered as it went down. "I'm not the right person to ask. I really know very little about Ellie's business dealings. She didn't talk about it much, at least not with me. I know she had some problem or other with James Edgerton, but I wasn't privy to the nature of it if that's what you're going to ask."

"What exactly *did* she say about Edgerton then, Mrs. Deardon?" Morales asked.

"All I recall is she remarked a few times in an off hand way about her frustration with him. If I ever asked specifics, Eleanor would just change the subject."

"What did you talk about when you met with her and Mrs. Highwater for lunch?" Cooper asked.

"I don't remember exactly. Just the usual chitchat, the kind we always had. We talked about the three of us going into San Francisco for a musical next month." She gave a brief, sad smile. "We were all so excited about it, we were going to see *Wicked*, at the Orpheum." Her smile faded. "She talked about her daughter a little. She made a remark about Maddie and her husband—their troubles."

"What, specifically, did she say?"

"Oh I don't remember," she said irritably, and took another large swallow of her whiskey. "I think it was something about how much she disliked him, and that Maddie had better get going on the divorce, stop dragging it out, something like that. I'm not sure, I wasn't really listening. I tend to tune out things like that…talking about other people's divorce troubles."

Cooper wondered about that comment but steered the conversation in another direction. "What about her other friends, acquaintances. Anyone you know of had a bee in their bonnet with Mrs. Abbott for some perceived wrong?" he asked.

Mrs. Deardon looked at Cooper, her head tilted. "Pardon?"

"Uh, anyone upset with her, or Mr.Edgerton." He saw her confusion. "Sorry."

"You're not from here are you, detective?" she inquired.

"No, ma'am, I'm not. Texas."

Phoebe Deardon sipped her whiskey and looked at Detective Cooper thoughtfully with red rimmed eyes. "I don't believe that Ellie alluded to anything of that kind, and certainly not among those she considered her friends."

"Are any of her friends having financial troubles that you know about?" Morales asked.

Mrs. Deardon laughed out loud. It was low pitched and throaty, sounding cynical, and completely without humor. "Most people who live in Los Gatos don't generally have 'money problems', detective." It surprised Cooper that the comment was delivered in a tone that somehow kept it from sounding elitist. She looked out the floor to ceiling glass walls at the hazy morning light. "I'm sure you will find during your investigation that not all of Ellie's friends were wealthy—of course, that depends on your definition, but they do well enough."

"So you believe she was on good terms with everyone?" Morales asked.

"I've been friends with Eleanor for over thirty years. We've been very close for most of those years. I probably know more about her than anyone else in our circle. Except maybe Ian." She sipped her drink. "But, she was also very private. She only let you so far in. Over the years she had problems with Clay. He was a scoundrel. A brilliant businessman, but a scoundrel." She shrugged as if to say what else can you expect, that's how men are.

"And she had to deal with the loss of her son. She worked hard all her life for what she had. She confided in me, but the truly deep important things she kept to herself. Perhaps she had learned to not trust anyone."

"Can you tell us about her son?"

Phoebe Deardon looked forlornly down at the glass in her hands, now nearly empty. "It was a tragedy. I'm sure you can find this out, it is in the records. It was a long time ago…I can't see what that could possibly have to do with her murder."

"In a homicide investigation, Mrs. Deardon, everything is important. What happened to her son?" Cooper repeated.

She looked at the detectives, brows pulled together and unhappiness etched in the lines of her face. "The boy, Michael, was born with 'special needs' I think they say now. He was developmentally delayed. It was just," she shook her head sadly, "dreadful. When he was about six years old, he drowned in their pool."

Cooper and Morales looked at one another. "It was an accident?" Cooper said.

"Well of course it was. Madeline was at home and was supposed to be looking after him. But she was only, what? Sixteen? For

God's sake. She left him for a just a few moments. He wasn't even in the pool. When she came back he was dead. Of course it was an accident."

The only sound in the room was the clink of Phoebe Deardon's ice cubes as she swirled what remained of her whiskey.

Cooper closed his notebook.

He said, "I guess that's enough for right now, ma'am, we'll see ourselves out. We really appreciate your being open with us. We may have further questions a little later on." Morales and Cooper managed to extricate themselves from the low slung chairs.

"I can't wait detective," Phoebe Deardon said morosely, looking up at him from the sofa. As they left she got up and went back to the drinks cart.

* * *

Cooper dropped Morales at the office so she could begin her research into those on their list. He headed to the Abbott mansion. The day was warming up, the temperature was near eighty when Cooper pulled into the courtyard at Raven's Nest. March weather was unpredictable. Cold and blowing one day, warm and sunny the next. He glanced at his watch. Eleven-forty five. The Abbott daughter was due around noon. He hoped her flight had been on time.

When he finally received a call from Madeline late yesterday, she had seemed calm, maybe a little too calm he thought, considering her mother was laying on a slab down at the morgue. Maybe it was shock. Or maybe she didn't care, he thought cynically.

Now he knew why the Abbott name had rung a bell, he had asked around the station. Clayton Abbott, Madeline Dean's father died in an automobile accident a year and a half ago. The detective who caught the case, Russ Mullins, briefed him.

"I was liaising with the CHP. It was a bad wreck. I guess he lost control on one of the sharp curves coming over the hill on 17, coming back from Santa Cruz. Went over the edge of the mountain in a nose dive. There wasn't much left of the guy's car, or the guy, for that matter." He shook his shaggy head. "Poor bastard."

"It looked like there *might* have been some tampering with the brake line and *maybe* the steering linkage had been messed with too. The car was so messed up you couldn't tell for sure. But Ralphie, the guy who towed it, said as far as he was concerned it had been messed with. He showed me cuts and shit that didn't happen 'cause of the wreck.

"Anyway it was late, really foggy… oh, and he'd been drinking. He wasn't drunk but his blood alcohol was a little high. We couldn't find enough solid evidence to make a case, but a rich guy like that, hell, you gotta know he had enemies." Mullins shook his head again. "That musta been one sweet car, though. Nineteen-sixty Austin Healey." He shrugged. "I worked that case a long time. It went cold."

In Cooper's naturally suspicious mind it seem unlikely the two deaths were not connected, even with the distance of almost eighteen months of time. The MOs were different but the motive seemed obvious: money. Or power.

Cooper put the car windows down and stepped out. There was little breeze and it was quiet. Far enough out of town where there was no traffic noise. He caught the scents of mowed grass and early spring flowers. He saw no one, no sign of the grounds keeper. Probably gets most of his work done early.

Insects buzzed on the warm air, and there was an occasional twitter of a bird. A late model black BMW sedan was parked nose in to one of the garage bays. He had noticed it yesterday. DMV records showed it was registered to Eleanor Abbott. As he headed toward the garage, his phone buzzed. It was the M.E., Walt Simmons.

"All done Detective Cooper. Everything exactly what I expected. Cause of death was blunt trauma to her skull. She took at least two, possibly three blows to the back of her head. Her skull was a mess. Massive brain damage. The thing is, the first blow would've killed her. This was overkill. The bastard."

Cooper cupped his free hand around his eyes to look through the windows of the first bay of the garage. Inside he could see a late model SUV, a Lexus. "Okay Walt, thanks for getting back with me."

"One more thing, detective. Mrs. Abbott had cancer."

"You're kidding."

"Of course I'm not kidding. She had lung cancer. Advanced. I'm no oncologist, but my guess is that she had less than a year."

Cooper, surprised, immediately began to wonder how this might fit into the puzzle, or possibly have a bearing on the will. "Okay, well, that's a surprise. Anyway, I appreciate this, the speedy turnaround."

"No problem, catch you later."

Cooper gazed behind the garage building several yards to where the hillside angled further upward. Between the garage and the terrace a path led to a stone stairway built into the slope of the hill. The switch backs zigged and zagged up to the top and disappeared into the trees. Cooper made a mental note to investigate it. A beautiful property. So much wealth. He sighed and continued his tour.

Everything was big. The size, the scale. The garage, originally designed for horse and carriage, now would house eight vehicles. Even though in immaculate condition it had not been modernized since being converted for automobiles. There was a staircase on each end of the building leading to the upper story. Maybe one or two apartments? He made a circuit around two other buildings, smaller and built of rough stone. Through one dusty window he could make out stacks of wooden boxes, cardboard cartons, discarded lamps and more detritus of living. He spied an ancient wringer style washing machine and laughed softly. Haven't seen one of those since I was last in my granny's wash house in Corpus Christi.

The cobbled courtyard was vast. East, far beyond the garage the wide terrace continued the length of the mansion. Past two towers and the irregular face of the mansion, French style doors from different rooms opened onto the terraced area. There was a large table and chairs, that were covered by a huge umbrella. Large pots of tall palm plants, citrus trees and other plants Cooper didn't recognize, were artfully arranged in groups with wicker sofas and chairs. It looked like the perfect place to sit with an ice cold beer and a book, he mused.

"You must be the detective."

* * *

Cooper whirled around with a start. A young woman stood a few feet away, a solemn expression on her face. His immediate perception: quite tall and attractive, good figure and lots of very long, curly dark hair. She wore a white cotton shirt tucked into a pair of slim, faded jeans. Sun glasses hid her eyes. How had he not heard her arrive? He looked past her and saw a small sedan parked next to his car.

"Oh, sorry, you startled me. Yes, hi, Detective Scott Cooper, ma'am, Los Gatos PD. He stepped toward her and extended his hand.

"Madeline Dean." They shook hands. Then she said, "Well actually, it's Madeline Abbott, or will be soon. I'm going back to my own name…" her voice trailed off uncomfortably. "Anyway, I just got here. I hope I haven't kept you waiting too long."

"No, I only got here a few minutes ago myself."

"Maybe we should, uh, I don't know," she hesitated. "Go inside? Is that alright?"

Madeline unlocked the kitchen door with a key from a large ring which Cooper noticed held many old skeleton keys and an assortment of modern keys. She paused to remove her sunglasses and look at the piece of plywood that covered the broken panes. One of the officers had swept up the broken glass. She set her leather handbag and sunglasses down on the end of the kitchen table.

Cooper said, "There was broken glass." He stood waiting, hands on his hips, looking awkwardly around. Finally he broke the silence with the only comment he could think of. "How was your flight?"

"It was pretty unpleasant, actually. The pilots always seem to wait until the very last minute before making their turn to approach the airport. It's always a heart stopping spiral, nose down." Madeline cleared her throat. "I'm not much for flying."

Cooper nodded, not knowing what to say. "I, uh, guess you would like some information. About what happened."

"I would prefer that I didn't have to, detective, but there's no getting around it, is there?" Madeline said softly.

"It was the library," Cooper said, with an awkward wave of his hand toward the door. Madeline followed him down the hallway. Outside the closed double pocket doors he stopped. "Of course the scene, hasn't been…well, it hasn't been cleaned up. If you would prefer to wait, we could just talk, we don't have to go in right now."

She stood still, looking at the doors, without speaking. Finally, taking a deep breath she said, "Let's go ahead and take a look."

Cooper pushed the massive doors apart. Many items had been bagged and removed, but other than the chair and the rug, which were stained with blood, the room looked essentially undisturbed.

Madeline's eyes locked immediately on the chair then drifted down to the blood stained rug. She didn't enter the room. Her face was pale.

"Mrs. Dean, if you would like I can explain what we believe happened to your mother."

"Please, call me Madeline." With a glance at Cooper she nodded and said, "Go ahead."

"It was Thursday evening late according to the medical examiner. Sometime after 12:00 a.m., your mother was here in the library apparently having a cup of tea. It appears someone broke in through the kitchen door, with the intent of robbery. Perhaps he didn't know Mrs. Abbott was home. It's unclear. But he managed to come up behind her somehow without alerting her, as she sat in the chair. She was struck from behind."

Madeline was silent, her lips compressed. She swallowed.

After a lengthy pause Cooper continued, "There are problems with that scenario however."

"What do you mean?"

"It looked like a robbery. Her purse had been gone through, probably cash taken, but unknown how much, if any, and credit cards. But this house…well, it's full of valuable things that could have been taken and sold. My question is, why weren't they?"

Madeline stared at Cooper. "You're saying it *wasn't* robbery?"

"I don't know yet. Why didn't she hear it when the window was broken? The kitchen is quite a distance away, yes, but the house was quiet. No television on, no music playing. She was here alone. Why didn't the perpetrator take jewelry that I found in her room? All the silver? The art? Why not take the expensive laptop that was sitting there on the desk?"

Madeline pressed her fingertips to her lips and shook her head, as if in negation of everything she was hearing and seeing.

Cooper pressed on. "I believe that this has been made to look like a robbery with the actual intent being an assault on Mrs. Abbott."

Madeline's eyes were once again on the wing back chair, but Cooper was sure she wasn't really seeing it. Her eyes, he noticed, were an intense greenish blue.

Finally, she spoke. "Why would someone want to kill my mother? She was just…just a little woman. Small. Defenseless. She couldn't hurt anyone. Wouldn't hurt anyone."

Cooper took her arm gently. "Let's go find somewhere else to sit down for a few minutes."

* * *

Madeline asked Cooper if he wanted coffee. Rarely one to miss the chance for coffee he said he would, thanking her. She set about making it while Cooper pulled out a stool and sat at the long table. He took out his notebook. "I'll just be making a few notes, Mrs.,…uh, Madeline, if you don't mind."

"Of course."

"My partner, Isabelle Morales, and I are taking this case. We will be working with the forensics team and others to determine who has done this."

Madeline turned and looked at him from the counter and nodded solemnly. "Alright, thank you."

"Your name is Madeline Elizabeth Dean, correct?" Madeline nodded. She turned back to the counter and scooped coffee into the filter.

"As I said, though, I will soon be going back to Abbott."

He nodded. "Okay. I understand you live in Eugene, Oregon?"

She started the coffee maker and sat at the table across from Cooper. "Yes." Madeline gave him her home address and cell number. "I also run my business there. Pacific Northwest Design."

"What exactly do you do? What kind of business is it—are you an architect?"

Madeline paused, thinking. "No, I'm not an architect although I did study architecture. In theory I restore and rehabilitate old, historic homes and buildings. I don't always get to do that, exactly. Mostly we get smaller jobs. Redos on bathrooms or kitchens, floor refinishing." Cooper caught a bit of a grimace and an eye roll there. "Anyway, you take what you can get in order to pay the bills, right?"

"I guess that's true. You've done this how long?"

"Over five years. I started PND when I got my Master's degree in Historic Preservation, from the University of Oregon. U of O is one of the better schools that offers a Master's in that discipline. I love old homes, well, any old building." She smiled slightly, the first one he'd seen on her face. "Plus, I like Eugene. It's far enough away, but close enough…well, you know."

Cooper nodded. "Yeah, I do." Of course, that isn't exactly how it worked out, when Cooper left Texas. Los Gatos certainly isn't an easy drive or short flight from his home in Texas.

"That's impressive. Must've been difficult," he added.

"It's not as glamorous as it sounds. It's been a bit of a struggle." She didn't elaborate. The coffee maker made gurgling and sighing noises as it finished brewing.

Cooper explained, "As I said before there are inconsistencies with the scene that have us puzzled. Do you know of anyone who your mother may have had trouble with? A business associate, an employee? Has she told you about anyone she's had trouble with?"

"Other than me, you mean?"

Surprised, Cooper raised his brows in question.

"Oh, we are like nearly every mother and daughter. We had our differences, occasionally." Madeline looked at Cooper intently. "Or, you think this could've been some former employee who had a grudge against her? That couldn't possibly justify murder, Detective Cooper."

"For a rational person, of course it couldn't. But we have to look at all possibilities right now, no matter how far afield they may seem." Cooper watched as Madeline got up and poured coffee into delicate flowered porcelain cups. She set the cup and saucer in front of Cooper and pushed a cream pot and sugar bowl over to him.

"Oh, no, thanks. I take it black." He sipped the steaming coffee feeling utterly silly. His fist looked like a canned ham next to the small cup. He couldn't get his finger tip completely through the handle. Cooper had a fleeting sensation of being at a Mad Hatter's tea party sipping from miniature cups.

"I didn't have the best relationship with her," Madeline said with a small shrug, as she blew on then sipped her coffee. "We weren't particularly close, and after my father died we seemed to drift further apart. I've never heard anyone say a bad word about her, but then maybe I wouldn't."

"Can you tell me who else was in your mother's circle? Who else was close to her, besides Arthur Selwyn. I get the impression they were close."

Madeline thought. "Yes, she and Arthur go back a very long way. Well, let's see. She hired a personal assistant last year." Madeline made quote marks in the air, around the job title. "She's just a young girl and she hasn't gotten along all that well with Mrs. Temple, I know that." Another brief smile.

Cooper checked his notebook. "Ms. Kenyon?"

"That's right. Diane." Madeline sipped her coffee. "And…there's mother's best friends, Ian Andrews, Phoebe Deardon, Helen Highwater. Mother and Dad's business partner, James Edgerton. I wouldn't classify him as a friend, though. There are others that they socialized with for cocktail parties, cards, you know."

Cooper nodded, as he drank his coffee. "Go on."

"Okay, well umm, Kathryn and Frank Van Gessler," she ticked names off with her finger tips. "Richard Kelsey and Sydney Poole; they're a couple by the way. There are others, but those are the ones she saw most often, as far as I know."

Cooper jotted them down, glad that so far the list Morales and he had compiled seemed correct.

"What can you tell me about her relationship with James Edgerton? Everything solid there?"

Madeline stared into her coffee, contemplating the bottom of the cup. Finally, she said, "I don't know. The company's doing great, I guess. It always does. My mother and James haven't always agreed particularly since my dad died. That's the feeling I've gotten from her."

She rose and poured more coffee in each cup. Cooper waited. She returned the carafe to the coffee maker and turned to face him leaning back against the counter.

"Mother told me that James has always been more—aggressive—in spending and investing than she was comfortable with." Madeline put down her cup and massaged her temples. Fatigue was settling on her like a heavy blanket.

"She seemed to become more conservative every year." Madeline shook her head. "Mother didn't seem to have the zeal for the business since my Dad died. She and Dad had their problems, but I know she relied on him. Maybe losing him just scared her." Madeline returned to the table and fell silent. Then she said in a near whisper, "It did me."

Cooper wished mightily he didn't have to mention the next thing, but knew he did.

"Arthur Selwyn has made the official identification. Of your Mother. You won't have to do that."

She remained silent for several seconds. The refrigerator hummed. Madeline finally said, "Alright," and looked away.

Somewhere in the distance, a clock chimed the hour.

Hearing the clock, Cooper glanced at his watch and decided this was enough for now. He stood and asked, "Where are you staying?"

She had her head in her hands and looked up at him from under a curtain of dark hair. "Here, why?"

"Oh. I didn't realize—"

"Can't I stay here?" she interrupted him. "Is there some reason why I can't stay here?" He heard anxiety in her voice.

"Of course you can." Cooper was taken aback. "Of course you can stay here, it's your house. We've finished with the scene. I just thought…" he shrugged. "Well, since it hasn't been cleaned up. Guess I figured you'd want to go to a hotel, or something, until things were put right."

Madeline gazed through the back windows, to the mid-day sun. She saw more than a dozen large ravens, perched atop the roof line of the garage, their coal black feathers glistened with cobalt highlights in the sun. Often groups of them gathered, and it always reminded her of the movie *The Birds*. She shivered involuntarily.

"Mrs. Temple will take care of it. She's good that way." Then her eyes met his. "This is my home. I don't want to go anywhere else."

He studied her face. It was pale and drawn, stress and fatigue written in the shadows around her eyes.

"Then you should stay here if that will make you feel better." He stood. "I have to go. Thanks for the coffee. It was really good and strong. I like it strong like that."

Wondering where *that* idiotic comment came from, Cooper went to the back door. He turned. "I have an appointment to see Arthur Selwyn tomorrow morning. Maybe after, later in the afternoon, you might have a bit more time? Once I've spoken to him, I'll likely have a few more questions."

Madeline tilted her head, and looked up at Cooper sadly. "Am I a suspect, detective?"

Cooper smiled at her and replied, "At this point everyone is. Goodbye Madeline."

The phone in Madeline's pocket began to vibrate. "Goodbye, Detective Cooper, I'll guess I'll see you tomorrow."

* * *

Madeline stood and watched the detective walk to his car. Tall, broad shouldered and slim hipped, brown hair. He was dressed so casually—jeans, tooled cowboy boots, a blue chambray shirt with rolled back sleeves. He doesn't look much like the police, more like a cowpoke. Of course, the gold detective shield clipped to his belt looked serious enough. She pulled the vibrating phone out of her pocket. David. Damn it all to hell.

"David."

"Maddie, I've just heard, I called the office and Nadine told me." His voice added to the growing personal hell of today. "What in the world's going on?"

Madeline answered dully, "Mother's dead, David. That's all I know right now. I just got here a while ago."

"What happened, for God's sake, how can she be dead?"

"She was murdered. Late Thursday night. They don't know anything else right now. They're investigating. But they're not telling me anything."

"Oh, my God, Maddie, I'm sorry. Who's investigating? Maybe I should come down. You'll need help dealing with this, it's no time for you to be alone."

For a fraction of a second Madeline considered the idea of David coming. The only advantage would be that she would not be alone, there would be another living body around the huge house. The idiocy of it made her want to burst into hysterical laughter for even having the thought. *If I need someone here, which I don't, it would not be him, of all people.*

"No, thanks. I appreciate it, but I don't need help. There are two detectives in charge of the case. There's really nothing that you could do, besides, Mrs. Temple is going to be here."

"That old bag? What good will she be? Look, Maddie, I can help with, I don't know…arrangements, right? You shouldn't have to face it alone."

"I said no, David! And shut up about Mrs.T, what the hell do you know about her anyway?" Madeline shouted. She rubbed her temple where a headache was beginning behind her right eye. "I prefer to be alone. The things that need to be done just require family decisions. And that's me." The enormity of that statement flooded over her as visceral as a wave of adrenalin. She slumped down on one of the kitchen stools.

"I wish you'd let me help. I loved her too, you know." Madeline rolled her eyes and sighed as hot tears spilled onto her cheeks. David Dean never expressed any feelings at all for Eleanor, except to complain that she seemed 'indifferent' to him. Which she was. Madeline was certain Eleanor had moved well beyond indifference in the last year.

"No." Madeline said. "You stay there and I'll wrap this up as soon as I can. When I get back to Eugene we'll get together. We'll have a meeting to get things sorted out. Get things finalized."

"Oh shit, Maddie, not that again. Not with this going on. I should be there—"

"David! I'm telling you for the last time. I said I wasn't going to argue with you about it ever again, and I meant it. And now, I have something much more important to deal with. My mother is gone." She felt a weird physical sensation, as if she was folding in on herself. "Son of a bitch…" Madeline muttered softly. Sorrow and loss broke inside her and tears rolled down her face.

The line was silent.

"I'm sorry, Maddie," David finally spoke quietly. "I shouldn't have said what I did. I apologize. I'll go now and give you some space. Call me if you need anything. Anything at all."

Madeline nodded wordlessly. David hung up.

Madeline finally became aware that she was still sitting on the stool, staring out the kitchen windows. She had been there motionless for nearly an hour. She stared into the courtyard, hypnotized by the sounds of insects and watching the cluster of ravens atop the garage. One would fly off, only for the group to be joined by two more. A half dozen would soar away, to be replaced by another matching set of three. Were they having a conference? Exchanging ideas about the hunt for dinner later on?

What was it they were called? She searched her mind for the word. Not a cluster. A murder? No, that's crows. She watched them as they appeared to chat with one another, and hop here and there, changing the line-up on the peak of the roof. Do you suppose there is a hierarchy? Surely there must be, there is in every group of living things.

Fatigue deadened her limbs, and she sighed. What was it…it was…the word eluded her. Unhappiness? No. Suddenly, it popped into her mind. Unkindness. An *unkindness of ravens*. Isn't that fitting, she thought miserably, because right now the entire world also seemed to be an unkindness.

She had to find the energy to get up.

With an enormous sigh, she scrubbed at her face and finally pushed herself up from the stool, her head pounding, her body stiff and aching like an arthritic old woman. She retrieved her suitcase and overnight bag from the rental car. She parked them in the kitchen and called Mrs. Temple.

"Oh, my Lord, Maddie, it's so good to hear your voice! Does this mean you're home? I was about to lose my mind, waiting to hear something, anything!"

"It's okay, Mrs. T., yes, I'm here now and we'll see to everything together, alright? Is Pancho with you?"

"Oh, good Lord, yes. He's been in a right state, too. Moping around, whining and whimpering…he knows something's terribly wrong—"

"We'll take care of him." Madeline cut her off, unable to care if she were being rude. She wasn't sure she would be able to finish the conversation with Mrs. T, before she fell over in exhaustion.

"I'm sure he'll be fine, once he's back home." She managed a smile at the thought of Pancho. "Why don't you come tomorrow, regular time, with Pancho. The detectives have finished here…with the house. We can start cleaning it up." Madeline paused. "We'll start with the library."

"Yes, well...yes, of course. If you think that's best, of course that's what we must do." Mrs. Temple, the most fanatically dedicated cleaning person she knew, sounded reluctant.

"I know we can take care of it together." She said it with more conviction than she felt. "See you in the morning."

Never in her life had Madeline felt less like doing something, than dealing with the library. But she was determined to stay in her home so—the library had to be cleaned up. The thought of what that entailed, bloody furniture, and carpets and fingerprint dust, caused bile to rise in her stomach. She swallowed and grimaced, before trudging up to her room.

* * *

Cooper swung by headquarters to pick up Izzy.

"How'd it go?" Morales asked from her desk. "You met the daughter? What's she like?"

"I met her, we talked for a while. I don't know why, but she's not what I expected."

"Okay, *amigo*, what do ya mean by that?" Morales asked with a smile. She sat, tapping a pencil on her notepad. "Just what did you expect? You mean you have a different idea of what a super rich lady should be like?"

"She seems nice, and frankly, lost. This is a huge deal being thrown in her lap, Izzy, think about it. Her mother's murder, her mother's business, and that house? That's a lot to take on, especially when it blindsides you."

"Okay, okay. You don't see her as involved at this point?"

Cooper thought about it. The fragile, miserable girl he met at Raven's Nest, didn't seem like the type of person who would set out to deliberately hurt another person. But, he'd been wrong in the past. "Not sure, but I don't think so. For one thing, what motive would she have?"

"The obvious one: money," Morales answered with a satisfied tone. "You know as well as I do, that money makes this old world go around, especially these days."

Cooper looked down at Morales with a shake of his head. "I don't know. Somehow, I don't think so. She's going to end up with it all anyway. Why would anyone risk screwing that up?"

Morales looked at her notebook. "Alright, maybe not, but she should still stay on the list. Anyway, I've called the Kenyon woman and left a message. We have an appointment set up with Helen Highwater, tomorrow morning."

"Fine. Right now we gotta get to Edgerton's."

"We're going to Edgerton's now? Hey, we need to get some coffee, something to eat. I haven't had lunch, you know. Or breakfast. I'm starving."

"I swear to God, you and the food!" Cooper laughed. Then he added: "After we're done with Edgerton, I'll drop you back here. I want to know more about the wreck that killed Eleanor's husband, Clay. Mullins seemed to think it could've been murder. See if you can find the wrecker that handled it, find out where they took the car, you know, see what he says. And, let's find out what more we can about the Abbott kid."

On the way to Edgerton's office, Cooper took pity on Morales and made a quick stop for a sandwich at a small convenience market called Zippie's (*Fast In-Fast Out!*). It was a small dive, converted from an old 1930s gas station. It had a lot of Art Deco style, with a curved roof that extended over where the pumps used to be. Zippie's had its charm, but its primary advantage was oddly enough, the ample parking. Windows were plastered with ads for every cheap beer ever brewed, along with every cigarette ever rolled, cigars, e-cigarettes, and don't forget sodas, energy drinks and candy. All the vices of modern man.

Cooper stood in a line, four deep, to pay for a couple of prepackaged sandwiches, two cans of soda and a bag of chips. He watched while the clerk laboriously entered prices in the cash register, tip of his tongue poking out between pursed lips. The guy, whose name tag declared him to be, ironically, Todd Bright, seemed confounded by the electronic cash register. He would painstakingly enter a price then whisper, "no, no," erase, and start over. Cooper rolled his eyes, and had to bite his tongue to keep from making a disparaging comment. Almost fifteen minutes later, he managed to pay and get out. So much for a quick lunch. Real *Zippie*.

They ate the ham sandwiches on a bench outside. "God, I'm hungry, even this crap tastes good. My blood sugar's low," Morales grumbled. "You know I get this way when I don't eat breakfast, then we put off lunch. I should've had some breakfast this morning. You didn't get any cookies or a brownie or something?"

"Oh, quit your bitchin'," Cooper said good-naturedly. "No, I didn't get any cookies. Hell, it took fifteen minutes to get outta there with this mess. It'll hold you," Cooper said. He picked soggy bread from his sandwich, which was dubiously labeled *Fresh Made Daily!*, and threw it to the gulls and pigeons strutting around their feet. They looked sleek and well fed, but Cooper wondered how healthy they were eating stuff like this every day.

"You know I get hypoglycemic if I don't eat," Morales looked at Cooper with a scowl. "Now I'll have a headache, and it'll ruin the rest of my afternoon." She was wolfing down the sandwich like she hadn't eaten in days.

"I swear to God, I don't know how you do it," Cooper said. "How can you eat so much, and still stay…", he eyed her petite and curvy but slender figure, "how you stay…uhh…fit."

"Watch it," Morales said, with a shake of her head. "I have a fast metabolism, that's all. Besides, it takes a lot of energy to do what we do. On the go all day long, you know."

"Whatever. Get your chips and let's get going."

* * *

"I'm sure this visit pertains to Eleanor, although I don't know what useful information I can provide, detectives. Eleanor and I never worked that closely."

Edgerton had opened the office door to them at 1:30 p.m. The building housed other independent business people. Cooper saw a couple of attorneys listed, as well as a consultant. Upscale. Very…new millennium.

He greeted them with an ebullient attitude of cheerful willingness and immediately showed them into his office. They didn't even have a chance to sit and cadge a cup of coffee. Too bad for Izzy, Cooper thought, and allowed himself a smirk. Cooper introduced them and each showed identification.

"Please, have a seat." Edgerton said, as he waved them into the pair of chairs facing his desk. He was of medium build and a few inches shorter than Cooper with thinning, grey blond hair, dressed casually in khakis and a short sleeved cotton shirt. Each item of clothing had a prominent designer logo. *What is it with some people? Even on weekends, they have to dress to impress?*

"We just have a few questions we need to ask. They are routine, to help us determine a time line. Where were you Thursday night?" Cooper asked.

Edgerton's cheerful persona rapidly faded, and he looked at the detectives askance. "Where was I? What, exactly, does that mean? You think I had something to do with this?"

"We need to account for the whereabouts of all people close to Eleanor, on the night of the murder. Since that also includes you, it means exactly what I asked."

"I was out to dinner with a friend as a matter of fact." Edgerton stood behind his desk chair and put his hands on his hips. "I don't know what you're on about, but this is ridiculous."

"And this friend can corroborate that?" Morales asked.

"I suppose so, but is that necessary? My God. I can't believe…"

Morales pulled out her notebook. "I need you to give me the name of the person you were with, and the phone number where he or she can be reached. We also need to know the location. For verification."

Edgerton's face took on a flush under the tanned skin. "Oh, fuck this. This is invasive, detective. I insist that this person be left out of this, since it has no bearing on the case."

Morales looked at him without responding. She wondered what about this relationship, could cause him so much consternation.

"Her name is Christina Bradshaw." Edgerton gave the contact information. They had been at a trendy night spot from eight until after eleven. He then muttered, "What the fuck this has to do with—"

"Who is Christina Bradshaw? A business associate? A friend?"

"She is a friend. It was a social event, not business. My God, you people—"

"You said you were with Ms. Bradshaw until eleven that evening? Where did you go after that?" Morales asked.

Edgerton's unhappiness at the questions came out dramatically in body language. His hands left his hips and clenched by his sides. He shuffled his feet, turning as if to walk away, raking his hair, hands clenching, hands back on hips.

"I went home. What in the hell are you saying?"

"Was anyone there, that can corroborate that?"

"Oh, goddamnit, I live alone. Sonofabit—"

"When did you last see Mrs. Abbott?" Cooper asked interrupting.

Edgerton tone was barely civil. "As I said, we didn't actually work together. Her office was in her home. When Clay was still alive, he and I had office space together. After his death, I moved here when I realized I didn't need that much space."

"And so, when did you last see her?" Cooper repeated.

Edgerton reddened again. "Alright, fine. Let's see." He made a show of thinking it over. "I guess it would have been weekend before this last, either Friday or Saturday." He scrolled through his phone. "My calendar says we had a meeting, on Friday morning. That would've been at her home. Yes, we met at 10:00 a.m."

"What was discussed, Mr. Edgerton?" Morales asked.

He looked at Morales. "Tell me what business that is of yours? When business is discussed, it is always a private matter."

"Look, sir, let's cut to the chase. We are investigating a homicide." Morales said. "The court can compel you to give us the details of the meeting, but it would be simpler, if you were more cooperative."

Edgerton looked from Morales, to Cooper, and back, anger making his jaw clench and twitch. "Alright, fine. The meeting was about my buying out Eleanor's interest in the business."

Cooper looked at his notes. "It's our understanding that Eleanor and Clay and yourself were equal partners, each individual owning one third of the business."

"Yes. When I came into the business, my capital investment equaled one third of the value of the business at that time."

"When was that?"

Edgerton sat down in his chair and put his elbows on the desk. "It's been over twenty years." His face finally relaxed slightly. A heavy silence overtook the room. "It's difficult to believe it's been that long. Sounds cliché, but time really does pass quickly."

"So, you were trying to get Eleanor to sell her interest, which of course with Clay's interest, is actually two thirds."

"That's correct."

"Why now? Why didn't you approach Eleanor when Mr. Abbott died?" Cooper asked.

Cooper watched, fascinated, as Edgerton carefully arranged his features into a solemn mask. Edgerton now braced himself against his desk, by the tips of his fingers, rocking slightly in his chair. "Believe it or not as you wish, but I was reluctant to intrude on her during that period of mourning," he said.

"It is difficult to believe. You don't seem to be grieving over her death." Cooper looked intently at Edgerton. "So you decided to wait until eighteen months had passed, and then you felt that the time was right."

"I did. Eleanor is not getting any younger—" he stopped abruptly. "That sounds incredibly crude, especially now. What I meant to say was, I thought she would be thinking about retirement soon. She must have been in her early sixties."

"So you approached her with an offer for her two-thirds share."

"Yes."

"That must be a great deal of money." Cooper said, his brows raised.

The flush of anger was now back on Edgerton's fleshy face. "Yes, it is."

Cooper, eyebrows still raised, tilted his head in question.

"Look, detective, I don't see how that information would have any bearing on the investigation, and it's information I would prefer not to become public. Surely to God, even you can understand." Edgerton protested.

"Your cooperation is what is important, as we said. It is our responsibility to decide what is, or is not, important to the investigation, Mr. Edgerton. We are simply gathering facts. I can tell you that…even *we*…are not in the habit of divulging sensitive information." Cooper replied.

Edgerton's face darkened and his lips thinned.

"I offered her just a bit less than one hundred and sixty-five million dollars."

The faint hum of traffic on the street never wavered or slowed. Other than that, the room remained silent, until Morales cleared her throat.

"You have that amount in cash?" Morales asked.

"Of course I don't have that all in cash, don't be ridiculous. I have bankers who are backing me. I had arranged for that to be made available, in the event I was able to come to an agreement with Eleanor."

"Was the offer accepted?"

"No, it was not."

Cooper and Morales stood to leave. Morales looked down at the seated man.

"Now, was that so hard?"

* * *

The large Victorian era home sat on a quiet street of comparable vintage homes, in Los Gatos. It was well tended, and beautifully landscaped with an abundance of rose bushes that were kept well groomed and healthy. If you could ignore the expensive SUVs and sedans parked on the street and in the narrow driveways, it was easy to imagine oneself back in the 1890s, so perfectly was the house restored. The entire street was similarly turned out.

Morales turned the knob that rang a mechanical brass bell on the door. It was answered by a very short and stout middle aged Mexican woman, dressed in a tidy black uniform. Cooper struggled not to laugh. She looked as if she came from central casting. She carried a cleaning cloth and lemon polish in her hand. Salt and pepper hair was pulled back severely from a pronounced widow's peak, low on her forehead, into a bun at the nape of her neck.

"Jes?" she asked, so short she had to peer up at them, even Morales.

They showed their identification, and Morales asked to speak to Mrs. Highwater. The housekeeper led them from the foyer, through double doors to a parlor and told them to sit. It was quite cool and dry. The air-conditioned air made the room comfortable after the warmth outside.

The room was also a step back in time. Authentic looking wallpaper and paint colors, along with all antique furniture and varnished woodwork made the room feel like a movie set. The tall narrow windows, each had vintage looking lace curtains and pull down shades. Old daguerreotype and tintype portraits (generations of Highwaters?) graced the walls.

They made their way to a pair of Eastlake oak chairs. They were complete with crocheted antimacassars on each arm that covered velvet upholstery. Intricately patterned oak floors, so beautifully refinished and waxed, they looked brand new.

It was quiet, except for the low ticking of a clock. Cooper gazed around and noted many framed contemporary photos, old fashioned porcelain figures and bric-a-brac. On the ornate marble mantel was the source of the ticking: a torsion clock under a glass dome. Its brass spheres rotated serenely, back and forth. Somewhere within the house could be heard the sound of soft rock music playing, that created a bizarre time warp effect. Cooper and Morales exchanged a glance, each unwilling to speak and break the silence. The house looked immaculate and smelled of lemon polish.

After a few minutes, footsteps could be heard coming toward them from the hallway. Helen Highwater entered the room in a flourish, apologizing for keeping them waiting.

"I'm so sorry for that, I was on the phone. I've just been making some arrangements in the city—San Francisco—for our shopping trip. Mine, and my son, Ben's. She added. "What can I do to help you?"

Cooper and Morales rose and showed their identification and introduced themselves. Cooper said: "We called yesterday? We're here about Eleanor Abbott, ma'am. As you are aware, she was murdered. We would like to know what you can tell us about your relationship with her, when you last saw her?"

Helen Highwater stood still, hands clasping a long rope of beads that hung down the front of her tastefully faded denim shirt. She was tall, probably five-nine, and although by no means heavy, she had a classic figure with an hourglass shape. Generous bosom, curving hips and a feminine, nearly unlined and very beautiful face. Cooper knew she was probably in her early fifties, but looked years younger.

Hearing his questions, her face clouded. "Yes, I can't tell you how shocking it was, to get your call. Eleanor, well, Ellie…she was one of my dearest friends. I've known her for many years. More than twenty, actually. I can't believe she was murdered. I can't fathom who would want to hurt her."

"That's what we're trying to determine. Where were you, Thursday night, Mrs. Highwater?"

"Oh, Thursday? I believe I was here at home. Why?"

"We have to have an understanding of where everyone was the night of the murder," Cooper answered.

"You want to know my whereabouts? I'm a *suspect*?!" Her blue eyes opened wide.

"Don't be concerned, Mrs. Highwater, we are asking the same questions to everyone who knew Eleanor, all friends, relatives, business associates. We are not singling you out, ma'am."

Hearing that, Helen Highwater, with a sigh, visibly relaxed.

"When did you last see Eleanor, Mrs. Highwater?" Morales asked.

"The last time I saw Ellie, would have to be the party she hosted a few weeks ago. We were all there, the usual gang. The kids joined us, for the meal anyway."

"Kids?" Cooper asked.

"Yes. Ben was there, of course. Also Phoebe's twins, Kassie and Kammie. They were going to be going out with Trent, well he's the grandson of Arthur Selwyn. He was visiting—well he lives in San Jose, and all the kids had decided to go out after the meal."

"All of the regular friends were there that evening?" Morales asked.

"Oh, yes. Those in 'our crowd', well, we rarely miss the parties. Everyone enjoys it so. We had food, drinks, you know. It was just a typical get together, like we always have. Everyone especially liked it when Ellie hosted, you know, because we all like Raven's Nest so much. Who wouldn't?" Helen Highwater paused and looked out the front window. She watched a car roll slowly down the street.

She seemed distracted for a moment, then, with a slight shake of her head she said, "Anyway, we ate dinner, and the kids took off. We had cocktails and wine, then played cards. We kind of split up, you know? Some like poker, some like rummy or bridge. It was pretty much like every other time. That was the last time I saw her." She pulled out a hankie from her jeans pocket and pressed it under her eyes and rubbed her nose. "We had planned to get together last weekend, but she called and canceled. Something came up, she said. Ellie didn't say what."

"You didn't see Mrs. Abbott last week? At a luncheon in town with Phoebe Deardon?" Cooper quizzed.

Helen pulled her brows together with a frown. "Oh, that's right! Oh, of course. We did meet for lunch, on Wednesday, I think. I'm sorry I had completely forgotten about it. I didn't stay with them the whole afternoon. I think they planned to do some shopping. I came home." Morales made a note.

"Did you see any change in her recently, Mrs. Highwater?" Morales asked.

"What do you mean change?" Mrs. Highwater asked, puzzled. "She seemed to be just the same as always. She did look tired and looked as if she'd lost some weight. As if she needed to, she's such a tiny little thing," Mrs. Highwater said with a slight smile. "When I asked her if something was the matter, she just brushed it off, saying she was having trouble sleeping and that she was worried about her daughter. I believe what she said was, she wanted Madeline to get on with divorcing David."

"Did she say anything more specific about her daughter? Anything about their divorce?" Morales asked.

Sensing more was coming, Mrs. Highwater sat down abruptly, on the edge of one of the chairs. "She didn't go into it much more.

She did say the marriage had been a mistake on Maddie's part, that the boy was no good. I couldn't understand it because my son, Ben, likes David, they're actually friends. They get together when David comes down here. He's a few years older than Ben, but they both like computers, computer games, all that online stuff, you know how kids are. Anyway, Ellie didn't dwell on it, and I didn't pry."

Cooper wondered how well the next bit would go down. "Had Eleanor told you she had cancer?" Cooper asked.

"Cancer?! Oh, no." Mrs. Highwater slumped back onto the chair. "Cancer? How…I mean, how bad was it?"

"The medical examiner determined that she had advanced lung cancer. He said that Mrs. Abbott would have had less than a year." Cooper said.

Helen Highwater looked stunned. "Oh…my God," she said softly. "I didn't know. I wish I would have known. The poor thing. I wonder why she didn't say anything to me about it. She must have known?"

"We haven't spoken to her personal physician yet, but I would assume that yes, she did."

A young man sauntered into the room. He was dressed in faded and artfully ripped denims and a black tee shirt with the tail hanging out. The tee shirt advertised a band Cooper didn't recognize, but then, he couldn't read the lettering anyway. He looked about twenty-five or six, a tall and muscular surfer type, bleached blond, and good looking, very much like his mother. He carried a cell phone in one hand and cigarettes in the other.

Cooper smiled inwardly at how different things were for kids these days. Cooper had begun smoking at sixteen, and hidden it from his mother for as long as he could, knowing he would have been whipped within an inch of his life, had she found out. He quit ten years later, but even now, five years on, just seeing a cigarette made him long to pick them up again.

Helen Highwater stood and introduced her son. "This is my son, Benjamin. Ben, these are the detectives investigating Eleanor's death…murder."

Ben nodded to Cooper and Morales. "How is the investigation going? Do you know who did this to Eleanor?" The lack of sincerity in his voice was surprising. He might have been reading cue cards. Cooper listened to his voice, and watched him closely while he spoke. His large, blue eyes looked empty and showed no care about the answer to his questions.

Cooper and Morales stood. "We have several leads, Ben. Do you know anything that might help us? Anything would be appreciated." Cooper said.

"Sorry, I don't. I'm usually busy with school, mostly. I haven't seen Eleanor for a while, so I don't know how I can help." His body language and voice conveyed no sorrow or concern over Eleanor's death. His only interest was finishing the conversation and leaving.

"Ben, where were you on Thursday night?" Morales asked.

Benjamin looked down at Morales, steadily. "I was out that night, with some friends. We went to the movies."

"Okay, let me know who you were with and how to contact them."

"I was with Kammie and Kassie Deardon and another friend. We met Jason in San Jose, and we went to the movies there."

"I expect we can get Kassie and Kammie's numbers. How do we get in touch with Jason?" Morales continued, her voice quiet, calm and businesslike.

He gave her Jason's number. "He's a busy guy. Might be hard to hook up with him." Ben looked very faintly pissed.

He turned to his mother. "Sorry, I have to go now. I'm going over to Kassie and Kammie's house for a while, Mom. I won't be too late." He excused himself politely, and headed out the front door, keys jangling in his hand. His mother watched, with a peculiar gaze Cooper couldn't name.

"This has really traumatized him. She's always been so good to Ben. He kind of thinks of her as a grandmother." She smiled sadly. "My mother died when I was a young girl, and Ben's paternal grandmother was killed in an auto accident when Ben was only five years old."

"That's too bad for Ben. Where is his father?"

"Greg is dead." She stated it with quiet finality. "He was an architect. He loved Ben so much." She stared, out the front window again, into a long distant past. The weird coldness of her tone, had Cooper making a mental note that there was more to the story. With a shake of her head, she continued: "Eleanor was so fond of Ben. And she and I were close. I thought of her almost as a mother. She was just a kind, considerate, woman."

"Is there anyone you can think of who may have wished Mrs. Abbott harm? Any person you know about that may have had issues with her, or held a grudge?" Cooper asked.

An odd look flitted over her pretty face. Cooper's intuition was on alert. Mrs. Highwater only said, "I have a hard time even imagining that any such person exists. She kept to herself a lot, but if you needed help, she was there for you. No, I don't think I do."

* * *

Madeline carried her bags up to her bedroom and heaved them onto the bed. She looked around. For most of her life, at Raven's Nest, her own rooms rarely changed. They were once redone almost fifteen years ago, and had remained the same since, reflecting her choices as a high school student. Now, she realized there was something comforting about the sameness. Pale yellow walls, dark English oak antique furnishings; bed, dresser, wardrobe, desk and bookcases.

She opened the window. It looked out over the lush front sloping lawns and gardens, and the large, forested area at the front of the property. Through the wooded area ran the serpentine drive. Warm, somnolent air filled the room. She stood at the window, mesmerized by the beauty of the grounds, breathing the clean air. Madeline shook herself, and realized that she had to keep moving until she was settled in, or the way she felt, it would never get done.

She unpacked the clothes she'd hurriedly stuffed into the bag back in Eugene, and put her toiletries away in the adjoining bathroom. She caught a glimpse of her face in the mirror over the sink. Oh, my God, I look like hell. Pale skin, dark circles under her eyes and grimy matted hair. She leaned in close to her reflection, pulled her lower lids down. They were red and bruised looking. No wonder that detective stared at me.

After she finished unpacking, Madeline collapsed across her bed, and laid her aching head on her arm. Other than the faint buzz of insects outside and an occasional bird call, the silence was so complete, her ears felt oddly muffled, as if she could hear nothing.

The finality of her mother's death swept over her again, like a wave. Gone. Just like Dad. How do I face it? Not so much that she's gone, but that now, there really is only me, I'm completely alone.

There is a certain distillation of feelings, when you lose someone, a parent, a sibling. All the things that you never took time to look at, think about, are suddenly there in your face, all you can think about. There's no escape. You can disappear maybe, with drugs, booze.

Should I try that, she wondered, put everything out of my mind by getting wasted? That's just what I need, to wake up tomorrow morning, hung over and sick, my head aching worse than it does now. The problem is, sorrow and regret are still there, to welcome you back. She stared up at the elegantly carved ceiling, while slow, hot tears leaked out of her eyes and rolled into her hair. Her chest hitched with a sob. After only a few minutes, exhausted, she slept.

A clock chimed at six, in the hall upstairs, and Madeline woke. She sat up, groggy and disoriented. It was dusk. Looking around the room, everything came back in a rush. She shook her head with a grimace.

After popping a couple of Excedrine tablets, she stood under a hot shower and vigorously scrubbed her body and hair. Under the spray, she turned the water up as high as it would go and hot as she could stand. She aimed the nozzle on the back of her neck, allowing the water to pummel her, hoping it would ease…something.

Once she had on pajamas and a robe, she actually began to feel nearly human again. The throbbing in her head had faded a bit, and she found herself hungry. She headed to the kitchen, to see what she might scrounge for dinner.

As she went down the hallway, two doors down and across the hall, she came to her mother's bedroom. The door stood open. She touched the switch by the door, that turned on the lamp on her mother's small writing desk. The soft light touched here and there, on her mother's bed, the crocheted pillow covers, her brush and comb resting on the vanity. Madeline stared with tearing eyes at the personal and private things that stood, waiting. A blue silk robe laid across the back of the vanity chair. A pair of slippers by the bed. All waiting for Eleanor, who was never coming back.

Even without entering the room, she could smell Shalimar, her mother's favorite scent. The bed was made, and the room was tidy. At least the detectives had not destroyed things during their search. She was reluctant to enter. Eleanor Abbott was private by nature and never allowed children to play in her rooms, so Madeline grew up rarely spending time in this room with her. From the door, she could see the residue of powder used for fingerprinting. It was on every surface.

She saw the door that connected Eleanor's room to Clay's, through a dressing room. It stood open. When the family first moved into the mansion, her parents had adopted the old fashioned practice of having adjoining, but separate, bedrooms. As a child, Madeline had thought it was because there were so many rooms, why not spread out? When she grew older, the truth became clear to her. They had separate rooms for very different reasons. She didn't know what the reasons were, specifically, and she still didn't know, but she was aware that part of their marriage had changed.

With a sigh, she brushed tears from her cheeks, turned off the light and went downstairs. In the pantry, she found a can of soup. Ten minutes later, using the back stairs, she carried a plate of cheese and crackers and steaming minestrone soup carefully up to her room and crawled into bed. Every time she came home, she felt the same crush of nostalgia when she climbed under the covers, remembering the nights her father would read to her at bedtime, when she was small. Her favorite was 'Where The Wild Things Are'. He had probably read it to her a hundred times. It was a wonderful memory, but it left her with a nearly unbearable sense of aching, hollow emptiness.

She turned on the small flat screen television which sat on the bureau across from her bed. The seven o'clock news was on so Madeline watched two channels rehash the same scant information about her mother's murder. There was little to report. An unknown intruder stole money, credit cards and committed the vicious assault. There were few leads. Hearing it again made her want to cry. She turned it off and tossed and turned for a short time before falling sleep.

CHAPTER SIX
Sunday

At 9:00 a.m. Sunday morning, police headquarters was already busy. Phones jangled and a handful of cops talked across their desks and across the room at each other. Isabelle Morales answered the ringing phone at her desk. "Los Gatos PD."

"Hello, this is Diane Kenyon. I'm trying to reach a Detective Cooper?"

Morales sat up abruptly, causing her chair to screech. She snapped her fingers to get Cooper's attention, as he stood filling his mug at the coffee pot.

"Ms. Kenyon, I'm glad to get your call, this is Detective Morales, Detective Cooper's partner. We've been trying to reach you, since Friday afternoon."

"Yeah, well, that's why I'm calling. I got your message. What can I do for you?"

Morales looked at Cooper with raised eyebrows and motioned with her head, to get him to come while saying to Diane Kenyon, "We need to talk with you concerning your employer, Mrs. Abbott."

Cooper sat at his desk and listened. Morales put it on speaker.

"What about Mrs. Abbott? She's my boss, I'm her administrative assistant. Is there some kind of problem—has she asked you to contact me?"

"It sounds as if you haven't heard, Ms. Kenyon." Morales paused. "We have some unfortunate news…Mrs. Abbott is dead."

"She's *what?!*" Diane Kenyon's voice rose to a shriek.

"She was murdered, sometime late Thursday evening, in her home."

"Is this some kind of a joke? This can't be…but…why would someone hurt Mrs. Abbott? Oh…" Diane Kenyon's voice fell to a whisper. "I, I don't understand."

"Ms. Kenyon?" Morales waited for the woman to respond. "Ms. Kenyon? Where are you right now? We need to talk to you as soon as possible."

"I went away. Mrs. Abbott said it was okay. She gave me the weekend off—and Friday, so I went to Napa. Oh, my God." In a rush she explained, "I usually work Monday through Friday, and Saturday if she's busy. Well, when she needs me. But she said it would be okay to take the days off."

Diane Kenyon caught her breath and babbled on, "I'd been working so much, and I've been so tired. Exhausted really. I just needed a little time off. Mrs. Abbott said I could go, she said it was okay. I wanted to meet a friend up in Napa, you know, just for a bit of rest, a bit of time off—"

"I understand, Ms. Kenyon." Morales interrupted her. "If you're in Napa, how soon can you get back here, to answer a few questions?"

"I guess pretty soon. I was going to come back later today anyway. I have work tomorrow… Wait, oh, oh God, I guess… I don't know what I'm supposed to do……"

"Okay, Ms. Kenyon? Take down this number." Morales gave Diane Kenyon her cell phone number. "It's important that you call me the minute you get back, alright?"

"Yes, of course, of course," Diane's voice was shaky and faint. "I'll call you. Goodbye."

Cooper leaned back in his chair, coffee in hand.

"You heard her. Apparently, she got the weekend off, per Mrs. Abbott, and went to Napa. She was coming back today anyway." Morales' and Cooper's desks sat side by side. She glanced over to Cooper. "She sounded pretty upset."

Cooper frowned and turned in his chair to face Morales. "She won't be working tomorrow now. Convenient. What do you think?"

"No, it sounds legit. Anyway, it's only about an hour and a half drive, depending on traffic." Morales replied. "No reason why she won't be here later today."

"Arthur Selwyn called and asked to postpone his interview until first thing tomorrow morning."

"What's his reason?" Morales asked.

"He said because of Eleanor's death, he needs to go to church, and spend the day alone to think and grieve. I told him that it had to be tomorrow morning then. Can't get to everyone in one day anyway."

Morales looked at Cooper with a frown. "That's weird. How long could an interview possibly take. Not like we would keep him all day."

Cooper had had the same feeling, but didn't think it was a good idea to refuse the guy. Death is hard, when it's a close friend. Who knows, maybe he really is grieving. They had plenty to do anyway.

"That Edgerton is a real asshole," Morales said.

"He was a bit nasty. I wonder if that's his every day niceness, or did we get something special."

"Don't know, but I was about to pop him."

"Calm down, Izzy. We'll do some looking into Edgerton—see if we can find out why he's being so difficult. Come on, let's go."

She stood, and her chair screeched again. "Where?"

Cooper got up and drank the dregs of his coffee. "First we'll swing by the watering hole Edgerton and Bradshaw used, Club Envy. Then, Kelsey."

* * *

With sketches in a portfolio under his arm, Ian Andrews stepped out into the cool, hazy air. He breathed deeply, invigorated by the clean early morning scents. Immaculately turned out, as was his way, he unlocked the door to his 1970 Mercedes sedan and slid in.

Los Gatos socialite, Fiona Abernathy, had requested conceptual drawings for a small pub she intended to open in the heart of downtown. Her Scottish great grandfather had had a pub in Edinburgh. Fiona wanted to recreate that homey feeling in Los Gatos. Andrews was thrilled with the idea and had come up with several interior plans to show her. She wanted hers to be as authentic a Scottish pub as could be made, and Andrews had done extensive research before beginning his sketches. The location she had in mind was large enough to create the look she was after, yet could achieve the cozy neighborhood feel.

He had been so relieved to get the call from Fiona. It came just a day after Eleanor's murder. The timing, for him, could not have been better. Strange, Andrews thought, how things happen……serendipitous. Hearing about Eleanor's murder, had thrown him into a devastating funk. He had plenty of work, but having a new job come his way, especially on the heels of such heart breaking news, well, it was a life line. A job that was so interesting and creative had really kept his mind busy for the last few days, thank God for that.

He backed out of the drive, onto the street, and put the Mercedes into gear. Oddly, nothing happened. Andrews tried putting it in park and then into drive again, but nothing. Now his car was sitting, idling in the middle of the street, with apparently no way to move it.

Am I going to have to push her? He sighed, set the brake, got out and opened the hood. Why am I doing this? I haven't got the foggiest idea what's wrong with her, and even if I did, I wouldn't know what to do to fix it. Maybe the transmission isn't even *in* the engine.

Ian Andrews was not a mechanical man, he was an artist. Some are put on this earth to create things, and some to fix things and he was not one of the 'fix things' types. Andrews pulled out his cell phone to call Eric Colby, who was a 'fix it' guy, the one who worked on his classic Mercedes when things went wrong.

Andrews stood near the front the car on the driver's side, peering into the engine compartment and searching for Eric's number in the contacts list. He found it and pressed to call. At precisely that moment, he became aware of the sound of an accelerating engine and heard the screech of tires. Out of the corner of his right eye, he caught sight of something moving, as the noise simultaneously increased.

In the blink of an eye, a nondescript car squealed down the street, pointed directly at him. Within the space of two seconds, it was upon him. Andrews stood, feet rooted in place, as the events unfolded, in weird, ultra slow motion. He took in the scene, stupefied, thinking for a fraction of a second, that he might be dreaming. Then, without conscious thought, Andrews sprang forward, hurling himself to the ground in front of his Mercedes. The impact of the fall caused the side of his head to bounce off the pavement. The car screeched by, where he had seconds ago been standing, impacting the left front of the Mercedes near the headlight, and grazing the back of Andrews' heel.

He lay on the pavement, shocked and unmoving, listening to the car accelerate away. In a few seconds the closest neighbor, retired college instructor, Edgar Gerhardt, came running. When he arrived and saw Andrews on the ground, he cried out, "Oh, oh no, Mr. Andrews, vhat has happened to you?" Gerhardt, a foot shorter than Andrews, managed to put his arms around Andrews and lifted the man to his feet. "Vhat was that? Did that car hit you?"

Andrews, wobbly and disoriented, could think of no reply. He tried to stand on his own, but pain shot up his right heel and made him cry out.

"I......I don't know what happened, Mr. Gerhardt. That car just suddenly sped right for me." He swayed slightly. His hand went to the left side of his forehead, above his eyebrow, where a knot was already forming and scraped skin oozed blood.

Edgar Gerhardt spied Andrews' cell phone, lying near the sidewalk, it had flown that far. He quickly reached for his own and dialed 911. After relating what he believed had happened, to the emergency dispatch, Gerhardt helped Andrews to the curb to sit. He could not stand, his foot was too painful.

Once seated on the curb, Ian Andrews, bewildered, looked down at his clothing and sighed. He had dressed that morning with great care. He chose a pair of black Armani slacks with a blue, bespoke, sateen shirt. The slacks seemed to have survived, other than street grime, but the shirt had taken a beating when he landed on his left side. He shook his head sadly.

Andrews said to Mr. Gerhardt, "Some days it just doesn't pay to get out of bed." Gerhardt frowned and nodded. He tried to move his foot, reposition it to get more comfortable, but grimaced in pain and left his foot still. His head was beginning to throb. He withdrew a handkerchief and gently dabbed at blood which had begun a slow trickle onto his eyelid.

An ambulance was on the scene within ten minutes, a police cruiser arrived even sooner.

Officer Ginny Bell took Andrews' statement, while the medics assessed his injuries. "Did you recognize the car, Mr. Andrews, any chance you got a license?"

He was regaining his senses and told her what he could remember. "I don't believe I've ever seen it before, officer. It was a small, rather plain car, nothing to distinguish it, and fairly old, somewhat beat up looking, was the impression I got. And, no it just happened so quickly, I saw no details."

"Color?"

Andrews thought about it, trying to rewind, and play back the images he remembered. "I would have to say it was a medium grey, possibly dull medium silver?" He could probably have given them the Pantone number if he thought about it for a while. The idea of that almost brought a smile to his face.

The medics had taken his vitals and cleaned the wound to his forehead. Andrews winced as they put his foot in a brace and prepared him for transport to the hospital. He protested.

"I'm sure that I'm fine, there's no need for this. I just need to get inside and put my foot in a tub of hot Epsom's salts."

The two beefy medics looked at each other with wry amusement, and finally burst out laughing. One said, "Don't you think we hear that all the time, sir? You've been injured in a vehicle accident, you need to be examined by a doctor. There may be hidden injuries. Besides sir, that bump is getting to be the size of an Easter egg, if you don't mind me saying."

Officer Bell chimed in, "They're right. You may be fine, but something happened here. At your age…"

"What? What about my age?" Andrews asked feigning an indignant sniff.

"At your age, sir," she continued, "respectfully, you must be checked out. I will continue with my interview after you've been seen."

After the two medics pushed Andrews' car back into the driveway, the ambulance departed for the hospital.

She turned to Edgar Gerhardt. "Thank you for your help today, sir. Can you tell me anything else, did you see what happened?"

Edgar Gerhardt was a short, thin man, with greying, receding hair and pasty skin, evidence of many decades inside classrooms rather than out in sunlight. He had been an instructor at West Valley College for over twenty years, but still retained a slight accent.

"As it happens I did see it, vell partly, anyvay. I had come out of my garage vith trash bins to put near the curb. I vas not looking toward Mr. Andrews' house, but I did hear the sound of a car, becoming very loud. We have little traffic on our street, so vhen the sound started, and then got so loud, I looked up."

Officer Bell was making notes as he spoke. She nodded. "Anything else?"

"At the time I looked up vas just vhen the little car was about to crash into Mr. Andrews. It hit his car, but thank goodness, he dived away, like that." Gerhardt shot one hand in an arc off the other palm. "I ran over to help him up."

"What did the car look like?" Bell asked. It never hurt to get more than one description.

"Oh, it vas grey, just like Mr. Andrews say. I think it was a foreign car, but don't know vich."

Officer Bell took Mr. Gerhardt's contact information and told him he might be required to come in to give a statement. He nodded solemnly. "Vhat is the vorld coming to, officer?" he asked rhetorically.

Bell looked at the little man with a weary smile. "I don't know, Mr. Gerhardt, but if you ever figure that out, will you please be sure to let me know?"

* * *

Club Envy was one of those night spots you don't see, unless you know it's there. In a basement space below a small boutique in the heart of downtown, customers have to go down two zig zagging flights of cement steps, to get to the entrance. So popular, that on weekend nights, the crowd spilled out, up the stairs and onto the sidewalk.

Inside was cavernous and black as pitch, even with the few lights that were on when Cooper and Morales arrived. Morales had called for an appointment to speak to anyone that was present on

Thursday night. The bartender agreed to open for them. They met him at the bar, and Morales made the introductions.

Bruce, the bartender, was small and wiry with muscular arms showcased in a denim vest. The bunchy arms were covered in tats that all resembled flowers. He asked if they wanted a drink.

"Sure thing, couple of sodas. Bruce, you were here last Thursday evening?" Cooper tried not to stare at the flower garden on the man's arms, as he settled himself on a stool.

Bruce looked at Cooper with surprise. "Hey, man, where y'all from? You sound like a southerner."

Cooper felt an immediate kinship in-spite of the tattoos. "I'm from Corpus. You?"

"Beaumont. Well, actually a bitty town to the east, almost to Louisiana." It came out 'Loosana'. "I'll be damned. Don't get too many of our type 'round here, know what I mean?"

"I do. Listen Bruce, we need to know if there was a particular guy in here, last Thursday night. Between oh, eight and midnight?"

Morales pulled out a photo of Edgerton and handed it over.

Bruce pulled it close and moved to be nearer one of the lights hanging over the bar. He studied Edgerton's face for several long seconds.

"You betcha. He was here. I remember, because of the lil' lady he had with him. She was quite a looker, if ya know what I mean." He pumped his hands out in front of his chest, indicating substantial bosom.

Morales rolled her eyes and sipped her soda.

"Do you remember how long he was here that night?"

"Well…I believe they took off around ten-thirty. She was drinkin' those whatcha call 'em, 'Nutmeg Nick' drinks. Why in the world anyone would want to drink sumpin' made with vodka, cream, syrup, vanilla and nutmeg…yuk."

"What makes you think they left at ten-thirty? Did you see them go?" Morales asked.

"Well, not exactly. They ordered their last round about ten-ish. They were sittin' down on that end of the bar." He gestured to the bottom of the long ell. "I made 'em up, delivered 'em and she says to me, 'This just *has* to be my last one or someone will just *have* to pour me into a cab', then she titters away." Bruce used a white towel to mop the bar. He shook his head and frowned. "She was three sheets to the wind when I gave her that last one, probably should have told her no."

Cooper drank his soda and waited.

Finally, Bruce said, "I was whupped, and had been clock watchin' all night, hopin' to speed the time 'til close. I looked up to check the clock and it was ten thirty-five. I saw a guy sidle up to one of the stools down there, so I went to wait on him. That's when I noticed they was gone. Left me a pretty nice tip."

With a handshake, Cooper and Morales left. Bruce promised to treat them anytime they wanted to come in.

Outside, they stopped on the sidewalk, eyes squinting after the darkness of the club.

"Ten-thirty. Edgerton doesn't really have an alibi," Morales said. "That's more than enough time to take the 'lil' lady' home and make it to Raven's Nest to kill Eleanor. Could be counting on a bartender to remember them, but not really remember when they left."

Cooper stood blinking, waiting for his eyes to adjust, thinking about what Bruce had told them. "Maybe. Maybe that's why Edgerton let her get that drunk. He could tell her anything, and she wouldn't remember anything different."

* * *

Madeline rose early Sunday and decided to go for a short run before Mrs. T arrived, and they started work. She needed the run, but she also knew that anything would work as long as it put off the inevitable. She donned her sports bra and shorts and ran a familiar course around the property, allowing the easy jog to soothe her mind and release some needed endorphins. She made it to the highest point of the property, which gave an almost bird's eye view of the mansion off to her right and allowed her to catch the slight breeze. She paused, breathing hard. The exertion felt good, and the uphill had made her legs burn pleasurably.

For the return trip, she ran down the hill through the densely wooded east side of the property, running along animal paths she'd always used. She crossed the road and continued for a short distance through the trees. As she came through the forest of live oak, Douglas fir and eucalyptus, she noticed a trampled and scuffed area, at the base of a huge and ancient cedar tree. It looked like someone had camped there, or at least had spent time loitering there. Under the branches of the cedar tree, copious needles dropped and nothing much grew. She studied the ground and saw scuff marks in the soil, almost footprints. Glancing up she realized the location provided a singularly good, albeit distant, view of Raven's Nest. The trees at this particular angle were oddly sparse, as compared to the rest of the forest. What you saw was not perfect, but certainly adequate. She then noticed several smudged burn marks, on the bark of the tree. Ashes. Someone had smoked here and stubbed out cigarettes. The detectives need to see this. This must have some bearing on what's happened.

She hurried back to the house, showered and dressed. She drove into Los Gatos to find the detectives, but they weren't at police headquarters. No one at the station could say where they were or when they were expected back. Frustrated, Madeline left a message that she needed to see them. She headed to her favorite coffee place, Diallo's Coffee House, to pick up a pound of beans. While there, she grabbed a cup, hoping they might call back while she was still in town.

Diallo's was a popular cafe on north Santa Cruz Avenue in downtown Los Gatos. Full of chic decor, it was 'the place' with young professionals and wealthy denizens alike, to be seen doing the trendy thing—drinking trendy coffee drinks. Diallo's served great coffee, which was the only criteria for Madeline. She ordered a mocha and a bagel with cream cheese. At a window table Madeline drank the coffee and watched.

People passing on the sidewalk looked like full time, professional shoppers, their hands full of bags, going from one upscale shop to the next. Madeline briefly thought about the concept of shopping as a pass-time. She knew there were some who indulged in it. She had close friends who loved it, Nadine came to mind. She also knew a few women for whom the compulsive need to shop, had developed into a real problem. Madeline herself, enjoyed a bit of shopping, when she needed something, but only when she needed something. Shopping as a way to spend your entire day? Uh—uuh.

The surveillance spot she'd found on the property, crowded into her mind. As she idly watched the shoppers walk by, Madeline tried to come up with a reasonable explanation for why someone would be watching, spying on Raven's Nest. There was no *reasonable* explanation. It was invasive.

Grounds keeper, Manuel Gutierrez, didn't smoke. He was the only person she could think of who would have any reason to be in such a place. He did periodically check the property for diseased trees, or occasionally for signs of trespassers or hunters. What did it have to do with her mother's murder? Was it before the night of her murder—the night *of* the murder? The idea was chilling. Madeline shivered.

When Mrs. Temple arrived Sunday morning, even though Madeline was out, she wasted no time. By ten thirty she had had workers from a restoration service remove the blood stained rug, and an upholsterer take the chair from the library for recovering. Even though it was a Sunday, certain customer's wishes were not to be ignored. By this time, everyone had heard of the murder of

Mrs. Abbott. Her community and charity involvement gave her special gravitas with most people in Los Gatos.

Normally off on Sunday, Manuel Gutierrez, brought a rug down from the attic and moved another wingback arm chair from the east parlor, to replace the missing one. It was the very least he felt he could do. Manuel was completely broken hearted.

Eleanor had hired Manuel after happening upon the fifty-five year old, sitting on a bench, outside the Los Gatos library. He had a small duffel bag that contained all his worldly possessions. She had asked what was wrong.

He related that he had come by bus, from Los Angeles. His son, Ernesto, was supposed to meet him there. It had been three days, and his son had not come. He was now hungry and without money, nor anywhere to go. Mrs. Abbott took him to Raven's Nest, fed him, then put him to work trimming shrubs and cutting grass. Within a month, she discharged the company she normally used and offered Manuel the permanent position as grounds keeper. That was six years ago. The son had never shown up.

Once the chair was in place and Mrs. Temple had vacuumed the newly placed rug, the room had begun to return to its former sense of peace. He and Mrs. Temple stood at the doorway into the library. Manuel held his cap crushed in his hands. They looked at each other, unmitigated sadness on their faces. They nodded and went back to work, each having decided to put in a full day.

Madeline had left a note for Mrs. Temple, saying that her mother's desk would be her job, so Alma Temple concentrated on the other rooms in the house, working briskly to clean away fingerprint powder. A worker from a glass shop in Los Gatos repaired the broken glass in the kitchen door with plain glass temporarily, promising that vintage beveled glass would soon be found, to restore the door. By mid day, the evidence of the break-in was eliminated in material ways, if not from their minds.

When she returned from town Madeline saw the replaced window pane. The plain, thin glass looked out of place next to the thick, one hundred twenty-five year old, beveled glass. She dropped her purse and coffee beans on the kitchen table and went looking for Mrs. Temple. She found her on the second floor, cleaning in her mother's rooms with Pancho helpfully watching.

Pancho heard Madeline before he saw her. He ran to her, barking, and he jumped and danced around her joyfully. Madeline knelt, brought him close and nuzzled his neck and stroked his head. He licked her face then broke away and raced down the hallway, his toe nails clicking madly on the wood floor. He slipped and slid as he tried to slow to make the turn, and then raced back to her, yipping with glee. She laughed out loud for the first time in days.

"Oh, Pancho," she gasped. "Settle down, for heaven's sake!" He continued to leap, prance and lick her hands and face until she could no longer take it. She stood up, and with as stern a voice as she could muster said, "Pancho! Settle down now, sit!" Pancho immediately sat straight upright at her feet and looked at her, his liquid brown eyes focused, mouth open and panting, his pom pom tail thumping a drum beat on the floor.

She turned to Mrs. Temple, who was watching from the door, a smile on her face and a dust cloth in her hand. "Good to see you Mrs. T. What are we going to do with him?" she said with a grin.

"I'm so glad you're finally home. He is surely glad to see you. He'll be better now, that's certain. Do you want some lunch, dear?"

"No, thanks, I had a bite in town. I think I'll just go to the library, work on Mother's desk."

"I'm going to keep on here and finish your mother's room before I stop for lunch." Mrs. Temple said, sadness in her face. "By the way, I will be calling the girls from town this week—if that's still alright," she added.

Mrs. Temple had three girls from town (although *girls* might be a misnomer as they were all close to Mrs.T's own age) that came a couple of times a month to help with what she called the 'big clean'. She and the girls would give all the rooms a going over, dusting and sweeping, even ones that were rarely or never used. They changed out linens in all bedrooms and bathrooms once each month, whether rooms were used or not. Eleanor could never bear the thought of the house not perfectly clean and ready at a moment's notice.

That created a mountain of laundry the day it was scheduled. They would sit at the table in the kitchen together, drink coffee or tea and fold the stacks of linen, gossiping, laughing. She had had the same three for over two years and was happy with them. Mrs. T. clucked over them and treated them like club members of a sort, enjoying their time together like a coffee klatch.

"That's fine Mrs. T. Go ahead and call them. In fact, if you need more help, call them in every week, if it's necessary. I'll be downstairs if you need me."

* * *

Madeline stayed in the library and worked for the next hour, concentrating on Eleanor's desk, cleaning each item meticulously. Every book, pen, pencil, picture frame was thoroughly cleaned then set aside. She used a cotton cloth with furniture wax and rubbed vigorously across the top and sides of the desk. She sat in her mother's desk chair and polished the fronts of the drawers, using cotton swabs to reach every tiny carved detail. It felt like penance.

She occasionally, trance like, slowed to a stop, and looked about the room. She could almost feel her mother's presence. I'm imagining it. Maybe not, though. Eleanor spent a large part of her time in this room, both working and relaxing. It was her favorite out of all the rooms in the mansion. I guess, Madeline mused, we were alike in that regard. We both admired this room.

How weird the circumstances of fate. Is that what this is? Fate? Was this whole thing fated to happen? Whose mother is *murdered?* No one Madeline knew, had experienced anything even remotely like it. Well, that's not strictly true. Ben Highwater's father died, a dozen or so years ago. But that was suicide, not murder. She continued to clean, slowly, methodically.

The repetitive nature of the work encouraged her mind to drift. Madeline knew the guilt she felt was a burden she would have to learn to deal with. Yes, she had been lax about coming home. Much of the reason for that was problems at PND. The business was important to her, important as a means to prove that she could be disciplined enough to create a successful business. It instead created conflict in her heart and mind. She knew her mother wanted to help, but Madeline wanted to succeed by herself. She now had a chance with the Litchfield job. Ironically, too late to have a wonderful conversation with Eleanor about the possibility of real achievement. She had to get over the guilt, but how, that was the question.

She got on her knees to polish the front of the desk. As she rubbed the satiny wood, she inadvertently glanced up from her work over the top of the desk, and her eyes came to rest on the mahogany paneled wall behind her mother's desk. She stared at the blank paneling with her eyebrows knitted, trying to understand what she was seeing. Or not seeing. Something was wrong.

In stupefying shock, she realized: The Cassatt was gone! The oil painting by the impressionist master, Mary Cassatt, the image of a young girl reading a book, was no longer hanging in its place behind the desk. Madeline raced around the desk scanning the rest of the wall space then made a hurried circuit of the entire library, hoping that her mother had simply taken the painting down for it to be cleaned. She found nothing. The painting was gone. All that remained, was the braided wire that hung from the picture rail above.

Madeline balled her fists as her eyes filled with tears of rage and frustration. Goddammit. Son of a *BITCH*! Whoever murdered her mother had gotten away with more than a few credit cards and cash. The Cassatt painting, in her family for two decades, was one of the family's most cherished pieces of art. She crumpled into a chair, consumed with feelings of hatred and violation. Every fiber of her being, urged her to grab her keys, jump in the rental car and drive back to Eugene. Back to where the biggest problem she had was how to keep her small business afloat. Not violent murder, not theft, not her beloved home being violated. She sat, jaws clenched, chin trembling, staring at dust motes floating carefree on the bright midday light. She viciously pounded the arms of the chair, until the pain in her wrists made her stop.

Madeline rested her head against the back of the chair. I have got to know who did this. It feels so personal. It *is* personal, goddamn it. If I just knew what to do and where to start. The first thing was to tell Detective Cooper. Besides the horror of murder, the painting's worth millions of dollars—that's enough of a motive for *anyone*. She sat until her anger had subsided enough for her think and speak rationally. What he doesn't need right now, a call from an hysterical woman.

She pulled out her phone and the detective's card and dialed. She got his voice mail and left a brief message. What were they doing, these detectives? Not at the police station, and not answering the phone. She remained sitting in the chair, willing herself to relax and focus. It seems as though that's all I've done for so long. Will myself to do things I don't want to do, or don't know how to do.

The Cassatt was her mother's first big purchase, with her own money. Eleanor loved fine art, everyone in the family had loved that painting. What if it is never recovered? What if it's gone for good? Madeline's insides were in a free-fall. What if, what if. Oh, dear God, she thought, what am I supposed to do? She had an overwhelming need to weep at the futility and helplessness she felt.

* * *

Richard Kelsey's condo, on one of the area golf courses, was as different from the Highwater Victoriana as it was possible to be. It was modern, sleek, and the grounds were meticulously groomed with a lush, tropical feel. Everywhere you looked were palm trees, bamboo, water falls and exotic plants. Cooper had never anything as large as this, called a 'condo'.

Cooper was surprised by Kelsey's appearance. Richard Kelsey on the street, could easily have been mistaken for a blue collar guy, a plumber, a city worker, so simply was he dressed. Ragged blue jeans (yes, that's the style, but still…), a wrinkled, cotton shirt that looked decades old and ratty tennis shoes. Athletic socks, the elastic long ago having given up, sagged in thin, limp folds around his skinny ankles. He was in his early sixties, but looked a youthful fifty-four, fifty-five. He welcomed them in casually and seated them in an informal grouping of leather furniture. Cooper and Morales identified themselves.

"I've been expecting someone from the police. This thing with Eleanor, well frankly, I just can't believe it."

"We have to ask you some routine questions, Mr. Kelsey. Where were you on Thursday evening?" Cooper asked, deciding on the direct approach.

Kelsey seemed happy, even eager to give answers to their questions. "Sydney and I were at her mother's house, in San Jose. I'll get that contact info for you."

Morales, surprised at his reaction to that question, "Thank you, that would be helpful. Can you tell us what you might know about Mrs. Abbott's friends and family that might be of help in the investigation? Do you personally know of anyone who might have had some reason to do something like this?"

"I wish to hell I did." He said it with such vehemence, Cooper was taken aback. Kelsey wrote the name, address and phone of Sydney's mother on a slip of paper and gave it to Morales. "The whole thing is sordid and awful. She is a wonderful person."

At that moment, a woman, who Cooper took to be Sydney Poole, entered the room. She was very slightly plump and had a face that held an assortment of irregular features that somehow came together to create an unusual, but compelling, beauty. Her nose dominated, with a Romanesque shape that was appealing. A cap of pale blond hair, cut in a modern bob, flattered her face. She was nearly the only person they'd met in the investigation so far that was not darkly tanned. Her skin was pearly and luminous.

"Sydney, these are the detectives that are investigating Eleanor's murder. Detectives Morales and Cooper." The detectives stood, and they all murmured greetings.

"Ms. Poole, is there anything you can add to what Mr. Kelsey has already told us? Can you think of anything that might be motivation, for the murder of Mrs. Abbott?" Morales asked.

"I can't actually, and Rick and I have talked about it a lot in the last few days. I've only known Eleanor for about five years, since Rick and I met." She looked at Richard Kelsey with a smile. "She was a very kind woman, so, no, I can't imagine anyone wanting to hurt her. Of course I've heard rumors. No one can resist gossiping, I suppose. Difficulties with her business partner. That's been discussed quite a bit. I've met him a few times, and I have to say, I wasn't all that impressed. It wasn't hard to imagine having 'difficulties' with him." Sydney Poole's fingers made quote marks. She glanced again at Richard Kelsey, who gave her a sympathetic smile.

Sydney Poole's voice was pleasant and melodious. She possessed an almost hypnotic cadence, that made listeners relax.

Cooper knew Sydney worked for Apple, but wondered if she had not missed an opportune chance as a therapist or even a hypnotist.

She continued: "She had some kind of a falling out with Helen Highwater, but that was a long time ago, before…well long before me." They smiled at each other again. "I do know she was very unhappy about her daughter's marriage. I don't think she liked him very much. The son-in-law, I mean. I had talked to Eleanor about this on a couple of occasions. It made her very unhappy. She wanted to do something, but didn't want to be perceived as interfering. I can't imagine how that could have anything to do with her murder, though."

Morales looked at Cooper. Then she said, "Do you remember anything specific, that she said about her son-in-law?"

"In one conversation, at a party—I think it was at Helen's—she said that Madeline needed to shake him loose, and fast. He was no good. You understand, I'm paraphrasing."

Cooper nodded, "Yes, please go on."

"I don't remember just why, but I remember thinking at the time that she must have found out something about the guy, that she didn't like. Maybe it was just a feeling I got from something she said."

Morales looked up from her note taking and nodded. She asked: "Have you met David Dean? Do you know him?"

Richard Kelsey answered, "We've met him on a few occasions. He's a different sort." He paused and rubbed his chin thoughtfully. "Honestly? He struck me a little like a spoiled, petulant boy. Seemed obsessed with 'things'. Every conversation was about stuff he had acquired or planned to acquire.

"It always seemed he was trying too hard. Anyway, whenever they were down for some family thing or other, we'd see him of course, but he didn't mix very well…with our crowd. And when he drank, he became boorish. I heard from someone, Ian, maybe, that he has an unusual background. Very underprivileged. Might account for the focus on money."

Then, Sydney Poole added: "I'm really the newest to the group, except for maybe Helen's boyfriend, William, so I'm probably not the right person to be asking. I don't feel like I fit in all that well." She gave a slight smile. "Most of them have known each other for decades…kind of hard to feel like part of things, when often you don't know all the old stories. I keep trying."

"You fit in just fine, Syd." Kelsey held her hand.

"About any of the other people in your group. Do you know of any animosity between Eleanor and her friends, acquaintances, maybe business? Anything?"

Richard and Sydney both frowned in concentration. Richard said, "I think she was more upset at the David kid, than even James Edgerton, truthfully. She was really worried about Madeline, she was frustrated that she couldn't do something without Madeline thinking she was butting in."

"I don't know what the problem was with Helen, Eleanor would never say. But I got the feeling from her that something happened between them—as I said, it was a long time ago."

Cooper signaled Morales it was time to wrap it up. He had one more thing.

"Were you two aware that Mrs. Abbott had cancer?"

No one they had interviewed thus far had known, and Richard and Sydney were no exception.

They looked solemnly into each other's eyes, and clasped hands. Sydney's eyes glistened with tears. Kelsey finally shook his head and said, "We didn't. What can you tell us?"

"It was discovered when the M.E. did the autopsy. Advanced lung cancer. She probably had less than a year."

They sat silently.

Eventually Sydney spoke, her voice low: "As gruesome as her death was, it may have been a blessing in disguise. That sounds horrible, I know, and I don't mean ill, you understand. But one of my closest cousins died of cancer. It was a lingering and painful death. It was just awful."

Morales stood and nodded at Sydney gravely. "Yes, my mother died of breast cancer. I know exactly what you mean." Cooper was unable to hide his surprise. Even after nearly two years, how much did he still not know about his partner?

"I didn't know you lost your mother to cancer, Izzy. Why haven't you told me?"

Morales glanced over at Cooper as she drove from the Kelsey and Poole home. "I don't like to talk about it. All of us were there at the end. Well, except for my papá. It was a sad thing."

"I'm sure it was tough. When was it?"

Morales stared out the windshield, unblinking. "A little over four years ago. Before I knew you. Before I met Alana." She shrugged. "Just as well."

"Why do you say that?"

"Because, my Mamá was a good Catholic. Very devoted."

"Oh." Cooper understood. "I'm sorry, Izzy."

They drove back to the office in silence, each wrapped in their own thoughts.

* * *

Sitting at this desk, Cooper opened his notepad and read what he'd written while at Highwater's house. "I'm not sure what to make of this yet, any of it." He frowned down at his notes. "Everyone speaks so highly of Eleanor Abbott. Yet, she's dead. What did you think about Highwater, Izzy?"

Isabelle Morales was a perceptive woman. Cooper listened, when she gave him her take about interviewees. She looked down at her desk pad and tapped on it with her pen thoughtfully.

"I wasn't impressed with her. She was polite and everything but…. The only thing that came out of her that felt honest, was the part about the boy and how he couldn't handle his father's death. That, she really seemed to be upset about."

"I noticed something off." Cooper frowned in concentration. "I can't explain it, but there was something...something. She said all the right things, but it was, I don't know," he shrugged, "hollow."

Morales smiled at her partner. "You're getting more sensitive, *amigo*, paying more attention. I thought so too, and there is a story behind the Greg guy's death."

Cooper looked at his cell phone and frowned. "My batt's been dead for two hours." He plugged it in to the charger he kept on his desk. "Will you dive in and look around about that Greg Highwater guy, see what you can find online? Pretty please?"

"Ugh. Stop that. Don't be a peckerwood."

"You calling me a peckerwood?" He grinned.

"Yeah, if you don't stop that crap. I picked that up from you, you yayhoo." She laughed out loud. "Jesus, obviously I've been hanging around you too long. I'll get on the Highwater guy. Why don't you call Kenyon and see if she's back yet. Then we'd better think about lunch."

Oh, yeah, lunch, Cooper thought, why didn't I think of that? He looked up the number for Kenyon and dialed. As it rang, Officer Ginny Bell walked up to their desks and tossed down a piece of paper. "The Abbott daughter was in earlier, looking for you two. She wants you to give her a call."

Cooper read the note. "Okay, thanks, Ginny. When was it?"

"Earlier this morning, I guess about nine-thirtyish."

"Okay, thanks."

The call to Kenyon went to voicemail. "This is Detective Cooper, Ms. Kenyon. We need to talk to you as soon as you get back. Please give us a call, it's very important." Cooper repeated the number.

Ginny Bell stood by their desks. "I think you'll want to know about the accident earlier today."

Cooper and Morales both looked up expectantly.

"One of the people on the Abbott interview list, was involved in a hit and run this morning."

Cooper shot out of his chair. "What?! Who, who was it?"

"Ian Andrews. Lives out on Azalea Drive, those old tracts east of town?" Those 'old tracts' of spacious mid-century homes on large lots that were now going for more than two mill. Old tracts, indeed.

Cooper looked at Morales. He sighed and canted his head. "Well, shit. What happened to him?"

Bell pulled out her notebook and read the details to them. "An unidentified car raced down the street, apparently right at him, looks like it was deliberate. He dove out of the away but it clipped him. He was transported to the hospital, but he wasn't seriously hurt, just banged up a bit."

Andrews, listed as a friend of Mrs. Abbott, was on their interview list, but they hadn't gotten to him yet. "Okay, Ginny, thanks for letting us know. Can you write up your notes and give us a copy?" She nodded and left.

A deliberate hit and run. "Well, Izzy, looks like someone is getting nervous. What does Ian Andrews know, that could make someone try to stop him from talking?"

"We should get to him as soon as possible—and—put a guard on him."

Cooper nodded. With both hands he vigorously scratched his head, raking his hair up into wild tufts. "Yeah, let's get an officer assigned to him. If he's still at the hospital, they're to stay with him until he goes home then stay with him there, until further notice."

Morales picked up the phone.

Later, he turned his chair toward Morales. "Okay, now, what was your take on Kelsey and Poole?"

Morales turned in her chair toward him. Her aging chair emitted a loud squeal. "I liked them. They seemed sincere." She shrugged. "They even seem to like each other. Go figure." She laughed. "Pretty unusual these days, no?"

"Oh, hell's bells and panther tracks, Izzy, that's not true. Some people do get along. My parents do." He was paging through the growing file on Eleanor's murder. "I got the same impression about them, but look into them anyway." He turned back to her. "Is there anything back from the techs? Anything found at the scene? Any fingerprints? Hair, fiber?"

"The place was as clean as a whistle, Scotty. That housekeeper, Mrs. Temple must run around on auto-pilot, constantly buffing every surface. *Jesus*, what a bore." She rolled her eyes. Morales occasionally enjoyed a bit of editorializing.

"The only prints were a few of hers, a few of Mrs. Abbott's, and a few that we don't have a match for, but probably they'll match Kenyon, since she worked there so much."

"Nothing on the bookend?"

Morales shook her head. "Blood was Mrs. Abbott's, and the hairs. So, whoever it was, wore gloves, hats…very clean. They knew exactly what they were doing."

He nodded, and sat quietly thinking. Finally Cooper slammed his hands down on his desk, making Morales jump.

"Izzy, look, the scene, it's wrong. That broken window in the kitchen. If they broke a window to get in, why didn't she hear? How could she sit there sippin' tea, until someone got close enough to her to beat her to death?

"What about all the stuff that wasn't taken, the jewelry, the art, and a new six thousand dollar laptop—oh, yeah, I looked it up. *Six grand*. Her cell phone just sitting there. And that's just for starters. Then they take whatever she had in her wallet……maybe a few hundred bucks and a few credit cards? I don't think so."

Morales's eyes studied the tip of her pen as she swirled it. "So how do you explain it? The way to explain it is, she let them in, or they had a key."

"If she let them in, then why? Why would she let someone in late at night—wouldn't it have to have been someone she knew? And trusted?" Cooper stood and paced quickly by the desks. "It would have had to be one of her so-called friends…or a family member.

"It's crazy. It was savage—literally a beating, and of a person everyone speaks so highly of." He turned to Morales again, and said, "I don't think she let them in. I think somebody got hold of a key." Cooper rubbed the back of his neck.

Morales sighed. She stared at her desk, drawing her brows together with a frown. "Then the killer is in her circle of friends. I'll bet you. We press them, hard, and find the skeletons, then we'll know who killed her and why."

* * *

Their work day schedule being what it was, the detectives always ate on the run. Cooper didn't mind so much. His time with Izzy, even lunch, was valued. If he went home, it was to an empty apartment and likely a cold cheese sandwich. Izzy never wanted to go home for lunch, because Alana was at work. So, today was another quick pit stop affair.

The detectives found a bodega on the way to Van Gessler's, where they each ordered an enchilada. They were prepared in a traditional way. Cooper also ordered a couple of fish tacos. They were served with spicy sauce, cabbage slaw and a big wedge of lime. He tasted and proclaimed them delicious, but not as good as Izzy's.

"Oh, you don't know what you're talking about," she said. But she smiled. Izzy liked to cook Mexican food and used her grandmamá's recipes.

"These are pretty good, but yours, Izzy…ummmm. Besides, not just anyone can cook Mexican." Cooper stated. "A lot of folks down home *think* they cook good Mexican food."

Morales grinned and said, "That crap's called Tex-Mex."

"No, I mean there are a few restaurants, you know in Dallas, San Antonio, Austin, that claim to make authentic Mexican. I guarantee I've been to all of them."

"Like I shaid, Shex-Mhex!" Morales said, with her mouth full.

"It takes a real Mexican with good cookin' skills to make good Mexican food. And I *know*. I'm like……I'm a gourmet." He laughed out loud.

"I doubt you could eat real Mexican, Scotty," Morales teased him, her mouth momentarily empty.

"You're as full of shit as a Christmas goose, Izzy. Every time you cook, I show y'all how *this* Texan can eat good Mexican food, don't I?"

It was really too breezy to be eating outside. There was no room inside, so it was outside or in the car, and Cooper disliked eating in the car. The wind was blustering a bit and clouds were accumulating in grey clumps, scudding across the sky. They sat at a cement table with matching curved benches.

They continued with their food in easy silence. Eventually Cooper said, "What have you found out about the Van Gesslers?"

Morales swallowed and wiped her mouth with a napkin. "Well, I know he's an investment banker. She's a real estate agent. Don't know much more yet. Haven't really looked at their personal life, but they are on the list of friends of Eleanor Abbott, even though he was her broker."

The continued without talking for a few minutes. Finally Morales finished her enchilada, wiped her hands and said, "Scotty, I don't think I like that Highwater kid. He struck me as pretty goddamn cold."

Cooper nodded. "I know. For someone who supposedly thought so much of Eleanor Abbott, he did seem," Cooper shrugged, "indifferent."

"The mother kept rattling on, about how much her murder has affected him, but I sure didn't see that. For all the sorrow he showed, he might just as well have been talking about a hamster. A hamster someone else saw die in the street, and then texted him about it."

Cooper smiled. "Well, he's a kid, Izzy. Maybe he's just keeping his feelings to himself. They do that you know."

He was still for a long while staring down at the crispy end of his fish taco. Finally he shook his head in frustration. "I don't know. This case is already buggin the hell out of me."

Morales chugged down the last of her soda. "Don't worry about it. We'll figure it out."

"You're probably right. Usually are." Cooper laughed. "Let's get up there and see if we can figure out where the Van Gesslers fit in."

* * *

The opulence of most of the homes they'd visited was beginning to rub Cooper a little raw. It was hard not to make a mental comparison to his cramped two bedroom apartment, when he saw how much of the rest of Los Gatos was living. This one was no different.

Frank and Kathryn Van Gessler's palatial new home, in a gated community, was intended to be awe inspiring. Stucco, in a warm terracotta color, was trimmed in two shades of pale cream. Huge palladium windows and crystal chandeliers were a few of the amenities Cooper noticed. When the detectives arrived, they were greeted by Kathryn and escorted through the main living area to the patio in the back. Frank was lounging by the pool at a large teak patio table with the remnants of lunch in front of him, along with a half finished beer.

He was of average build (with a bit of a belly, Cooper noticed), average height and average looks. Greying brown hair and very tanned skin. Cooper wondered again, if everyone in Los Gatos spent their off hours in a tanning bed.

In sharp contrast to this, was his wife. Slender, petite five-four-ish, maybe one hundred-ten pounds, and very beautiful. She looked like an even prettier version of a young Ann-Margret. Thick auburn ringlets cascaded down her back. Cooper allowed himself a male chauvinistic moment thinking what in the hell does she see in *him*? Both were dressed ahead of the yet to arrive California summer in shorts and cotton tee shirts. The summer like attire was odd given the cloudy skies and the cool breezy air. Maybe wishful thinking. The detectives showed their identification.

"As you know by now, Eleanor Abbott was murdered. We need to ask a few questions about when you last saw her," Cooper began.

Morales jumped in: "Where were you both last Thursday night?"

Frank Van Gessler said with a concerned frown, "Where were we? Uh, well, let's see…Kath, is that the night we were out shopping?"

Kathryn shrugged, and answered in a manner that suggested no interest in the conversation. "I think so. I think that's the night we were out looking for a birthday gift for Ruth."

"Ruth?" Cooper asked.

"My friend, Ruth, she's one of my group. Realtors? It's her birthday in a couple of weeks…" Kathryn's voice trailed off. She studied her French manicure, the tips of which were blindingly white.

"When did you last see Eleanor Abbott?" Morales asked.

"We haven't seen Eleanor in a few weeks, actually," Frank Van Gessler said. He sipped his beer. "We were at her place for a get together a few weeks ago. Eleanor was the host this time for a casual dinner party."

"At Raven's Nest? When was this?" Morales asked, wondering if they would supply details that matched what others had given.

"Oh...well, let's see, it was on a Saturday, so I guess it was three weeks ago last Saturday," Mr. Van Gessler said. "It was typical—lots of food, wine. We played some cards." He smiled. Then, as if realizing that might be an inappropriate response, stopped smiling and fixed Cooper with a serious gaze.

"Did Mrs. Abbott seem to be bothered or upset about anything at that time?" Cooper asked.

"Eleanor didn't seem different at all. She seemed just like she always does—did, friendly, gracious."

"Have either of you heard of anyone who might have a reason to harm Mrs. Abbott? Someone with whom she had problems? In business, or friends?

The Van Gesslers exchanged a glance. "No, I've never heard anyone say anything like that, have you honey?" Frank Van Gessler asked his wife.

"Of course not," she answered. Another shrug. Kathryn Van Gessler picked up an issue of DOLCE magazine and began thumbing through it.

Their remarks sounded rehearsed to Morales. She changed tack. "What do you do, sir?"

"Do?" he looked at Morales with surprise. "Oh," he laughed. "You mean, what do I do for a living? I'm an investment banker. In fact, I worked closely with Clay—Eleanor's husband—before he died, and also for her, in more recent time. I invest for her, stocks, bonds, technologies."

"You're personally in charge of her portfolio, of her market investments?" Cooper asked as his cell phone rang.

"Yes. Well, I have been...I guess that has changed now, of course," he replied.

"Excuse me," Cooper said and stepped to the other end of the patio.

Morales turned to Mrs. Van Gessler. "What do you do, ma'am?"

Kathryn Van Gessler looked up from her magazine, surprised that anyone would be asking her a direct question. "I am a real estate agent, although, right now I'm only working part time." Her tone was indifferent.

"Where is your office?"

"My office?"

What the fuuu.... Do they not understand English? "Yes. Do you have an office, and if so, where is it located?"

"Oh. Well, since I'm part time, I work mostly here. I am affiliated with the Mountain Realty office, in town. Where Ruth works, the group I spoke of."

Morales, who was making notes, paused, and asked for the office number. Mrs. Van Gessler seemed to be put off by the questions, but answered.

Cooper came back.

"You have a beautiful home," he said. "How long have you lived here?"

"Oh, not long," Frank Gessler said, expansively. He seemed to glow with the perceived compliment to their good taste. "We built this just a year ago."

The fenced property was beautifully landscaped, with the swimming pool, a koi pond, slate walkways and well designed lighting and seating areas. The landscaping alone would have cost tens of thousands of dollars. And that didn't include all the expensive outdoor furniture, which didn't come from the local discount store. The property looked to Cooper like it was at least an acre of land.

"Was there a particular reason why you chose to build here? A gated community, I mean," Cooper said.

Van Gessler frowned, as though he was giving his answer serious consideration. "I guess we liked the look of the place. The lots are large, and you have to build a certain size and type of home. The Association doesn't let just anything in." He then shifted in his seat, self-consciously. "Well, you know what I mean. There are certain standards."

"Yes," Cooper said. "I understand."

Van Gessler continued explaining, this time trying for what, he thought, might be a more acceptable reason. "We were concerned about the increase in crime. The statistics are not real encouraging."

"Were you, at some point, the victim of a serious crime personally, Mr. Van Gessler? Was that what prompted the decision?" Morales asked.

"Not us, specifically, no. But you listen to the news and it's hard not to get worried," he replied. "The world is changing. We felt it would just be safer here. You have to do what you can, to keep your family safe, don't you?" Kathryn Van Gessler had not yet bothered to look up from her magazine.

"We won't take any more of your time," Cooper said finally. "If we have further questions, we'll be in touch."

The Van Gesslers rose, and Kathryn Van Gessler showed the detectives back through the house, to the door. On her way back to the patio, she grabbed another beer for Frank. They sat opposite each other at the table. "We've got a problem," Frank said.

* * *

In the library, Madeline finally pulled herself wearily to her feet. *I've got to focus. Finish the desk at least. I can't expect Mrs. T to do everything by herself.* With a deep sigh, she went back to begin again on her mother's desk.

Madeline moved around to the back of the desk. She ruminated, going over and over what had happened, hating the feeling of defenselessness. Her weakness, constantly dwelling on things, was a fault she continually tried to correct. But, with increasing frequency, she found herself in an endless loop, rehashing, rethinking, usually leading to more anger and frustration.

In an overwhelming burst of rage, she began buffing furiously, taking every named and unnamed embitterment out on the desk: the murder, the stolen painting, the spying, the finger printing dust. She banged her fingertips violently on the drawer handles bruising them, bent them hard on the inside edges, broke a couple of fingernails, then cried out.

She stopped and sat back on the floor, weeping again quietly, the fit exhausted. She knelt at the desk, wishing she knew how to pray. Her religious upbringing had been one of benevolent non-involvement. Her parents had wanted her to grow up and decide what, if anything, she believed. They provided her with dozens of fine books, on philosophy, all types of religion and metaphysics. Madeline read them all. Her Dad often said that when the time was right, and she was mature, she would develop her own personal beliefs.

That was well and good, but it left her unsure of how to deal with important issues of loss and sadness, particularly when her father died. And now, with her mother's death. What did faithful people do, when they found themselves in need of comfort? They relied upon their faith, right? Prayer, fellowship? Right now, she desperately wished she believed in prayer, because she needed some kind of help. When the tears stopped, and she finally calmed down she returned to the cleaning at a normal pace, being mindful of her aching fingers.

In an effort to be thorough, Madeline intended to clean all the surfaces, including the inner surfaces of the kneehole. On the inner surfaces of the drawer and edges, her throbbing fingers ran over what felt like a knob or a small button, just behind the left front edge of the center drawer. Madeline bent over and tried to see it, but it was too dark to make it out. She pulled out her cell phone and used it as a flashlight to peer up underneath the front edge. She saw what looked like a small push button, on/off switch. She pushed it gingerly and heard a click. The left side wall of the knee hole angled out slightly, just enough to get her fingertips in to pull it fully open. It leaned out, opening a cubby hidden between the inside wall and the left hand stack of drawers. It was not large, only about two inches deep by fourteen inches square. Her curiosity piqued, she aimed her phone flashlight at the dark space and could see a leather volume resting inside. She pulled out a fine grained, black leather book, with the name Eleanor Abbott in gilt lettering on the front. Uneasy, Madeline opened the book. Inside the front cover it read: "January 1st through———" A simple lined journal without preprinted dates. A diary.

Madeline moved over to a window near the fireplace and opened the book. The writing was her mother's small, neat script, written with her fountain pen. She began to read:

January 4—

Another new year. I know I say it every year, but I hope desperately that I can make amends and see the fruit of my efforts. Clay has been gone for over a year now. I never thought I would be alone. I thought I would go first. I hoped I would. With everything happening now, it's ironic that I didn't. I have decided to tell Madeline the truth. It isn't right that she go on believing one version of her personal history when it isn't true. But, is the time right? It never feels right, and she comes home so infrequently. What impact will it have on our relationship? I fear it may damage it beyond its already fragile state. Anyway, I have to tell her. Everything. And it must be soon. I suppose if it destroys us, it will be my own fault for the part I have played. Maybe that's why so much misery and pain have ended up in my lap. There is trouble brewing. James is taking more liberties than he ever did while Clay was alive. He thinks I don't know, maybe he thinks I don't care. He will soon realize just how wrong he is.

Madeline collapsed into a nearby armchair. Her spinning mind could hardly process what her mother had written. The truth? What truth? What in the hell is she talking about, my personal history? So this is why she has been so insistent that Madeline come home for the last few months. She quickly turned the page to the next entry.

> *January 19—*
> *James thinks he's going to buy me out? Has that been the plan from the day Clay died? He's power mad. The partnership was the worst decision Clay and I ever made, bringing him into the business. It was about money. He had it, we needed it. Sadly, everything's always about money. I've heard rumors that he's scouting financing for something big. Since we haven't talked about any large projects, I assume a buy out, is the money he's looking for. The man's delusional. Besides being strange and getting stranger every year. I finally got a call from Maddie. It was brief, but she seemed fine, if maybe a bit overwhelmed. I know it's about her business. She doesn't know that I'm aware she's struggling. I asked her to come home, and she's promised to try to fit it in sometime in the next few weeks. Even though she was home over Christmas, it was not enough time, and there is so much—— Well, I didn't even know then.*

Madeline leaned back in the chair and closed her eyes, a wild ride of emotions made her feel dizzy. And it left a bitter taste in her mouth. I don't know if I want to keep reading, she thought. Do I *want* to know what the hell she was talking about? Madeline felt a shiver of fear in her stomach. Then she sat up abruptly, opening the book to the first entry. "Another new year…" There were more? Past years? The first entry sounded like a continuation. Something pricked in her memory. Of course there were. Her mind suddenly flooded with a collage of faint images in which she now saw her mother writing in notebooks from time to time over the years. She, as a child, too self absorbed to be curious about what Eleanor was writing or why.

Where are they? Madeline hurried back to the desk, and used her phone flashlight to look in the hidden cubby again. Empty.

She searched every desk drawer. That's silly, if they had been in the desk drawers, the police would have found them, and the detective said nothing about finding diaries.

She checked the time. Past four-thirty. I have time to take a look in her bedroom, although probably no chance anything is there. The police have been over all of it. She found Mrs. Temple in the billiard room, and told her that she was going upstairs to continue cleaning. Madeline headed up the grand staircase.

Reluctantly, she entered her mother's room and began. She checked under the mattress and under the bed itself, the armoire, inside hatboxes in the closet, even inside luggage. Madeline rifled through the drawers of the vanity.

She found small vintage photo frames with pictures of Michael and her, as small children. She had not seen them in years. One was a hinged, four frame set, with two panels for each of them. She looked at her brother's face. A sweet, angelic face, with a thatch of dark, wavy hair spilling onto his forehead. Large blue eyes, that peered into the the camera lens with a not quite focused look, and a gentle smile on his lips. Seeing them brought up old feelings of guilt, sorrow and anger. Madeline folded the small frame and returned it to the drawer.

She found assorted jewelry boxes with some of Eleanor's lesser pieces of jewelry. Madeline knew her mother had many fine pieces given to her over the years by Clay, diamonds, some stunning sapphires. They were kept in the safe built into the wall of the library.

There was tons of costume jewelry, from the 1960s and 70s, enamel, rhinestones. All the rage now. There were various cosmetics and lotions. No diaries.

After an hour of fruitless digging through her mother's private things, Madeline gave up and sat slumped on the side of the bed. Where did the afternoon go, she wondered, glancing out the windows. It was blustery, and the sky was dark with clouds.

She unconsciously massaged her aching fingers. She peered at them, and noticed they were already showing bruises. It was nearly six o'clock and time to think of dinner, or so her stomach told her. Fading light of early evening came in, mist like, from the windows. It did nothing to alleviate the deep shadows around the room.

Mrs. Temple silently materialized and spoke from the door. "I'm going to go home now, dear."

Madeline started. "Oh, God, Mrs. T, I didn't hear you come up."

"I've finally finished cleaning every room downstairs." She sighed deeply. "Amazing how…thorough…the police were in their searches of the house."

"I know Mrs. T., it's a bit disheartening, but we can finish the upstairs tomorrow, then maybe we can begin to…you know, to move on."

"I think you're right, dear. I wasn't sure before…but, you're right. It does help, to get everything clean again. Work is good for the soul."

Before Madeline could respond, she heard the front door bell chime faintly.

Mrs. Temple added, "I'll be back in tomorrow morning, regular time?" It was more a statement than a question. Madeline got up and herded Mrs. Temple out to the hallway. "Yes, that's fine. I'll see you then. Goodnight, Mrs. T."

"Goodnight, dear." She patted Madeline's arm and headed for the back staircase that led to the kitchen.

* * *

Madeline went down the main stair, with Pancho by her side, and opened the front door to see Detective Cooper, leaning casually against the door frame. It was dusk now, and with the cloud cover, it was nearly dark. She studied him in the lights of the stoop. He wore his regulation blue jeans and boots, with a white dress shirt and a sports jacket.

"Hello, detective, I'm sorry, I thought you would be coming here this afternoon. I stopped by your office, and I also called this afternoon." She glanced at her wrist watch. "It's nearly six o'clock."

"I'm sorry for the delay, but Izzy and I have been busier than a one legged man at an ass kickin. Hey, Pancho!" He tousled the poodle's head, then looked into Madeline's eyes and smiled. "Is it too late?" Cooper asked.

She continued to gaze at him as he stood in the porch light. With a wry expression and a sigh, she finally stepped back and waved him into the foyer.

"I got your cell phone message just a while ago. My phone was dead," he said sheepishly. "You've discovered a painting missing?"

"Not just any painting." Madeline led him to the library and pointed to where the Cassatt had hung. She explained about the piece and its history. The longer she spoke, the more grave his expression became.

"You're right, this does change things. From the beginning I felt the scene was staged, like I told you. Nothing had been taken that justified the break-in, much less murder. A priceless painting certainly could. If it's worth millions, and the person who took it could find a fence? Who knew the painting was here?"

"Oh, hell, everybody," she said, anger returning to her voice. "Everyone who is a friend of the family. People my mother met with in her work, her charities. The library is her office, so dozens, if not hundreds, of people have seen the painting hanging there."

Cooper stood with his hands on his hips, shaking his head. "Well that'll make for 'dozens if not hundreds' of possible suspects. Shit. Sorry."

Madeline smiled for the first time all day. "Oh, it's okay. Anyway, there's more."

He tilted his head. "Oh, God. What?"

"Well, something interesting I found today while cleaning in the library. But, that can wait. Do you mind if we just take a small break from this…this craziness? I'm hungry. I was just going to make myself some dinner." She hesitated before asking, "Have you eaten?"

"Actually, no. Well, not since Izzy and I had tacos, around eleven."

"That was your lunch?" She shook her head and smiled. "Well I'm not a great cook, but I can put something together. Mrs. T usually keeps the kitchen pantry and fridge well stocked. Then we can talk."

Madeline told Pancho to get into his bed, in the corner of the kitchen, and donned an apron. She scanned the contents of the refrigerator and pantry, then tasked Cooper with choosing a red wine and setting places at the kitchen table, while she prepared the food. She sent him to the wine cellar through a door off the larder. He descended the spiral, stone staircase.

It was an incredible, medieval looking place, exactly like what he expected a wine cellar to be in a castle. Stone walls kept the cellar cool, and antique sconce lights made it dim and mysterious. There was an old, heavy oak table with four chairs around it. Cooper wondered if this is where secret parties where held? It seemed a little like something from Alice in Wonderland. One cabinet held an assortment of different sizes and shapes of wine glasses. Dozens of them.

Three long walls held rack after rack of wines of every kind. They were all covered in a mist of dust and more than a few cobwebs. Cooper spied a section marked 'everyday reds' and took the hint. He selected a Beauleiu Cabernet, a name he was pretty sure he'd heard of before, and headed back to the kitchen.

"Quite a nice cellar. Your family must really love wine," he said. He squeezed his eyes shut, immediately wanting to stuff the words back in his mouth. "I'm sorry, Madeline, I wasn't thinking."

She looked up from the sink, where she trimmed a head of cauliflower. "That's alright," she said softly. "I know what you meant, and yes, we all did…do, love wine. I was raised to appreciate wines. Hard not to, growing up in this area. Do you enjoy wine, detective?"

"I do. I don't know a lot about wine but I enjoy red wine, and some whites, if they aren't too sweet. And, please call me Scott. Izzy calls me Scotty. I answer to either," he said with a grin. Madeline noticed he had a beautiful smile. He uncorked the bottle. "Can I help you?" he asked.

"No, it's a really simple meal, but you can go ahead and pour, and set the places here at the table." After a pause she said: "Do you get on well with Detective Morales?"

"Izzy and I have been partnered for about two years. Yeah, we get on really well. She's an interesting person. She's had her share of trouble with the Los Gatos PD, but she lets it roll off. I respect her."

Madeline nodded. "That's a great advantage in your work, I would think. She must be extremely capable."

"I trust her with my life. Every day. She's one of the best detectives I've known. Fearless."

Madeline continued working at the sink for a while, then said: "In case you're wondering, we're eating in here because I don't like eating in the dining room unless there are enough people to keep it from seeming…well, ridiculous. The dining table can seat twenty-eight without crowding. Thirty-two, if needed. It can be intimidating. When there's only two, it just seems silly." Madeline said.

"I was in the dining room Friday. I understand."

He poured wine and sat to watch Madeline prepare the food. She seemed comfortable and unselfconscious puttering around, cleaning vegetables, making salad and grinding herbs. If she had reservations, about a police detective being in her kitchen she hid it well.

Cooper couldn't help but notice Madeline wore faded blue jeans. The kind that got that way when you like them and wear them often, not because some fancy-dan designer bleached the shit out of them, then added two hundred dollars to the price and put their name on the hang tag. Smart woman. A simple blue silk blouse complimented her eyes. She looked really pretty.

Some people just have it, I guess, Cooper thought. Then he caught himself and chided his line of thinking. Hardly professional, he thought with a smile. His curiosity was roused, when she finished up by making some kind of sauce with brandy. The pan burst into flames and smelled fabulous.

In less than thirty minutes, she had the food plated and served, and was sitting down taking a grateful swallow of her wine.

Cooper was suddenly starving and dug in. "This is great, what is it?" he asked around a mouthful of steak. He would have to pace himself.

"It's called, Steak Au Poivre." Madeline said. "You make it with a fillet cut from the beef tenderloin. You cover it with a kind of crust of fresh crushed peppercorns, then grill it quickly and serve it rare with a brandy cream sauce."

He took another morsel. It was incredibly tender with a sharp bite of pepper tempered a little by the creamy sauce. "Whatever it is, it's fantastic," he said nodding his head. "Oh, and the roasted cauliflower and the salad are good too. Why would you say you're not a cook?" Cooper grinned at her.

Madeline's green-blue eyes looked at him over the rim of her wine glass, her dark lashes creating fluttering shadows. She took a sip and said, "It's one of the few things my mother and I enjoyed together. She liked to cook and taught me when I was young. Thank you."

They ate for a while in silence. Cooper felt comfortable with her. Not a bunch of inane and mindless chit chat. That didn't always happen with women. Especially beautiful ones who had just cooked a fantastic meal. She refilled their wine glasses. Finally, Cooper pushed his plate away with a sigh.

"God, that was great. Best meal I've had in a long while."

"Really?" Madeline laughed. "You should get out more. There are some great restaurants in this area."

"No time. Besides, I'm not crazy about eating at a fancy restaurant alone."

Madeline looked over the rim of her wine glass again. Her intense eyes studied at him quizzically. "Why alone. Surely you have a......someone," she said.

"Didn't you tell me you were splitting with your husband? Well, I've already been there."

Her dark brows rose and she nodded slowly. "I see."

* * *

Suddenly embarrassed, Cooper felt himself squirming on his stool. To change the subject he said the first thing he could think of. "Tell me about this house. How did y'all end up with such a huge place?"

"It has a very interesting history. It's mysterious…sad." She looked around, as if seeing it with new eyes.

"Raven's Nest as it is called, was built in 1893 by William Dalton Knox. He started out around 1880 in New York and amassed a huge fortune in the railroad industry. He decided to come west and expand into mining and ranching. He bought the original six hundred and forty acres here sight unseen. Knox wanted to build something similar to what other wealthy industrialists were building in New York and Newport."

"Mission accomplished, I'd say."

"Yes, well, it didn't quite go as planned."

"How do you mean?"

"Knox was thirty-two when he came out to California, in 1888. He had a clear idea for the kind of house he wanted, he even made sketches of what his vision was. The architect he hired began developing the plans. It was to be a wedding present for his fiancé, and they would marry once the house was finished. Building began in 1891 and was completed in '93. When it was finished Mr. Knox went back east to marry his sweetheart and bring her to her new home. But she refused to come west." Madeline sipped her wine.

"Why not? With a house like this to come to?" Cooper was astonished.

"Apparently, the new Mrs. Knox was a beautiful, pampered, twenty-two year old socialite from an old and wealthy family. She balked at the idea of living in what she believed was the 'wild west around the wild Indians'. She told him that she was terrified because of the stories she'd heard. She thought she would be killed or scalped, or maybe 'taken' by the Indians."

Cooper shook his head. "Unbelievable."

"Well, Knox was devastated. He sold this property and he and his wife never lived in the house, not even one day. In fact, she never even saw it."

The idea that a woman would be so…Cooper couldn't come up with an apt word. Spoiled? Demanding, self-centered…maybe, impressionable? He said, "So, what happened to it? Who ended up with it?"

"Knox sold to a pair of brothers. Confirmed bachelors, I understand. Couple of good ol' boys who wanted to build a big ranching empire of cattle and horses. Not all of the original six hundred forty acres is hilly, like around the mansion, lots of it was good pasture land. They weren't buying the place for the house, just the land. In fact, they didn't know what to do with the house. A house this big, this…well, you know."

"I get the picture." And he did. The idea of a couple of rough and tumble cowboys in a house like this was laughable.

"So, they closed off most of the house so they didn't have to heat it. They chopped firewood on the fireplace hearth, in the library, and ruined it. Several of the art glass windows were damaged." Madeline smiled. "Cowboy thugs."

"When did your parents buy it?" Cooper asked.

"They got a really good deal on it in 1988. Of course, by then, only about fifty acres remained. The rest had been sold off over the years, to pay for upkeep and taxes. It'd been used for a convent, a home for girls, someone even made a half-hearted attempt at a Bed and Breakfast. My Dad and Mother had their eyes on the property for quite a long time. It had been empty for probably ten years, when they decided to buy it. They barely saved it from being razed."

"That's hard to believe, why would anyone want to do that?" Cooper was incredulous.

"It had become derelict. Everyone who looked at it only saw how degraded it had become, how much work and money it would take to restore it. My parents put a ton of money into restoration, basically from the ground up. Including central heat; when they bought it, the only heating was the fireplaces. The house had been electrified decades before, but that had to be redone of course.

"That's really where I got my love of old houses, it all started with Raven's Nest. I got to 'help' a bit, but I was just a little kid. I remember that I loved this house so much, right from the start, all the rooms, the staircases. There's even a few secret passages."

"Secret passages, huh? Ooooh. Just how big is it?" he asked.

"It's three storeys, well in some places four, and a bit less than forty-five thousand square feet. Give or take." She smiled.

"Jesus!" Cooper let out a low whistle. He couldn't get his head around that. He said, "I like the castle look."

"The architectural style is an eccentric mix of Gothic Revival and English Tudor. It has English influences…stone work, timbering, towers, lots of woodwork, but it also has elements of Gothic, arched windows…." She waved her hand, as if pushing all of that away, and said with a laugh, "Too much information."

"No, not at all. Why 'Raven's Nest'?" Cooper asked.

"Mr. Knox christened his new home Raven's Nest because of the extraordinary numbers of huge ravens that he saw in the forest, when construction started. They are indigenous, but there have always seemed to be so many around. Also, there is another story…it's a little strange, but it was written about him at the time."

"Alright, let's hear it."

Madeline sighed, smiling. "If you won't laugh."

Cooper shook his head. "Absolutely not."

"Okay, well, apparently, while he was on the property one day, around dusk, he said he saw a big cluster of ravens, in the lower branches of a live oak tree. A large group together is called an 'unkindness' of ravens, by the way." She paused, and frowned, then took a deep breath and continued.

"As he watched, he said that they all took off from the branches in a mass, swirled around, and began settling on the ground, not twenty feet from him. As they did, he said they sort of……turned into a figure. An Indian man. He looked at Knox and made a gesture with a spear in his hand. After that he turned and took a step like he was walking away, but then, he just became a huge group of ravens again. They soared away. He talked about how real the man was. He said it was just like an actual person was standing there."

Madeline stared into her wine, then tilted it up to drain the glass. "Natives in the area said it was a 'skinwalker' or a 'shape shifter'. Knox wrote about it in his diary, wrote letters to friends." Madeline added with a smile. "I guess the new Mrs. Knox didn't like the name Raven's Nest at all anyway, so she sure as *hell* wouldn't have liked to hear something like that."

"I've heard stories like this, told by the Comanche and other tribes in Texas. It is a part of their culture and history."

"Do you believe it?" she asked.

"I keep an open mind," he said solemnly. "Native Americans have a very old history, with a great respect for nature, for life and death, for their elders. Who am I to say, what is or isn't true?"

"It certainly put this property, this house and the story, on the map around here, so to speak," Madeline said with a low laugh. "Somehow it has grown to be such an integral part of this place, that I can't imagine it being called anything else."

"I like it," Cooper said. "It adds mystery." He sipped some wine and said, in a lower voice, "Do you know what you're going to do with it? Now, I mean?"

"I don't know. It takes a lot to maintain it, as you can imagine. I don't know if I can manage it. I've got my business in Eugene…" Madeline stared down at her hand, twirling the stem of her empty wine glass. "One more of hundreds of decisions to be made."

* * *

After refilling their wine glasses, they went into the library and Madeline showed Cooper her mother's diary. Even though it was only March, there were several more entries, after the two in January. Madeline had not yet read them all, but the ones she had, were mundane references to the house and some committee work.

"This does seem to imply that there are other journals. You've looked?" he asked.

"In the obvious places, yes." She showed Cooper the cubby. "I've been through her room, but no luck. Besides, I don't know that the diaries would shed any light on her……murder." Madeline had difficulty saying the word.

"We've talked to Edgerton. It's true that he was trying to buy your mother out. However, that all changes now because you will be inheriting the estate, and he will have to deal with you from this point. If you find the other diaries, it's possible they would shed light on what's happened."

Madeline took a seat on one end of the sofa, carefully avoiding the wingback chair that sat in place of her mother's chair. Cooper sat on the other end of the sofa. Pancho curled up on the rug between them. The fire that Mr. Gutierrez or Mrs. T had built, was still burning, but had dwindled down.

"I need to tell you what happened today." He twirled his glass and watched as the wine spun in a small tornado. He studied the flames of the fire through the wine. "Ian Andrews was injured, in a hit and run accident. Although, Izzy and I are certain it wasn't an accident."

She sat up abruptly and turned her stunned face to him. "Is he badly hurt? Is he in the hospital?"

"I think he's likely back home by now, he was not seriously injured." Cooper related the details. "The thing is, someone was making a deliberate attempt on his life. My guess is, that someone is afraid that he knows something pertinent to your mother's case."

Madeline's heart sank. The insanity of her mother's death was now being brought to Ian as well? "Ian is a gentle, lovely man. I can't imagine someone trying to kill him!"

"He was very close to your mother, right?"

"Well, yes he was. I'd say even closer than Arthur. In a different way."

"We have a police guard on him and will have until this is over."

She closed her eyes and sighed with relief. They drank their wine in silence for a while.

In a low voice, Madeline said, "I've talked to Arthur. He says we can read the will anytime. I thought it just as well to get it over with. I also have to plan her funeral." Madeline grew quiet. "I assume there is no reason why I can't do that, is there?"

Cooper uneasily spun his wine glass, finally raised his eyes to hers and said, "No. No reason at all. I'm very sorry, Madeline."

She nodded. "Thank you. I'll keep looking for the diaries and let you know if I find them. Did you say you were going to see Arthur tomorrow? I thought you were meeting him today."

"Yeah, but he wanted to postpone until tomorrow. Something about going to church."

"Well, I'm going to his office in the morning, my appointment's at eleven. Maybe you should hear the information about the will. I don't have a problem with that, if you think it would help."

After the detective left, Madeline cleaned up the kitchen. Pancho didn't seem interested in helping, but he did enjoy the last of the brandy sauce. As she washed the dishes she reflected on Detective Cooper and the meal they shared. It had been very pleasant and left her feeling more relaxed than she'd been in days.

He was tall, boyishly handsome, and the soft drawl was appealing. She wondered about his background and how he came to be so far from his original home. The southern accent sounded like Oklahoma or Texas, and he had mentioned Texas. She had met a few kids at the University of Oregon that were from the south, and his voice reminded her of them.

Her thoughts moved to Ian. She was frightened for him. He was a sweet man, and her mother had loved him dearly. Now, someone was taking their problems with the Abbott family out on him. It seemed that she took two steps forward and three back. She felt that she was trapped in an horrifying dream from which there was no waking.

Since the detective had left at eight-thirty, Madeline decided a movie might keep her mind off things, if only for a while. Still have to find those diaries, she thought, but there's always tomorrow. God, I sound like Scarlett O'Hara, why do today what you can put off until *tumarrah*?

During the mansion's heyday, the billiard room was a male bastion, full of everything then associated with men. Huge billiard table, large, deep armchairs, cigar humidors, leather, liquor cabinet, low lighting and dark, rich colors. During the restoration, every effort had been made to bring the room back to its original condition.

Madeline's father, Clay, had loved the room and spent many evenings there, sipping whiskey and teaching a young Madeline to play pool, on a restored professional sized billiard table from 1900. He loved it, so she loved it. A couple of years ago, after Madeline had nagged him relentlessly, he caved in. He had a huge, state of the art digital flat screen television installed, along with a surround sound system. He found a talented wood craftsman, to cleverly build the entire unit into the original paneling. When it wasn't in use, it was invisible.

There was a half dozen theater chairs, custom built with mohair upholstery, to look like vintage arm chairs. They too, looked like they had lived there since 1900. Her dad had secretly loved the TV, and they shared movies every time she came home, right up until his death.

Madeline made microwave popcorn. Pancho watched attentively as she filled a bowl (he loved popcorn) and together they went to the billiard room. She browsed the movie collection to find something to watch, that was neither too lighthearted nor too morose. She settled on *Moonstruck*, not exactly sure why the story appealed to her. Pancho sat at her feet and waited patiently for his share of the popcorn. After snuffling and crunching a couple handfuls, he curled up on her feet.

As she watched, she become vaguely aware of the rising wind. It made the usual howling and sighing noises that were caused by the shape and size of the house. The way the house was situated on the property, and the height of the surrounding mountains seemed to affect winds from the coast. Madeline was accustomed to it. But, tonight, when she realized that was what she was hearing, it left her feeling edgy and spooked.

When the movie ended, she was momentarily cheered by the romance between Cher and Nic Cage. She turned off the lights, and she and Pancho headed up the main stair. She briefly considered making a cup of tea, but decided against it. *It's too late and I have to meet Selwyn tomorrow. I wish to God I didn't have to go.*

The mansion, filled with darkness and deep black shadows could confuse or even frighten a visitor, but Madeline knew every square inch and could find any room blindfolded. As she reached the landing, she heard a noise, a tapping, coming from somewhere downstairs. She padded back down, listening hard. There it was again. Pancho whiffled softly. The tapping sounded like it was coming from the ladies' parlor. She crossed the foyer and went down the gallery, pausing at the double doors to the parlor. No light came in through the windows, but she could make out the furniture groupings, the fireplace. Nothing there. The stillness in the house was absolute. The only thing she could hear was the blustering wind.

As she headed up the stairs again she heard it once more. Tapping. Irregular. Sometimes hard, sometimes soft. Was it now coming from the back of the house? This time, Madeline headed toward the kitchen and the utility rooms. *There must be a branch blowing against a window*, she reasoned.

Sound carried through the huge old house in odd ways. Maybe it wasn't even in the back of the house, but as far away as the east wing. Madeline was puzzled by her own reaction. She had spent years in this house and never once been frightened. Odd noises were to be expected in a house as old as this, but this felt different. This felt *unnatural*.

By the time she got to the back of the house the noise had stopped. She held Pancho's collar, unlocked the back door in the kitchen and stepped out onto the stoop. Gusting wind buffeted her.

The light over the back door illuminated the cement stoop and broad stairs down to the terrace. Lights that shone from each corner of the garage, created small pools of light over the cobbled drive. Nothing. Her mother's car, and her rental, were parked side by side, eerily illuminated by the yellowish lights. She sensed......something. Was someone out there, a prowler? What a ridiculous notion. But what of the surveillance post across the road? If she hadn't seen it herself, beneath the cedar tree, she wouldn't have believed it. Someone had been watching she just didn't know when or why. Or more importantly, who? Madeline shivered, and the hair on the back of her neck stood up. She quickly pulled on Pancho's collar, stepped back inside and relocked the door.

Madeline and Pancho went to the front foyer and peered out the window. The front stoop was lighted by wrought iron sconces on each side of the huge oak door. As far as away as she could see into the darkness, in the lawn and garden area, there was no one. If someone lurked beyond that, in the woodland, it was impossible to know. Once again, she felt something weirdly...wrong.

She was turning when she caught a glimpse of something, lying under the edge of the mat outside. Glancing around again to be sure there was no one about, she unlocked the door. It looked like a letter. She quickly snatched it up. It was not postmarked nor addressed, other than one name: *Madeline*.

Madeline closed and locked the door. She held the letter in trembling hands, afraid to open it, afraid to put it down, afraid to look at it. What could it possibly be, who could have left it? Cooper left through this door at eight-thirty, and it *wasn't here*. No one knocked or made their presence known. It was unlikely to be an invitation to a masquerade ball or garden party.

She went to the kitchen and poured a glass of wine and sat at the table and drank, with the envelope laying on the table in front of her. She stared at it. She didn't recognize the handwriting. She finished the glass and poured more. Finally with a deep breath she opened the envelope.

* * *

Do you know why your mother was killed? The same reason YOU will be killed. It's what you deserve. And nobody will ever know who did it. You aren't safe. You'll never BE safe. Especially here.

Madeline stared at the words, stunned. Uncertain that she read it correctly, she read it again. A wave of nausea hit suddenly and violently. She jumped from the stool and barely made it to the sink before vomiting up the popcorn, wine and the supper she had enjoyed with Detective Cooper.

After she cleaned up, Madeline selected another bottle of wine and walked on shaky legs to the library, where she and Pancho sat together. She was at a loss. *Is this someone's idea of a joke? Cruel and awful as it was, she felt it must be a joke simply because it seemed so utterly unbelievable. Why would anyone deliberately choose to harm my mother—or me? And then taunt me about it? It was cruel. It made no sense.*

Pancho sensed something was wrong. He sat on the rug next to Madeline, as close as he could get, his body leaned against her legs, his head rested on her lap.

She poured a glass of Merlot and drank. *Now, is this something more that I have to give to the detectives? What can they do with it? Probably nothing. It's just a dead end that will lead nowhere.* Everyone in town knew about her mother by now. No matter how much Eleanor had done for Los Gatos, every town had its share of crazies, didn't it? *It has to be a thoughtless prank, some kid's absurd idea of fun.* Madeline got up and paced the room. Her now empty stomach sent the wine quickly into her blood stream, and she began to relax. She drank another glass.

Why bother giving the detectives with this note because it isn't real. It can't be real, she reasoned. With my luck they'll think I wrote it myself, just to get attention. That's the way it is in the movies, right? She sat on the sofa and talked it over with Pancho. What is the point of this, she asked him. If this isn't some kid's prank, then what is the point? Pancho didn't have any answers. Her feeble attempts to make herself feel better didn't work. The longer she thought about it, the more sure she was that someone was just attempting to frighten her, here in her own house. The idea of that infuriated her, more than frightened her. She poured more wine.

She pulled out her cell phone and called David. He answered on the second ring.

"Maddie! I'm glad you called. How are you?"

"Where are you, David?"

There was silence on the line. "What do you mean, where am I?"

"I meant just what I said, where are you?"

"I'm at home, Maddie, why? Do you need me? Do you need help?"

"No, I don't need you, David. I just got an anonymous letter. A threatening letter."

"Jesus, Maddie, you're kidding! Are you all right? What can I do?"

"Nothing. You can do nothing, David, absolutely nothing. I'm telling you that you had better not have had anything to do with this. If I find out you're the one responsible for this, you'll regret it."

"I don't know what in the hell you're talking about, Madeline. I'm in Eugene, I'm not at Raven's Nest, as you well know. You sound like you've been drinking, what's the matter?"

"I just told you, I got a threatening letter, and I'm pissed about it."

"Maybe I should come down and help you, I can—"

"NO. Never mind. I'll talk to you later."

"Maddie—"

Madeline hung up. One thing about cell phones, they just don't have the same impact when you're angry with someone. Not nearly as satisfying as slamming a regular phone down. Damn it, I wish I'd called him on the land line. She snickered.

She couldn't think of another person in her life that might have a reason to do such a childish, foolish thing, and be stupid enough to actually do it. David fit that bill pretty neatly.

Madeline poured another glass, and wondered if she believed him. Her cell phone rang, and the caller ID said David. She ignored it.

What to do now. Was there any point in even telling the detectives about the note? If she kept it from them, she would probably never hear the end of it. On the other hand, if it is just a joke, it will just have them racing around, spending time away from what's important, finding out who killed her mother.

She finished the bottle and decided to open another. The troubles of her life were slowly slipping away. She re-read the note. Now it looked different. She realized it looked, well, pathetically amateurish. Who in the world would really write something like this? The more she looked at it, the more absurd it looked. Ridiculous even.

I'm so lucky. I have a life truly worth being envious of, don't I? My entire family is now dead. I have a huge business I have no understanding of, and I'm now going to be responsible for, a tiny somewhat insignificant business I'm still responsible for—along with all the employees. The question of who murdered my mother and why, and some anonymous idiot threatening my life for kicks. Madeline poured another glass.

Pancho sat patiently at her feet, looking at her with a puzzled expression. "I can't help it Panch. I'm sick of this mess. What am I supposed to do?" He woofed softly, as if to say, "I wish I knew."

She sipped her wine. Now, to top it all off, someone has tried to hurt Ian. Kind, gentle and funny Ian.

It isn't right to be afraid in your own home. In the more than twenty years that this has been my home, I've never been afraid at Raven's Nest. Ever. And now, someone is trying to make me afraid of my own shadow. What is being gained by doing that?

In another half hour, she had finished off half of the second bottle. Madeline's head was fuzzy but pleasantly unconcerned with everything. Nothing much mattered now, other than getting upstairs, washing her face and crawling into bed. She and Pancho went upstairs together, she a bit unsteadily. Madeline cleaned her face, drank a glass of water and took a couple of aspirins, deciding maybe it would help with what she already knew to be inevitable.

That night, even having had so much wine, she barely slept. She would just be about to doze off, and she'd hear odd, unidentified noises. Every one made her start and pick her head up from the pillow and listen, hard. Even though it was strictly forbidden, she brought Pancho right up onto the bed with her. He made no protest. He laid by her side, between Madeline and the door.

CHAPTER SEVEN
Monday

Detective Scott Cooper called Morales on her cell phone and asked her to meet him at Diallo's, at seven-thirty. "Have you heard from the Kenyon woman?"

"No, she never called me back. I called her again late yesterday and got no answer. Left another message. She's giving us the run around."

"We'll catch up with her today. We're going to Selwyn's office at eleven, meeting Madeline there."

"Madeline, is it now?" Morales asked with a smile in her voice.

"Oh shut up, Izzy, I'll see you shortly." Cooper felt his face get hot, thankful Izzy wasn't around to see it.

Like Cooper, Isabelle Morales was a coffee junkie. She loved good coffee and liked Diallo's coffee enough to make it a regular haunt. She rushed in fifteen minutes late, stopped at the counter to order a latte in a to go cup and a bagel with cream cheese.

"Sorry I'm late."

"Domestic issues?"

Morales looked at him askance. "What makes you say that?"

"I've just had the feeling you and Alana are having issues. You've been on edge, lately. What's up?"

"We aren't having issues," she said, her tone was defensive.

"Then why the touchiness in the last week?"

Morales looked out the window at the overcast sky. The winds from the previous night continued and had blown in clouds making the sky a solid, leaden grey. She looked back at Cooper. Her voice softened. "Have I been touchy? Maybe I'm just not happy having to work with Willis, you ever think of that?"

Cooper sipped his coffee and pulled his thoughts together before replying. "Willis is an asshole, but you can't let him get to you, Izzy, it's not worth it."

The waitperson brought Morales's coffee and bagel. She immediately dove into the latte. "I get tired of fighting it, that's all. Racism, homophobia. It wears me out. Did I tell you, Alana wants me to find other work? She's afraid for me. I've worked hard to get where I am, and I like my job." After a pause she said: "I like working with you."

Isabelle Morales had been in a relationship with Alana Greeley for two years, since shortly before she was partnered with Cooper. Although Izzy kept her personal life strictly private, things always have a way of leaking out. It exacerbated her situation on the force. Willis wasn't the only officer who had a problem with Morales, he was just more obvious about it.

"You just keep being professional, and he'll come to see there is nothing to be done about it. He'll have to learn to get along." Cooper snickered. "Maybe he was absent the day they taught that lesson in kindergarten."

Morales sat silently, trying to remain serious and not to smile at his remark. She studied her coffee, as she pulled her bagel into manageable chunks. Her smooth brown brows were knitted together as she thought about what Cooper said. Finally she sighed. "I'll do my best, Scotty, but I'll only be pushed so far." Morales looked at him intently, her dark brown eyes stared into his blue ones as if searching for an answer.

Cooper said: "I've got your back, Izzy, you know that."

Her slender fingers circled her latte and gripped it like a lifeline. "I know."

"Okay, then, let's go over what we know."

Morales opened her notebook. "So, we talked to Richard Kelsey and Sydney Poole. The stats on them: he is sixty-one and she's forty-seven. They live together, not married. He is a high priced attorney, and she is a computer analyst working for Apple. She telecommutes. They told us they were at her mother's house in San Jose Thursday night and it checks out."

A gain for Apple, but what a loss for all the folks looking for therapy in the form of a kind, thoughtful ear—and voice, Cooper thought.

"What did you think of them?"

"He's quite a bit older than she is. But, he's kinda good looking, I guess I can see it. Of course, he's rich, which helps. He's a defense attorney so he pulls down loads of dough." She paused the added, "I don't know why I say that, she makes a hell of a packet with Apple. As we both saw, they seem happy together."

Morales grinned, then read from her notes. "Richard's known Eleanor Abbott for almost twenty-eight years. Only been involved with Sydney Poole for about five years. He was divorced a long time ago. He owns that huge condo they're living in. Very expensive. At this point, I don't see what motive they could have. They did seem genuinely upset about her death."

"Okay, were you able to get to the Van Gesslers?" he asked checking his notebook.

"I did. I found out that basically what they told us is true, he's a banker she's in real estate. They seem to be financially well off, he's got quite a number of clients. None as wealthy as the Abbotts, nowhere close. I didn't really find out anything about them personally yet or about their relationship with the Abbotts. I'm still on their finances."

"Well, listen to this. Madeline called yesterday. She's just realized that an old and pretty valuable painting is missing. She didn't notice it when I met her there Saturday."

"A painting. Which painting?"

"It's by an Impressionist painter, Mary Cassatt. I'm kinda familiar with her work. I seem to remember her from an art history class in college. Anyway, it's a valuable painting that hung behind Mrs. Abbott's desk in the library, and now it's gone. Probably worth millions."

At that Morales raised her brows and said around a mouthful of bagel, "So *that* was the reason for the break-in? Hoping to fence a multi-million dollar painting? Well, *if* they could fence it…"

Cooper nodded and frowned. Finally, he said, "Maybe. Probably. But, something still feels wrong about the whole thing. Like I said, how in the hell did he get in without her hearing, to come up behind her to beat her to death? And besides, if what he wanted was the painting why kill her?"

Morales shrugged. "Umm hmm, why kill her when you could, I don't know, knock her out, or tie her up?" She sat munching the bagel, staring at Cooper. "You think he, or she, had a key, don't you? That the whole thing was set up to misdirect."

"Yes. I also think it's more than one person, but out of this group, who?"

Morales shrugged. "Maybe we'll know after we talk to Kenyon. Her being in the thick of things every day with Abbott, access she had as the PA, maybe *she's* in it up to her eyeballs.

"Oh, Bell said that the Andrews guy didn't have to stay at the hospital. Just a badly bruised heel bone. He went home, escorted by a uniform." Morales drank some coffee. "God, this is good. The bagel really hits the spot." Then she added offhandedly, "By the way, you went to talk to her yesterday? The Abbott woman?"

Cooper squinted at Morales, senses on alert, and slowly said, "Ye-e-s-s. That's what I said. And her name is Madeline."

"So what happened? She told you about the painting?"

"Yeah, she told me about the painting. I saw where it had been hanging. Also, she found a diary, kept by her mother." Cooper explained about what Madeline had learned by reading the diary and that she was looking for others.

"Sounds like that might be something. What else?"

Cooper looked at her warily, and with a slight shrug said, "Nothing else. That's all she said."

Morales shook her head vigorously. "Ohh, no. Come on, *amigo*, you told me you didn't get home till after eight-thirty. I don't think it takes two and a half hours to look at an empty wall and one diary." Morales tried hard not to smile.

"Jesus H. Christ, Izzy. Yes, I was there for a while. Okay, you want the truth? She cooked some supper, and we ate it. Drank a couple glasses of wine. Got anything else to add?"

"Oh, nothing," she said airily. "Can't wait to meet her."

"Why do I tell you anything?" Cooper groused, his face reddening. "We might as well go over to Kenyon's place, before our appointment with Selwyn. If the little lady's not going to return our calls, maybe we can catch her at home. Grab that coffee. Let's go."

* * *

Diane Kenyon's apartment complex was a stucco building dating from the late 1970s and was as utterly, bland and featureless, as an old shoe box. Covered in grey-tan stucco, it had unpleasant swirls of mold decorating the lower third, along with bedraggled unkempt rhododendrons. The layout was a ubiquitous two story rectangle, around which all units opened onto a courtyard. In the middle sat a swimming pool, empty other than a two foot deep puddle of scummy green water at the deep end.

They spied Kenyon's apartment number opposite a wrought iron entry gate, that, because of a bent hinge, wouldn't quite close completely.

Morales knocked on the door and called out, "Ms. Kenyon, it's Detective Morales and Detective Cooper. We've come to talk to you about Mrs. Abbott." There was no response. The sound of a television game show came faintly from inside.

The cement area around the pool was empty. A few battered lawn chairs leaned crazily at angles, on bent and broken legs. A faded and tattered plastic fire engine, rested near an apartment door across from where the detectives stood. All was quiet, except for the sound of traffic rushing on the thoroughfare next to the complex. The gusting wind kept dense grey clouds moving across the sky, and created an odd blueish light that reflected off the cement. From somewhere came the plaintive wail of a baby.

Two units down from Kenyon's, the door opened, and a young Mexican woman peered out. She had a sticky faced toddler clinging to her leg working studiously on a sucker.

"What do you want?" she asked.

"We want to talk to Ms. Kenyon. Have you seen her?" Cooper asked.

"No. I haven't seen her in many days. I think she's gone."

"She was supposed to be back yesterday," Morales replied.

Something in the back of Cooper's mind was sending off an alarm.

"Where can I find the manager?" he asked.

"Diez." She pointed with her chin to unit ten on the corner of the other side. She abruptly stepped back and shut the door without saying another word. Cooper heard the lock engage.

Cooper knocked on number ten.

The door was answered by a tall cadaverous man, late sixties, wearing a yellowed and badly stained undershirt and dirty khaki shorts. A cigarette dangled from the side of his mouth and nicotine stained whiskers bristled from his face. He stared at them with malice and said, "Yeah?"

They showed their identification and Cooper said, "I'm Detective Cooper, this is Detective Morales."

Without looking at the IDs he said, "Yeah, so? Whaddya want?" Fetid body odor finally escaped the apartment and wafted over them.

"What's your name, sir?" Morales asked, trying to breathe shallowly.

He stood, looking from Cooper to Morales. It seemed at first he might not answer. Finally, he said, "Truitt. Merle Truitt."

Morales made a note of it, asking as to the correct spelling. He stared silently at her, through the thin, grey ribbon of smoke from the end of his cigarette. Finally, he complied. He spoke without removing the cigarette, and its jerking dance, caused an inch of ash to fall to his undershirt. He brushed at it, making a smear. It blended right in.

"We are looking for one of your tenants, Diane Kenyon. She was supposed to get in touch with us yesterday. She isn't answering her door. Have you seen her?" Cooper asked.

"Ain't my job to keep track 'a renters. Why do the cops want her anyway, what's she done?"

"We aren't at liberty to say. We just need to talk with her. Would you please let us in to her apartment?" Morales asked.

He looked at Morales then back to Cooper. "Dontcha need a warrant?" He said it, 'wornt'.

"Well, Mr. Truitt, we can get a warrant, sure," Cooper said reasonably. "But I think it might be better if you were cooperative with us now and not have to deal with a charge of obstruction later." He smiled. "Sir."

With a grunt Truitt turned to get the key and began a coughing fit that lasted until he retrieved the key and returned to the door. He proceeded to hurl a gob of spit into one of the few areas of dirt available, an untended planter full of lifeless brown plants. He trudged across to Kenyon's apartment, cheap rubber flip-flops slapping the cement.

Morales looked at Cooper and rolled her eyes. He lifted his eyebrows, sighed and shrugged.

At the door to Kenyon's apartment Cooper said, "Just unlock it, and we will take it from here." He was unsure of what they might find and wanted Truitt gone. After unlocking the door Truitt held the key up to Cooper with a sour look. "Bring it back." He went back to his apartment coughing and spitting and slammed his door closed.

They opened Diane Kenyon's door to the sound of Wheel of Fortune playing on the small flat screen television resting on a low bookcase opposite the sofa. The apartment was exactly like ten thousand others. A small living room with a dining area adjacent to the small galley kitchen, making an inverted L shape. It was tidy and decorated with feminine touches, of poster art and pillows on the sofa and chair, the kind you find at Pier One. Diane was obviously working hard to make her home as comfortable and attractive as she could on her income.

The small wood dining table was clear, except for a couple of place mats and a decorative pottery bowl. The bowl held a miscellaneous assortment of the odds and ends that everyone accumulates: a few loose coins, a few rubber bands, a handful of paper clips, a beer opener with a restaurant logo, a tiny photo, battered and scuffed. Cooper used a pen to stir the items around as he looked. The photo was one of the small ones, taken at a photo booth. It showed a young blond woman in most of the frame, with part of a man's face, half obscured by hers. They were making idiotic expressions for the camera.

The galley kitchen was tidy, sink empty, no dirty dishes or stale food. The trash can at the end of the short counter, lined with a plastic bag was empty. The worn counters gleamed. The fridge held a quart of milk, a few Amstel beers, a couple of pears and some sliced cheese and a bottle of white wine.

The short hall had three doors. The bathroom was empty and dry. The small sink vanity held a dispenser of liquid soap, neatly folded towels hung from a bar over the toilet.

A small storage closet had a vacuum, a few folded towels and bathmats, toiletries and extra bedding. They last door they opened was the one bedroom. A young woman's body lay at the foot of the double bed, feet on the floor. As if too tired to continue, she simply sat and leaned back to rest. Long, straight blond hair framed a conventionally pretty face. Blue eyes were open and clouded, staring at, but no longer seeing, the bland popcorn ceiling. A large knife handle, protruded from her upper abdomen.

* * *

Blood had pooled around her body and soaked into the mattress. A suitcase and overnight bag were between the dresser and the bed. Each had been opened and savagely rummaged. Clothes and toiletries were strewn everywhere. A straw purse had been dumped on the dresser. A pair of sunglasses, lay broken, next to the purse.

Cooper strode to her side and felt for a pulse. Her body was cool, but not cold. "She hasn't been dead that long." He said to Morales. He stood with his hands on his hips, shaking his head. "Son-of-a-*bitch*." He called it in.

While Cooper made the call, Morales pulled on gloves and made a quick search through the items from the purse. The wallet contained a small amount of cash, a couple of credit cards and a driver's license, belonging to one Diane Lee Kenyon, age 23.

They stood outside and waited for the forensic team to arrive.

"What did it look like to you, Izzy?"

"Looked like the girl in that little photo."

"Yeah, I thought so too. No, I meant, what did the scene look like to you?"

"Someone went through her stuff in a hurry. Looking for something."

"Did you see her cell phone there?" he asked.

Morales shook her head.

"I didn't either. So he took it, or it's still somewhere in the apartment."

Ginny Bell and another uniform were first to show up and began to cordon off the area with tape. By the time the photographer and forensics arrived, activity and hubbub caused a few curiosity seekers to venture out of their doors. They huddled in groups, whispering. Cooper and Morales split up and began the questioning.

Information was thin. Diane apparently didn't socialize with other residents, in fact, few even knew her name. In Cooper's mind it seemed that Diane's not mixing with her neighbors, keeping herself apart, was self protection, of a sort. She was trying to disassociate from her surroundings, hoping for a life more in keeping with where she worked, not where she lived. Everyone had dreams.

Merle Truitt continued being unpleasant and intractable. He claimed to know nothing about Diane Kenyon, other than the fact that she paid her rent on time. "And that's friggin' unusual, in this Godfersaken place, let me tell ya," he said with a snarl that exposed yellowed teeth, what there were of them.

Medical Examiner Walt Simmons strode into the courtyard and with a nod to Cooper and Morales, went directly in.

"It's almost eleven. We gotta get over to Selwyn's place, Izzy. I'll tell Simmons to phone when he has something."

Inside, Cooper told officer Ginny Bell that she was in charge of securing the scene, when forensics was finished. "Oh, and look for her cell phone, and let me know right away if you find it."

She nodded. "I'll take care of it."

He went into the bedroom and spoke to Simmons. "Walt, Izzy and I have to go. What can you tell me, just by your first look?"

Walter Simmons peered up at Cooper from his position, kneeling on the floor next to his equipment case. "I've been seeing more of you than I'm seeing of my wife, detective," Simmons said. "Is this related to the Abbott murder?"

Cooper nodded the affirmative then said, "But let's keep it quiet, for now. So, what can you tell me?"

"What I can tell you is that she's dead." Cooper usually enjoyed Simmons' quirky sense of humor, but today was not one of those days.

"Think I got that one, Walt. When, d'ya think?"

"My guess is, just a couple hours ago, or less. What a fucking shame. She's so young."

"Okay. Call as soon as you have something. The quicker the better."

"But of course," Simmons said, with only a tinge of sarcasm.

Outside, Cooper and Morales returned to their car and sat for a moment quietly, each thinking similar thoughts.

Morales finally said: "She knew something and became a liability."

"Like Ian Andrews is a liability?"

Morales nodded.

"But who did she know? Some of Mrs. Abbott's business people? And, who knew her? Who do we know that would know anything about her?" Cooper mused.

They looked at each other and said at the same time, "Mrs. Temple."

"When we're through at Selwyn's place, I'll go out to talk to Mrs. Temple."

* * *

The detectives entered a waiting area at Selwyn's office. A receptionist or secretary sat at a large oak desk at one side of the room. She introduced herself as Ms. Morgan, and asked them to please sit, Mr. Selwyn would be with them in just a moment.

The office struck Cooper as being so......plain, for an attorney. Usually attorneys had money to burn, and liked spending it, buying the best: the most expensive furniture, art, rugs, lighting. This waiting area could have been a dentist or a new wave health practitioner, maybe a reflexologist or a naturopath. Plain furniture, beige walls, vapid floral art prints that you've seen a hundred times.

They had been there for less than five minutes when his office door opened and Phoebe Deardon exited. Cooper stood and greeted her. She seemed flustered to see him, and after a brief hello she left. Cooper and Morales exchanged a glance.

Ms. Morgan motioned them into Selwyn's office. Selwyn, pale, gaunt and somber, stood with an enormous amount of effort. He greeted them and waved them into chairs around his desk. Cooper introduced himself and Morales to Selwyn, adding, "We've spoken on the phone."

Selwyn murmured, "Yes, yes." Selwyn's demeanor was one of utter devastation. When he sat down again, he heaved a dispirited sigh.

"I had hoped we would be able to speak a few moments before Mrs. Dean arrives," Cooper said. "There are some questions we need to ask."

Selwyn nodded. "Go ahead. I'll be happy to help in any way I can."

Morales looked at Selwyn, her hand poised over her notebook. "Where were you on Thursday evening, Mr. Selwyn, from eleven p.m. on?"

He looked at the detective sadly. "I know you have a job to do, Detective Morales, but I wish you could know how completely ridiculous it is, to suspect me of harming Eleanor."

"We need you to answer the question," Morales replied evenly.

"Alright. I will. I was at home. Alone. I have no way for you to verify that. But I will tell you this. I loved Eleanor. *Loved* her. I would have married her, if she had only said yes. And I asked her many times over the years. I'm older than Eleanor, several years older, but I don't think that was the problem."

Cooper and Morales exchanged a quick glance and waited, knowing instinctively there was more coming.

"I asked her forty years ago. I asked her while she was married to Clay, much to my embarrassment. You see, I knew the trouble they had. I knew he was not faithful to her, the miserable bastard. She said no. I asked after Clay died. She said no. I believe that Eleanor held the notion that she had made her pact, as it were, and was going to stick it out. But I have never stopped loving her. I will never stop loving her." The statement was so simple, direct and heartrending, that Cooper felt the urge to excuse themselves and leave.

A tap on the door interrupted the conversation. Ms. Morgan escorted Madeline in. Cooper stood. She greeted him, quietly, indifferently, her face ashen.

Puzzled, he extended his hand. "Hi, Madeline. This is Detective Isabelle Morales, my partner." Madeline, a head taller than Morales, put out her hand and they shook with a murmured greeting. Madeline turned and took a chair. Morales looked at Cooper, pumped her eyebrows a couple of times and smirked. He shook his head, feeling his face get red again. They retook their chairs.

Cooper frowned at Madeline's demeanor. Something was wrong.

Once everyone was settled, Selwyn said: "Madeline, you wish to have the detectives here for this? You are not obligated to do so, reading the will is a private matter."

Madeline looked at Morales and Cooper, then back to Arthur Selwyn. "I don't have a problem with it, Arthur. How complicated is the will?"

"Not terribly complex. There are some bequests to others, a few to Ellie's favorite charities, but the bulk of the estate does go to you, of course." He unfolded the document and smoothed it on the desk. For an uncomplicated will, it certainly looked substantial. Cooper estimated thirty to thirty-five pages.

"There are bequests to Phoebe Deardon, Mrs. Temple, of course, and Mr. Gutierrez, Ian Andrews, Sydney Poole and Richard Kelsey, Helen Highwater and others."

Madeline barely glanced at Cooper but, as if reading his mind, said, "Can you go ahead and spell out what those bequests are?"

"Of course." He perched a pair of bifocal glasses on his slender nose, and began.

"This is the most recent version of her will, updated in January of this year. There are provisions for your children when and if you have them, that will be required to be made from your portion of the estate upon the birth of those children and that is specified here. The other bequests are as follows:

"Mrs. Alma Temple, is to receive $250,000.00, post tax. She is to receive this bequest when she chooses to quit working, and that is at her discretion. Until that time, she is to be paid her regular salary."

"Mr. Manuel Gutierrez, is to receive $250.000.00, post tax. He is to receive this bequest when he chooses to quit working, and that is at his discretion. Until that time, he is to be paid his regular salary." Selwyn peered over the bifocals at them, then continued.

"Phoebe Deardon, is to receive $150,000.00 and Helen Highwater, $150,000.00."

"Mr. Ian Andrews, is to receive $250,000.00, Mr. Richard Kelsey and Ms. Sidney Poole, are to receive jointly $250,000.00"

Selwyn paused and then added, "There is a generous bequest to me, in the amount of $250,000.00."

"Mr. Frank and Mrs. Kathryn Van Gessler, were to receive jointly $150,000.00, but at the end of February, Eleanor asked me to amend the bequest."

Everyone looked at one another. Selwyn said, "They are to receive $1.00."

Cooper and Morales exchanged a look, then Cooper turned to look at Madeline. Her face had gone white, but she did not speak.

Selwyn cleared his throat and continued. "The balance of the estate which includes the property known as Raven's Nest, the property on the northern California coast, referred to as Black Oaks, all other liquid assets, bank accounts, stocks, artworks, furnishings, vehicles, jewelry and two thirds ownership in the business and properties known as Abbott & Edgerton Developments, is bequeathed to Madeline Elizabeth Abbott. These stipulations go into effect as soon as Madeline Abbott has finalized her divorce from David Dean, but not until such time as the divorce is finalized. Until then, she has limited access to assets as necessary, up to $40,000.00 per month for employee salaries, household maintenance, taxes and expenses. This and any other financial requirements, will be by agreement with the executor, Arthur Selwyn. The estate remains in trust, until the requirement of the divorce is accomplished.

"With careful determination of the current market value of all these assets, the value is placed at approximately $213,227,581.00 as of the last quarter."

* * *

Silence in the room, stretched out for a full minute. Before the will was read, Cooper had no idea what the scope of the Abbott business and other holdings amounted to. It could have been any number, he had no idea. Yes, the mansion property was huge, but the extent of the estate left him nearly speechless. When he could find his voice, he said, "There are large differences in the bequests. Do you know why?"

Selwyn said, "As far as I am aware, Ellie thought that the bequests should reflect each beneficiary's current personal financial picture. Some 'need' more, others less. As far as my portion of her estate is concerned, Ellie was completely aware that I did not necessarily need the money. I believe it is a gesture of our long friendship and fondness for one another. My guess is that the same holds true for Ian. She had fond regard and respect for both Mrs. Temple and Mr. Gutierrez and their years of service. I know that she wanted their retirement years to be easy."

Cooper and Morales again glanced at one another, then at Madeline. She sat perfectly still with her hands clasped tightly on top of her handbag, which laid in her lap. She stared out the windows behind Selwyn's desk, her expression one of bewilderment and Cooper could see, fear.

He asked, "Mr. Selwyn, about the Van Gessler's bequest, can you—"

"No, I'm sorry, I cannot. When Eleanor came in several weeks ago to ask for the change, she made it clear that she didn't want to discuss the matter. My sense was that something was amiss, but I have no knowledge what it could be." Selwyn took out a handkerchief and wiped his eyes and nose.

"Mr. Selwyn, have you been in contact with the beneficiaries, to tell them about their bequests?"

"No. I was obliged to wait until I had spoken to Maddie, of course. Now the will has been read, I will be contacting them, via certified mail, later today."

"I must ask that you not send the notification to these beneficiaries until I get back in touch with you. Revealing this information might compromise the investigation." Cooper said.

"But I don't see how this is in any way connected to Ellie's murder, detective."

"Did any of them know before Mrs. Abbott died, that they were to receive something upon her death, Mrs. Deardon, perhaps?" Cooper asked.

Selwyn looked askance at the detective. "What are you implying?" He removed his bifocals, laid them gently on the desk and sat back in his chair. "Are you saying that someone on this list is responsible for Ellie's murder? Mrs. Deardon was here on a private matter, Detective Cooper, as I am her attorney. Besides, that's unthinkable." His already pale face, had taken on a grey tinge.

"Murder is committed every day for far less than even the smallest of these bequests. It has to be considered, sir," Cooper said. "Did they know?"

"I don't know," he responded, rigidly. "If Ellie chose to tell them that was obviously her right, but I wasn't privy to it. I knew about the bequests, of course, because I drew up the document. But it was privileged information between me and my client, and I kept it privileged.

"I was included in this version of the will. All of these bequests were introduced into her will in the most recent version, last January. Before that date, Eleanor had a more 'standard' will in which nearly all of the estate was to be inherited by her daughter. It was at the beginning of the year that she came to me with a desire to make changes to the existing will."

Madeline left Selwyn's office at eleven-forty-five, without speaking to Cooper and Morales. She walked directly to her car with her head down. She slid behind the wheel and drove slowly away, in her rental car, headed in the direction of Raven's Nest. Cooper watched her go solemnly. The wind was coming up again and dark heavy clouds hung over the mountains.

"There's something wrong. Madeline's acting strange."

Morales watched the car disappear and said, "She had a pretty good motive, Scotty. But, the bit about the Van Gesslers?"

"It's not her, Izzy. And yes, we've got to find out what happened with the Van Gesslers."

"Don't just overlook Madeline, she may have been angry at her mother, for giving so much of it away." Morales said as she climbed into their car.

"She has over two hundred million—surely a couple million more is not enough to make someone commit murder, especially a family member.

"Yeah? Well, I don't understand that kind of money. I can't even imagine that high."

Cooper started the car and put down the windows. He smelled rain in the air. "I think these murders are all about money. Besides, I just don't think she's capable."

"Come on, Scotty, make sure it's your *brain* that's doing the thinking, okay? Nothing that's happened is beyond the ability of a woman, and you know it."

"We need financials on all the beneficiaries, right now. Start with the Van Gesslers. Must be something going on with money that will point us in the right direction or show us who among them had the most to gain. Get on the computer." Izzy was a wizard at computer research. It was a good thing she was, because Cooper certainly wasn't. In that, he relied heavily on Izzy. "And, let's keep checking alibis."

"I did get hold of the Highwater woman late yesterday." Morales said. "Told her we needed to ask a few more questions. She said she could see us tomorrow."

He rolled up to police headquarters and said to Morales: "Get on the computer and get started. I'm going back by Selwyn's with a few more questions, since we got interrupted. He might know something important, that he doesn't even know is important. Then, I'm going out to see what the hell's wrong with Madeline. She was upset about something, just now at Selwyn's. That'll give me a chance to speak to Mrs. Temple again."

"Okay, *amigo*, let me know if you need help." Morales grinned salaciously.

"Izzy, get your goddamned mind outta the gutter, will ya?"

"What do you need now, Mr. Cooper? I've given you all the information I have. Allow me some peace." Cooper understood his curt behavior, but knew he had to ask the questions.

"I'm sorry, sir, but you have to understand that we're trying to find out who did this to Eleanor. We don't mean to insult you. It's possible that you know something that can help us solve this case." Cooper seated himself in the chair he was in before. "I think you should know that, just before we arrived at your office earlier Morales and I were at the scene of another murder."

Arthur Selwyn sat heavily in his chair and regarded Cooper with bloodshot eyes. Cooper pressed ahead. "The young woman, Diane Kenyon, Eleanor's personal assistant? She was stabbed to death, earlier today."

Selwyn was clearly having a difficult time absorbing this information. "What? What did you say? Another murder? Not Diane Kenyon, oh, dear God."

"Yes, and we believe it is connected to Eleanor's. Also, Ian Andrews was the victim of a hit and run. Actually, we believe it was an attempt on his life."

Selwyn managed a strangled, "Oh, oh, no. Is Ian alright?"

"He was taken to the hospital, but the injuries were minor, thankfully."

Arthur Selwyn sat, immobile, his face expressionless as if in shock.

"I assume that you know all of the people Eleanor saw socially, as you were part of it." Cooper made it a statement not a question.

Selwyn started, as if someone had roughly awakened him. He frowned and studied his bifocals resting on his desk, playing with the ear pieces. "I've known Eleanor for such a long time detective. You have to understand the dynamics. If you love someone as I loved Eleanor, then it follows that you will come to know all those others who orbit around that person. Eleanor made many friends, but she was still reserved. She wasn't one to allow a lot of people to be really…close. Not intimately close. Oh, I don't know if I'm explaining this properly," he said with a sigh.

"I think I understand what you mean. She liked people and became friends, but only a select few were allowed to come to know her deeply."

He nodded. "She was very close to Ian. Oh, poor Ian, my God. And me, of course. Odd, but I don't believe that any women were in that 'close' group. I don't know why."

"Go on," Cooper said.

"This group of people have been socializing for years and years. You could say, that we all 'grew up' together. There have been changes over time, naturally. Greg died. Eventually Helen found someone else, she's beautiful, so finding companionship has never been difficult for her. She's had a couple since Greg died. She's had her new man, uh, William, William Gray, for a while. They seem well suited." He paused, as if realizing that he might just be getting off topic. He took a deep breath.

"Richard divorced years ago. His wife, Rebecca, left him after having an affair. He was so crushed by that experience, that he stayed single for a long while. Oh he dated, of course, but he seemed reluctant to become committed to a particular woman. Then, Sydney came along." Selwyn attempted a feeble smile. "She's a dear girl. I like her. I think everyone in the group does.

"Phoebe Deardon is divorced too, but that was long ago as well, when her girls were just babies. Her's was quite non—traumatic. Phoebe and Doug just couldn't stand one another, simple as that." That brought a hint of a smile to his beleaguered face. "She sometimes brings a date to our gatherings, but often comes alone and doesn't seem to care one way or another."

"I've heard different stories about difficulties with Edgerton, some tiff with Helen, her problems with her husband Clay, worries about Madeline." Cooper tented his hands under his chin, and regarded Selwyn. "We've heard so much conflicting anecdotal information, it's hard to sort it all out. I'm wondering what, if anything, you might now about these relationships that could help us. And yes, we do believe that the person responsible for Eleanor's murder, is among her circle of friends."

Arthur Selwyn rested his head in his hands and massaged his forehead and temples. Finally, looked up into Cooper's eyes. "As hard as that is for me to believe, detective, I promise you that I'll do anything I can to help you. At this point, I can't think of anything that stands out in my mind, that would point to any of her friends, I'm sorry. But, I promise I will give it serious thought and contact you if I think of anything."

Cooper rose to leave. "I'm sorry Mr. Selwyn to ask this of you. Were you aware that Eleanor had cancer?" He regretted having to utter the words. The look on the old man's face was one of indescribable sorrow. He stared at Cooper, head cocked slightly, as if perhaps, he had heard incorrectly.

"Please tell me what you mean," he finally said.

"During the autopsy, she was found to have advanced lung cancer. The M.E.'s estimation was that she likely had less than a year to live."

Tears welled in the Selwyn's eyes, making the faded blue pupils look like floating pieces of agate. "I wish I had known," he said. "Why didn't she tell me, was she afraid of hurting me? Surely, she must have realized I would know eventually."

Cooper looked down a him in sympathy. "I'm sorry, Mr. Selwyn, I really am. Eleanor apparently told no one. Perhaps she was hoping to get Madeline to come home, to tell her first, I don't know." Cooper leaned across the large desk and extended his hand. They shook. "If you think of anything, anything at all, please get in touch."

He left the office as the old man mopped his eyes with his handkerchief.

* * *

When Madeline returned to the house after the meeting with Arthur, she saw that Mrs. Temple had arrived while she was out. It was past one-thirty now, but she didn't feel hungry. She didn't feel anything at all. Well, maybe sorrow. What she heard at the office was beyond belief. She knew that her parents were successful, but they had never discussed the estate she would inherit. With Michael gone she was the only one left, but it had simply never occurred to her to wonder at the size of their business, their estate. And of course the stipulation that she must finalize her divorce in order to inherit. Very, very smart, mother. Raven's Nest was going to be hers. This huge business, her responsibility.

With the note that showed up magically last night and now the will, Madeline felt she might be going mad. It was becoming difficult to tell what was real. Is someone in my mother's will actually capable of committing *murder?* For money? And the note. I have to stop focusing on it, just stop thinking about it. Put it out of my mind. Easier said than done.

Was the business what her mother wanted to talk to her about? The important thing that she alluded to in the phone message? That phone message, only what, five or six days ago? It already seemed like it was in the foggy mist of the long ago past.

Maybe she wanted to talk about David. She knew her mother didn't care for David, but respected Madeline enough not to push her about it. Madeline had told her mother months ago that she and David had separated, and felt sure they would end up divorced. She chose not to rush into it. She wanted to be sure she was right about it. As she grew more afraid of David's anger, the drugs and drinking, the fact he couldn't hold down a job, it became clear that divorce was the only option. She wondered bitterly, how he managed to always have money for drugs and booze if he didn't work. She had shared all of it with her mother on the last visit at Christmas. I guess it really was the last visit she thought morosely.

She turned off the whistling kettle, and got out the Belleek set her mother always used for tea. She preheated the pot and made her favorite, English Breakfast tea. Just as she was about to pour a cup, Madeline heard the electric buzzer in the kitchen, which indicated someone was ringing the front door bell. She glanced at her wrist watch. It was ten to one. She couldn't think of anyone due to come by.

She opened the front door and was stunned to see David on the front step. He wore wrinkled and torn blue jeans and a grimy ZZ Top tee shirt. His light, faintly reddish blond hair, uncombed, stuck out in all directions from his head, and there was at least a day's stubble on his face. He held a duffel bag in his hand. Her first reaction was a panicky cramp in her gut which she strove to hide.

"What are you doing here, David? I told you, I didn't want you here," she said with as much calm as she could manage.

"Hi, Maddie. I thought it over and decided it just wouldn't be right for you to be here all by yourself, dealing with everything you're having to deal with." With that he started toward her to come into the house.

"No, David, no." She shook her head and put her hand on his chest. They were nearly the same height, but he outweighed her by over fifty or sixty beer drinking pounds. "I said I just want to be alone now. I told you that clearly."

David Dean stared at Madeline, his face surly. With a sigh, he took out a cigarette, lit it and took a long drag.

"Look, Maddie, I'm just here to help," he said, smoke shooting from his nostrils in great plumes. "Surely you can understand that I want to be of some help to you. Your mom has just died, you've had a break in. It's probably not safe for you to be here alone. Come on, just let me stay here and help you."

Stay *here?* she thought. He's insane.

As David uttered the words, there was the sound of an automobile on the driveway. She recognized the detectives' car and relief flooded her. David turned and looked at the approaching vehicle. "Who's that?"

"It's the detectives who are working on the case," she said. She fanned the smoke away. "Get that away from me."

David took another hefty drag, tossed the butt down and gave it a twist with his toe. He didn't pick it up.

Cooper parked near the porte cochere and got out. He was alone.

"Hello, Madeline," Cooper said as he ambled to the front door, sizing up the situation. "How are y'all, this afternoon?"

David Dean turned on him with a sour look, and said belligerently, "And who the hell are you?"

Cooper looked calmly at David then stuck out his hand and said with a level tone: "I'm Detective Scott Cooper with the Los Gatos PD." And although he had guessed, he added, "And you are?"

"I'm Maddie's husband. David Dean." He hesitated, but finally shook Cooper's hand. Cooper studied him. He looked like he hadn't slept in a couple of days, eyes bloodshot, mottled skin, nose red. Cooper knew a coke user when he saw one.

Cooper turned to her. "Madeline is there anything I can do to help y'all?"

"No. We *all* don't need any help. If she needs help, I'm here now, I can help her," David said preemptively.

"Actually, Detective Cooper, David was just leaving." Madeline said. "Right now."

"Maddie…" David swung back to her, and at the same time reached out to take her hand.

Madeline jerked her hand away and said heatedly, "Don't David, I told you before I don't want you here."

Cooper took an involuntary step toward him then stopped.

"What's it going to take, to make you understand?" Madeline's voice quivered.

Cooper saw she was striving to keep control and decided it was time to intervene. He bent over and picked up the remnants of the cigarette. "I think you should do as Madeline says, Mr. Dean. She's under considerable stress right now, and this is not helping. Maybe you could wait until she gets in touch with you, at a later date?" He held the crushed cigarette butt out to David, for a few tense seconds until David raised his hand. Cooper dropped the butt onto his palm.

David's face already ruddy, flushed bright crimson. He pursed his mouth and scowled. Then quickly, a change came over him. His face calmed and he deposited the cigarette butt in his pocket.

"You're right, of course. I'm sorry, Maddie, I've just been so upset and worried about you. Maybe I shouldn't have come. I've just been so worried, you here alone in this big old house, not knowing who broke in and killed your mom. I just want to help."

He hitched up his duffel bag and turned. "I'll go back to Eugene. I'll be there if you need me for anything. I just wanted to help you," he repeated. David hurried to his car, got in, made a sharp turn that made his tires squeal, and sped down the serpentine drive until they could no longer see him through the trees.

* * *

Madeline relaxed and let out a shaky laugh. "Thank you, Detective Cooper. I guess I'm lucky you happened by. Sometimes I don't know about David. Mostly, he bugs the hell out of me."

Cooper smiled. He could see that her face was still very pale and her eyes looked as if she had been crying. "Good timing, I guess. I came to ask some additional questions and maybe talk to Mrs. Temple, if she's available?" Seconds ticked by, as he stood with his hands on his hips. "Is it okay if I come in?"

Madeline, suddenly aware that Cooper still stood on the front stoop, stepped backwards quickly, with the door. "Oh, of course, please come in. Sorry, I just was caught so off guard, David showing up like that. I've already told him that I didn't want him here. And yet, here he is." She lifted her hands and shook her head.

He came into the foyer and glanced around, in awe again at its size, the beautiful paneled walls. A fresh arrangement of mixed flowers filled the crystal vase on the table in the middle of the space. He could smell the fragrance from the doorway.

"What did he want?" Cooper asked.

Madeline sighed. "He said he was here to 'help' with everything, you know, but it's the same old crap. There is a long version, but I won't bore you with it. The abbreviated one is, I've told him that I want to finalize our divorce. He's told me that he doesn't. And that's basically it." In her voice he detected a note of despair.

"David has anger problems, among many other issues. Sometimes I get a little bit afraid of him, but I don't think he has enough guts to ever really do anything. Maybe he is just, I don't know, insecure?"

Cooper thought there was more instability in the guy than Madeline believed. A very unpleasant feeling emanated from him in the short time Cooper stood by him on the front steps.

He said, "Still, I think it would be better if you were not here alone with him. If you see him here again, just call me or Izzy. We can be here quickly and maybe that might be all it would take to diffuse a, uh, situation."

Madeline shook her head with a rueful expression on her face. "If I can't handle David, then I'm in trouble." Cooper thought that might be more true than she thought.

"Oh, I'll go get Mrs. T. Why don't you go ahead into the kitchen? I won't be a minute."

"I made tea a while ago, but it's probably cold," Madeline said as she and Mrs. Temple entered the kitchen. "I'll make some coffee, but first I'll go check the mail and give you some privacy."

Mrs. Temple sat warily across from Cooper and dried her hands on a kitchen cloth. "What can I help you with, detective?"

"Mrs. Temple, what can you tell me about Mrs. Abbott's assistant, Diane Kenyon? We need to know who she knows, what friends she has around here. What do you know about her?"

Alma Temple nervously twisted the cotton cloth, wringing it as if it were a chicken neck. "I don't know all that much," she said, "I know that she thought pretty much of herself, if you get my meaning." This was delivered with a sour look and a bit of a huff.

"What, exactly, *do* you mean?" Cooper asked.

"She hardly had the time of day for anyone," she declared, "me, Mr. Gutierrez, and other of them that helps out around here, from time to time, that's what. Above it all. She was always, 'Oh yes, Mrs. Abbott, oh no Mrs. Abbott, of course Mrs. Abbott'. But when Mrs. Abbott wasn't around, she acted like she owned this place." Harrumph.

"Anything else?"

She leaned across the table toward Cooper, with a conspiratorial look. She lowered her voice as if there might be someone listening outside the doorway. "Well, you tell me how a *secretary* can afford the clothes she's always wearing? She has expensive tastes, that one, but I happen to know that she doesn't make all that much money, in her salary, you know."

"You know that how?" Cooper asked, curiously. Apparently Mrs. Temple was going to be a fountain of information, but just how did she come by it?

"I'm telling you, it was an accident, like. I happened to see her paycheck one Friday. I was dusting in the library and I saw the checks. Mrs. Abbott wrote out our checks herself. One for me, one for Manny and one for her," Mrs. Temple said. "Hers is not even as much as mine, and I can tell you, I don't go out buying all the fancy shoes and purses and clothes." Mrs. Temple sat back with a sharp and self-satisfied nod.

Cooper looked down at his note pad, trying to hide a grin. "Okay, that's interesting, Mrs. Temple. Was she involved with helping Mrs. Abbott run her business, do you know?"

"Not nearly as much as she would've liked. She was just a secretary! She was always trying to act like she was doing more than she really was, that one. Do you know what I mean? And, a few times, when Mrs. Abbott had left the house for a quick errand in town, you know how you do, I saw her going through Mrs. Abbott's desk, and looking in that computer on Mrs. Abbott's desk. I ask you, what business did she have doing that?"

Cooper glanced up at Mrs. Temple from his notes. "How do you get along with Ms. Kenyon?"

Mrs. Temple scowled and unconsciously began twisting the kitchen cloth again. She said, "I just try to stay away from her. Manny does too, he has no use for her. But I should've told Mrs. Abbott about her snooping and sticking her nose in where it didn't belong. Isn't a secretary supposed to be, you know, *confidential*, like? I should have told Mrs. Abbott, I should have. Now it's too late," Mrs. Temple said sadly.

"What can you tell me about about Diane Kenyon's friends? Do you hear her speak about or talk to friends?"

"Not really. I'd hear her talking on a cell phone to some man. You can always tell when it's a man. Maybe more than one, if you get my meaning. Her voice will get all drippy, like honey. 'Bout made you want to be sick. She'll be on that cell phone, you know, making plans to meet for drinks, but I've never heard her say a name. Something about meeting at a club in town. I heard that a few times."

She paused and Cooper opened his mouth to ask another question, when she abruptly started: "Seems like I can't get away from her. Even when I'm cleaning somewheres else in the house I'll run into her! Why do you suppose she needs to go upstairs? I'll be cleaning and I'll come out of a room, and boom! There she is. What do you make of that?"

It was odd, Cooper thought. "Finding a ladies room?"

"There's two perfectly fine bathrooms downstairs. One just by the silver room across the hall," she pointed toward the door behind Cooper "and another off the billiard room, and she knows it. I don't think that's it." Her woolly, grey brows pulled together as she frowned. "Nope, she was snooping."

Cooper decided to change tack. "How did she get on with Mrs. Abbott? You ever hear Mrs. Abbott being cross with her?"

"I think they got on just fine. I think Mrs. Abbott was sort of taking her under her wing, so to speak. That's the way she was, kind like that and good to people. That's what made me so mad when I saw what that Kenyon girl is up to, snooping, peeking and sticking her nose in places that aren't none of her business. Like she's using Mrs. Abbott. It's just plain wrong."

Cooper thanked Mrs. Temple, who, now thoroughly grumpy, retrieved a pre-made sandwich from the refrigerator, and left for parts unknown in the huge old mansion.

While he waited for Madeline's return, his phone rang. It was Walt.

* * *

He sat on a stool at the kitchen table and once again watched as Madeline made coffee. She wore the clothes she had on that morning at Selwyn's office, a pair of linen slacks and a white silk blouse. When the coffee began brewing she sat down across from him. The latest news from Walt Simmons was not going to be included in what he planned to tell Madeline this afternoon.

"What questions do you have for me, Detective Cooper?" she asked, looking intently at him with a puzzled expression on her pale drawn face.

"Scott, please."

"I'm sorry. Scott." She barely smiled.

"First, there are a few things I need to tell you. Unpleasant things."

The tiny smile she had given him disappeared.

"What? Something about my mother?"

"Diane Kenyon." He paused. "She's dead. She was murdered."

Madeline's eyes widened with disbelief. "No," she said softly. "No."

"I'm afraid so. She's been murdered, sometime within the last twelve hours. Naturally, we believe this murder is directly related to your mother's. It's possible—no, probable, that Diane knew something about Eleanor's murder, and it got her killed."

Madeline shook her head and seemed unable to speak. She got up and poured coffee into the same porcelain cups she had served him coffee in before. As she set the coffee down on the table, the cups clattered noisily in their saucers. She sat back down.

"I don't understand. How could Diane be a threat? I don't think my mother gave her access to sensitive information. You know, potential purchases or money being invested in various projects. How could she be involved?"

"We aren't sure right now, but she must have known something, or someone. Do you have any knowledge of who she came in contact with through her job here?"

"I'm sure she did mostly secretarial work, phone calls, typing, filing, that kind of thing. Possibly computer research? Although, she probably met everyone my mother dealt with. She likely knew, at least superficially, most of my mother's business associates and friends, calling to confirm appointments, invitations, things like that."

"Did you know anyone who was close to her, friends with her? She told Izzy she had been given the weekend off by your mother and went up to Napa with a friend, maybe a boyfriend?"

"I'm sorry, no, I don't. I'm sure she had friends, but I don't know about that, I didn't really know her. We spoke a few times when David and I came down or during the last year, when I visited by myself.

"Actually? She seemed fairly sharp. Seemed to have a quick mind. I heard from someone that she studied to be a CPA. So I guess she would have had to be sharp or competent or my mother wouldn't have hired her." Madeline frowned. "God, I can't believe it."

"I'm concerned now about your safety, Madeline. I believe the murders are about money, your mother's estate, and we don't think the person, or persons, responsible is going to stop."

"But I'm the one who will inherit most of my mother's estate. By that logic, *I'm* the one who should be the prime suspect!" There was a sudden hysterical note in her voice.

"Look, there are several people who benefit from your mother's death, as you heard this morning. My gut is telling me this isn't about your parent's business, or disagreements with Edgerton, it's about money. I don't see all the angles yet, but your inheritance is important financially to a lot of people." Cooper looked at Madeline's sorrowful face. "Look, there's more. I'm really sorry to have to bring this up now."

Madeline's expression turned wary as if she feared an attack. "What?"

"Had your mother told you she had cancer?"

Her wariness turned to stunned shock. Dark brown brows knitted and her eyes filled with tears. "Cancer? Oh my God, no.... What...?"

"I'm sorry. It was discovered during the...autopsy." Cooper said the word as softly as possible. "She apparently had lung cancer. Fairly advanced." Cooper waited as the horrifying words sunk in. Madeline looked down at her hands circled around the coffee cup. Her chin trembled.

"I...I didn't know. Lung cancer? She didn't even smoke. Why didn't she tell me? Maybe she would have if I had made time to come home occasionally," she said, bitterly. "I'm so caught up in my own world, my own problems. I couldn't be bothered." Madeline wiped at her eyes angrily, and sat in silence.

Cooper feared confiding in her any more. If he didn't tell her, he wasn't being honest, but he dreaded hurting her more. He began, "Madeline, I don't want to add to your distress, but there is something else that I think is important that you know."

Madeline looked up into his eyes, her cheeks wet with tears. "What now?"

"Izzy and I believe there is a very good chance that your father's car accident was not an accident." He paused. "We believe that it may well have been murder and that all these deaths are linked. If that *is* the case, then all of this" he spread his hands, "is a long term plan by someone to devastate the Abbott family." Cooper said this as gently as he could.

"You must be wrong. Why in the world would anyone want to hurt my father? He had a car accident, they told us it was an accident!" Her voice rose and tears began again. The news that her father could have been murdered brought on a fresh wave of anguish.

"I know. I know that's what they thought at the time, but I've spoken to the detective who investigated. He saw suspicious things, evidence that your father's car had been tampered with. He saw things that didn't add up. He worked the case for a long time. There were few suspects, and no concrete evidence." Cooper put his hand on her arm. "I'm so sorry, Madeline. I really am."

She wept silently for a few minutes. "Why didn't I just come home when she asked? If I had, maybe none of this would have happened."

"Don't say that. You can't start blaming yourself." He reached across the wooden table and covered her hands with his. Hers looked pitifully small enfolded in his.

"Look, it's easy for all of us to get too busy, get too wound up in our lives that we don't think we have time for other things. I've been guilty of that too."

After a time her crying slowed, and she became quiet. Madeline looked up into his eyes, hers huge and glittering with tears. "So, along with my dad dying, oh, wait, being murdered, mother had to bear getting cancer all alone. I should have been here for her. I should have." Another tear slid from each eye and down damp cheeks. Cooper felt unutterably sad.

"Please don't be so hard on yourself," he said. "We all make mistakes, and thankfully, parents are way more forgiving than we think they will be. You're here now, helping us in finding out who did this. That's important."

Cooper sat, holding her hands gently without talking for another quarter hour before he said a quiet good-bye and left. It wasn't until he was back at the office that he realized he had not asked Madeline what had been troubling her earlier at Selwyn's. He almost got back in the car to return to Raven's Nest, but decided she had been through enough for one day. He'd ask about it tomorrow.

* * *

Back at the office, Morales was eager to spill on the Van Gesslers and started to fill him in the minute he sat at his desk.

"Wait, Izzy, wait. While I was out talking to Madeline and Mrs. T, I got the call from Walt. He said Diane Kenyon's cause of death was a single stab wound to her upper abdomen. Lacerated her liver, but also cut her aorta, she bled out fast."

"You know, Scotty, I think I figured that one out," Izzy said.

"One other thing, though."

"What? That's not bad enough?"

"She was pregnant. About three months along." Cooper said.

"*Madre de Dios*, no."

"It's possible that whoever she was in Napa with is the person who killed her. We've gotta get up there and see if we can find anyone who might have seen her, seen who she was with up there. Did they find any records in her purse? Motel or food receipts? And, we have to find her next of kin, asap."

"There may have been some receipts. I haven't heard anything yet, I'll call and push forensics, see what they've found so far."

"We need Kenyon's cell phone. Bell is supposed to call if she finds it. Whatever's on that cell should answer a few questions, at least."

"She did call, Scotty, I'll tell you that bit in a minute. You've gotta hear this now——what I've found on the Van Gesslers," Morales said.

"They built that big house last year, right? But there doesn't seem to be a mortgage on it. It probably cost more than six mill, but where did the money come from?"

"How in the hell can they have no mortgage?" Cooper asked. "Where does anybody get six million in cash. And why would they, anyway?"

"Well, it looks like they got it somewhere. Last year there were periodic payments to a construction company, one to the consortium that owns the development, you know, the land. Somewhat interesting that it *wasn't* Abbott and Edgerton. Anyway, lots of payments to other companies. Mostly, I think they were for custom things like flooring and fixtures."

Morales continued, "Their income seemed fairly steady until about three, four years ago. They were doing alright, nothing dramatic. After that there have been several substantial amounts deposited into their personal account three or four times, or more, annually. About a half million each time."

Cooper whistled. "You've traced where the money is coming from?"

"Oh, yeah. I think the deposits were coming from an offshore account. But, what's important is where the money came from to put *into* the offshore account. I've got Phil in computer forensics doing the accounting of Van Gessler's computers, his banking and so on. And by the way, Van Gessler apparently was no genius in hiding the money.

"Anyway it's really a formality because I'm certain Van Gessler has been embezzling from the Abbott's investment accounts for at least a few years. Millions. That's how they built that house and

God knows what else. He does alright as a banker, but I think he saw an opportunity. Maybe thought the Abbotts wouldn't notice if he was clever enough. Then when the husband died he must have felt Mrs. Abbott was really distracted, because that's when the amounts got larger."

Cooper frowned. "If he thought he could get away with that kind of scheme, I suspect he very much underestimated Clay and Eleanor Abbott. Good work, Izzy. After Phil gets the details out and we have them in hand, we'll bring him in."

"Okay, about Bell. She found Diane Kenyon's cell at the apartment. It was in the pocket of a jacket, behind the chair in the living room. It must have slid off behind the chair. Anyway that's why it wasn't found by whoever killed her."

"A lucky break. We could use one," Cooper said.

"Bell has gone through the phone and listed all the numbers and names in the contacts, and she called the phone company to get a list of all calls for the last two months. Smart woman. She'll make detective one day. When I talk to her, she actually acts like she knows what she and I are talking about.

"Anyway, the two most often called people in her phone were......can you guess? David Dean and Van Gessler. In the last thirty days there have been no fewer than thirty calls *to* Diane Kenyon. All of those were *from* Van Gessler. Of course, there's almost that many from Dean." Morales grinned at Cooper.

"Shit, Izzy." He sprang from his chair. "You know what this means? It means Kenyon probably discovered what he was doing."

Cooper paced by their desks. "Madeline said she was sharp, you know, with numbers and wanted to be a CPA. Mrs. Temple said she'd caught her snooping around on Eleanor's computer more than once. What if she got curious about the Abbott investments? Maybe on a lark she decided to snoop and managed to hack into the investment accounts and figured out what Van Gessler up to? He would've been ripe for the pickin'."

Morales shook her head slightly and frowned. "Blackmail? Seems a dumb move. Besides she had something going with David Dean. Do you think he might've been in on blackmail? I think Dean was who she was with up in Napa. Maybe that means Dean is involved in her murder."

Cooper scratched his head with both hands until his hair shot up in waves from his head. "Don't know. Diane thought she was clever. She…or they, didn't realize who they were dealing with, if she was blackmailing Frank Van Gessler. He must have gotten desperate. Maybe Diane just pushed too hard."

There was comparative silence in the office as they thought through the Kenyon angle.

Morales broke the silence by saying: "Scotty, that doesn't explain Mrs. Abbott though."

Cooper continued pacing. "I know."

Morales tilted her head and gave Cooper a serious look. "You may think I'm wrong, but I think we're making a mistake not looking closer at the kids. Mrs. Deardon's twenty-four year old twin daughters. They live here in Los Gatos and they share a condo."

"How nice for them." Cooper said sarcastically as he imagined what the shared condo probably looked like, in comparison to his small apartment. "What are you thinkin' that has to do with anything?"

"These particular 'kids' have been in trouble before. Kammie and Kassie. They are involved with drugs—pot, pills…coke, who knows what all. They were busted for dealing once a few years ago. Because they were first-timers and so young, they had to do treatment and got probation. No doubt Mom got them a top notch attorney too. Anyway, rumor is, that didn't stop them."

Morales looked up at her partner. "Don't you get it? The girls are friends with Ben Highwater, and since Dean and Highwater are buddies, is it much of a leap to put Dean and the Highwater boy and even the twin girls into this? I have a feeling they're involved."

"No wonder Phoebe Deardon's hitting the sauce so hard. Those girls must be driving her crazy." Cooper felt like some of the crazy aspects of the case might be coming into focus.

"If they're all into the druggie thing together, which my guess is they are, and all buddy-buddy, maybe it's somehow connected to Mrs. Abbott," Morales said.

Cooper frowned. "But how? What are you sayin'?"

Morales wheeled her chair to face him. It erupted with a loud squeal that made Cooper flinch. She looked at him steadily. "How do we know they're not responsible for it, or in some way connected to the murder?

"Sure their parents are rich, but where do they get the kind of money it takes to live the way they do? Not one of them has a job. The two girls *each* have a new Mercedes SUV and Ben, Highwater's boy? He drives a one year old Beemer. I mean, I guess they probably have an allowance but it takes a lot of money to support a drug habit…." Her voice trailed off.

Cooper pondered that for a few moments. He'd heard of stranger things in his relatively short career. Children of wealthy parents often didn't know the meaning of 'doing without' or 'making do', both common phrases to him growing up. Being involved with a murder for money when you already had so much? Still, it seemed unlikely.

"I'm not sure I see a viable connection. What reason would they have to be mixed up in something like the Abbott murder. That's serious stuff. Besides, it's a generation removed from them. Or two," he said skeptically.

"I don't know, but I'm going to keep looking around, see what I can see."

"I still need whatever you can find on Edgerton right away. Also anything more on Helen Highwater. Don't forget," he added, "now we gotta get on Diane Kenyon, asap. Next of kin, especially.

Finances, anything, okay? Meantime, I'm going to see Ian Andrews."

"Okay, *amigo*." Then Morales smiled. "Be careful-l-l...."

"What the hell are you talking about now?" Cooper said, exasperated.

"From what I hear, he's ...well, you know."

"No, I'm afraid I don't."

Morales grew more serious. "I've heard he's gay. You know how people are. Obviously I don't have a problem, but with this police department, I just want you to be careful. People talk, they insinuate. Whether it's true or not. People here are supposed to be liberal. I know they aren't." Her tone had hardened.

Cooper rolled his eyes and tried to lighten the mood. "Izzy the poor guy is injured. How much trouble could I get in? Remember, I'll have police protection. Get on that computer and get what we need. And oil that damn chair." He picked up his notebook and left.

* * *

Cooper knocked on the elegant and imposing double doors at Andrews' glaringly white stucco mid century ranch style home. It was true California style: white quartz rock in place of grass and dotted with succulents, palm and eucalyptus trees. Bright coral pink bougainvillea climbed up the stucco walls and a couple of shrub azaleas introduced a brilliant splash of color. He felt like he had walked onto the set of *Gidget*. Except for the black and white cruiser parked in the drive.

The door was opened by a uniformed officer that was over six feet, over two-twenty and sported a vaguely menacing look. Cooper forced himself not to reflexively take a step back. He didn't recognize the officer and showed his identification.

A tall slender man limped in to the foyer with right foot wrapped in ace bandages and enclosed in a brace. In his mid sixties, with wavy salt and pepper hair, green eyes and dark tanned skin, he was film star handsome and in fact reminded Cooper of 1940-50s movie idol Farley Granger.

Ian Andrews was impeccably dressed in crisp linen slacks and dress shirt with a white sweater casually draped over his shoulders. And, Cooper noticed, on his one good foot, an expensive leather loafer, one of a pair that probably cost the entirety of Cooper's salary for two weeks. Ian Andrews smiled at Cooper and started talking before the detective had a chance to speak.

"Hello, hello, hello, you must be Detective Cooper! Ian Andrews, come in, come in." He shook Cooper's hand and waved the detective through a tiled foyer. A wave of cool air met him. "I hope you have come to tell me that you know who has done this dreadful thing to Eleanor. I can't imagine such a horrible, horrible thing to have happen to someone you know and love. Please, please do come in."

The officer went back to his position: sitting on a chair in the dining room with a cup of coffee and a book.

Using a cane, he limped ahead of Cooper from the entry into a spacious sunken living room filled with spare, modern furniture, everything an explosion of color.

A low teal green sofa anchored one side of the room. Grouped around were four chairs, two of sea green and two of pink. The gleaming hardwood floors were covered with a large area rug in bright golden orange. Modern lamps with white shades glowed. A low glass coffee table held bright ceramic 'objets d'art'. Modern paintings caught the eye from every wall. It was nearly overwhelming but somehow, Cooper realized with surprise, it worked.

"No, sir." Cooper finally answered, as he pulled his eyes from a painting that looked like an original Jackson Pollock. "I'm not here to tell you who committed this murder. I wish I could, but no. I'm here to find out what I can about your relationship with Eleanor

Abbott, and any other information you can give that might help us."

"Please sit down, Detective Cooper." Andrews waved him to a chair. "Let me get us some refreshments." He had no sooner said the words than a young man materialized from the direction of the dining room, a questioning look on his face and deference in his posture.

"Jeffrey, could you please bring some drinks. What would you like detective? Coffee? Iced tea? Beer?"

"Iced tea would be fine, thank you, sir." Cooper said. Jeffrey nodded and left.

Cooper began, "Mr. Andrews, first I must ask you where you were on Thursday night."

Ian Andrews looked down at his slender fingers. "I was home that night. Unfortunately I have no one who can corroborate that. Jeffery is my secretary and day time help, but," he looked significantly at Cooper, "he does not live here."

"All right, Mr. Andrews, tell me everything you can tell me about the relationship you had with Eleanor Abbott."

"Please. Call me Ian. If we're going to talk in this vein, I'd prefer to assume a friendly attitude."

"All right. Ian. And I'm Scott."

Andrews nodded and sat on the sofa, made an attempt to cross his legs elegantly, but ended up simply lifting the right leg up onto the sofa with a grimace. He loosely clasped his hands in his lap and began speaking in a quiet voice, free from the affectation of moments before.

"Eleanor and I have known each other for over thirty years. She was one of the first people of her—circle—that accepted me and viewed me as worthy of being known. Her death has been a terrible blow." He sighed. "I am an interior designer you see and have achieved some success. I lead a certain lifestyle. In the arts, music and design communities I am accepted, even held in esteem.

But in the world of 'society', for a person such as myself, well, that is not such an easy thing to accomplish."

Cooper knew a little of what Izzy and Alana had to deal with. Oddly, in a state like California, it is assumed that problems like that are rare, but they are not.

He nodded. "Go on."

"I met Eleanor quite by accident. She saw my work—an interior I did for another woman. She contacted me and asked if I could provide her with some sketches for the design of a large building she planned. A complex of buildings, actually. It was to be an organization for women. A multi-faceted charity designed to give women the help they needed to stand on their own feet, survive spousal abuse, make a new life.

"It was to include a suite of offices and conference rooms, battered women's shelter with children's daycare and indoor and outdoor play areas, psychological counseling, even physicians and nurses were associated with the project. There was to be job training, a library, computer sciences, and so on. It was extensive. She wanted a mix of beauty and functionality. Very forward thinking at that time. And, Eleanor assured me that the cost was not the first consideration. I was flattered and honored to be considered." Andrews shifted and moved his bandaged foot slightly.

"Then, as it often does, something happened to spoil everything. Concurrent with my work for Eleanor, there was an incident with a young man, extremely bad timing. The young man brought charges against me. They were unfounded of course but Eleanor's husband, Clay, learned of the whole sordid affair. By the time I had cleared myself and shown the man to be the gold digger he was, it was too late. Clay was adamantly against me. He was worried about the Abbott name being connected however tangentially, with something so scurrilous. Eleanor stood by me. That said everything to me about her as a friend.

"Over time, she managed to soften Clay's feelings toward me. I wouldn't go so far as to say he is—was—homophobic, but he could be difficult to be around. In truth, I was her friend but not necessarily his. In the end, she did engage me to do the designing for her, and she was very happy with it. So was Clay when all was said and done."

Jeffrey glided quietly into the room with a tray holding two tall glasses with tea in crushed ice. "Would you care for sweetener?" he asked Cooper.

"Oh. Yes, sugar if you have it." Cooper replied. He watched Jeffrey add two teaspoons of sugar to each glass and stir. He put down coasters in front of Cooper and Andrews, along with small napkins. Suddenly and silently he was gone.

"Did Eleanor ever confide in you about other relationships? Family? Her daughter?" Cooper asked.

Andrews stared into his tea glass, swirled it gently and finally set it back down on the coaster. "Eleanor was not a demonstrative person. She loved her family very much. They had their own problems of course, like every family. But she had suffered many personal setbacks. Her son's problems and of course his death. Clay's infidelities." With a shake of his head, he retrieved his glass and drank more tea. "She was a strong woman, but anyone would be brought low by problems of that enormity."

Cooper asked gently, "What can you tell me about the death of her son? We haven't gotten much detail about it during the investigation."

"It happened quite a long time ago. Michael was only six, I think. Yes, Madeline was about fifteen or sixteen at the time, so it's been over thirteen years. Lord," he pondered, "has it really been that long?

"Madeline was supposed to be watching the boy while he swam. But, he was out of the pool when she went back down to the house—I'm don't know—to get something? She was only gone a few moments, but when she returned Michael was face down in the water. They believe he may have had a seizure which caused him to fall into the pool."

Cooper sat, tea glass in hand, thinking. Once again, he felt a surge of pity for Madeline. "What was the outcome? Was it determined to be an accident?

"Yes, it was. Madeline of course called 911, which brought the ambulance and police. At least she had the presence of mind to do that as well as try to perform CPR on Michael. It was too late." Andrews' face was full of sorrow. "I was so very sorry for the family. Eleanor came home from a trip into town just about the time the emergency people had arrived. I know she called Clay, he was at the office. She called me and Arthur. I honestly thought she was going to lose her mind."

"What was the boy's problem? You said he had some kind of problem?"

Andrews looked at Cooper thoughtfully. "Michael was born with a developmental disability. He was a little slow, but he was a sweet, dear boy. He was functional, just a bit slow. He was prone to occasional seizures, but it wasn't epilepsy. Michael always had the best tutors and was enrolled in a special school. Eleanor and Clay did everything they could for him, gave him every kind of support that doctors determined could be of help. It was devastating, really. When you think of all the tragedy that the family has endured."

Andrews sipped some tea and said, "By the way, Scott, are you aware that Madeline was adopted?"

* * *

Cooper stared at Andrews, stunned. "No, no I wasn't aware of that."

"No one talks about it much. In fact, I'm not sure that all those in our circle even know. I know because Eleanor confided in me and about many of her 'secrets'. I believe she thought of me as safe, you know? She knew my secrets and I knew hers. The truth is, we had a great simpatico relationship. I felt I could tell her anything, and I guess she felt the same. I already miss her desperately."

"When was Madeline adopted?"

"I suppose it isn't any longer a betrayal of confidences as Eleanor and Clay are both now gone…," Andrews said quietly. "It is a tragedy that could have been written by Shakespeare. As I said, Eleanor confided in me about her marriage." He shifted in his seat, his foot apparently bothering him.

"One evening many years ago, Eleanor and I had gone out to a club for drinks and a bit of a natter. Clay was away on a business trip. The children, still small, Michael was just a baby, were with a nanny." Andrews sipped his tea. "That night Eleanor told me that Clay had had an affair—as it turns out, one of many—early in their marriage. There was a child born. A girl. Clay wanted children badly and Eleanor had not become pregnant. Clay convinced her they should adopt the baby so they could raise it. He convinced the woman too, obviously. He brought Madeline home when she was barely a month old. And, no, I don't know how the adoption was handled. When there is a lot of money, things can be 'fixed', can't they?"

Cooper could hardly believe his ears. "Does Madeline know?"

Andrews nodded. "But, she doesn't know that Clay was her real father. Not that the whole adoption thing mattered to either of them. I've never seen a pair so close. He adored her and she him. There's more, Scott." Cooper raised his eyebrows in question.

"When Madeline was around ten, Eleanor did become pregnant." Andrews shook his head and sighed. "This time it was she who had the affair. Eleanor took no precautions thinking that she couldn't become pregnant. When Michael was conceived, she ended the affair, naturally, and was overjoyed at the prospect of having a baby."

"Oh, Jesus." Cooper muttered.

"Yes, well, she didn't tell Clay the baby wasn't his. In fact, as far as I know, he died believing that Michael was his son. Anyway, Clay was devastated when it became apparent that Michael had problems, but it was nothing compared with how badly it effected Eleanor. She adored Michael but never seemed to be able to come to grips with his disability. To her, it was as if a curse had been put upon her. To know that Madeline was Clay's and the son he loved wasn't his and would never be 'whole', well, it was more than she could bear. It took many, many years of therapy to even *begin* to deal with it. I believe it had a seriously negative effect on her relationship with Madeline." Silence settled over the room. Cooper set his tea glass down.

"What an incredible story, Ian. I wonder if any of it has to do with the murders," Cooper's last remark was mostly to himself, but Andrews picked up on it.

"Murders? Are we talking about more than the murder of Eleanor?"

"I'm sorry, I was thinking out loud." Cooper paused a few moments, then said: "We believe that Clay Abbott's car accident was actually murder." He looked intently at Andrews. "Just this morning, Eleanor's PA, Diane Kenyon, was found stabbed to death." Cooper wasn't sure why he was giving Andrews this information. He had a sixth sense about the man and liked him already. "We have to consider that the attack on you was perpetrated by someone involved too. It was no accident."

Andrews was shocked speechless, his green eyes glistened. Finally, he swallowed and said, "Dear God, this can't be true. Why?"

"We have a few ideas we're working right now, but we're pretty certain these murders are all linked, and money is the motivating factor. We aren't sure what the hit and run has to do with it yet. Is there something you know about Eleanor that someone might be reluctant for you to speak about? Do you know of anyone, anyone we haven't been made aware of, who may have had a reason to hurt Eleanor?"

Andrews was silent, a frown on his handsome face. Finally he said, "You might talk to Edgerton. I know that Eleanor was concerned recently that he was attempting to make run at her—buy her out. He's power hungry, that man." Disgust was ripe in Andrews' voice. "She wasn't going to sell her shares to him even if hell froze over. She wanted all of it to go to Maddie." He shook his head again. "Eleanor had a falling out with Helen many years ago, you know how friends do, but that was resolved long ago.

"I also know Eleanor was very upset with the status of Madeline's marriage. She thought that David Dean was an awful mistake on Madeline's part. She didn't trust him. Period. In recent weeks she had said to me that when Maddie next came to visit she was just going to put it to her straight: Get rid of him, basically, or else. Oh, I don't think Eleanor would have been that harsh with her daughter, she loved her deeply. But I know she was very concerned about Madeline. Poor Maddie, well, the whole family. They've had so much misery. It's proof, as if you needed it, that having a fortune doesn't keep evil at bay."

* * *

It was after five-thirty, and still Madeline could not rouse herself to do anything. Mrs. Temple had gone and now she sat in the kitchen trying wrap her mind around what the detective had told her. Another murder. Her mother had been dying of cancer. Madeline could barely comprehend it. And the detective tells her, her father's death had been murder, not an accident. It appears I've been living in a pretend world for nearly two years. Maybe longer, maybe all my life. Nothing I thought or believed, was actually true.

Madeline shook herself. I have to get my head out of my ass and think, for God's sake.

It was time she touched base with PND. She picked up her cell phone and called Nadine.

"Nadine, it's me."

"Oh, my God, girl, I'm so glad to hear from you. What's going on? What are you doin?"

"Everything's fine, fine. I'm okay. It's just, you know, put one foot in front of the other until you get through the day. Is everything okay there? Payroll went out okay? Any problems?"

"Oh, hell no. You remember when you helped me do it once before, that makes me an old hand." Nadine kept her voice light. "I got it done in about forty-five minutes, checked the figures twice and handed them out. We're cool here." Her voice became quiet. "Tell me how you are. Please don't say I'm good, I'm fine. This is Nadine you're talking to. Tell me what's been happening, how you're really doing."

Sympathy in her voice brought stinging tears to Madeline's eyes. "I really am doing okay. There's nothing to tell at this point. The detectives are investigating, I'm trying to help as much as I can. Apparently there are some diaries that my mother had been keeping for years—I hadn't really remembered that until now—and it looks like they might have some information that might help."

Madeline wiped away one tear that had escaped and took a deep breath. "Anyway, I'm just staying busy. Tomorrow I'm making the funeral arrangements. I should be able to come back to Eugene soon. Oh by the way, David showed up here a while ago. Did you know he was coming down here?"

The lengthy silence that followed made Madeline think they'd lost the connection. "Nadine? Are you still there?"

"Yeah, I'm here."

Madeline immediately sensed something and said, "Nadine? Did you know David was coming to Los Gatos?"

Finally, Nadine said, "I thought he might. He's been acting crazy since you've been gone and before you left."

"What in the world do you mean?"

"Sorry, that probably sounds weird, I know." Nadine grew quiet again.

"Nadine, what's going on?"

Madeline heard what sounded like a snuffle. "Nadine?"

"Oh, Maddie, I'm so sorry, I really am." Madeline could hear the tears in her voice. "Things have just been so hard."

"Okay, start at the beginning, and tell me what the hell you're talking about."

More snuffling, some background noise. She heard Nadine's muffled voice tell Jamal to go to his room.

"Okay, I'm back."

Madeline waited. Finally, she said, "What?"

"I wanted to tell you before you left. I tried, really. I tried to talk to you a couple times. Then your mom died. Shit, I just felt so lousy, then you were gone…"

"Nadine! What are you talking about?"

Madeline heard a huge intake of breath. Finally Nadine said, "A week or so before you left David had been in to see *me* a few times, at the office, always while you were out. It was weird, like he knew when you were here and when you weren't. A couple of times we went out for lunch. He'd been calling too. He was asking about Jamal, asking about me, asking how we were doing. He seemed so nice, he seemed to care about what was going on with Jamal and me."

Madeline froze with the phone to her ear. "He did *what?*"

"He had called, and he asked me out…" Nadine's voice trailed off and stuttered to a stop. After a long pause she said, "He asked me to dinner. Just dinner. He said he wanted to talk about Jamal and that he was concerned about him. Oh, nothing happened, Maddie, I promise. He was so nice. He asked to take Jamal to a soccer game, and I said yes. I thought it couldn't hurt, Jamal needed to spend some time with an adult that wasn't me. I thought it wouldn't hurt, really… Oh my God…"

Dumbfounded, Madeline asked, "Did he talk about me when you went out with him? Did *you* talk about me to him?"

"Oh, no, Maddie, no. Honest to God, I would never do that. I never said anything personal about you. We talked a little about *PND* and what was going on there. Nothing else important, I promise."

Madeline was silent as she processed the information. What in the world is he up to? Why Nadine? Suspicion gathered in her mind and made her feel slightly sick. David Dean was like any man, so it wasn't beyond him to hit on Nadine—she was a beautiful woman. But Madeline knew, she *knew* this was about something else entirely.

"Maddie? Are you there? Tell me you're not mad at me, please. I'm sorry. I've just been lonely, and Jamal has me so worried, so I told David about Jamal's troubles. I thought it would be nice to talk to someone even though I knew all along I shouldn't be talking to him, of all people, what with all your problems with him and the divorce and..." Nadine blubbered on.

"Nadine! Nadine, stop. It's all right. I'm just worried about the you and Jamal. David is not to be trusted. You must not allow Jamal to spend more time with him. He's......Nadine, he's not the kind of man you want influencing Jamal. David's involved in drugs. I don't think he would do such a despicable thing as push dope onto a little kid, but, I do know David can't be trusted. I can't tell you all the details right now and I can't ask you to stop seeing him, but I do know that he's probably up to no good. I really don't think it's a very good idea."

"I know, Maddie, I'm sorry. I'm really, really sorry." Madeline heard a stifled sob. "I tried to tell you before but I was so afraid you'd hate me and think...oh, I don't know what I thought. He told me he was going down there to see you and not to call and tell you. He wanted it to be a surprise."

"Well, it certainly was that. Look, this decides it. I'm going to get the arrangements taken care of for my mother's funeral tomorrow then I'm coming back to Eugene. I won't be able to stay long but I want to talk to you, and obviously I'm going to have it out with David." She paused. "When he left here he said he was headed back to Eugene so he'll likely be around tomorrow. If you see him, steer clear. Don't say a word to him about this. Don't tell him we've talked. Are we clear on that? Nadine? Are we clear?"

"Yes, we're clear. I won't say a word, I promise."

"Okay. I'll catch a flight tomorrow afternoon or Wednesday morning. Remember, not a word."

"Yeah, not a word," Nadine muttered miserably, but Madeline had already hung up.

* * *

Reeling from the conversation with Nadine, Madeline slumped onto the sofa in the library. If David was manipulating Nadine to try to get to her, it meant real trouble. It was obvious that he would go to any length to prevent her getting the divorce. Certainly getting information was the reason he was hanging around Nadine, but Madeline couldn't figure out what else David thought Nadine would do for him. And why would David struggle so hard to keep a marriage together that clearly wasn't working? When he knew she no longer loved him? Why would any two people stay together when there is so much animosity? Madeline rubbed her temples trying to ward off the headache that seemed to be coming. Goddamn it, she thought miserably, goddamn it all to hell.

She decided on a light supper and an early evening. With so much to do the next day, all the funeral arrangements, going to Eugene, what Madeline really wanted to do was get in bed and pull the covers over her head. Instead, she went on to the next thing on the list she had to get done. She picked up her cell phone again and called Phoebe Deardon.

"Phoebe, hello, it's Madeline."

"Maddie, oh good heavens, what a surprise, thank you for calling. It's so good to hear from you, how are you?"

"I'm doing all right, Phoebe. Just trying to keep going. You know."

"Yes, I do know. I'm so sorry, Maddie, I'm really very sorry. I would have called you earlier, but I didn't want to intrude. Your mother was such a dear person and such a good friend. You must miss her terribly. I miss her so much…"

"Yes, well, so far it's just been a blur. I haven't had much time to process it. That's partly why I'm calling. I was hoping I could ask a tremendous favor of you. Could I get your help in dealing with, well, the arrangements. I'm sure I don't know all the people who should be invited to the service. I wouldn't want to leave anyone off the list. I was wondering if I could count on you to help with that? I mean, I know it's short notice but…"

"Oh my sweet girl, of course you can count on me. I'd be pleased and privileged to help you. Why don't you just leave that part all to me? Where is the service to be held?"

"The Unity Church of Palo Alto. They have pretty large facilities, and my mother liked them, I believe."

"That's a beautiful church, I know Ellie would love that. It can hold a lot of people, and there will probably be a couple hundred attendees. Just like your father's service. Your parents are so loved," Phoebe said.

Madeline's head swam at the thought. She pressed on. "I'll be arranging the rest of the details tomorrow, before I have to head back to Eugene for a short while. I've spoken to the church. They can accommodate the service next Saturday. Two o'clock? I've already called a florist and made those arrangements."

"That's just fine, Maddie. Don't you worry about the people. I'll see to publishing the information in the newspaper tomorrow, and I'll get in touch with Helen. We can combine lists. Your mother and father had so many friends. Because time is a bit short, Helen and I will divide the lists and make personal calls. Don't you worry a bit."

Phoebe made it sound like all I have to do is just 'not worry', like it's a simple matter of thinking of something else, Madeline thought. She's trying to be helpful, she wants to do something constructive to help get me through the bad time, be a part of it for Eleanor's sake, I get it. But forgetting or not worrying is not such a simple matter. Her head now aching, Madeline tried to come up with something simple to fix for dinner and tempting enough that she wouldn't skip the meal altogether. Once again, she hadn't had anything but coffee since breakfast, and her stomach growled fiercely.

Okay, okay. Grilled cheese sandwich? Simple, easy, and even sounded kind of good. She headed to the kitchen. In ten minutes she had grilled a sharp Cheddar cheese sandwich, put some corn chips on the plate (might as well go all the way) and had poured a glass of lemonade.

In her bedroom she sat in bed, propped up by pillows and devoured the sandwich while she watched the news. Suicide bombings and unrest in the middle east, the kidnapping of a wealthy bank executive somewhere in New York City, and of course, local coverage of her mother's murder. On that subject the media representatives for the police said several leads were being investigated. It went on for nearly four minutes. Boy, they're really good at saying something without saying anything at all. For the gossip mongers there were several pictures of the mansion, a picture of Eleanor at one of her charity events and a short clip from the District Attorney.

Cooper is sure the murders are connected. It's someone who has been mentioned in mother's will. Madeline shook her head. To get their hands on a pot of money? It seemed so implausible.

A friend of Madeline's in college once said something to her that now came to mind.

"The only people who *don't* think of money as the motive——for just about everything——are those who have always had plenty."

At the time, the comment made Madeline feel somehow guilty, and a little angry, although she couldn't exactly say why. The friend came from a good, solid, well known and well liked family. Upper middle class. Apparently the friend realized even if Madeline didn't, the differences between them.

Madeline leaned back on the pillows behind her head. The stress of the last several days, reading the will, finding the watcher's nest, the murder threat, all of it, was grinding her down. The headache had lessened since she ate, but she was bone tired.

I've got to find those diaries, even if I'm afraid to. What if I can't deal with the 'truth' Eleanor hinted at. Maybe I don't want to know the truth. I am who I am, are the diaries going to change that? I may not be able to handle whatever it is my mother wanted me to know. Or worse, she suddenly realized, what if there's nothing in the diaries to tell me what she hinted at? Oh, my God. What if I *never know?* The possibility that the knowledge she hinted at may have died with her mother made tears fill her eyes.

What if the diaries could lead to the killer? The detective thinks there may be a clue to what's going on here. To Madeline's mind it seemed absurd. If her mother had been in danger, surely she would have said something. Wouldn't she have talked to Arthur, or Ian? Why not just call the police?

Cooper. Her mind flitted to him. He is so kind and empathetic. Strong. And handsome… those blue eyes… she drifted off.

* * *

Madeline came awake and found herself slumped over on the pillows, the television still on, a bit of drool on her pillow. Ugh. She wiped her mouth and clicked off the late movie with the remote. She pushed the food tray onto the bedside table. Her body and mind ached to get in bed, pull the covers over her head and sleep for a week. Instead, as she knew she must, she set the alarm.

Madeline clicked off the bedside lamp and started to crawl into bed when she heard it. Her head flew up. Was it the tapping noise again? She went to her windows and peered down to the front lawns. There was little light and she could see nothing. Pancho was up, shadowing her movements. She spoke to him softly, "Let's go downstairs, Pancho."

She and Pancho made their way in darkness, silently down the back staircase that led to the kitchen. Madeline looked out the back door but saw nothing. "I'm hearing things, Pancho," she whispered as she rubbed his fluffy head. He whined softly.

Out of habit, her hand went to the lock to confirm it was engaged. It was unlocked. Surely I just forgot to push the deadbolt over. No. Absolutely not. She was certain she had done it. As that clear memory surfaced in her mind, Madeline froze and her body trembled.

I *did* lock that door this afternoon when Mrs. T left. She stood rooted in place, furiously thinking about what to do while a cold sweat broke out over her body. There was someone in the house. Sensing her distress, Pancho escalated from a whine to a low growl. How would someone have gotten into this house? Someone has a key, *who?*

With her hand on Pancho's collar, Madeline shushed him quietly and turned left out of the kitchen and silently followed the hallway, passed by the bathroom built under the structure of the main stair. Then by the silver storage and the butler's pantry and a couple of utility rooms. She glanced in each of the rooms quickly. Empty. At the east gallery they turned right in the direction of the front of the house.

They passed the formal dining room which was shrouded in darkness. Thirty-two carved walnut chairs stood on each side of the massive table. Large sideboards, housing massive china sets, were ghostly shapes hugging the walls.

Next they went to the billiard room. She slowly and noiselessly pulled open the pocket doors a couple of inches. She peered in, but saw nothing in the room other than the murky shapes of the billiard table, arm chairs, liquor cabinet and tables with lamps.

The mansion was utterly silent as they continued down the gallery to the east parlor. Here the doors were open already, and again she saw nothing. They padded noiselessly on in darkness until they had nearly reached the foyer. Madeline, trembling and terrified, held Pancho's collar with a sweaty hand. They stayed close to the paneled wall of the grand staircase, and she realized how glad she was she had on her old dark blue robe. It would be difficult for anyone to see her in the darkness. She heard a very soft sound, like the single tread of a foot. Then, a faint creak. Silence for several long seconds. Then, she heard another longer and barely audible creeakk. Madeline tried to determine where it was coming from, but gave up, it could be anywhere.

Pancho began a low growl. Madeline tugged his collar. He stopped and sat quietly. She swallowed. The sweat that had popped out all over her body Madeline could now feel trickle down her spine like an icy finger, to the small of her back. Then came another single sound, like a footfall. But she still couldn't pinpoint where the sound had come from, upstairs or down.

In the blink of an eye a large, dark shape crashed down the main stairs to the foyer and made a hard right turn. Without thinking, Madeline screamed "HEY! What the hell are you doing here?!" She raced along the length of the paneled stair and around the bottom, holding Pancho's collar. The smell of stale cigarette smoke hung in the air. The figure sped along the hall toward the back of the house. Madeline instinctively ran after. Pancho began barking furiously and pulled free. He charged after the intruder.

A deafening explosion rocked the hallway as the trespasser fired a gun back toward Madeline. She felt the push of the air current as the bullet narrowly missed her left arm. She simultaneously heard the sound of breaking glass. Terrified, she crouched and screamed, "Stop, Pancho! Come!"

In the darkness ahead she could barely make out the figure running away and lost sight of him at the dog leg in the hallway nearer the back of the house. She saw a faint, partial figure sprint through the doorway into the kitchen. She heard the kitchen back door open, and then very faintly, the sound of pounding footsteps receded.

Pancho came to her immediately, with a combination of whining and growling. "Oh Pancho, Pancho, my God, are you okay? Huh? Are you?" Madeline's voice shook as she hugged him tightly, petting and stroking his body to make sure he was alright. Pancho licked her face and with a small whimpering sound then suddenly, as if saying, *I can't take any more of this*, he collapsed to the floor, and put his head on her lap. "Stay right here Pancho, stay." Madeline wanted to go lock the kitchen door but she could barely move. It was all she could to retrieve her purse from the foyer table and get her cell phone. She nearly didn't make it back where Pancho sat before her trembling legs gave out. She dialed Cooper.

* * *

"Jesus H. Christ on a crutch, Madeline, you could've been killed!" Cooper was nearly shouting.

"Scotty......Scotty, take it easy," Morales said in a soothing tone.

"You should never chase an intruder! You don't know if they're armed! As this one was!" Cooper said as he paced, hands on his hips.

Cooper and Morales were both at Raven's Nest within fifteen minutes. Officer Willis followed in a patrol car. Madeline sat with Pancho in the library giving a statement, while Willis gathered what evidence there was which was pitifully little.

The bullet had gone through the windows adjacent to the door, so there was no retrieving it, and there was no shell casing. No fingerprints. Morales called a locksmith to replace all the locks.

Madeline sat with her mother's lap rug around her shoulders and Pancho on her feet. Cooper finally sat next to her on the sofa. Madeline now regretted deeply having put on the old blue bathrobe.

"I'm sorry, but I was just reacting, I didn't think. I couldn't believe there was someone, some *person*, inside my home, for Christ's sake," Madeline said. Her eyes were weighted with dark circles that stood out from her pale, drawn face. "It scared the shit out of me."

"Can you remember anything about the person you saw?" Morales asked, her voice calm and quiet.

"It happened so fast. I was getting in bed and I heard a noise. Pancho and I went downstairs and looked around but didn't see anything. I found that the kitchen door was unlocked. We went along the back hallway to the east gallery. We checked the rooms then headed up toward the foyer. We were standing next to the stair. I could hear some small sounds, creaks, footsteps? All of a sudden, there was just a big shape, thundering down the stairs, and running up the hallway toward the back of the house. It was pitch dark. All I saw was a shape. But I think it was a man. It was large, you know, bulky, and when he ran, it sounded like heavy boots. Oh, I could smell smoke after he ran past."

"Smoke?" Cooper asked.

"Yes, you know, old cigarette smoke. That smell."

"Okay, that's good. So it was a man, and a smoker." Morales said.

"You're sure you locked the door today?" Cooper asked, more calmly.

"I'm positive. I remember distinctly locking it after Mrs. T left. So how in the hell did someone get in this house unless they had a key?" The idea of someone having a key to one of the locks in her home was frightening in the extreme. Madeline had never once felt anything but utterly safe at Raven's Nest. That feeling was changing.

"The doors haven't been jimmied, so who has keys to the house except you?"

"Other than my mother, just Mrs. T and I. No one else as far as I know. I guess it's possible mother may have given a set to Arthur Selwyn for emergencies? Possibly Ian Andrews? But I don't think so."

Cooper got up and began pacing again, thinking. "No spare hidden outside?" he asked.

Madeline shook her head. "No. It's odd but, you know, I heard noises last night too. It turned out to be nothing, but it was weird. Gave me the creeps. Sometimes sound travels funny in this house. It will sound like it's close by then somewhere else entirely."

"Did it sound like what you heard tonight?" Cooper asked.

"Well, yes, sort of. But like I said you can't tell where sound is coming from or even what kind of noise it is. I think last night was a tree branch tapping on a window."

"What else?" Morales asked.

"I heard something, and again, it sounded like a tapping noise, like a tree branch tapping on glass. I just went downstairs, like tonight."

Cooper waited. What was she holding back? "What happened?"

There was a knock at the front entry, and Morales let the locksmith in. She began to explain where the locks needed to be replaced and led him to the kitchen door first.

"What happened, Madeline?" Cooper looked at her intently.

She had decided to give the letter to the detectives while she was waiting for them to arrive. She had it in the pocket of her robe. She gave it to him.

He read the note and turned to look at her. "When did you get this?" He pulled out a plastic evidence envelop and sipped the note in, trying not to touch it.

"When I heard the noises last night. I looked out the front entry, and it was under the mat on the stoop. It was put there sometime after you left and before I went up to bed."

"Why didn't you call me?" Cooper's worries about her safety had just skyrocketed. If she wasn't going to be more forthcoming, how was he going to keep her safe?

"I didn't see the point. What can you do about it? There's no way to know who wrote it."

"Maybe, maybe not. We can have forensics take a look at it. Anyway, you should have told me."

Cooper sat down again next to Madeline and took her hands. "Are you really okay?" he asked softly.

She looked into his eyes and saw concern and worry. "I'm okay. It was just so damn scary." She felt something funny happening in her chest. Cooper kept staring into her eyes, as if searching for evidence of injury, something to fix. To break the tension she did the only thing she could think to do. "I'm glad Pancho was with me." She disengaged her hands from Cooper's and pulled the dog's face up to look into his eyes. "You're a good puppy, aren't you, Pancho?" He whined and licked her hands.

"Look, I don't want you staying here until we figure out what the hell is going on."

"I'm not leaving Raven's Nest."

"Madeline..."

"No. I don't want to let a bastard sneak thief run me out of my house. And, the locks are getting changed as we speak. Someone may have a key, but they won't after tonight, right? Besides I'm not alone, I have Pancho."

"I don't think stealing was what they had in mind. I think it's about you, and maybe they lost their nerve. Next time, maybe they won't. This note takes things to another level." He looked down at the dog. "And, Pancho's a great guy, but he's not all that much in a crisis, now is he?" Cooper gave her a faint, lopsided grin.

Madeline pulled the blanket around her shoulders and hunched down. "I'm not leaving."

With a theatrical sigh of defeat, Cooper stood. "Alright Madeline, you leave me no other choice. I'm staying with you."

Her head flew up to stare at him. "What?"

"Are you saying you have no room to put me up?" He spread his arms expansively to take in all the space in the huge room.

Her pale face flushed. "Of course I *can*, but it's not necessary, I'll be fine."

"Since you're not in charge, I guess what you think doesn't matter. I would rather feel confident that you're safe, and if that means you have to find a way to *shoehorn me in somewhere*," he turned slowly, three hundred and sixty degrees around, arms outstretched, "then so be it."

Madeline rolled her eyes. Inside, her heart thumped wildly.

* * *

An hour and a half later, the locksmith had replaced the locks at all three of the keyed entrances to the mansion. Madeline felt a little more secure, but the puzzle of how the person got in was all she could think about. They couldn't suspect Mrs. T, surely.

Cooper had called Selwyn, related what had happened and asked about his having a spare key. He told Cooper that yes, in fact, he had had a spare set of keys for many years. One for each of the keyed exterior doors. He checked and they were still safely stored in a locked drawer in his desk. "Is Maddie okay, really okay?" he asked.

"Yes, she's fine for now. I don't want her to stay here but she is refusing to leave, so my partner and I will be here with her, at least for the time being. I'll be here for the shift tonight."

"That's a good idea, detective. Let me know if there's anything I can do to help."

"I'm going to talk to Selwyn tomorrow," Cooper told Madeline as he sat back down on the couch.

"It wasn't Selwyn I saw." Madeline protested. "He's what, seventy? Older? He couldn't have moved that fast, and frankly, the person was way too big. It had to have been someone a lot younger."

"He could have given the keys to someone. Also, I'll be interviewing Mrs. Temple again, as well."

"It makes no sense. What could be gained by breaking in here now? Nothing was stolen. What was the point?"

"I don't know," Cooper said. "What are your plans for tomorrow?"

"I have to finalize the funeral arrangements." She paused and stared intently at her hands clasped in her lap. "I have set the funeral for Saturday, at two o'clock. Unity Church of Palo Alto. Do you know it?" she asked Cooper quietly.

"I know of it."

"Perhaps you and Detective Morales will come?" She turned to look at him. He exuded strength, dependability, and a certain undefinable essence that made Madeline feel calm.

"We'd be honored to be there," Cooper assured her.

Morales came into the library. "It looks like the locksmith is all done." She handed Madeline three sets of each of the three new keys. "The locksmith has checked each of them, they work properly. Willis has everything he's been able to find. Being his usual assholey self. You ready?"

Just as Morales asked the question, Willis lumbered into the library, already talking, toothpick jumping around the side of his mouth. "I didn't find any fingerprints, no footprints outside of course. Door wasn't jimmied, so it was unlocked or they had a key. Basically nothing. The kitchen door was standing open, again. That's about it."

Cooper nodded. "Okay, leave a copy of your notes on my desk. You can go on." Willis stared at the two detectives. Finally turning on his heel, he trudged through the foyer, and Cooper heard the front door close.

Morales closed her eyes for a moment then shook her head with a sigh. "Okay, as I was saying, you ready?"

Cooper stood. "Change of plans." He showed Morales the note.

Morales frowned at it and at Cooper. "What the hell?"

"We'll take it in and have forensics look at it. Madeline doesn't want to leave Raven's Nest, and I don't think she's safe to be here alone, even with the change of locks. I'm going to be staying. You take the car back into town. If she's still here, maybe you can be here for a shift tomorrow night, Izzy."

Morales gazed at Cooper with an unreadable expression. Finally, she replied, "Sure, we can work that out, it's no problem."

"Oh, no, you don't have to do that. I've told Detective Cooper that I'm perfectly alright by myself, I can—"

"It's already been decided," Cooper interrupted.

"Okay, well then, good. I'd like to confer with Detective Cooper before I go. Goodnight Madeline, take care, see you tomorrow."

Cooper and Morales walked from the library toward the back of the house. Once in the kitchen Morales turned and looked up at Cooper, arms crossed over her chest and spoke, her voice low. "What the hell are you doing, Scotty? Is this a good idea? It seems like you're getting a bit close to our victim."

Cooper stood, hands on hips. "You heard what she said, Izzy. The shot barely missed her. She felt the air current from the bullet! She could've been killed. And this letter? You think it's some kid's practical joke? I don't. She's scared to death, even if she pretends she's not. Since we don't know what's going on, I think it's safer to have somebody here."

Morales' eyes met his steadily for several long moments. Finally she threw up her hands and said, "Oh, for Christ's sake, Scotty, I understand. Just be careful, will ya? You don't know her."

He put his hand on her shoulder and gave it a squeeze. "I'll be careful. Why don't you come pick me up in the morning?"

"All right, *amigo*, but just remember. We don't know who was in here tonight. We don't know if *she* knows. And we don't know what's next. Stay alert. See ya tomorrow." She left. Cooper locked the back door behind her.

* * *

It was after eleven when Cooper made a final round to check that all the new locks had been engaged. Madeline brought a bottle of wine from the kitchen to the library and poured two glasses. She sipped her wine and sighed. "This has been one hell of a day. I am pretty sure I won't sleep—if I don't have a glass of wine. God, what does that say about me," Madeline smiled wanly.

"I agree with you, it's been a very, very long day. But do you think anyone would be able to do better, after being shot at?"

She shrugged and spoke softly. "I wish I understood what's going on. It's only been a few days and I feel like I won't to be able to cope much longer. I feel so guilty, my mother should have had someone to depend on."

"Madeline, I promise you we will find out who's at the bottom of this. We're already making headway." He related what they had learned about Frank Van Gessler.

"You suspect him of murder as well as embezzling? That's so—surreal, I know the man."

"He thought it was going to be a simple thing to embezzle from your mother and father, thinking he was clever. Then after your father's death, it looks like he upped his take, he decided that she would be too distracted to pay attention or look closely at things. He didn't count on Diane Kenyon."

Madeline nodded her head sadly. "She was so young. And, it sounds like, a bit of a risk taker. By the way, after I finish the funeral arrangements tomorrow, I'm going back to Eugene."

Cooper looked sharply up from his wine. "You are?"

"I have to deal with some issues there, namely, David. Now he's causing problems for people other than me. I think he's trying to get to me through one of my employees." Madeline rubbed her neck. She could feel the effects of the wine spreading like a warm wave. "I have to get him to settle the divorce, one way or the other."

"When will you be back down?"

"Mother's funeral is Saturday, as I said, so I'll certainly be back by Friday. If I can get cooperation from him. I've got lots going on at work. I was starting an important bid process just as all this started." She sipped the Cabernet. "It shouldn't take more than a couple of days to deal with some of the work related stuff and say my piece to David."

Cooper stared at her earnestly. "I want you to be careful, Madeline. With him, I mean. I got an awful bad feeling from him today." Oddly, to her, the incident with David Dean earlier today seemed another time, already a long ago. She nodded.

In one of the upstairs hallways, Madeline walked into a spacious closet (much bigger than Cooper's own bedroom) that held vast quantities of linens of every kind. Well organized into type, size, description, and beyond that by color. Mrs. T was nothing, if not efficient.

"You have two choices," she said. Then, with a laugh that was almost a hysterical giggle, "What am I saying? There are at least twenty-two unoccupied bedrooms upstairs at last count, so I guess you have more than two choices. Anyway, you can take some sheets, blankets and pillows from here and sleep in the ladies' parlor downstairs, or pick a room up here." She glanced at Cooper sideways. "The large sofa in that parlor is very comfortable, it would certainly fit you. I've napped on it before. Of course, it's not as good as a bed."

Cooper peered into the linen closet. Then he glanced both ways down the hall. Opposite the staircase, the hallway disappeared into semi—darkness, only one small sconce a dozen yards away gave out feeble light. "Where is your room?" he asked.

Madeline waved back toward the stair landing and replied, "Third door on the right once you're up the stairs. Oh never mind, come on." She turned off the light, closed the linen closet and headed down the corridor and opened an oak paneled door, seemingly at random. She pressed the light switch and a soft glow from a bed side lamp illuminated a beautiful room. "Will this do?"

Cooper took in the antique furnishings, lamps and draperies. The room so impressed him that, "Wow. Great," was all he could think of to say. He walked around the room, examining the mission oak desk and chair and the oak bed. He looked out of the windows onto the back terrace, garage and outbuildings.

"There is a bathroom through that door." She pointed. "You'll find plenty of towels. There's spare everything: toothbrushes, toothpaste, shampoo, razors, shave cream, anything you need."

He turned to her and with a smile, eyes slightly squinted and asked, "Is this S-O-P?"

She looked at him, brows pulled together quizzically.

"Standard operating procedure. Do you outfit a bedroom like this in the off chance that someone will drop in who is homeless and penniless?"

Madeline laughed out loud at the comment. "My mother and dad thought that if you're going to have a home like this, that you had better be ready for any contingency. *All* the spare bedrooms are like this."

"No freakin' *way*."

"Yes, way." She said, laughing at their use of teenage vernacular. "Believe it or not, they used to have weekend long parties, where many of the rooms got used." Bemused, she added, "Really used, if you know what I mean. Just think of poor Mrs. T. She has to keep them all dusted and swept and scrubbed."

"In spite of the possibility of putting Mrs. T out......I'll take it," Cooper grinned.

Madeline turned to leave. Cooper strode over to her. "Madeline, wait," he said, very gently. "I'm sorry for all your troubles. Izzy and I, we'll do all we can to find out who's responsible."

Madeline sensed a sudden charge in the atmosphere, and was petrified but forced herself to look Cooper in the eye. "I'm sure you will, I appreciate that."

He reached out and gently brushed the dark hair back from her face. Then to her shock, Cooper bent and pressed his lips to her cheek. She smelled his clean scent. His hand slid down her arm to grasp her hand briefly. "Goodnight."

She nodded wordlessly and carried her flip flopping heart down the hall and across to her room and closed the door. She heard his close.

CHAPTER EIGHT
Tuesday

Madeline was up early, busying herself with coffee and breakfast. Mrs. Temple would be getting there soon, so she unlocked the newly keyed kitchen back door. Since waking up, her mind had been consumed with the moment last night when Cooper kissed her cheek. Finding herself daydreaming, she chided the behavior. *I'm acting like I am a teenager not just talking like one, for Christ's sake. He was just being kind.* When Cooper came into the kitchen, she avoided his eyes.

"Good morning, Madeline." He somehow managed to look fresh and clean, even in yesterday's clothes.

"Oh, good morning, she said, attempting an offhand tone. "How'd you sleep?"

"You kidding? It was like a five-star hotel. The shower's fantastic."

"Coffee's ready. I hope you like a mushroom omelet Detective Cooper," she said as she beat the eggs.

"That sounds great. I'm really hungry." He went to the coffee maker and poured a cup then stood by her at the stove. "You said you'd call me Scott, remember?"

Unnerved by his proximity, Madeline glanced up and said, "Sorry, of course I remember. Scott." Pointing with the spatula to the drawer he'd been in before, she said, "Would you get out some silverware?"

Cooper set the places and soon she served up a steaming fluffy omelet, oozing cheese and sautéed mushrooms. They ate comfortably in silence for several minutes.

The back door clicked and in one smooth motion Cooper wheeled around, simultaneously raising and aiming his Beretta.

The door opened to reveal Mrs. Temple. She started and dropped her purse and newspaper, and let out a shriek. "Oh, my dear Lord!" she said, her eyes wide and terrified. "Oh, dear God. What…? What in the *world?* What's going on? Madeline?"

"It's okay Mrs. T., it's okay." Madeline patted the air to quiet her. "We just had a bit of trouble last night, and the detective is here providing protection."

Cooper had immediately re-holstered his weapon. Mrs. Temple raised her eyebrows at Madeline's remark, but proceeded to pick up her things and deposit them on the end of the table. She thumped her chest and took a huge breath. "Goodness gracious! That gave me an awful fright." She exhaled shakily. "Something happened last night, Madeline? Were you hurt? Are you alright?"

Cooper related to Mrs. Temple an abbreviated version of the night's events. Madeline handed her one of the new keys, while Cooper asked her about her movements the night before and where she kept her set of keys.

"Well, I was at home last night, where else would I be? I never go out at night if I can avoid it, you know. The nighttime is when all the crazy people are out. And, those keys never leave my purse. Ever. Well, of course they do when I'm unlocking the door," she frowned briefly at that, "but beyond that, never!" Mrs. Temple had regained her composure and helped herself to a cup of coffee. She pulled out a stool and sat at the table. She then rummaged in her bag and showed him her set of keys. She then proceeded to exchange the old key for the new.

"Alright, Mrs. Temple." Cooper said agreeably. He settled himself across from her. "Is there any chance that anyone could have access to them?"

"I don't see how. I live by myself. I have a grandson who visits every now and again, but I haven't seen him in almost a month. Why would he want keys to this house?" She snorted at the absurdity of it.

"What's his name, and how old is he?"

Mrs. Temple said, "You can't be serious. He's just a boy. His name is Willy, well it's really Wilfred, but he likes Willy. He's named after my husband."

"How old is Willy?"

"He's only seventeen. He lives with his mother, in San Jose. He's just a boy and has nothing to do with any of this."

"You know I have to ask, Mrs. Temple, we have to cover all the bases. It isn't just you, we're asking everyone, ma'am." Cooper added.

Mrs. Temple looked at Cooper with an expression between a scowl and a frown. "Yes, well…"

There was a tap on the back door and Morales came in. "Morning all. Scotty, you ready?"

Madeline took that as a cue. "Hello, Detective Morales, good morning. Help yourself to some coffee." She rose and stacked their breakfast dishes in the sink.

Morales pounced on the offer of coffee. With a cup in hand she sat next to Mrs. Temple. "How did things go last night?" She asked with a serious tone, but there was a playful smirk around her mouth.

Madeline couldn't see either detective's face. Scott delivered his comment to Izzy with a black look, "Everything was quiet, thankfully. You have anything new?"

"I've got a few things, I'll fill you in on the way into town."

"Detective Morales, I'll tell you what I've already told Detective Cooper. I have to get down to the funeral home. When I'm through there, I am going to get a flight back to Eugene. I'll call to let you guys know when I'll be able to come back. Should be Thursday. Friday at the latest," Madeline said.

She turned to Mrs. Temple. "Mrs. T? Can you take Pancho with you until I get back?"

Mrs. Temple, still a bit out of sorts over the key issue and the Willy issue, agreed, patting his poufy head and loving on him. "That's never a problem, *he's* a gentleman." The obvious implication in her tone being that certain other males in the world might not fit that description. Cooper tried and failed to hide a grin.

Morales gathered the coffee cups and deposited them in the sink then headed for the back door. Cooper looked at Madeline seriously. "Okay, remember what I said about David. Don't go anywhere with him alone. If you think you need help, I can make a call to someone at the Eugene PD."

"That won't be necessary, but thanks."

At the door he turned and said quietly. "Please be careful. And don't be gone too long."

Madeline watched the detectives walk to their sedan, her brows furrowed, her mind musing on the strange way of circumstance and what he may have meant by that remark.

* * *

Morales drove down the serpentine drive. "So, you can tell me now. What happened?" she asked.

Cooper kept his eyes out the passenger window looking at the forest of trees. "I don't know what you mean. Nothing happened. I told you. Thankfully, it was quiet."

"I'm looking for details, *amigo*. Details."

"Jesus, Izzy. We drank a glass of wine. She gave me a room to bunk in. End of story." If only that was actually the end of the story, he thought. But no......not by a country mile. Last night he had wanted much more, than to simply kiss Madeline on the cheek. Is it her vulnerability, her beauty? Cooper knew this was dangerous ground, but she brought out something in him. Maybe Izzy was right, maybe he was becoming more sensitive to people and their feelings. But this particular person? Oh, hell.

Morales lost the kidding tone. "I'm sorry I pushed, I shouldn't have. I can tell something's up. I know you too well," she said softly. "Are you getting stuck on her?"

Cooper looked out the window without responding. Finally he said, "When I'm around her I feel…oh, I don't know. It doesn't bear talking about. What difference does it make? She's in the middle of a divorce."

Morales kept her eyes on the road and drove in silence for a few minutes. She finally said, "The status of her divorce has nothing to do with it. What's important is how you feel about her. How she feels about you."

Cooper glanced at his partner. Izzy could really cut through the crap.

It was not yet eight o'clock, so they swung by Diallo's. Cooper wondered, quite seriously, if Morales would actually keel over if denied coffee—or food—for more than three hours at a time? The woman could eat and drink more than any man he'd ever known. How she stayed slender was beyond him. She was only five foot five, give or take, and no more than one hundred and fifteen pounds. And it had to be all muscle—she was strong. She made use of the PD fitness facility occasionally, but not religiously, so that couldn't account for it. Just good genes, he supposed.

"If you remember, I didn't get a fancy omelet for breakfast." she said. "We have a busy day, so don't gripe about me having some food. And coffee."

"Yeah, yeah, fine. Let's see where we are."

Morales was scarfing down an apple fritter, literally as large as her head. She sipped her latte and pulled out her notebook, flipped a few pages, then saw Cooper's face. "What?" Morales asked around a mouthful of fritter.

He pulled out a plastic evidence bag with the note in it. "Let's not forget this. We need to find out who wrote it, if possible. We'll drop it off with forensics."

Morales nodded and munched. With her mouth full she said: "You think it's a joke?"

"No, I don't. I'm worried about her, Izzy. It's a direct death threat, plain and simple. They, whoever they are, say they're going to kill her. What has she done that would make someone want to murder her? It's money, just like I've said from the beginning.

"I haven't figured out what's been buggin' me. After I talked to Selwyn again yesterday? Something he said made the whole thing start nagging at me. I wish I could figure out what it is…" Cooper's voice trailed off.

"Who benefits from murdering Madeline, though? Oh, but, well…she's divorcing David Dean. But still, what would he get out of it?" Morales asked.

"What he gets is, he wins, money-wise, if he can keep her from divorcing. Short of that, he probably thinks he would inherit if she dies before a divorce can go through. He doesn't know that *she* doesn't even inherit until after she divorces him."

"God, what a screwed up mess."

"I think his main problem is, he wants to control Madeline. I'm not going to let that happen. He's not getting his filthy hands on her."

"Hey, power down, *amigo*. When she gets back from Eugene, we'll take turns staying out there." She grinned. "Unless you want all that duty."

"Cut it out, Izzy." His face grew thoughtful and he became quiet.

Morales looked up from her fritter at him and asked, "What?"

Cooper held up a finger. "Hang on a sec." He dialed his phone.

"Hello, Ian, it's Detective Cooper. Yes, Scott. How is your foot? Oh? Uh huh. That's good, glad to hear it. Listen, would it be possible to talk with you again, later today?" He nodded and grinned. "Okay. Yes. It might be late afternoon. I look forward to it too."

"What's that about?"

"Just something I'm kicking around. First, we will make a quick trip up to Napa. Well, not quick maybe. After we get back to town we'll run out to Andrews' house. You can meet him. You'll like him, Izzy."

"Okay, if you insist." Morales smiled. "What are you thinking?"

"For one thing, there is something about this tiff between Eleanor and Helen Highwater. I think Andrews can fill in the blanks."

"You think Highwater's involved? You don't think *she* murdered Abbott, do you?"

"No, I don't think she's the killer, but I'm thinking she might be part of it. I think Ian Andrews has details he didn't share when I first spoke to him. Come on, grab that coffee. We gotta drop off the note and get on the road."

"I told ya. A full day."

* * *

It was a long two hours up to Napa to visit the B and B on the receipt found in Diane Kenyon's effects. Traffic on the 680 is bad, no matter what time of day. The fallacy of there being a rush hour, and it being the worst time on the freeways, is just that—a fallacy. There might actually *be* a rush hour. But the truth is, there's just traffic. Lots and lots of traffic, nearly all the time. It ranged from slow moving, to creeping, down to one long parking lot, which is the incongruously named 'rush hour'.

The Berkley Inn on a main thoroughfare in Napa, was a two story craftsman style home, situated well back from the street in a quiet neighborhood of similar vintage homes. It boasted immaculate landscaping, manicured lawns, slate walkways and an abundance of roses and hydrangeas.

Inside the spacious foyer, a well dressed, well groomed and pleasantly plump older woman greeted them. She introduced herself as Mrs. Whitman, the proprietor of The Berkley Inn. She reminded Cooper of his grandmother. Shining silvery hair, rosy cheeks and the cheerfully expressive eyes of someone who loves people.

They showed their identification and explained what they were after. Morales showed the woman a photo of Diane and the innkeeper recognized her immediately.

"Oh, yes, she was here, I remember her," said Mrs. Whitman with a smile. "She checked in mid day, on Friday, with her boyfriend. I can show you the register."

"That's great, Mrs. Whitman, we'd appreciate it," Morales replied.

As she bustled toward the reception area, she called back over her shoulder, "What has this young woman done, officers? She seemed very sweet and extremely polite."

"It's not what she's done, Mrs. Whitman, but what's been done to her," Cooper answered. Mrs. Whitman paused at that, then stepped behind the counter with a frown.

She opened a drawer and thumbed through a card catalog. She glanced up at them with a sheepish look. "This must seem terribly antiquated to you. I just don't like computers, you know? I guess I was just born too soon," she said with a small laugh.

"I try to convince myself that people who enjoy a Bed and Breakfast experience, appreciate the slower pace and maybe don't expect simply *everything* to be computerized. Although," she whispered, as if it were a secret, "we do have WiFi. Here we are." She pulled out a card, printed with a logo, especially for her establishment, with lines for guests to fill in their information.

Cooper scanned the card. All the details pertained to Diane herself, with the exception of number of guests. Two. "Did you say Diane Kenyon called for a reservation and asked for a room for two?"

"Oh, yes, she called a couple of weeks ago. I guess she had to arrange to get the days off from work, you know? She said she would be here with her boyfriend, and they would stay Friday and Saturday night and leave Sunday at checkout time."

"Would it be possible to take a look at the room, ma'am?" Cooper asked.

"I don't see what good that would do, detective." She seemed miffed at the very suggestion that there would be anything to find. "I'm very thorough when I clean, you understand."

"Likely you're right, ma'am, but if you don't mind, we'd like to take a look."

The landlady sighed, looking from Cooper to Morales and back. "Oh, alright. Come on."

She led them past the reception desk to the broad oaken stair. Their steps were muffled on a floral carpet runner. At the top of the stairs was a spacious landing. She turned right and went down a hallway. Cooper noticed that each door was embellished with a beautifully hand carved wooden plaque. At the second door he saw the plaque identified this as the 'Pinot Room'. Whitman opened the door and stood back. "I'll let you take a look. I'll be at the desk."

Cooper nodded his thanks. The room had a window that faced the front of the house and one that looked down on a side yard. It was spacious and bright, with a couple of wicker arm chairs with foot stools, a desk, a queen size bed sporting a beautiful quilt and fluffy pillows.

They looked around the room, in drawers, in the bathroom adjacent. The desk held an easel backed Lucite box containing brochures on area points of interest. There was a laminated copy of information about the history of the house and another with times for breakfast service, wine and cheese hour. Other services the Inn offered were included, like boxed lunches, bicycle rentals and of course, check out time. Every single thing was gleaming and in perfect order. Mrs. Whitman was right. The place was immaculate.

"God, Scotty, this must rent for a fortune. You don't think Kenyon paid for it?"

"We can ask. The point is, what happened here? Who was she with? Did she tell him she was pregnant? Was she hoping to get him to marry her? If it was David Dean, that means he wasn't around Los Gatos on Friday, but it doesn't necessarily mean he wasn't there Thursday night."

"True," Morales said, "but they might have taken off Thursday, stayed somewhere for a night on the way? Damn, too bad the landlady didn't see the guy."

They went downstairs and met Mrs. Whitman at reception. "Y'all sure have a beautiful home Mrs. Whitman," Cooper said by way of mending fences a little. He added, "You were absolutely right. That room is as clean as a whistle." He paused. "I just want to ask again if you remember seeing Diane's friend at all. Do you remember anything?"

She shook her head. "I'm really sorry I can't be of help to you, detective. I realize now, looking back, that they really were keeping quite a low profile. Normally my guests come down to the parlor in the evening, have a glass of wine, enjoy some cheese, you know. That is part of the cost of the room." At this bit of advertisement for her establishment, she preened, ever so slightly. "I think it's important to give people a little more than they expect, you know? But, not them. They just stayed out of sight." She gave a short laugh. "Almost like honeymooners."

"Can you tell us who paid for the room?" Morales asked her.

Mrs. Whitman looked again at the card that still rested on the counter. "It looks like they paid with cash. However, I do require a credit card on file. Well, that's for incidentals. Damage to the room. You can never tell about people. I've just always felt it is better to be safe than—" Cooper cut her off smoothly, "I'm sure you are right about that Mrs. Whitman. So, the card holder's name?"

"The imprint on the card she gave was, Diane L. Kenyon."

Cooper and Morales looked at each other in defeat. "Would you contact us, Mrs. Whitman, if you think of anything at all?" Morales handed her a card.

"Oh I certainly will, detective. You know, it's funny. One thing I remember thinking at the time, was that they were both so light haired, you know, blond. I only caught a glimpse, mind you, but I remember thinking, they could've been siblings."

* * *

"Who was he, Izzy?" Cooper asked as they headed back to Los Gatos.

"I don't know. Ben Highwater's blond. The other kid, Selwyn's grandson, don't know what he looks like. There's Madeline's ex, he's blond, and a strong contender. But was in Eugene. Supposedly."

"Except, of course, when he wants to show up on Madeline's doorstep," Cooper said testily. "That proves he can drive down from Eugene pretty easy. High on coke, he can probably make the entire drive without stoppin'. Madeline has told me that he has a long time drug problem. Nice to have something in common with his buddies down here."

"Doesn't it seem odd to you? To carry on that kind of a long distance friendship, especially when David and Madeline are a married couple, none of these others are married. Hell, they're just kids."

"But," said Cooper, "Madeline and David have been split a year."

Morales shrugged. They drove on in silence, until Morales suggested a pit stop for restrooms and coffee. Cooper sighed, but pulled off the 680 near Concord and into an In-And-Out Burger.

Morales had no intention of allowing a great opportunity to pass by. They ordered hamburgers, fries and sodas. "Man, I'm so hungry." Morales said. "That apple fritter, without enough icing mind you, was a long time ago."

Cooper, preoccupied, wasn't listening to Morales. She continued, "What would Madeline's ex get out of hitting on Kenyon, if it was him? Was he just being, what do you call it? A horn dog?

"Or, was he getting info about Eleanor's business from her? Maybe Diane wasn't doing the snooping for herself, maybe snooping for him, for David. Or someone else? Maybe that's why he's giving Madeline such a hard time with the divorce."

"What?" Cooper looked up from his tray of food. "What did you say?"

"I said, why was he hitting on the Kenyon woman? We think he was trying hard to keep Madeline, or at least keep her from divorcing, until she comes into her inheritance. So what would be the point of risking screwing that up, to go after Kenyon. The only reason he would be involved with Kenyon is to get to Eleanor through her, and hope like hell Madeline never found out about it."

It was nearly five when they got back from Napa and arrived at Andrews' home. They were greeted this time by officer Ginny Bell. She showed them in and went back to her station, a different chair, book and cup of coffee.

Cooper's mind had been occupied from the time they left the burger joint. He realized Morales might be right about David Dean. Was it Dean who was involved with Kenyon, or maybe it was but only for what he could pry out of her. Financial details?

To what end? What could a bottom feeder like Dean do with that? And what about her pregnancy?

Ian Anderson, still walking with the assistance of a cane, showed them into the living room. Cooper introduced Izzy.

"I'm very happy to finally meet you, Detective Morales. I hope you will call me Ian. I don't like all the formality. You're Isabelle? That's a lovely name."

Morales reddened and shrugged. "Thank you...Ian."

They settled in the living room and Jeffery came to take refreshment orders once again. Morales naturally voted for coffee. Everyone else went along.

"What can I do for you today, Scott? Do you have further information about Eleanor? Or possibly something on who tried to run me down?"

"I think you can help me, Ian. At least I hope so." Cooper frowned slightly. "I'm reluctant to ask you, but we need help and I think you have details that may prove important."

Andrews' eyebrows pulled together but he said softly, "Go on."

"When I was here before, you told me that Eleanor and Helen had a falling out some years ago."

"Yes, and it's true, they did have a serious falling out, but it's been, what, twenty years?"

"Can you tell us what was the trouble? We have heard the same thing from several others, but no one has given us particulars as to the nature of their disagreement." Morales asked getting out her note pad.

Ian Andrews rose with difficulty, and limped over to a large window that faced the front quartz rock garden area of the home. He gazed out with one hand on his cane, the other in his pocket, his natural ebullience gone. No one spoke.

The silence was broken when Jeffrey came back with three coffees on a tray. This time he left everyone to make the coffee to their liking, and with a polite minimalist bow, left the room. The detectives rescued two cups from the tray.

Andrews, still at the window, eventually turned back to them and said, "You think this has to do with Eleanor's murder?"

"I think it may," Cooper replied.

Andrews sighed and returned to the sofa. He picked up a coffee and sipped. "The problem they had was Eleanor's affair. I told you about it, if you recall."

Cooper nodded.

"Her affair was with Greg Highwater." Andrews stated quietly stirring his coffee.

Cooper and Morales exchanged a look. Morales said, "Please, go on, sir…Ian." The second it was out of her mouth she realized how ridiculous the flub sounded. He wasn't a British peer. With a sigh, she began her note taking.

Andrews gathered his thoughts for a few moments then began. "Alright. It started early in 1996. It lasted only a few months. I'm certain the affair was Eleanor's attempt at retribution. At Clay. She was so hurt and angry, and had carried it around with her for years. Plus, she saw Madeline every day, a constant reminder."

"Eleanor became pregnant, as I said. Once she was, she broke it off with Greg. Truly, I think she was so shocked at the pregnancy, she couldn't figure out how to handle it. She had been married to Clay for almost twenty-four years and had had no children. I think she believed it was her problem, and that she could not get pregnant." He drank more coffee.

"Oddly, as an aside, to my knowledge they never went to a doctor to investigate why they weren't getting pregnant. I've never known why that was. They just didn't." Andrews paused to drink again from his cup. "Anyway, I know the whole thing just destroyed Greg. It ruined his and Helen's marriage. There was talk of divorce. The boy, Ben, knew something was terribly wrong with his parents. Almost immediately, Greg and Helen had problems with him."

"We understand Greg committed suicide. What do you know about it?" Cooper asked.

"Have you asked Helen?"

"Yes, but she won't talk to us about it. If you don't want to share the information, we will have to get a court order to compel her to answer."

Andrews waved this away. "No, no. I'm not trying to make your job more difficult. It's just that, well, we're speaking about people I've known for years. They've been through hell." Andrews changed positions and propped his right leg on the sofa.

"Greg Highwater was an interesting and intelligent man. He was an architect professionally and extremely creative. Also, he was a highly talented musician, a violinist. He experienced emotional problems throughout his life. Depression, anxiety. Most of his adult life, he struggled with severe melancholia...up, down. Never as much 'up' as 'down', you understand."

Andrews contemplated the coffee table objects, as if they were all the disparate characters in the current drama. He reached over and moved one just a fraction, then continued. "I'm sure that played a part in why he had the affair with Eleanor. I believe he truly loved her." A long silence followed as he seemed to decide how to phrase his next thoughts. "Greg committed suicide about six years after the affair ended. He knew Eleanor's boy was his son. Helen found out as well. He felt overwhelming guilt about it."

Andrews absently rubbed the back of his neck. Watching his action was almost as contagious as a yawn, Cooper had to struggle not to follow suit.

"However, to his credit, he worked hard in the following years, to repair his marriage to Helen and his relationship with his son, Ben. I guess they did everything they could think of to do. Helen tried to reassure him that the past was forgiven, but somehow that reassurance was not enough. They struggled on for six years. Unfortunately......it didn't work. Even with therapy, religion...well, he ended it by putting a gun to his head. The worst part? He did this at home, and Ben found him that day, after school."

* * *

Morales had managed to talk Helen Highwater into another interview with Cooper. He dropped her off at the office before going. He knew some of the parts of the puzzle now and thought it was time Helen came clean. She wasn't quite as nice as during their first visit, but she agreed to see him.

When he rang the mechanical bell, the maid came to the door, as before. "Jes?"

"I'm here to speak to Mrs. Highwater again."

"O-kay. Come this way," she said and led him to the same parlor.

"I'm sorry," Cooper said. "I didn't get your name when I visited before." He looked down with a grin on the short, wide woman. She raised her heavy brows in surprise.

"Jue want to know my name?"

"Why, yes, I do. My name is Detective Cooper. And you are?"

With a shy smile she told him, "I am Maria."

"Very good. Maria.." He said the name out loud as he wrote it in his notebook. The act made her blush. He thanked her, "Gracias, Maria."

She made a tiny giggling noise, then said, "The Missus will be with jue in just a minute." She left.

Cooper smiled to himself. I've still got it.

In another two minutes he was joined by Helen Highwater, who appeared to skim into the room like a swan, much as she had on his first visit. He was struck again by her beauty. She was lightly tanned had glowing, finely textured skin any woman would envy and a classically proportioned face and figure that belied her years. Strangely, she did not seem to have the same overly flirtatious bent of many beautiful women. That was a plus as far as the detective was concerned.

"Good day, Detective Cooper, how are you today? What can I do for you?" Business like, she took a chair opposite him.

"Oh, I just need a bit more information for our investigation, if you don't mind." Cooper kept his tone light.

She sighed and replied, "I'm not sure what more I can tell you, detective. I've explained my relationship to Eleanor and about the last time we were together."

"Why don't we start by you telling me more about Ben. What does he do?"

She frowned, but answered, "Ben is enrolled in college classes, at San Jose State, so I guess you'd say he's a student and what he does is go to school."

"What is he studying?"

"He's very interested in computer technologies. I think that's the field he will be going into. What does this have to do with your case, detective?"

Ignoring her question, he asked, "Would you say he is good friends with the Deardon twins? Do they spend a lot of time together?"

She appeared to think that over. "Yes, they're good friends. Neither is a girlfriend, I wouldn't say. But they go out to eat together, movies, to clubs and the like, you know, like young people do."

"Uh huh. And they know David Dean, correct? Madeline's husband?"

"Oh, yes, Ben and David get together when David's down this way." She didn't elaborate.

"Can you tell me a little about your husband?"

She gave Cooper a beautiful smile revealing perfect teeth, and said, "Oh, I'm not married. William and I are just…you know, dating. We've been together for more than three years now, and I'd say we're pretty serious. He does stay h—"

"I meant your previous husband," Cooper interrupted.

Her reaction was immediate and absolute. "My husband? You mean *Greg?*" She looked shocked. "My husband has been dead for several years, Detective Cooper, I don't see what he has to do with anything, and I don't appreciate your dredging up unpleasant subjects." Her face flushed with pinched white areas showing around her eyes and mouth.

"We need to fill in the blanks about all the persons close to Eleanor. Greg's name came up as someone who knew her, so naturally I need to ask."

"Yes, he knew her. But he......died many years ago." Her anger seemed to soften and she looked lost. "It was a difficult time for me, for Ben. He was just a young boy."

Instead of responding to that, he continued, "How was your relationship with Greg?"

"We had our difficulties, like any marriage, but we loved each other."

"At what point did the 'difficulties' begin for you, Mrs. Highwater?"

Her hands were now tightly knotted in her lap. She stared down at them avoiding Cooper's eyes. "That's a very personal question detective, and pertaining to a time long ago. I don't see what bearing it has—"

"It may have a great deal of bearing on this case, if he was unfaithful to you. With Eleanor."

Helen Highwater looked at him as if he had slapped her. Anger simmered in her eyes. "How dare you. Who told you that?"

"If you look long enough and talk to enough people, you will eventually get to the truth," he replied. "He was involved in a relationship with Eleanor Abbott?"

Helen Highwater looked once again out the front windows. Her eyes appeared to be searching for something. Sorrow and defeat radiated from them, as well as a glimmer of tears. She plucked up a transient piece of thread from the arm of the chair.

Finally she said, "Yes, he did. It was a mistake, a terrible mistake. Greg was a good and decent man. He just got confused. Sidetracked."

Cooper spoke softly. "He committed suicide?"

After a few moments she spoke, her voice was nearly inaudible. "Yes, he committed suicide. He left us, Ben and I, and took the coward's way out."

"Out of what?"

"In the end, he just couldn't find the courage to face the consequences of what he'd done. We had a good marriage and we had a son we both adored. I found out about his affair with Eleanor. I found out about her pregnancy. Oh, she broke it off after a few months. When I confronted him, he begged me to forgive him.

"And I did, I *did* forgive him. I loved him, but it simply wasn't enough. Greg knew it was impossible for things go back to the way they once were. It's funny", her tone implying it was anything but funny, "I didn't realize at the time, my life was essentially over. I struggled so hard, trying to hold my family together. It took six more years before my life was finally ended. Greg and I tried everything: we had professional marriage and psychological counseling, we attended church regularly and even had counseling with Father Carmichael......we did everything I could think of to do. We struggled on for *six years* trying to mend something that apparently couldn't be mended. That's when he did it."

"You blamed Eleanor?"

"Of course I blamed Eleanor! Why would I not blame her? She was my friend. But I didn't kill her if that's what you're implying. For a long time, I hated her. As time went by we managed to move beyond it, she and I, but it was not easy and it took a long, long time. It was never again the way it once was between us, really, how could it be?

"But, she was always good to me, and to Ben. Was it out of guilt? I don't know. It was awful to lose your husband, the father of your child, as well as your good friend. You can't imagine."

He saw sorrow etched in her face. "As it happens, I can imagine," Cooper said softly, as he thought of Angie and their final words at the Dallas-FT. Worth Airport two years ago. He had often wondered if that knot of sadness would ever leave him.

"So," he continued, "What did you do?"

Helen Highwater sat worrying the small piece of thread, pulling at it, twisting it around a finger. Several moments of silence later she finally said, "After Greg's death, I began picking up the pieces of our lives. Mine and Ben's. It was Ben who found his father's body. *That*, I will never forgive Greg for. The trouble in our marriage, the talk of divorce and everything we struggled to do to repair our lives, took a toll on Ben. But he was so traumatized by what his father did, his suicide, finding his body......he began to turn inward. He became sullen and angry and began acting out.

"Remember, he was on the cusp of adolescence. His behavior was understandable given his tender age and the circumstances. So I did what I thought was right—I put us both in counseling again, with the top psychiatrist in the fields of grief and suicide. It has taken us years, detective, years to begin to pull our lives back together."

"Do you believe it has helped you? Ben?"

Helen Highwater stared out the parlor's front window, pulling absently on the piece of thread. After a moment she shook her head. "I don't know, Detective Cooper. I don't know."

* * *

Madeline had managed to finish the rest of the heart rending decisions with the mortuary in time to catch a flight up to Eugene. She had brought a simple cream silk suit for her mother. Forlornly, in her mind, she felt sure that it would have made no difference to Eleanor at all.

Mr. Bayless, a tall skeletal man in his forties, met her at the door. His simply cut somber black suit and grey tie told the story of his profession. If ever a description like 'the guy looks like an undertaker' fit someone, it fit Mr. Bayless. His skin has a translucent blueish tinge and looked as if it had never once seen the light of day.

Madeline handed the garment bag to him, and he thanked her quietly. His slender pale hand touched her shoulder gently. As he turned back to his office, carefully holding the garment bag as if it were a priceless antiquity or art object, tears filled her eyes. She put on her sunglasses and left.

By the time she landed in Eugene, retrieved her car from long term parking and got to town, it was past eight and she was exhausted, emotionally, mentally and physically. She drove directly home. Her mail had been picked up each day by Nadine. It rested on the entry table. She thumbed through it without interest.

Madeline poured a glass of red wine and crumpled into her chair in the living room. As she carefully avoided looking at the land line and its blinking light, she considered how to approach David.

Maybe the best way to deal with him is through the attorney. Let her do the confrontational bit. The attorney can inform David that there can't be anymore stalling, and that if he will agree to finalize the divorce, then a settlement can be reached. Maybe you wave a stick with some money on the end at him, and he'll finally cooperate. With the decision made to call her attorney first thing tomorrow, Madeline crawled gratefully into bed.

Instead of sleeping, she laid awake, her mind whirling chaotically. David's unreasonable anger, his back door attempt to gain information through Nadine frustrated her. Bizarre scenarios of who her mother's killer might be also churned through her mind. Each person she tried to make fit into the picture seemed beyond ludicrous. These people were her parents' *friends*, for God's sake, most of them Madeline had known for years, if not most of her life.

As a child, Madeline had spent a great deal of time in the company of her parent's friends. Raven's Nest was just isolated enough that other children usually weren't around to play with. The Deardon girls were younger than her by enough years that they never seemed like much fun. Selwyn had a grandson but he was too young as well. Ben Highwater was never around, period. Madeline never bothered to wonder why.

She spent much of her free time reading or drawing. Her creative streak had her constantly making things: elaborate puppet shows, stage plays, figures out of clay or PlayDoh. Mrs. T was usually her audience, since her parents were always working.

Summers away from school were long idyllic seasons that Madeline loved. Another child might have been lonely, but Madeline was not. She easily filled her own world with creativity and had the added spice of living in a fantastic and huge old house. She read hundreds of books, including all the Nancy Drew and Hardy Boys mysteries.

Sometimes when Clay and Eleanor hosted the parties at Raven's Nest, Madeline's imagination would go into full swing: she would snoop. Her knowledge of the house came in handy—she used the back stairs, the hidden passages, out of the way nooks and crannies. She imagined herself a spy, with the code name 'Raven'. She used her father's binoculars, a magnifying glass and kept notes on the all the adults. She examined coats and purses. She wrote elaborate dossiers for each person and imagined all manner of crimes and wrong doings. She had so much fun, and they never suspected. She got along well with the adults in her parent's group. She liked them.

From the perspective of twenty plus years on, none of these people seemed to have the mind set for such brutality. Had she so completely misread them all these years? Had her parents? Madeline respected her parents enough to doubt that they would have chosen friends that had a streak of malevolence and not recognize it. So what is different now? Has one of them changed and now become a murderer? Not once, but twice?

* * *

Cooper found Izzy still working on the computer at the office, at the end of the day. He sat at his desk and related what he'd found out from Helen Highwater. "What do you think that would do, Izzy, to a little kid? He would have been, what? Twelve? Thirteen?"

"My guess is, he would be looking for someone to blame." Morales turned in her chair to face Cooper, the squeal set his teeth on edge. "Little kids don't have what it takes to process something as awful as that. I think he would look to blame someone, and someone not his mother. Little kids don't understand the relationship between their parents. I know I didn't."

"What do you mean?"

"My papá was a true Mexican, in every sense of the word. He took the macho crap seriously. He lived it. I don't know how my mother stood it. But in her generation women just did. Well, hell, some of them do even now."

"What happened to him?" Cooper asked.

"He got mixed up in a drug thing down south. This was when I was only about fifteen. We never heard from him after that. I don't know if he's alive or not. Don't even know if he knows about mamá dying. Anyway, what I'm saying is, when you're little, you don't get all the dynamics of an adult relationship. You only know that something's wrong, someone's to blame. I wasn't much older than the Highwater kid when my papá made his mistakes. It was hard."

Cooper shook his head sadly. He liked Izzy so much and hated that she had had such a hard row to hoe. "I'm sorry, Izzy. They say that what doesn't kill ya, makes ya stronger, but I don't know about that." In Cooper's mind, frankly, it sounded pretty much like bullshit.

"I guess you just have to keep trying. Right, *amigo?*" She laughed softly.

Cooper said, "Do you think the Highwater kid could have gotten over what he saw, and stayed, I don't know, normal?"

"I don't know a kid *would* be able to get over it, regardless of therapy or church or mother love. It's one thing for your father to just...disappear, like mine? Seeing your father with his head blown off? Ugh." She shuddered.

"Okay, it traumatized him. How traumatized? As a little boy, what could he do? Feel helpless, angry. Now, a dozen years later, has that anger just been bubbling along, under the surface, waiting to explode? We know he had counseling. By himself and with the family. But, outside the influence of professionals, we don't know what Helen's said to him over the years, what kind of propaganda she might've exposed him to. Has she somehow allowed her own anger and resentment to color his perception? Has she made things worse by talking about it? Her, the psychiatrist, the church, whoever else put in their two cents worth?"

"Exactly how do you think this fits in to Eleanor's murder, meaning if they're involved, who did it?"

"I don't know how. But they—mother and son—have the strongest motive for Eleanor......revenge. The problem there is, why wait all these years?"

They got ready to leave. Cooper turned to Morales and said, "I'm beggin' ya, Izzy, oil that goddamn chair."

CHAPTER NINE
Wednesday

Divorce attorney Deborah Walker's office was located on Olive Street in Eugene. She came highly recommended by a friend who had recently been through a contentious divorce. Was there ever a divorce that *wasn't* nasty, Madeline wondered. Maybe if you're a celebrity. They always split with talk of eternal and blissful friendship, deep respect for one another, have only the best in their hearts for their children, blah, blah, *blah*. If any of the drivel were true, then why bother to divorce?

When Walker and Madeline met the first time, Madeline had not been keen on her. At first impression she seemed distracted and hopelessly scattered. Her reputation was good though, known as a pit bull, a fighter. Hoping the scatterbrain thing was just an act, Madeline stayed with her. Now she just wanted the woman to push things along. Madeline had reached her limit with David. With her mother and everything else on her plate, she just wanted this one thing to be done.

She had gotten a ten o'clock appointment and it started right on time. A good sign. Deborah ushered Madeline into her office and asked her what was prompting the urgency.

"I'm ready to move on, Deborah. My mother just…died. She was murdered." Deborah's head snapped up from the papers she was shuffling around to stare at Madeline. "I'm very sorry, Madeline. I hadn't heard."

Madeline met her gaze. "I just have to get this situation settled with David. I've got too much else to deal with and think about. Can we do something to speed it up?"

"I understand. Okay…it's pretty simple. He's received the papers, correct?" Madeline nodded and refreshed Walker's memory on the date. "If he received them and hasn't signed, then what we do now is file a default and the court will finalize in due course. If there are no disputes, then it can proceed without his cooperation."

"I don't know if there *are* disputes. He's never been willing to sit down and discuss it with me. He just keeps harping on getting back together. I'm willing to agree to some kind of settlement, but he won't even get to that point."

"After we file default, he won't have any other option. He'll finally come to understand that it's the only thing he can do."

Relief flooded through Madeline in a wave. "Oh, I didn't realize that was the case. He's been stalling from the beginning, trying to wheedle his way back in. At first it wasn't bad, I wanted to make sure I was doing the right thing. Now I'm sure—and have been for more than two months, but he is so goddamn stubborn. He's trying to convince me that he's going to somehow magically make things 'different' and that everything will be fine."

Deborah looked at Madeline with a faint smile. "Do you have any idea how many women have sat in that chair and said the exact same things to me? 'We'll work it out…I'll make it all better. I'll never do that again…he says he will…fill in the blank. The problem is that ninety-nine percent of the time they're saying it to convince themselves. In truth, it's mostly BS."

Madeline slumped back in the chair. "Oh, I feel so much better. Should I try to talk to him again while I'm in town? Should I tell him what's going to happen?"

"Certainly, if you want, but it's not necessary. He's had plenty of time to respond. You can give him a bite of a reality sandwich, and let me and the court handle it. I'll file the default immediately. That'll really give him a jolt." She laughed. "You'll have to appear before the court, I'll let you know when."

"Great. I'll probably be down in Los Gatos, but I can be here with a day's notice. Thank you, Deborah. I can't tell you what a load you've taken off of me."

* * *

At six-thirty Wednesday morning, Morales checked email with her phone and found:

March 22.
To: Detective Squad, Los Gatos PD.

You might do well to look at Kelsey

She made a quick stop at the office. She pulled up the email on her computer and stared at it. Anonymous. She tried every trick she knew to determine who sent it, with no luck. If someone is trying to help us, she mused, who and why? She printed out a copy and headed to Diallo's.

Morales arrived at Diallo's at seven-thirty on the dot. Cooper still beat her and was sitting at a table in the back, half way into his first latte.

"You aren't going to believe this, Scotty."

He looked up at his partner as he forked up a mouthful of cinnamon roll. "What?"

She handed him the print out. "I checked email this morning before I left. Someone's trying to steer us."

"Where did it come from?"

"Don't know. I did everything I could think of to find out, but it's anonymous. There *are* anonymous email services, you know. They are encrypted and can't be traced. Anyone can do it I guess, if you understand computers well enough you can send things without leaving a trail." She grinned. "Apparently it has its uses. Hang on I'm getting coffee and whatever that is," she said pointing to his roll.

"It's a double-cinnamon, cinnamon roll. Pretty damn good. Cinnamony," he added, nonsensically.

Morales went to the counter and ordered, while Cooper munched and stared at the print out. She returned with a latte and two double-cinnamon cinnamon rolls.

Cooper eyed her plate, then looked at Morales. "You gonna eat both of those?"

"Well of course I am. I'm really hungry," she answered. Morales set down her coffee and rolls and settled in a chair. "So. What do you make of it?"

"Not sure. The wording's funny."

"Oh, you mean that weird wording?" Morales had already attacked the first roll.

"Yeah, who phrases sentences like that? 'You might do well..' Sounds formal, not like every day speech."

"Right, it sounds strange. So, it's not a kid, someone older?"

Cooper nodded and drank his coffee. "Maybe educated. Or, it could be misdirection. What if someone's just trying to throw a wrench in the works, using an anonymous emails and odd language. Trying to make us chase our tails."

Morales sipped her latte. "Well, Andrews gave us some good info. Maybe now we should take a little time to do more looking at Kelsey."

Cooper shrugged. "I don't know. Have you found anything about their finances, Kelsey, Poole, that would point to them? Are they having money troubles?" He finished the last bite of his roll.

"No, they aren't. It's always possible this isn't about money. Maybe there's something in the past with Kelsey? Anyway, I'm serious about checking out the kids. All of them. Deardon's two, Ben, find out what we can on David Dean, maybe even Selwyn's grandson. Don't know where it might lead. Maybe they just irritate me," Morales said.

Cooper raised his brows. "Okay, fine. But I think this email is just trying to get us to waste time." He used his fork to scraped the last crumbs of cinnamon and said, "Why do you suppose Highwater didn't tell us the details about the husband, the suicide. Kind of a big detail to leave out."

Morales shrugged. "Ashamed? Still angry? Embarrassed? Whatever she thinks of him now she must be happy about her money situation. Greg must've been worth a bundle because they are sitting pretty good, to the tune of almost eight million, and that's just what's in the bank. Don't know yet about investments. They were by no means ever poor. His architect work provided pretty well."

"Anything else?"

"No life insurance. They had it of course, but as you know suicide invalidates most life policies. That probably pissed her off. And now, of course, she's got herself a rich boyfriend too. Some guy who's a world traveler, invented some computer gadget that made him a fortune." Morales checked her notes. "His name is…William. William Gray. They've been together for a few years."

"So, she's got money, he's got money……and yet, I do think Eleanor's murder is at least in part about money."

Cooper rested his chin on his fist and gazed out the windows at the front of the cafe. Some clues seem to bear no relation to one another. Every one in the group seemed to have plenty of money. So why does it still feel like Eleanor was killed because of money? Why…because you can never be too rich? He couldn't get his thoughts off of it.

"I don't know, Izzy. Most people are quick to point out Edgerton. What motive would he have to kill Eleanor? Madeline inherits so he still has to deal with her. Unless he thought she would be easier to manipulate. Or maybe, he is just the squeaky wheel. Gets everyone's attention because he's the loudest." He sighed heavily. "Let's look at the kids like you say, and see if it leads anywhere."

"We have what we need now to bring Van Gessler in," Cooper added. "Let's take care of that later, after we see the twins. Can't wait to get my hands on the guy though."

"It ought to make for an interesting interview," Morales mused. She took a huge bite of her cinnamon roll. "They could've put more icing on these you know," she said with disappointment.

Cooper looked at Morales with a grin. "You know, Izzy? There's an old saying down south and it fits you to a T, especially when it comes to food. 'You'd bitch if you were hung with a new rope'."

Cooper called Phoebe Deardon to get contact information on her twin daughters. She was surprised to hear from the detective, and especially so when she learned that his interest was in the girls.

"Why would you want to speak to my daughters, detective?"

"We are covering all our bases, Mrs. Deardon. We understand that your daughters know Mrs. Highwater's son and possibly David Dean, Madeline's husband. There are a few questions we have to ask."

"I don't know...I'm not sure what they could have to do with anything. Should we be contacting our attorney?"

"Mrs. Deardon, that is certainly your right, ma'am. These are informal questions, trying to understand all the relationships surrounding Eleanor Abbott."

She finally gave the contact information, but asked that he talk to Kassie and Kammie at her house. "I think they would be more comfortable here, if you don't mind."

He agreed to that, thanked her and hung up. He called the cell phone numbers he was given and one at a time made the same appointment with the girls to meet at their mother's house in an hour. He called Phoebe Deardon back and informed her that he and Morales would be there in an hour for the interview.

When Morales and Cooper arrived at the Deardon home, a new Mercedes SUV sat in the drive. The vanity plate read, 'KASSIE'.

They were greeted at the door by Phoebe Deardon. She was subdued and frowning and seemed to have aged since they saw her only a few days before.

In the living room the twins sat side by side on the white sofa, one paging through a Vogue magazine, the other fiddling with a phone. He was startled at their looks. They were identical twins, and they looked so much alike, Cooper could discern no difference between them. Even the makeup they wore looked exactly the same. The detectives showed their identification and introduced themselves.

He knew the girls to be about twenty four, but they looked older. Older and mature in a way he had trouble defining. It wasn't wrinkles or lines. Their grey eyes held no youthful innocence which would have been expected in twenty-four year old kids. The expression that sat upon the faces of each was bored indifference. He wondered how people so young could be either.

Slender to the point of emaciation, they had lank blond hair, each one bleached in the exact same way, and (what else?) tanned skin. They wore skin tight jeans and tee shirts which emphasized two sets of breasts that had been vigorously enhanced.

"Thank you for seeing us. Who is Kassie?" One raised her hand.

The other, apparently Kammie said: "Kammie," and gave a limp wave.

"Okay, we just have a few questions for you, shouldn't take much time. Where were you girls the night that Mrs. Abbott was killed?"

There was a sharp intake of breath. One of them, Cooper thought Kassie, said "We were here with Mom, watching a movie that night."

Phoebe Deardon interjected. "I believe I told you that, detective."

"The questions are for your daughters, Mrs. Deardon," Morales said. Phoebe Deardon threw Morales an irritated glance.

Cooper looked down at his note pad thoughtfully. He scribbled some nonsense words. "Okay, good. Now, how well do y'all know Ben Highwater?"

Since he couldn't tell one from the other he just listened. With a giggle, one finally responded, "We know Ben. He's our friend."

"Do either of you, you know, date Ben? Like a girlfriend?" Morales asked.

The girls exchanged rather nasty smirks. One said, "No one 'dates' anymore, detective. We go out. Everyone just, like, goes out. Together."

"So, neither of you are 'with' Ben?"

"Like we said. We just go out."

"Where?" Morales asked.

"We go to movies, shopping, clubs, you know, like, just hang out."

Morales made a show of flipping her note pad a few pages back. "Do you girls know David Dean?"

Their faces froze. Several seconds went by. Morales said, "Did you hear me? Do you know David Dean?"

Partially recovered, one of the girls finally spoke, "We know him, but that's about it." Their expressions were both visibly concerned.

"Is he with you when you all 'like, hang out'?" Morales asked.

They looked at each other again. Cooper decided they needed a bit of a push.

"Do you girls know what the penalty is for obstruction of justice?"

Before either girl could answer Phoebe Deardon stood up quickly. "Alright. That's it. That's enough. If you want to ask more questions, detectives, you will have to wait until we have our attorney's council."

"That's perfectly fine, Mrs. Deardon. We'll be in touch for another interview at a later date. We'll see ourselves out."

* * *

Frank Van Gessler arrived mid day for an interview at the station. He was accompanied by his attorney. The interview was recorded.

Cooper started the interview by reading Frank Van Gessler his Miranda rights.

"Why do you need to read me my rights?" Van Gessler asked.

"That's so anything said in this interview can be used later if it should become necessary," Cooper responded calmly.

Van Gessler went pale beneath the tanned face. He glanced at his nattily dressed attorney, who simply nodded at him. Cooper began.

"Mr. Van Gessler, where were you yesterday morning at approximately nine a.m.?"

"Yesterday morning?" he asked with a confused frown. "Well, it was Tuesday? I was at home, I believe, until just before lunch. Why?"

"Can someone corroborate that?"

"Of course my wife can, detective. What's this about?"

If that was true, it cleared him for the attack on Ian Andrews. Cooper didn't answer him, but instead rapidly changed tack.

"Mr. Van Gessler, you told Detective Morales and me on a previous visit to your home, that you are an investment banker. Is that correct?"

Van Gessler nodded, his expression relaxed somewhat, as if he felt like he was on more solid ground. "Yes, that's correct."

"And you have been the Abbott's investment adviser for a number of years as well?"

"I have been, yes. Since about 1995. I got their account and was very pleased to be of service to them. We became personal friends also."

"What changes took place when Clay Abbott died?"

"Changes?" Van Gessler looked puzzled. "What do you mean?"

Cooper wondered if Van Gessler was really dense or trying to obfuscate. "I mean how did your relationship with Mrs. Abbott change?"

"It didn't really. I continued to work for her investing her more liquid assets."

"She put a limit on you, didn't she? An amount beyond which you were not allowed to go without prior approval?"

Van Gessler's face flushed. He was silent.

"The records would indicate that she didn't have complete faith or trust in you by stipulating such…limits," Cooper said.

His attorney leaned in and whispered to him. Van Gessler finally said, "There was a change to my handling of her accounts. I believe it was simply a reaction to the loss of her husband. She was in mourning, and I believed that his death served to make her feel that she was losing control of her life." Van Gessler nodded as if to himself. "I don't think that behavior like that is all that uncommon." He sipped from a cup of water.

Cooper stood and paced a few moments, hands on hips.

Morales cleared her throat and spoke. "Mr. Van Gessler, you explained that you and your wife Kathryn, built your home last year in the Village of Greenhills subdivision, a gated community. Is that correct?"

"Yes, we did."

"And how much was spent on the construction of your home?"

"As I said to you both before, I don't know the actual figure. I guess around four million," he said testily.

Cooper sat back down. He looked Van Gessler in the eye. "I believe that we can produce documents that would show that figure to be quite low. What is your annual income, sir?"

Van Gessler shifted in his seat and looked at his attorney. The attorney whispered again.

"I don't know exactly. Due to the nature of the work, it varies. About $200,000.00., not including the income my wife earns." The response was barely audible.

"Who holds the mortgage on your house, Mr. Van Gessler?" Morales asked.

"My what?" Van Gessler looked at Morales with a frown. "My mortgage?"

Morales sat calmly with her head cocked slightly, frowning at Van Gessler. "Yes, sir. The mortgage on your new home."

Van Gessler glanced over at his attorney. The attorney leaned next to him again and whispered.

Cooper plowed ahead. "Perhaps you can explain why you have been receiving lump sum deposits into your personal accounts as many as three to five times times a year for the last few years, each in the neighborhood of a half million dollars?"

Finally the attorney spoke. "I'm going to advise my client not to answer that question, sir."

"We have this documented, forensically. Unless Mr. Van Gessler can give us an accounting as to where those funds originated, legitimately, and that they did not come from skimming from the Abbott's accounts, then I'm afraid he's going to be charged with embezzlement." Cooper replied.

Morales continued with another question.

"Do you know Diane Kenyon?"

Van Gessler's eyes became unfocused, his face took on a distant look, one that settled into resignation. He was ghostly pale. He swallowed.

"I knew of her."

"What exactly does that mean, Mr. Van Gessler? Do you know Diane Kenyon personally?"

"I wouldn't say I knew her personally. I knew her because she worked for Eleanor. We have spoken to each other on several occasions."

"Knew? Worked?" As in past tense? Why is that Mr. Van Gessler?" Cooper asked.

"Well, I...I don't..."

"Can you explain why your personal cell phone number was found in her cell phone? Can you explain why more than three dozen calls transpired between your cell number and hers in the last thirty days? The most recent of which took place Monday morning, about an hour before her body was discovered stabbed to death at her apartment?"

Frank Van Gessler didn't respond. Morales asked another question. "Where were you Monday morning, and can anyone vouch for your whereabouts?"

His attorney leaned in and whispered to Van Gessler. Van Gessler did not answer, but put his head in his hands and wept.

* * *

With a new lightness in her step Madeline headed to Pacific Northwest Design. When she pushed open the office door Nadine sprang from her chair and hugged her fiercely, not wanting to let go.

"Oh, Maddie," she whispered into her friend's ear with the hug, "I'm so glad to see you! I'm so sorry for everything. Please forgive me."

Madeline gently disengaged from Nadine with a laugh. "It's okay, Nadine. It's okay." She held her friend at arm's length and looked into her eyes. "I just want you and Jamal to be safe. The rest...well, don't think a thing of it. We'll talk about it later. Did you call everyone in for the meeting?"

"Yes. They're all due here in..." Nadine glanced at her watch, "about forty minutes."

"Good. I'm going into my office to check my desk and return calls. Let me know when everyone's here."

Madeline sifted through the calls and returned the critical ones and put the rest back in the pile. It almost felt like an ordinary day at the office. She'd only been gone for a few days, but so much had happened, it might as well have been a month.

She waffled back and forth about confronting David. The idea was terrifying. Avoiding him solved nothing, but Deborah said she didn't have to talk to him at all. It seemed so much like the gutless way, the Madeline way, she berated herself. David wouldn't hurt her, he was just verbally abusive. A walled off part of her mind continued mulling it over while she caught up on work. Finally, she sat back in her chair. She decided she would find the nerve to do it. *I'll try to talk to him, I guess I owe him that much. Try once again to make him understand.* That feeble inner declaration made her feel a bit sick. Madeline glanced at her watch. She didn't have any more time to spend on David right now. Nadine just buzzed. It was time for the meeting.

"I'm back as you can see, sadly only for a short while," Madeline said to the group, the small conference room once again jammed with people. "Thank you all for your kind words about my mother, I really appreciate it." She paused to cough and clear the lump that had risen in her throat. "Timing could not have been worse as far as preparing a bid for the Litchfield job, right?" She looked around at the faces. "But that's life, I guess." Madeline cleared her throat again. "I understand that work has gone on in my absence, which is good, thank you all for that. Charles?"

"Yes, Miz Dean. First I want to let you know that the Stanley floor was finished. Correctly and on time. Mrs. Stanley was happy with everything, so it's a done deal.

"Cally and I met at the estate on Saturday, as planned. Wow, what a place!" He grinned. "There were several subs there. We, and they, got a quite a bit of work done, assessing the damage, trying to get a handle on the scope of it. Cally took a lot of detailed photos and has put them on a thumb drive for you to take a look at when you have time." Cally handed the drive to Madeline.

Charles continued: "She and I managed to get measurements of the main house and a small cottage, a lengthy list of the worst problem areas, but there is quite a bit more to be done before we have an accurate assessment. I've started the project management software and broken it out in all the different trades—electrical, plumbing, roofing and the like." Charles continued the briefing, covering the state of the original tile roof of the house and outbuildings, the failing septic system, need for new plumbing, wiring, insulation. The age old question of whether to trade original windows with high efficiency replacements came up, as well as the serious wasp infestation in a corner of the garage and the issues with the crumbling foundation of the old cottage, originally for the caretaker.

Murmured comments began, but Madeline waved them down. "Hold on, hold on. Thank you, Charles. It sounds like you got quite a lot done. It's going to be a huge project, and we'll need to be sure that all data is entered correctly in the PM software, no mistakes. But I'm eager to get to it. I think that I'll be done in Los Gatos by the end of this weekend. If everyone will pitch in, I'll be back to help with whatever's left by Monday. Everybody? You're to follow Charles' instructions, he is in charge while I'm absent, he will be handing out further assignments. When I get back, I can start the assessment and begin working up the bid. In the meantime I think I'll give the Litchfields a call and let them know we've had a bit of trouble, but that our bid will be in very soon. Are there any other problems I should know about?"

"I think you should go back to Los Gatos and take care of your mother," Charles said gently, the kindness in his voice almost brought Madeline to tears. "We can handle PND. Take all the time you need, Miz Dean. You shouldn't be worrying about this anymore until that's all settled, don't you think?"

Madeline pressed her lips together to keep them from shaking. Looking around, she took a few deep breaths. When she finally had control of her voice she said, "I think I might just have the best damn crew in all of Eugene." With that the tension broke and everyone enjoyed a little subdued laughter.

* * *

He felt he was losing control and was growing tired of the whole thing. They were meeting in a pizza place in the heart of Los Gatos. It was loud and not a single patron took the slightest notice of the group, but they still hunched over the table speaking quietly. Everybody around them was busy eating pizza, drinking beer and playing noisy electronic pin ball machines. It was the middle of the day, and this was a popular lunch spot.

Many of the group were bitching about how long everything was taking. The leader shushed them. "We're doing everything we can to move things along. We had no idea she was going to be so…resistant."

"Yeah, well, I don't like this. Those detectives are doing a lot of poking their noses in places. I think they might be starting to put two and two together."

"That's right," another spoke out. "We thought there would be money before now. What the hell's *going on*, for chrissakes?"

"The detectives won't be putting anything together, trust me. They are looking at Van Gessler from what I hear. The old boy has apparently royally screwed himself." He wanted to laugh. Van Gessler was a pompous social climber who thought way too much of himself. "I know someone inside the police, so I have gotten some info. It has been suggested that it's time for other measures," the leader offered.

"Oh yeah? That bit about Van Gessler—who told you that? Those two detectives are doing way more than that, believe me. Besides. I think David is losing his nerve."

"You shut the fuck up!" David snarled.

"David's done everything we discussed and agreed on, and more. She just isn't budging. She seems to have grown a set of balls."

"Oh, yeah? Okay, what about that Kenyon girl? She was *murdered!* We never talked about that. You didn't say we were going to *kill* her. I thought she was just being used as a way to get info. Killing her just made more police snoop around!"

"Yeah," another protested. "Is that what you mean by other measures. I don't like the sound of that. We can't have any more people dying. I don't want to end up in prison. This was supposed to be a simple thing. Knock off old lady Abbott with a robbery thing, and David would be right there with Madeline to get control of the estate."

"I didn't kill Diane Kenyon, I've told you that!" David said, his voice nasty.

"Yeah, but you were putting it to her, right? You took her to Napa, or did you forget that? And, I heard through the grapevine that she was pregnant!"

"Yeah, well I only just found out she got herself pregnant. That wasn't *my* fault. I was using her to get info, that's all, you asshole. Thanks to me we knew when that old bag, Temple, was going to be there and when she'd be gone, when that stupid mutt *wasn't* going to be there. Lot of thanks I got for that."

"Alright, settle down. Stop your whining and complaining," the leader said. "Look, I don't know what happened with Kenyon. Something's gone wrong there. That doesn't mean the plan doesn't work. I'm talking about taking things in a different direction, if that's what's necessary," he said.

Four pairs of eyes were fastened on him.

They traded looks. David said, "We've already taken too many risks. Madeline was almost shot."

"Look, if it gets us where we all agreed we wanted to be, then...that's what we're doing."

"Yeah, well, I thought we would get the money, you know, right away. I need it, you know? But I didn't know that it might mean, well, hurting people, right?"

"You're getting the money. There's going to be more than just the seventy-five grand. A lot more. You just have to be patient for a while longer. And leave the details up to me. Now, who wants pizza and beer?"

Later, at the Highwater home, they sat down in the dining room to talk.

"Are you certain this is what you want, Helen? We could stop it now. It doesn't have to go any further. If it doesn't, I don't think they will be able to connect us to Eleanor."

She stared at her hands clasped so tightly on the table before her, her knuckles were bloodless. "This is what I want. I've watched that family for years, doing things, going on just as if nothing had happened. I wanted Eleanor to hurt like I hurt. Like my *Ben* has been hurt. I thought I would feel vindicated when your man fixed Clay's car. I would have been happy if he had ended up a cripple and she would have had to tend him the rest of her life. But we were lucky, and he died.

She paused, took a deep breath and continued: "I'm so goddamned angry! I wanted her to feel the never ending pain and loneliness I've felt for so many years. So, no, his death wasn't enough. Her child wasn't a *baby* when she lost her father, like Ben was. She was a grown woman, she was better able to deal with that kind of loss.

"I'm worried about what the detectives may have learned from Ian. He knows. If anyone of this group knows, it's him. If only that plan had gone right. Goddammit. I just want something to go right. Or it's going to be too late."

"I understand, Helen. I do. You've been through hell. Will killing Madeline put an end to your suffering?"

Helen rose and went to the bay window and looked out into late afternoon light. She saw a pair of western stellar jays, flitting around the rose garden area that nestled against the bay.

He studied her from where he sat at the table. She wore a beautiful silk evening dress of sea green, it draped around her body like a sensuous river. An emerald choker decorated her substantial décolletage, and matching earrings glowed regally on her ear lobes in the subdued light. She was the most beautiful woman he'd ever known.

She turned from the window and looked at the ruggedly handsome face of William Gray. "Ben thinks that access to lots of money will make him happy. We have enough money. I don't want her money. He thinks that will give him power. Make up for all that's happened to him." Helen shrugged.

William looked into her face with love. "You know, don't you, that all the money in the world will not make up for what happened to Ben. He is a confused and angry young man. Do you understand that I care about you, and I want to do what I can to help you?"

Helen walked back to the table and took his hand. She held it to her lips and kissed. "I know darling. I know."

"What I really want," she said, "is to be able to know, really know, that Ben's going to get over this. Put the hostility and anger behind him. How can he do it, if *I* can't? I've watched him for the last dozen years, fury building in him about the whole sorry mess. And nothing that I've done has helped. Either of us."

"You know Ben is not the only victim. You are a victim, and you both will remain so until you can let this go. And what about David?" William said, "David is just as mixed up as Ben. He is obsessively focused on Madeline. He says he wants the estate, the money, but I don't know if what he's really talking about is Madeline."

"What will David Dean do with all of that, the Abbott estate?" Helen scoffed. "He's not very smart, you know, not much intellect. Yes, he is completely obsessed with Madeline. I don't know if it came down to it, whether he would choose the money or control over *her*. All he would do with a business like that, is probably drive it into the ground. Oh, hell, I don't know why I'm even thinking about it, it's not my problem. But I'm so worried about Ben. I think this thing is making him crazy. I'm afraid of how it will end. For both of us."

* * *

David Dean lived in a duplex off Barger in West Eugene. It was in a modest neighborhood of well kept homes interspersed with multi family dwellings. When Madeline arrived she saw his car was not in the drive. She knocked on the door anyway. No answer. She retrieved the emergency key she knew was under a potted plant near the door, and without thinking it through, let herself in.

The apartment was a shambles. It had the rotten smell of dirty socks, spoiled food and unwashed dishes. What is it about men? Like frat boys forever, she thought. She tried David's cell, but was sent straight to voice mail.

"I'm here at your place, David. I wanted to talk to you before I have to head back to Los Gatos. Where are you?" She hung up and glanced around the murky, shadowed room. Greasy pizza boxes and leaking Chinese takeout cartons along with empty Heineken and Amstel beer bottles littered the coffee table. Flies the size of hummingbirds, buzzed lazily around the left over food. Dozens of old newspapers sat in haphazard stacks on nearly every surface.

Madeline ventured down the hallway and stopped at the door to the bathroom. She flipped on the light and grimaced at the filth.

David had never been a housekeeper, never shared the duties when they still lived together. Somehow by tacit agreement, those tasks were relegated to Madeline. If they had not been, their bathroom would have looked like this one. She turned off the light.

She passed one bedroom that David euphemistically described as his office. It was primarily a dumping ground for anything he didn't know what else to do with. In the corner a bicycle had clothing hanging from the handle bars, a couple of broken down chairs, stacks of porn magazines and boxes still packed and sealed from when he moved in.

She continued to the master bed room. The curtains were drawn and the room was in darkness. She walked across to the window and pulled the curtains apart, allowing light to spill into the room. This room, like the others, looked like it had not been cleaned in months. Clothes were piled everywhere, and the room was suffocating. The closed up, dirty clothes and dirty sheets stench (she didn't want to dwell on *that*) almost took her breath away. She wondered who did his laundry. He certainly didn't, and the way it smelled indicated it hadn't been done in ages. Madeline cracked open the sliding window. Clean, rain moistened air flowed in, and she gratefully took a few deep breaths.

She turned back to the room and noticed the sliding closet door partially ajar. Idly, she pushed it fully open. On the top shelf Madeline spied a box stuffed under a sweatshirt. She pulled it out. It was a old dented metal container that advertised it had once held Christmas butter cookies. Inside was a large bag of weed, rolling papers, a roach clip, a bag of pills and another bag of something she thought was probably cocaine. Meth? Heroin? Madeline has so little experience with drugs she had no way to know. There were even a few small disposable syringes. With a shake of her head, she stuffed the box back where she had found it. I should just call the cops. Wouldn't that serve him right? Her eyes traveled down.

A few shirts hung sloppily on bent metal hangers. Jesus, has he always been such an utter slob? As she had done on numerous occasions in the past year, she wondered again what had ever appealed to her about David. They were so completely different. Even at thirty-one, he seemed so immature. He appeared incapable of conducting his life like an adult. Then there was the abysmal way he treated her. Controlling, manipulating. Because they met when he was in school, still with a bit of external direction, perhaps he had seemed different, maybe even *been* different? Madeline hadn't been able to see the truth of his character, maybe he was just successful at hiding it from her.

One pair of slacks was pushed to the left side next to a ratty sport coat. Her gaze wandered down to the floor. A couple pair of grimy and worn denims lay crumpled next to (but not in) an open clothes hamper. There was also a mixed heap of shoes, a half dozen pairs of expensive sneakers and several pairs of boots. You can't live in the pacific northwest without hiking boots, but four, five pairs?

On the floor at the very back, something caught her eye. She bent over and peered into the shadowed recess of the closet. Leaning against the back wall was what looked like a rectangle of old wood. Something pricked at her brain. There was something familiar about the size and shape. She reached in to grasp the object. As she pulled it out away from the wall it fell backwards into her hands. Horrified, Madeline held the missing Cassatt painting.

* * *

She stumbled out of the house, locked the door behind her and nearly fell in a hurried attempt to return the key to its place under the pot. The minute she was in her car, she pulled out her cell phone and called Cooper. She related what she'd seen, in a jumbled, frantic explosion of words.

"Hold on, Madeline, hold on! It's okay, calm down. You're certain it is the missing painting?" Cooper asked.

"Of course I'm sure!" She cried, her breath coming in heaving gasps.

"And you put it back? Just as it was?"

More erratic, gasping breaths. She thought briefly about what she had actually done and said, "Yes, yes. I put it right back."

"Okay, calm down, and listen to me. You have to get out of there now. Don't wait, just go. Call me after you're somewhere safe and we'll talk."

Madeline drove, too fast, weaving wildly in and out of traffic on the Beltline toward Delta Highway and on to her house. Her mind raced with the knowledge that David had the missing painting. How was it possible? Why? *He's* mixed up in this? He killed my mother?!

Just as she pulled into her driveway, her cell phone rang. It was David. Petrified, Madeline stared at the ringing phone lying on the seat next to her as if by even touching it David would be able to get to her. She let it go to voicemail and once inside her house, she locked herself in.

She ran directly to the kitchen and poured a large glass of wine. She stood at the counter looking out the window at her backyard. Madeline was suddenly overwhelmed by the bizarreness, the strangeness, of what was happening in her life. In a short week, her life was turned upside down by things she didn't understand, that seemed to have no basis in reality. Unbelievable, horrific things. And yet, look out there, she thought. Today was a completely normal day in beautiful Eugene, Oregon. A day just like any other. It was lovely outside, the weather was perfect. The air clean and fresh from a rain squall that had passed through just a couple of hours before. Normal ordinary people were outside, going about their lives, driving to the market, going to work, running errands. Everything that we see every day and never stop to consider, really *think* about. How quickly and senselessly it can change.

Madeline saw her retired next door neighbor, Clete, calmly puttering about getting tools, wood and supplies together, apparently to make repairs to the fence that ran between their two properties. His wife, Virginia, sat in a patio chair, reading in the shade of their apple tree. Lovely people. Great neighbors. And there……sweet and delicate hummingbirds, enjoying her plastic feeder, just like this was any normal day.

Zombie like, she walked back to the living room and sank into her arm chair, staring at the cell phone in her hand. She took two large swallows of Cabernet and when it sank like a warm blanket through her chest, tears filled her eyes. She looked down at the phone in her hand and watched it as it weirdly wobbled and swam. Finally, a ragged cry broke from her throat, and tears coursed down her face.

"I don't know what to do," Madeline said to Cooper a short time later. She struggled not to weep again.

"I think you should just come back down here. We've arrested Van Gessler so far. Murder and embezzlement. We'll figure out the rest soon."

"But…what about the painting?"

"I don't know, Madeline. David is obviously mixed up in it somehow. There's gotta be a connection between them. Do they know each other?"

"David and Van Gessler? Oh, I don't think so, or maybe superficially. I mean, I'm sure they've met at family functions, parties, things like that over the years," Madeline said.

"Izzy and I are going to push on. Things are coming together finally. Avoid David. We don't know how he fits in, but he does somehow *and* I believe he's unstable. I don't want him to know you've seen that painting."

"You'll get no argument from me. The only reason I was there was to talk him into signing the damn papers. My attorney is going to file a default. I thought he should know."

"Just stay away from him. God, I feel helpless with you so far—uh." Cooper stopped abruptly. "Anyway, when will you be coming back?"

Madeline caught what Cooper had said. Unsure, couldn't speak. "Madeline?"

She spoke in a rush, the first thing she could think of. "I'll get a flight back tomorrow. I've taken care of things at work for the time being. I thought I'd be settling stuff with David, but I guess not… Anyway, I'll see you when I get back." She hung up without saying goodbye.

Cooper stared at the phone and cursed his stupidity. "Izzy always tells me that my mouth will get me in trouble, and she's right," he muttered.

Changing out dirty clothes for clean ones and packing them in her suitcase, Madeline prepared for her return to Raven's Nest. She added a couple pairs of blue jeans and some tops and a sweatshirt, stuffing them mindlessly into her suitcase. *I could have done all this by phone*, she thought as she selected her outfit for the funeral. She chose a navy blue sheath dress with a short jacket and leather pumps. She arranged them in her garment bag and added a small clutch bag.

*The trip was a waste of time. What if I had found David at home, with what I know now…*the prospect chilled her to the bone. The sound of a gunshot from outside made her leap for the corner of the room and cower. Several seconds went by and she ran to the kitchen. Madeline saw Clete using an air compressor and nail gun to attach boards to the fence. Another explosive noise echoed as he shot another nail into the fence. He glanced up just at that time and saw her through the window. He waved gaily and smiled. With herculean effort, Madeline returned the smile and waved back. Just another day. She turned around, inhaled mightily then exhaled and slumped against the counter.

I've got to calm down, or I'm going to jump out of my skin. *CRACK!* came the next nail shot. Her head jerked.

Madeline called the airline and booked a flight for the next day. The rest of the next two hours she listened to the gunshot sounds from next door, flinching at each one. Later in the evening she stayed in her bedroom with the lights off, blinds closed, every door and window locked. She tried to read with a small book light but concentrating was impossible. Every noise, every creak or car door slam made her heart race.

* * *

Morales' home phone rang at nine-thirty. Cooper had tried her cell, but it was off. Izzy and Alana rarely answered the land line at night, but they did always check caller ID. Alana paused the television.

Morales answered. "Hey, Scotty, why are you calling me so late, *amigo?*"

"Izzy, I gotta tell you this, it couldn't wait until tomorrow. You won't fucking believe it." Cooper said.

"Yeah? Well Alana and I happen to be busy. We're binge watching Law and Order on Netflix. That's as close as I can get to talking with her about crime," she said laughing. "We're also stuffing our faces with popcorn. You know how women are. What's going on?"

"Sorry to interrupt. Tell Alana I'm sorry. I got a call from Madeline. You know she went up to Eugene and all the shit she's having with the ex—getting him to sign the papers, right? Well, I guess she stopped by his apartment to try to talk to him. He wasn't there so she let herself in."

Morales, puzzled by the story, gave Cooper a tentative "Yeaahh? So the first question I'd ask is why, why let herself in—"

"Wait, Izzy, listen! When she was in his apartment, looking around I guess, she found the missing painting in a closet."

"She *what!?*" Morales exclaimed. She looked at Alana, shrugged and held up her hand as if saying, 'what the hell?'. "She found the goddamn painting in the ex-husband's apartment?"

Alana turned from the television and watched Izzy, trying to interpret what was going on from the one sided conversation.

"I know, I couldn't believe it either. But she did find it there. Somehow this puts Dean smack dab in the middle of things. The break-in, the murder? I don't know. Van Gessler's swearing he had nothing to do with the Abbott murder. Madeline doesn't think Dean and Van Gessler knew each other well at all, but they must be linked.

"Jesus, I can't believe this. How did she take it?" Morales asked.

"Well hell, she was scared, she bolted and called me. She said she was going to come straight back in the morning."

"*Are* we looking at two unconnected crimes? Van Gessler not connected to Eleanor's murder at all seems……improbable. But, still, who is it that had a beef with Eleanor enough to kill her? Maybe he figured Eleanor was onto him. Plus, listening to all these so called 'friends' talk about her like she was a saint. Obviously *somebody's* lying." Morales said.

"Something we've heard or seen in the last couple days is the key to this. I just haven't been able to dredge it up."

"Okay then, let's sit down and go over the notes of each interview, one at a time. That should bring whatever it is back to you."

"Coffee before we go in tomorrow?"

"Yeah. Diallo's. Seven-thirty." Morales decided at that moment she would do what ever it took to beat him there tomorrow.

"Okay, tell Alana I'm sorry, and I owe her."

"Oh, I'll tell her, *amigo*." Morales snickered.

CHAPTER TEN
Thursday

"Scotty, what in the hell is going on with this case? Van Gessler—and Diane Kenyon—do we really think it's not connected to Eleanor Abbott? He was embezzling. He would certainly have motive if she found out about the it through Diane. And now Madeline's soon to be ex-husband has the missing painting in his apartment? That's pretty unbelievable."

Cooper sipped his latté and considered Izzy's question. "One thing I find interesting on that subject, before we go on to the murder is, I don't know how, but Eleanor *must* have found out about the embezzling recently. Hence the $1.00 bequest. Had she not been murdered, she would have undoubtedly commenced legal action. Surely she would have since she knew she was dying of cancer.

"If Van Gessler found out that she knew, it's possible he could've killed Eleanor, but I tend to believe him when he said he had nothing to do with it. I would be interested to know how she found out. It probably has nothing to do with anything, but I'd still like to know. I think someone else did the murder and took the problem right out of Van Gessler's lap. He was no doubt breathing a sigh of relief.

"But he did have to put a stop to the blackmail. He thought that he could get away with it, that with Diane dead no one would put them together. If he had found her cell phone he might have succeeded. He thought, wrongly, that the embezzlement wouldn't be discovered."

They drank their coffees, thinking.

"So," Morales finally said, "let's look at the interviews we've done and figure out what it is we're missing."

"We've talked to everyone who's close to her. It was murder, and murder isn't done for no reason. And the only person or persons who could conceivably have any reason to harm her is…?" Morales paused and sipped her coffee and looked through her notes. She said, "We've got the bad blood between Eleanor and Edgerton, and Eleanor and Highwater at some point."

"I don't think the thing between Eleanor and Edgerton has anything to do with this, Izzy. The more I learn about her the more I think it's unlikely. Eleanor was a strong woman. She wouldn't have been intimidated by a guy like Edgerton. He may have been a pain in the ass to her, but I don't think she was afraid of him. No, I think that it's possible that what happened to Eleanor and Helen all those years ago has raised its ugly head…again."

"But, *why*. Why wait twelve years to get revenge for an affair?" Morales shook her head. "I don't know…."

Cooper was quietly thinking. He sipped his coffee. "Don't forget, for six of those years, Greg was still alive. They were 'working' on their marriage. Helping Ben recover from the upset to the family. It was after Greg's suicide, that was the turning point. I think that was when the Highwater family reached a point of no return."

"So in the last what, twelve years, after the suicide, the boy has been growing up, but not getting better, in spite of all the therapy and devotion of his mother?"

"Maybe Ben has gotten to an age where he believes that he can finally do something about those events. And, I think he's a very, very angry young man."

Morales said slowly, "The problem Madeline's having with David. What does that have to do with Ben? It has to have *something* to do with it--he has the painting! That alone proves he was somehow in on the murder. God, I hope that's not true, for Madeline's sake."

"He doesn't have the balls to commit murder, Izzy. I'd bet on it. I've been around him. I've heard Madeline talk about him. He's a bully, a verbal bully. He talks big, but murder is another thing altogether. So, he has the painting. There's something we don't know yet, that will make it make sense."

"Maybe he talked the Highwater kid into stealing the painting? Maybe it wasn't taken the night of the murder. Maybe Mrs. Abbott took it down and planned to sell it. But that's not logical. And, she sure as hell didn't need the money," Morales said.

They sat drinking their coffees when suddenly Morales looked up at Cooper. "Hey, maybe Eleanor planned to give it to David Dean as an incentive to agree to the divorce." Even Morales thought that was a pretty absurd notion.

Detective Cooper leaned back in his chair, coffee in hand. Absently took a bite of his cinnamon roll. He finally sighed and shook his head. "No. I don't think she would have sold it and certainly not without mentioning it to Madeline. They way Madeline talks about the painting it is unlikely they'd ever sell it, and the way she felt about Dean, I think Eleanor Abbott would have cut off her own hand before she would have given the guy anything, especially something that valuable."

* * *

Madeline breathed a sigh of relief when she boarded her flight to San Jose. As much as she disliked flying it allayed her fears a little to be on the plane, in a place she knew David could not reach her. She had risen early and got ready as quickly as she could, doing the minimum to be presentable. She was too frightened to listen to the voicemail from David, even holding the cell phone and looking at the notice of a voicemail from him made Madeline feel strangely vulnerable. She couldn't shake the feeling that he was watching her. Once dressed, she prowled about the house for an hour carefully peeking out the curtains of one window and then another. Finally she decided that she'd feel safer if she left the house even though her flight wasn't scheduled to leave for three hours. When she was ready to go she peered out the window for signs of David—or even any of his friends—before sprinting to her car.

Madeline drove to a nearby city park after picking up a large mocha. As she drank her coffee, true to form, she couldn't help dwelling on the mess her life had become. The minute she stopped moving or wasn't engaged with some kind of busy-ness, the mounting problems spun ceaselessly through her mind.

The now certain knowledge that David was involved in some way, brought on intense feelings of rage. Although it did serve to reconfirm the rightness of her decision. If she had even the slightest doubt about moving on with the divorce this latest turn of events dispelled it. Who would be involved in something so heinous against someone they professed to love? Anger was like a palpable, molten ball in her stomach. Her shoulders ached with tension and stiffness. She could almost feel the weight of her unhappiness physically pushing down on them. No matter which way she looked at recent events they made little sense. Instead they served to make her feel stupid and helpless. After having slept so fitfully the night before she eventually dozed, sitting in the car with her head against the window glass.

The sound of a child's scream of glee startled her awake. Two little girls, maybe four and five years old, were racing across the grass heading for a play place jungle gym and a set of swings, their mother pushing a stroller behind them. Madeline heard the young mother call out the universal cry for them to be careful.

Madeline looked at the young mother. She was city chic in L.L.Bean fleece and spandex jogging pants. Well put together and just frazzled enough to make her motherhood look real. She sat near the play area, keeping a watchful eye on the girls and talking to the baby in the stroller. That kind of life is so far from mine as to be unimaginable, she thought.

Madeline's eyes then looked on the children. Beautiful, healthy and energetic. She felt a stab of overwhelming envy. They looked so free. They were so young, innocent, so joyous. How long has it been since I've felt that way? The girls played together, chasing each other up and down the slide, through the small playhouse, across the tiny suspension bridge. They played without stopping— —falling, getting up and running again. They screamed with joy. Tears welled in Madeline's eyes at their unbridled happiness. She brushed them away impatiently.

A glance at her watch told her it was time to head to the airport. As she drove, her eyes nervously jittered from the road to the rear view mirror, but the trip was uneventful.

Once seated and buckled in, she still carefully watched each person as they boarded the small plane. When the staff came by to take drink orders she asked for two of the small bottles of red wine. All they had was white Zinfandel, her least favorite. White Zinfandel? It's a contradiction in terms! With reluctance, she took the two bottles and nursed them throughout the flight. She tried to make them last till the end and the gut wrenching, fast spiral pilots on this flight use to land at the San Jose airport. She really hated flying.

Madeline arrived at Raven's Nest after four-thirty driving another rental car. She supposed she could have had Detective Cooper pick her up, but after the last phone call and the implications of the end of their conversation she felt it was not a wise idea. Madeline needed time to think.

She was tired and grubby, and wryly thought to herself that it seemed to be an exact replay of last Saturday. *I feel like I'm in the Groundhog Day movie.* This time though, there was no bloody stains in the library, and Mrs. Temple was here with Pancho. With a huge sigh, she noticed a real wellspring of happiness the minute she walked in the door. She adored her home and enjoyed a feeling of peace that came over her. All the upheaval and tragedy aside she was still so glad to be home.

Mrs. T and Pancho greeted her as though she'd been gone a week instead of just a little more than a day.

"Oh Maddie, I'm so glad you're back!" Mrs. Temple beamed. "What do you want for supper? I got a nice big piece of fresh caught salmon at the market that I should use today or free-eeze?" Her comment ended on a tantalizing up note.

"Mrs. T, that sounds delicious, it really does, but you needn't worry with it. I'm not going to be hungry for a while yet. Why don't you go ahead and quit for today? I can just pop it in the oven later when I'm ready."

"Alright dear, if you wish," she said, patting Madeline's arm. "That lady detective called me this morning and asked me questions about Mr. Dean, about that Kenyon woman, oh I don't know what all," she grumbled. "I don't know what's going on, but I sure wish they'd get the whole thing settled, if you know what I mean."

Madeline nodded. "I know, Mrs. T. Maybe they're making some progress on the case. Perhaps it will be over soon." She didn't mention to Mrs. Temple the part David apparently played in it. How could she explain it to her when Madeline herself couldn't understand it? Just bringing those thoughts to the front of her mind succeeded in dampening her once happy mood.

Mrs. Temple gathered her belongings and said goodbye, and with a pat on Pancho's head, left through the kitchen door. Madeline immediately locked the door behind her.

* * *

In the library she sat with a glass of Merlot in the wing back chair opposite her mother's chair. The chair in which her mother died, was returned from the upholsterer sometime while she was gone, and the fabric had been replaced. It almost looked like nothing had happened. As she sat with her glass of wine she thought of the wine on the plane and couldn't help but smile. I've become a bit of a wine snob, I suppose. Never cared all that much for white wines, most of them just too sweet. Nothing wrong with having a preference, is there? White Zinfandel just wasn't her…cup of tea. But, at least it helped crutch her through the flight and landing. She smiled again.

Madeline sat and enjoyed the wine while bright afternoon sun streamed in. The sun caused brilliant colors and rainbows from the stained and leaded glass in the windows to play across the furniture and rugs. It was mesmerizing and delightful. Madeline relaxed back in the chair and rested her head against the wing, idly watching the play of light while running scenarios through her mind about the murder. Pancho was curled on her feet asleep.

As her mind pondered her unthinkable situation, Madeline's gaze browsed around the beautiful room, resting here, then there, mostly unseeing. Finally her mind registered something odd on the area of paneling where the Cassatt painting had hung. It took a few seconds for it to sink in. She was seeing a dark line, perhaps an extra shadow? The afternoon light struck the paneling at just the angle to create a shadow, but she saw *another* line, inside the narrow one made by the batten. One she had never noticed before, probably because the painting itself was what you were drawn to look at. She squinted across the room to the wall behind her mother's desk. Must be just a weird double shadow. She shrugged and sipped her wine. She continued to peer at the line across the room. She blinked and squinted again. Too far away to see it well, she set down the wine and went to study it more closely.

At the wall behind the desk she peered at the mahogany paneling. The wire that had suspended the Cassatt from the picture moulding above the paneled wall was still hanging against the wood. Now she could see a very narrow space between the panels and the battens or frames. It encompassed two entire square panels. It was not more than a thirty-second of an inch, the width of a pencil line. How had she never noticed this before? Naturally when the painting hung there, it was all you could look at.

Madeline tentatively touched the side by side panels. They felt solid, but now she could clearly see the tiny gap in the wood. It was not solid. She ran her fingertips along the frames. Nothing. She moved her fingers onto to the panels themselves, running from corner to corner. She tried putting pressure on the wood. When her fingers met the lower outside corners of each of the two square panels, she heard a soft click and the panel came ajar, just like the cubby under her mother's desk. She lifted and the two panels rose smoothly and quietly as one, until, above her head, they were perpendicular to the wall.

Madeline stood frozen, gaping at what was before her. Pancho came and stood beside her, looking up to see what was in the wall. Behind the opening in the library paneling was a rectangular space approximately sixteen inches tall by thirty-two inches wide. The size of the two mahogany panels. The bottom edge was just about her shoulder level. She stood five foot ten. Her mother, only five-three. She would have had to use a stool to access this cubby. She was rooted to the spot, staring at more than thirty leather volumes. She knew, without picking one up, that she had found her mother's diaries.

With a trembling hand she chose the last one in the line. It leaned toward the other volumes to hold them in place. Just like the one she had found in the desk cubby, it too was smooth, expensive leather, inscribed in gilt, "Eleanor Abbott". She looked at the inside page. "January 1- December 31." Madeline fanned the pages and saw that many entries had been made throughout the year. The book was quite full, each entry written in the same neat script and with Eleanor's preferred fountain pen.

Hot tears began stinging her lids, and she felt a physical ache in her heart yet she wasn't sure why. Perhaps in finding the diaries it was as if she had found her mother, with their complicated relationship, their unsaid goodbye. She clasped the diary to her chest and walked aimlessly about the room Pancho steadfastly at her side. She circled the entire library ending up in front of the hidden space. She stared into the space again. Pancho, unsure what was happening, looked up too. She counted the volumes. Forty-two. Madeline and Pancho walked on. Finally she stopped at the chair where she had been sitting and picked up her glass of wine. With two swallows, the rest of it was gone. She poured another glass. She sat back down in the chair and drank that glass, poured the next, which finished the bottle. Pancho sat erect at her feet. He stared sadly, blinking, feeling her upset. His eyes liquid and nearly crying, tried to understand. Finally he curled up on her feet.

It grew dark. In her pocket, her cell phone rang. She made no move to answer it. She opened a second bottle of wine and began again. She sat in the same chair with her mother's diary clutched to her chest, occasionally looking at the hidden cubby that still stood open. Forty-two volumes. Oh, no, wait. Forty-three with the one currently held firmly to her chest. She drank.

Eventually Pancho decided it had to be supper time. His stomach was growling, but he worried about leaving her alone. He moved off toward the kitchen to check out his bowl. Surely the grey haired lady would have filled it?

At six-thirty Pancho padded back to the library. He sat at attention at her feet, wanting to help. He blinked his eyes, sighed and snuffled. Madeline's cell phone rang again. She pulled it from her pocket and looked at it through bleary eyes. Detective Cooper. One other missed call. Why talk to him? He will only tell me something has gone wrong, or some other disastrous thing has happened. "You know Panch, there must be a comet hursling toward ush. Or, maybe, theresa zombie apocalisp starting." Madeline, her lips ever-so-slightly numb, giggled and shook her head slowly from side to side. Befuddled with wine and sorrow, she hadn't the capacity to think clearly and didn't want to. As the call went to voicemail, she rose unsteadily and went upstairs to her room, to wash her face and take a scalding shower. Pancho stuck by her side.

* * *

Cooper rang Madeline a second time and when he still didn't get an answer, left a voicemail. "Madeline, it's me, Scott. I'm calling to see if you've gotten back home okay. Please call me if you have time."

He was puzzled because she had assured him she would call them as soon as she got into Los Gatos. He called Morales on her cell.

"Izzy, have you heard from Madeline?"

"No, why?"

"Where are you?"

"I just got home. It's almost six-thirty, you know. We *are* supposed to have a life. We're cooking. I'm making chili rellenos and Alana is making Mexican rice with cilantro sour cream sauce. Hey, why don't you come over and have dinner with us, we're making more than enough."

"Thanks, Izzy. It sounds great, but I probably shouldn't. I can't seem to get a hold of Madeline, and she promised to call us when she got in. Her flight was due in by three, I think. It's six-thirty and she must be back. I've called twice, but she never picked up and hasn't called back. Maybe I'll run out there, just to check things out."

"*Amigo*......" Morales said in a soft chiding voice. Cooper heard Morales take a drink of something. "You're worrying too much, dontcha think? She'll call you. Give her some time. Maybe she just needs time to, I don't know, think things over."

"I'm worried for her to be there on her own."

"She has new locks, Scotty, remember? Pancho's probably with her. You know, why don't you ask whoever's on rota to drive out and take a look?"

"Maybe you're right." Cooper paused and thought. "Yeah, Izzy, you're right. Of course you're right. I think your old buddy Willis is on tonight. That'll really frost his balls," he said laughing.

"Don't you know it? It'd piss him off royally. And all the while, we'll be here, having good food, laughing our asses off, while he's driving the streets." Izzy was snickering.

"Okay, Maybe I will come over. You sure it's okay with Alana?"

Cooper heard Izzy call out to Alana, "Alana, honey, what do you think about Scotty coming over for dinner?"

He heard the reply faintly but adamantly, "If he doesn't get his ass over here, right now, he's gonna be sorry!"

"Okay, okay, fine." Cooper said. "What should I bring?"

"Just your handsome self and you'd better be hungry. I'm making guacamolé too. If you want something to drink other than Negra Modelo, you better bring it, 'cause we ain't serving lemonade," she said with a laugh.

Pancho escorted Madeline to her room. She dropped the diary on the bed and toppled over next to it. So much for washing my face and taking a shower... She was asleep in seconds.

Cooper thought it over and decided he was being paranoid not to mention over protective. It will only make her angry if I show up there carrying on because she didn't call me. She's probably just tired. I'm acting like a juvenile. Izzy's right.

The problem with all this rationale was that it masked the real feelings behind his worry. Copper knew that he had—what was it Izzy said—gotten 'stuck' on Madeline. He wasn't sure how it had happened so quickly, but he knew it was true. And he truly feared she was in some kind of danger.

He called Willis.

"You're on tonight, Willis, right?"

Cooper heard a three second belch. Then, "Yeah, that's right, why?"

Cooper could see him in his mind's eye. Willis, sitting with his gut wedged behind his cruiser's steering wheel, stuffing his pie hole with a greasy burger or a dozen doughnuts. Not a pleasant vision.

"Okay, I want you to take a drive up to Raven's Nest once you're on. Just drive by, check on the place, make sure everything's quiet."

There was silence on the end of the line. "Willis?"

"Yeah, I'm here. Sure, okay, I'll go." Another belch.

Sweet Jesus. "Okay, you've got my cell number. Call me if you see anything."

He made it to Izzy and Alana's a little after seven and brought his appetite as requested. Cooper thought it was high time for a little relaxation. He and Izzy had been working long hours, days straight with no time off. Well it was time now. Izzy was a great cook and had the entire spread ready when he got there. The place smelled tantalizing.

He greeted Alana with a hug and a kiss on each cheek. "How are you, Alana?" he looked into her grey-blue eyes.

"I'm good, Scotty, good. Worried about Izzy, as usual."

"Don't get her started, please. She spends too much time on that subject as it is," Izzy chimed in from the stove.

Cooper helped set the table which brought on a chuckle. He'd spent an awful lot of time lately putting dishes and silverware on tables. Alana put a small vase full of daisies on the table. She put out fresh, cold Negra Modelos at all three places.

The pair lived in a Spanish/Mediterranean style duplex that Izzy bought after making detective. It had been built in the 1930s and had nice terracotta tile floors, stucco walls and cool arched windows. They had really done a good job fixing it up. They had a retired lady renting the next door unit which helped pay the mortgage as well as gave them a reliable watcher if they were gone.

The three sat in the kitchen around a small round table and Izzy began dishing up chili rellenos and rice, guacamolé with chips. Cooper popped the lid on his beer and dug in. Spicy, cheesy, incredible. The guacamole' was fresh and perfectly seasoned. Just enough garlic and onion. Just enough lemon. He was in hog heaven.

"Shit, forget this detective thing, Izzy, y'all should open a food place," Cooper said sincerely with his mouth full of guacamolé.

She blushed. "Oh, stop it, for cryin' out loud." But she looked pleased.

They talked and bantered, joking easily with each other. Scotty asked Alana how her job was going. She was a nurse at the Los Gatos hospital. A very busy place. Luckily nearly all of her shifts were days so it mostly coincided with Izzy's schedule. She talked easily about her duties and some of the cases she worked.

"I was on duty when they brought in Ian Andrews," Alana said. "He's a funny guy."

Cooper nodded. "I've talked to him a couple times, he seems like a decent sort."

"Yeah, well, he was awful lucky. That whole thing could have ended pretty badly, from what I heard about it."

Cooper and Izzy looked at each other. "Yeah, he was lucky." Cooper agreed.

Cooper then made a conscious effort to talk about things other than his and Izzy's job; it was too easy to get started and stay on that subject all night. Alana didn't like it, and it was clear to him that she preferred to stay completely away from the subject of law enforcement. He wondered how they would keep their relationship alive if Alana couldn't handle Izzy's profession.

In the back of his mind was his concern for Madeline. It simmered along as the talk turned to upcoming plans for summer vacations. Izzy and Alana were planning a week long cruise to Alaska and were excited by the prospect.

"Have you ever been to Alaska, Scotty?" Alana asked.

"No, Los Gatos is as far north as I've been," he said with a laugh. "But I wouldn't mind seeing Alaska. I hear it's full of beautiful scenery. Never been on a cruise either."

"Well, we're going in two months and eight days, and I can hardly wait," Alana tittered like a school girl. She reached over and squeezed Izzy's hand. Izzy grinned.

"Hey, *amigo*, when this is over maybe you can take the lovely Ms. Abbott on a trip like this…eh?"

"What?! What's going on?" Alana looked at Cooper with her brows raised.

Cooper frowned at Izzy. "Don't start that now."

Izzy sighed and blinked. "Our friend, Scotty, needs to take a vacation, I think. Get away." She looked at Cooper. "Just saying that having someone to go with is a lot more fun than going alone, am I right?" Then she said to Alana with a grin, "I'll fill you in later."

Cooper wondered what he *would* do with his vacation this year. He only had one week. He supposed he could go back to home to visit family. The idea of that left a pall of loneliness over him. Everyone would jump on him about Angie, the blame would start. No, not Texas. But then, if he didn't go home, there would be no end of hell to pay.

Take Madeline? Oh Christ, he scoffed to himself. I doubt that very seriously...

Before he knew it his watch told him it was nine-forty. He helped clear the table and under protestation left without helping wash dishes.

* * *

Willis hated the night shift and constantly bitched whenever he was scheduled so everyone knew it. It wasn't like he had the night shift all that often, but in his mind having it at all was having it too much. He had been on the force for fourteen years and had never managed to advance further than uniform officer level. Willis blamed the situation on women officers. What other answer could there be? It had to be fucking equal opportunity he grumbled to himself for the hundredth time. Why were women in law enforcement anyway? The subject infuriated him.

Now, here was Cooper pushing his own work on *him*. Why doesn't he drive out to that massive dump and check out the lady if he's so worried? He jammed a new toothpick in his mouth. Fuck it. He took off on patrol. I'll go *if* I get time, he decided.

They met for the finalization of the plan. The twins were much less enthusiastic since the murder of Diane Kenyon. After all, she was their age, younger even. Twenty-three. And she was dead. And no one seemed to even know who or why.

"What do you have with you?" William asked.

Ben said, "I have a three fifty-seven and plenty of ammo, William, what else do I need?"

"Where did you get it?"

Ben was affronted. "I have connections, don't you worry about that."

William shrugged. "Fine. Sounds like you are set. David? What about you?"

David's face was sheet white. He looked ill. "I was able to get a twenty-two pistol."

Ben looked at David with a sneer. "We wouldn't be in this position if you had been able to do what you said you could, namely get her to come back and stop the divorce shit."

David came alive and responded hotly, "I did everything I could. What'd you want me to do, beat the hell outta her? You think she wouldn't have called the cops on me? I tried to scare her, tried to spook her. Thought if she got scared and everything, being at the old place alone, she'd want me to come help."

"Yeah well, she didn't scare did she?" Ben looked at David with contempt. "You made it sound like you would get the whole estate." He made a snorting noise. "But you couldn't, could you? Shit, you couldn't even kill the old woman."

William broke in. "There's no time to go into that now. Quit your bickering. If we want to get this done, we have to get started. The girls are going to park on the road as lookout. They're going out before us. You two are going into the house. Ben? You have the key?"

Ben gave a malevolent smile that turned his handsome face ugly. "Yeah, I got it. That dork, Willy Temple, is such a dumb ass he wasn't even suspicious—didn't ask a single question." He laughed rudely. "He *likes* David. I told him that David had his feelings hurt, waaah, because the locks were changed and he couldn't get in anymore. He snagged the key outta his old granny's purse, went down to ACE hardware and copied it. Had it back in thirty minutes. I only paid him fifty bucks too."

David Dean looked at William and said: "Have you written the ransom note?"

"It's done. Ben has it."

"What about Mom?" Ben asked.

"She's at your house and that's where she stays. She's our alibi. She's calling in enough pizza for all of us, just like we're having a party. Everyone's cars will be parked there. We're taking two 'borrowed' cars."

"You mean the two your friend stole?" Ben snickered. "We better hope the cops don't ever find that one we used to mow down Andrews or they'll find evidence on it and we'll be sunk."

"Just shut up, Ben. Learn to keep your fucking mouth shut when you should." Ben's faced reddened and he scowled.

"Anyway, we go back to Helen's house after. Looks like we're all set."

* * *

The stolen cars were two completely nondescript beater sedans, both very small. The one the girls drove stank of beer and vomit. The other was so small that the three men were crowded in like sardines. David, in the back seat had to wedge himself in sideways. The car's right front fender was badly crunched from its crash into Ian Andrews' Mercedes.

The men each dressed in all black clothing, black knit caps. They wore gloves and had the weapons in a small carry bag. It never occurred to the girls or David, to ask where they would be taking Madeline during the time she was to be held captive until the 'ransom' was paid. Being with Madeline again, the opportunity to show her how changed he was—and easy money—danced in David's head. In Ben's head was the fulfillment of years of rage. And money.

Willis had been on duty for only a short while when he thought again about Cooper's request. It had been a quiet shift so far, he had no real reason not to do as Cooper requested. His nature compelled him to be obstinate.

He had written a speeding ticket, two parking tickets and he had pulled an old drunk off the streets downtown. Son. Of. A. *Bitch*. He really didn't want to drive out to the sticks and check up on somebody who would likely be asleep. He glanced at his watch. Ten-forty. Hmm. Maybe I'll get a coffee before I drive out. Maybe I'll get a call to another situation, and I won't have to go at all. Willis tittered. Oh, yeah...

Kammie and Kassie pulled off the edge of the rural road about twenty yards from the stone columns which flanked the drive up to Raven's Nest. It was very dark and there was light, chilly rain falling. They had been instructed to keep the car radio off, not to use their phones, and to slide down in the seats so that in the unlikely chance that a car passed the driver wouldn't see anyone. Their job was to keep an eye on the road after the men got to the mansion and alert them by text if anyone showed up. Simple.

That was well and good for the first five minutes of their duties. By that time they were bored senseless and one of them, who knows which, decided it was time to spice things up. She dove for her bag.

"What the hell are you doing?" the other one asked with a giggle.

"I'm not going to sit here bored out of my mind for God knows how long without a bit of diversion," the other responded.

"You didn't bring the pens did ya?" the second K girl asked with another giggle.

The first K girl dug in her ten gallon Michael Kors handbag and pulled her hand out with a flourish. "Of course I did!"

In her fist was a baggie with four slender black vapor pens. The twin in the passenger seat popped up and looked out the car windows, warily, as if a DEA agent was going to suddenly appear and draw a weapon on them. Darkness everywhere. They could barely make out the mansion up the hill. "Well.... Oh, fuck it. Sure, why not? They aren't even here yet, anyway," the girl in the passenger seat said.

K girl number one handed a pen to K girl number two and they simultaneously clicked them on. Within a couple of minutes, the girls were vaping THC oil with relish.

"Ah...," K girl number one exclaimed.

"You know, they didn't take me seriously when I said I was pissed that we hadn't gotten the money we were promised. Do they think these babies come cheap? Hell no," K girl number two complained.

"I know. The last ones I bought were $175 a pop," K girl number one replied. "I don't think it would go over well if we went to Mom and said, 'Look Mom, we're out of dope, can you spare a few hundred?'" This remark brought both to a fit of laughter.

Then K girl number two leaned back and scrunched against the seat in the smelly car and agreed, "Mmm.... Better." They both slid down just as instructed. "Maybe in a few minutes, we won't notice how putrid this car smells." That produced another fit of giggles.

They busily vaped and by the time the rest of the crew arrived thirty minutes later, the two K girls were too stoned to know it, or care.

Ben, David and William pulled into the driveway to Raven's Nest by eleven. They saw the car the twins were driving, parked off the edge of the road just as they were told. William could see no sight of them. At least they were paying attention to what they were told to do. With headlights off, they drove up the winding drive past the porte-cochere and made a large circle to point the car backward down the drive. Silently the three men got out with their weapons bag and approached the back door.

At the door William motioned them to stop. It looked like all lights were off in the mansion. "She's here, isn't she?" William whispered.

"Where else would she be?" Ben asked. "She was supposed to come back today, right David?"

"I didn't talk to her. She left a message on my phone saying she was leaving Eugene to come back here. I called her back but she never picked up. That's all I know."

"Maybe she's out on a *date*." Ben sniggered at David. Ben rarely missed an opportunity to push David's buttons. Their once close friendship had soured over the last couple of years each believing it was the fault of the other. Ben was aware of David's raw nerves where Madeline was concerned and got a great deal of pleasure in insinuating things about her just to enjoy the rise it got from David.

"She's not out on a fucking date," David snarled at him. "What are you saying?"

"Shut up, both of you. Keep it down." Once again, a bad feeling rose in William about the whole mission. These two are too volatile, unable to keep their emotions under control. I could pull the plug now before we go further.... He recalled what Helen had told him and with a reluctant sigh, headed up the stairs.

Ben pulled out the copy of the new key. William took the key and slowly turned it in the lock. "I'm going to stay here by the door. You go on and get it done." He gave Ben a significant look, which Ben returned with a nod.

* * *

Willis got his coffee and a couple doughnuts but, damn it, had had no more calls. It was five minutes till eleven. With a dispirited sigh and a gigantic belch, he pointed his cruiser toward Raven's Nest. He arrived shortly after eleven. He saw a sedan parked on the shoulder a few dozen yards down the road from the drive, but could see no one in it. Maybe someone ran outta gas, he reasoned. Sensing something, he turned off his cruiser lights. He crept slowly up the drive and to the porte-cochere where he spied a beater sedan, pointing the opposite direction. Ready for a quick get away. This looked like no car he could imagine being in *this* place. He radioed in the plate. In just a moment or two it came back stolen. He called Cooper.

After the unintended nap—that lasted more almost four hours—Madeline got out of the shower feeling a little better but her head spun. She braced herself against the wall and dried off. I should probably eat something, might make me feel better. In her bedroom, she saw the diary lying on the bed where she had dropped it. She squeezed her eyes closed to block the image. She swayed like a leaf in a breeze.

All she wanted, she realized, was another glass of wine. So that's it, I'm giving up. I can't handle this shit anymore, and I just want to give up.

She opened her closet and saw a set of flannel pjs on a hook by the old blue bathrobe. She reached past them and pulled out a pale green silk nightgown and matching robe and slipped them on. Where is that handsome detective now that I'm dressed decently? She tried to twirl in the generously flowing silk. OOOh, my head…nope. She laughed softly as she steadied herself.

Pancho met her on the stairs. He was agitated. He wandered down a few steps and back up, nudging her hand and whining low and quiet. She paid him no mind but steadied herself by holding on tightly to the stair rail and continued toward the library. The pale green gown and robe flowed and swirled around her, ghostly in the darkness. She paused at the bottom of the stairs and detoured to the kitchen, going past the billiard room to the east kitchen doorway, closest to the refrigerator. A couple pieces of cheese will do me a world of good, especially if I'm going to have more wine.

She and Pancho stopped in the hall outside the kitchen, Pancho making a faint noise in his throat. Madeline heard another noise. A muted screech that sounded like the metal stools at the table. Then came a sound of a person sitting on the stools, a muffled creak. She inched into the kitchen doorway just far enough to peer around the edge of the cupboard. There was a man sitting on one a stool, his back to the back door. There were two more about to leave the kitchen and enter the hallway by way of the door opposite her. She pulled Pancho quickly through the door to the pantry and seconds later the two men glided silently past as they made their way down the hall. They came within a couple of feet of her. The stench of smoke hung in the air after them. Pancho began a low noise again. Madeline knelt down and whispered to him, "Shush, Pancho, you have to be quiet."

Silently she edged back out into the hall and looked around the corner again into the kitchen. She couldn't see through the murky darkness well enough to identify the person sitting at the table. She edged back and tugged on Pancho's collar to make him sit.

Fury was gathering into a molten knot in her chest. The fucking bastards are *in my house again!* She stood perfectly still trying to decide what she could do. How in the hell did they get keys, *new keys!* Goddamn it!

I've got to call Cooper. Oh *hell*, my cell phone is upstairs in my room. If I go to retrieve it, I might run into them. I don't know where they are, upstairs or down. Or where they're going, and more importantly, *why*. Well they're obviously not here for a social visit. They're here to steal or to hurt me or both. If I can get to my phone, I can get the police. Without a weapon going upstairs is out of the question. However, I *am* close to the gun room…

Back at his apartment, after dinner with Izzy and Alana, Cooper checked his voicemail and saw nothing from Madeline. He tried not to overreact. He paced.

To distract himself, he thought the case over for the hundredth time. In his mind he went over the statements that had been made, picking at this fact, that remark. Something they'd missed or not paid attention to floated around the edges of his brain. If only he could——he abruptly stopped pacing. It was something Selwyn said when Cooper had gone back to his office to talk with him further, something that had clicked in the back of his mind when he said it. About Eleanor's cancer......what had he said? He said, '*I wish I had known*'. When Selwyn said it, it had sounded like extreme frustration at being left out, not being trusted with the sorrowful news, not being there to help.

Cooper knew he had heard the same comment or something like it somewhere before...who had said it? Someone they had talked to in the last week. Someone said...*what?* What *was* it?

He paced the living room of his small apartment. He retrieved a beer from the refrigerator and continued mulling as he paced.

It was a similar comment he had heard from some other person connected with the case. It was not what had been said, but the way in which it was said. Finally, it came into focus. It was the same comment Helen Highwater had made when she heard about Eleanor's having cancer. 'I wish I would have known.' It had sounded so odd at the time, so cold. As if she meant something different than the meaning of those simple words. It was the tone with which Helen said it? Did it mean that things would have been handled differently had she, Helen, known Eleanor was dying?

Was Eleanor murdered in revenge for the perceived wrongs of having had an affair with Greg? An affair which led to Eleanor's pregnancy. An affair which led to Greg and Helen's marital problems. Which in turn, exacerbated Greg's guilt, depression and suicide. And, ultimately, led to Ben's mental and emotional problems.

Cooper felt sick. He continued pacing. How does this relate to Dean? The threats and the attempt made on Madeline proved that Eleanor's death did not end things, it was not the only and ultimate goal. But how was it all connected?

Madeline is in danger, why else would there have been the break-in, the threatening letter? She tried to brush it off, make as if it were a child's prank. He was certain now that it was not that. It was either an attempt to frighten Madeline, or a true threat, which meant that someone was going to make another attempt on her life. The fact that he hadn't been able to get her on the phone terrified him.

Cooper made one more call to Madeline. It was after eleven now, but again there was no answer. He was sure something was wrong. She would not have ignored all these calls. Surely she wouldn't.

Cooper flinched when the cell phone in his hand rang. His first thought, Madeline. But it was worse. It was Willis. He listened as he hurriedly dressed, pulled on his boots and got his shoulder holster. Then he called Izzy.

"Jesus Christ, Cooper, what the friggin' hell? I'm sleeping!" Izzy answered after seeing the caller ID.

"Izzy, I just got a call from Willis. He drove out to the house. There is a sedan there, plates say it's stolen. He says there are no lights on. He's waiting for us and back up. I think I know what's been going on."

Izzy was already pulling on clothes. "I'm on my way."

Alana, awake now, sat up. "What's going on?"

Morales strapped on her weapon and put on a jacket. "Something's going on out at the Abbott house. Scotty's on his way out there. Everything's okay. Go back to sleep. I'll be home soon as I can."

"Sleep. Right," Alana said and pulled on her robe. "As if."

"Stay by the phone then. I'll call." Izzy kissed her.

Using only a small penlight, Ben and David crept through the kitchen. David motioned them left out of the kitchen, and down the back hallway to the gallery so they could check the billiard room. David knew Madeline liked the room and in fact had watched movies with her there. A long time ago now. The room was empty and dark. They continued silently until they came to the foot of the stairs and David motioned for them to go up. At the landing, they stopped. David whispered, "She must be in her bedroom. It's the third door on the right." He had no sooner whispered the words than the very faint, muffled sound of a cell phone ring could be heard. They both darted up to the top of the stairs and over against the paneled wall to be completely in darkness.

"It's coming from her room," David hissed. "I don't hear her talking."

"Let's get in there," Ben replied, his voice barely audible.

* * *

Cooper had never driven out to Raven's Nest so fast. Thankfully there was very little traffic and once out of town, none at all. He turned off his lights before turning in and proceeded up the drive until he was parked behind Willis' cruiser.

Willis was crouched behind his cruiser with his service weapon drawn.

"What's happening?" Cooper asked quietly.

"I don't see anything at all. There's no sound, no lights. If there's someone in there besides Ms. Abbott I don't see no sign of it."

Cooper studied the mansion. It did look as if the household was peacefully asleep. The house was totally dark, eerily so. But why a dump of a car, a stolen one at that, parked on the drive? His first thought was maybe David had somehow come to the house and forced Madeline into something. His mind was reaching for a link to what he now believed was happening.

"Willis, stay where you are and wait for Morales, she's on her way. I'm going to take a look around the back."

Willis, amazingly without comment, nodded and remained crouched down.

Not knowing what to expect, the detective edged around the corner of the northwest corner of the mansion. With his weapon drawn he made a circuit of the sedan, there was no one. He slid along the wall of the house until he came to the single window that was west of the door in the kitchen. Carefully he peered around the edge of the window. At the wooden table a figure sat on one of the stools, a man with his back to the door. Cooper couldn't make out who it was, but in the murky light he was able to make out the gleam of a hand gun resting on the man's thigh.

Madeline held on to Pancho's collar like a life line and hurried to the gun room. In one cabinet were three handguns that her Dad had taught her to fire. She picked the Smith & Wesson .38 revolver. She had not fired it for almost three years, but it fit her hand well and the grip felt secure. There was a box of bullets in the drawer. She loaded it with shaking hands and hurried back to the door. The longer she thought about the situation the more furious she became. If they think they can just waltz into *my* home, whoever they are, to hurt me, to steal from me, they have another think coming.

Through a bare slit of an opening of the door, she peered down the hall and listened carefully. There were very slight noises now upstairs. Slight and muffled creaks and squeaks like careful footsteps on the carpet runners or doors opening and closing. Madeline had to strain to hear them. Instead of going toward the billiard room she went back to the kitchen with Pancho in tow. At the kitchen door she again edged around the corner. The man was gone from the table. He must be upstairs. I'll wait for them in the library and shoot them all when they come down. Fury propelling her, she was no longer aware if her thoughts made sense nor what the consequences might be. The anger she felt was so overwhelming and sense of violation so complete, she didn't care if she killed them. She just wanted to repay their intrusion in kind. After she shot them, she'd go back to the library and have that glass of wine. Madeline continued down the hallway and turned left toward the main hall.

Cooper watched as the man left the kitchen. He quickly went to the corner and looked down the drive, and saw that Morales had pulled up. He jogged down to the cars.

"Alright. There is one man I just saw sitting in the kitchen. He's armed. Couldn't tell who he is but he left the kitchen just now. There's no sign of Madeline. I'm going to make entry through the back door and head to the main foyer and unlock the front door. Izzy, I want you and Willis to keep your eyes on that front door and make sure no one exits that way. When I unlock it I want you to spread out in the foyer and gallery area, but try to stay out of sight. We don't know if there is more than one of them, but in all likelihood there will be. Izzy, if you haven't already called for back up, do that now before you make entry."

Cooper hurried back to the kitchen door and after confirming the room was still empty he silently let himself in. He slipped off his boots and padded noiselessly up the hall to the foyer and unlocked the front door. Noiselessly, Morales and Willis came in and spread out, weapons drawn. It was quiet. He signaled that he was going to check the other rooms downstairs. He headed to the ladies' parlor.

Ben and David approached the door to Madeline's room. David opened the door slowly and used the pen light to look around the room. Madeline was not there. Her cell phone rested on the bureau. David picked it up and pressed the button to light the screen. It showed a missed call from Scott Cooper. David exploded.

"Fuck! The stupid bitch, she thinks I'm going to put up with this shit?" He seethed with rage, as Ben leaped on him and put his hand over David's mouth.

"David, you damn jackass, you've gotta be quiet. We don't want her to know we're here until *we* want her to know. Where's she likely to be?"

"I don't know, and I don't give a flying fuck." David stood in the darkness looking at Madeline's cell phone as if he were considering hurling it against the wall.

"Well, you'd better care, buddy, this was partly your thing remember, you wanted this."

William pushed open the door clearly exasperated. "What in the hell is taking so long?" he whispered.

"She's not here. Everything's dark so we aren't sure where to go from here. David says he doesn't know where she might be."

"Well, it's too bad this isn't a little tract house in Timbuctoo that you can look over in two minutes, but it isn't. So let's look around up here, make sure she's not in another bedroom. Come on, hustle, make it quick."

In the library, Madeline took up a position inside of the double pocket doors, to the left. She could see the end of the stairs and most of the main hall from there. The house was deathly quiet, with the exception of very soft and random creaks, clicks and muted squeaks seemingly emanating from upstairs. But she couldn't be sure where the sounds came from. The only thing she was positive of was that the intruders weren't in the library.

She heard no one speaking. Suddenly Pancho was up, stiffly at attention with a low noise in his throat again. As Madeline watched, a tall man crept up the hall from the direction of the kitchen toward the front of the house and unlocked the front door. She could see he was armed. She raised her gun. As she tried to aim, she realized he looked familiar.

Madeline stood staring, astonished. It looked like Detective Cooper. He opened the door and from the light coming in through the front windows she saw Morales and a uniformed police officer enter quickly. Finally, after having had quite enough an ear splitting series of bellowing barks erupted from Pancho. Loud, commanding and ferocious.

* * *

The three men spread out and quickly and efficiently made a circuit of most the the second floor and realized that Madeline was not going to be found there. Ben told William that he and David had already checked the billiard room. That still left several possibilities: the ladies parlor, the west parlor, the library, the music room and the conservatory. There were other rooms but David thought these were the most likely.

"Why is the whole house dark?" Ben asked. "If she's not sleeping, I mean."

William looked at Ben and whispered, "You have a limited imagination, Ben. There could be any number of reasons why she would be sitting somewhere without the lights on. Anyway David, how do I get back to the kitchen the quickest?"

David pointed to the end of the hall. "There's a back stair that takes you right there. You want the left one. The the middle one goes to the conservatory and the other one leads to the ladies' parlor."

William walked down the hall and was quickly swallowed by the darkness.

"Okay, let's go find her," Ben whispered.

They were at the top of the stairs when violent, bellowing barking tore through the silence. Chaos began.

"What the fuck? That's the goddamned dog! Wherever he is, that's where Madeline is," David screamed. David and Ben ran hurriedly down the main stair to the landing. Suddenly, cruiser headlights with light bar flashing and siren blaring came up the mansion drive. The lights shone through the front windows illuminating the foyer. David saw the two armed officers and called shrilly to Ben, "Cops! Ben, the cops are down there!"

Willis, standing just to the right of the stair, was silhouetted and utterly exposed. Willis saw the men on the landing were armed. He raised his weapon, assumed his stance and aimed at the two men. He cried out, "Stop! Los Gatos PD! Put down your weapons!"

Morales saw the two on the landing at the moment the headlights lighted the foyer. Cooper, running up the gallery from the back of the house saw Madeline appear in the foyer, near the entry to the library. Madeline raised her gun and aimed at David. Pancho was standing in front of her in a rigid stance barking furiously upward toward the stairs.

Willis boomed out again, *"Put down your weapons!* Los Gatos PD!" Ben swiveled and pointed his 357 at Willis. David turned and pointed his twenty-two at Madeline. Morales reacted instinctively. She dove toward Willis and fired her weapon at Ben as the gun in his hand went off. Willis was stunned to find himself on the floor and a wounded Morales lying on top of him. Cooper watched them go down in slow motion.

Nearly simultaneously he called to Madeline, "Don't, Madeline, put your gun down." And in a fluid motion he aimed his weapon and fired, sending the gun in David's hand flying before David had the chance to pull the trigger. David screamed out and grasped his hand. Momentum caused him to fly backwards and crash into the suit of armor, cursing and crying. The armor created a loud crashing sound like cymbals. Ben, who had been standing close to the top stair, crumpled to the ground then continued a painful bouncing journey to the bottom of the stairs, screaming and holding his right arm.

After the clanging of the medieval armor and the deafening sounds of the gunshots, Madeline stood with her firearm now at her side looking in shock at the scene in front of her. Her head swinging to the right, then the left then up the stairs and down to the bodies. She watched as Detective Cooper ran to where Madeline could see two people lying in a tangled heap on the floor. She sat abruptly down on the black and white marble tiles. Pancho's barking had stuttered to a near stop punctuated by occasional chuffing and snuffling. Finally, he laid beside her, his head in her lap. The tile was cold to her skin. Madeline began to shiver.

Cooper knelt by Morales. She was bleeding heavily from a wound to her left shoulder. Willis, back to his senses, said, "Is she okay, Cooper? Oh, shit, oh shit. Sonofabitch...is it bad?"

Cooper pulled her jacket back and saw that she had taken the hit about an inch below her collar bone near her left shoulder. She moaned. Back up officers were coming in the front door. Cooper screamed at them to call for an ambulance. He told Willis to go find a couple of towels in the kitchen. He was back in less than a minute. A record for him, Cooper thought.

Willis pulled off his own jacket, folded it and slipped it under Izzy's head.

"Hey *amigo*, did we get them?" Morales whispered to Cooper.

He put one towel under her shoulder. He could feel warmth of Izzy's blood as it flowed rapidly through his fingers. Using the other towel he applied pressure to the wound. He tried not to cry when he responded, "Yeah, Izzy, you're damned right we got them."

"Is Madeline...is Madeline alright? Her words slurred.

"She's fine, Izzy. Don't talk now, don't worry about anything." He turned to the officers who were wrapping the wounds on Ben and David. "Where the hell is that ambulance?"

"It's coming, detective. Any second." They finished the temporary bandaging and cuffed them.

"You tell Alana, *amigo*, you tell her......" Izzy lost consciousness. Cooper pressed the towel harder against the wound and began to pray. He heard the ambulance siren.

William had slipped out the back door as soon as he heard Pancho's bark. By the time he got in the stolen sedan and headed down the driveway the back up officer's cars were pulling in. He had no where to go. He was arrested.

The Deardon twins were an easy arrest. In fact, they missed all the excitement. Once the others were detained two officers approached the car, one on each side. One tapped on a window. No reply. They each opened the front doors and found both K girls snoring in their respective seats, clutching their vaping pens. The two officers looked up at each other across the top of the small sedan and burst out laughing.

CHAPTER ELEVEN
Friday

Izzy went into surgery Friday morning at about three. She had sustained a devastating wound from the .357 magnum. In her favor was her youth, her fitness and general health. Still, she was in surgery a long time.

Cooper sat in the waiting room with Alana, both of them stone faced. Before five, Willis showed up and sat beside them.

"How's she doing?" he asked solemnly, his face grey and slack.

"They say she lost quite a bit of blood. I guess the round did a lot of damage," Cooper answered.

"Is she going to be okay?" Willis' voice shook.

"I don't know."

"D'ya suppose I can give blood?"

Cooper was so surprised, he turned and stared at the man. "I'm sure they would be happy to take your blood, Willis, whether or not it's a good match for Izzy, it will be a help to someone."

"If she hadn't tackled me, it would be me in that operating room. Or on a slab at the morgue."

Cooper stared at him hard. "I know. She was doing her job, Willis."

Willis nodded without speaking. Finally, he got up and trudged off, disappearing down the hall.

Cooper leaned over with his arms on his knees and stared at the floor. Alana, all cried out, rested her head on his shoulder.

"The guy is a surprise. He's always been so hard on Izzy…, funny how something like this changes your perspective," Cooper said.

Alana looked at Cooper and smiled wanly. "No offense Scotty, but men are difficult. If it's not their macho upbringing it's their so-called friends that they feel they have to act out for. Maybe Willis isn't such a hard ass after all."

They sat for a long while in silence. *If they don't tell me something pretty soon I'm going to*—Cooper's thoughts were interrupted.

"Hi, Scott." Madeline stood in front of him with an arrangement of flowers.

That was the first time he ever heard her use his first name without him requesting it. It made his heart ache even more. He stood and they looked at each other for several long moments. She stepped forward and took him in her arms. "Thank you, so much. You saved my life. I'm sorry about Detective Morales."

He returned the hug and held her fiercely. Cooper fought the tears that burned his eyes.

Cooper had the presence of mind to introduce Madeline to Alana. She took Alana's hand, held it and said softly, "Alana, I'm so very sorry."

They all sat back on the bench. Madeline said, "What have you heard?"

"Nothing. It's been a very long time. Alana and me…well, I don't know what to do."

She took Cooper's hand and held it. "We'll all wait together."

* * *

The next afternoon the temperature was mild, the sun was out and only a few puffy white clouds marred a perfect sky. The crowd that converged on the Unity Church in Palo Alto was impressive, and it frankly surprised Madeline. She gave the eulogy at her mother's service talking about who her mother was and what a strong and generous person she was. It overwhelmed her, mostly because she found herself meaning all the things she said. She also spoke about her father and how much her parents loved each other. She hoped they were at peace now. It was a difficult thing, but she made it through without so much as a pencil to hold in her hands.

She greeted all the attendees, a task which she found emotionally grueling. All the close friends of her parents (well, almost all), hugged Madeline and whispered condolences and good wishes to her. Arthur Selwyn was in tears.

"Maddie, I loved your mother so much. Did you know that? She was a very important part of my life. I miss her," he said simply.

Madeline nodded to him, tears in her eyes as well. "I know Arthur. I do too."

James Edgerton came by near the end of the line and shook Madeline's hand with sincerity.

"I'm very sorry, Madeline, I really am. Your mother and I didn't always agree, but I worked with her for years. Even if we didn't see eye to eye, I knew she was an honest person, an upfront person. I think I made her angry in the last few years, and I regret that. I didn't do enough to meet her halfway. I'm so sorry. I will miss her." Madeline believed him.

By his own design, Detective Scott Cooper was the last person in line. He took her hand and said, "I told you we would get them, Madeline. It's a relief to know you're safe now."

"How is Izzy?" Madeline asked.

"She's still in recovery. She's weak, but they think she'll be okay."

Madeline smiled at him. "I'm so glad, detective."

Cooper winced inwardly at the formality of her tone to him. He acknowledged his feelings for her to himself. Cooper thought she was a woman he wanted to know. He decided to risk it.

"I would really like to take you to supper sometime, once things have settled down for you. Please call me."

Later

Isabelle Morales was in the hospital for two weeks. However, by the fifth day, she was complaining at every meal about the food and had nothing good to say about the coffee either. It was at that point Cooper breathed a sigh of relief. He took to sneaking in a latté each day to her, and once brought in one of the big—as—your—head fritters she was so fond of. She was ecstatic and was able to eat almost all of it before dozing off.

Del Willis visited Izzy every day. He brought fresh flower arrangements several times and was introduced to Alana. They sat in Izzy's room, a curious threesome. They played cards, rummy or poker, nearly every day. They used toothpicks for betting.

Frank Van Gessler confessed and was indicted for the murder of Diane Kenyon. Cooper had been right. Diane Kenyon discovered the embezzlement and had been blackmailing Van Gessler for months. At first it was small amounts, a few thousand here, a few there. Just enough to keep her in some designer clothes.

According to Van Gessler, the pressure kept mounting with Kenyon becoming greedy when she saw her success at the scheme. She kept asking for more and more. When she found out she was pregnant with David's child, she told him she had to have $500,000.00. She had confided to Van Gessler that she believed she could convince Dean to leave with her and had to have a half million.

When Cooper heard this tidbit, her naiveté astonished him. But, when Van Gessler heard it, two weeks prior to her murder, it sealed her fate. Van Gessler realized he was in a no-win situation. All he could see was years ahead, of Kenyon threatening exposure and wringing him dry of resources. You just never know what a person is capable of when pressure overwhelms.

Along with murder charges Frank Van Gessler was charged with embezzlement and conspiracy. Kathryn Van Gessler claimed no knowledge of any of it but with the evidence, both email and cell phone, the prosecutor didn't buy that. She too, was indicted on conspiracy and embezzlement.

Ben Highwater, David Dean, William Gray and Helen Highwater were indicted on conspiracy, attempted murder, burglary and grand theft. Ben had the added charge of first degree murder of Eleanor Abbott. Because David was present at the time of Eleanor's murder he faced an additional charge of accessory to murder.

The trials wouldn't commence for a long while. There was a great deal of legal wrangling. Expensive, high powered attorneys were hired. David Dean, in jail, finally signed the papers for divorce. He had no funds to procure top attorney representation and Madeline was in no frame of mind to help him financially. Nor were any of his co-conspirators. He ended up with court appointed representation. Madeline's and David's divorce was officially granted. Eleanor Abbott's will went into probate.

The Deardon twins were indicted on conspiracy. Phoebe pulled out all the stops and got one of California's best defense attorneys to represent them. There were rumors that the twins' father contributed to their defense expenses. Since their actual participation was limited, Phoebe's attorneys managed to get their charges reduced by the girls agreeing to give evidence against the rest of the group. They would have reduced sentences but were also required to do rehab again. Cooper allowed as how he thought it was a waste, throwing good money after bad, but it wasn't his money, so…

Two weeks after Izzy was released from the hospital, Madeline called Scott. They had not spoken since her mother's funeral. Scott was concerned that he had not heard from her. He wanted to see her but was reluctant to intrude, so he waited. He was excited when she finally called. She said they should go out for dinner, and would he please ask Izzy and Alana. Cooper had had something quite different in mind for his first date with her but agreed and tried to sound enthusiastic.

Cooper made reservations at a swanky restaurant in downtown Los Gatos, and the four of them had a fabulous meal. As Madeline knew it would, conversation came around to the case.

"I don't understand why any of this happened," Alana said. "If Mrs. Highwater had been able to get over her husband's suicide, the anger over the affair with Eleanor, the jealousy, it might have been avoided. Couldn't she see what it was doing to her…and her son?"

Cooper thought differently. "I believe that Ben Highwater was the driving force behind it. He was so destroyed by what happened between his Dad and Eleanor and what it did to his mother *and* his father that I think those feelings of hate and abandonment just festered. Eventually he was old enough to actually do something about it. In fact, it may have been *his* inability to let go that continued to fuel Helen's rage."

"Yeah," Madeline added, "then, unfortunately along the way, they met David. Maybe he was the catalyst, like putting a match to a fuse. They found they were kindred spirits. Devious and manipulative. Different goals, but they certainly thought the same." She shook her head. "All David wanted was to manipulate me, keep me under his control. And the money, of course."

Cooper decided to venture a comment. "So, the divorce is over? It's all settled? You must be feeling good on that score, at least."

Madeline slid a look his way. "Yes, it's finally over. I admit it was truly a relief when the judge made that a legal declaration."

Alana and Izzy exchanged a quick glance.

"How did the painting figure into this?" Alana asked.

Madeline shook her head managed a small laugh. "David was the one who was supposed to do the murder, kill Eleanor. They all agreed that it was his 'duty' to take care of her. His mother-in-law, his problem. I guess he initially agreed to do it but when push came to shove he didn't have the guts. He's always been an awful bully, but it's just a bunch of blow. He decided to take the painting because he knew it was important to me, to my mother. It's very valuable. He figured he could sell it and have more money than he could ever need, in the event anything went wrong. Like an insurance policy. Obviously he never gave it much thought or he would have realized how hard it would have been to find a buyer for a painting like that. Anyway, he went with Ben that night, just to steal the painting."

Cooper looked at Madeline. "Well, it's back now in its rightful place, and I'm glad for that."

Izzy had been quiet. She finally said, "So, what now for you Madeline? What are you going to do, have you decided?"

Madeline looked around the table. "It's hard to leave friends. Besides Raven's Nest, I've inherited another house up on the northern California coast. It needs restoration. So, I guess I have to say, I'm not sure yet. I'm just not sure."

CHAPTER TWELVE
Later that Fall

The wind was gusting as she drove up the serpentine cobbled drive of Raven's Nest. Red-gold leaves fell in swirling drifts from the cottonwoods and maples in the woodland that surrounded the mansion. Madeline loved autumn, especially at the estate. It added to the pervasive, mysterious sense of the place, as grey clouds covered the sun and darkened the stone of the mansion.

It had been over six months since her mother's murder. A long spring and summer saw the recovery of Detective Morales. It went slowly and with (seemingly) never ending physical therapy. Izzy and Alana went on their much anticipated Alaskan cruise with Izzy getting stronger every day. While Izzy was out on leave, Del Willis was 'partnered' with Cooper, much to Cooper's dismay. Why didn't they give him Ginny Bell? In the end, he decided his best move would be to do all he could to have a positive influence on the bruiser. Cooper did see minor improvements. Nothing like a brush with death to change one's attitude.

Madeline began, with tentative steps, learning the ropes of her mother and dad's vast business interests along side James Edgerton. During the summer James Edgerton married Christina Bradshaw, a woman less than half his age, with whom he had been sporadically—and secretly—dating for two years. Her divorce had just been finalized. They dated while she was still married. During the investigation he had been petrified that that would become public knowledge. Since that happy event, he was (almost) a joy to work with.

Madeline's company won the bid on the Litchfield restoration. In order to manage everything, she had come up with what she felt was an ingenious plan. She offered a part interest in Pacific Northwest Designs, jointly to Charles, Cally and Nadine. They would own one half of the company with Charles the on site President. The first thing Charles did was formally show the Carsons the door.

The three had all the day-to-day decision making responsibilities but could contact Madeline at any time if they felt the need for further input. Madeline was technically still overseeing the Litchfield project until its completion, spending every other weekend in Eugene, conferring with the group. In between those weekends lots of time was spent exchanging information via email and phone. After that restoration project was finished, the transition would be complete. The sub contractors had managed to get a great deal of the exterior work finished during the good weather months. As winter approached they would be focusing on interiors.

Just after the end of the case and before she had begun reading her mother's diaries, Scott Cooper's persistence paid off, and Madeline agreed to a date with him. Alone.

Scott took Madeline to a restaurant where they dined on tapas, sampled wines of different vintages, and in general had a marvelous time. She enjoyed being with him. She felt...secure. And with David in jail, she had no more worries about him. They were divorced. It was over. With Scott there was no badgering, no bullying. He was so different from David. They talked easily as if they were old friends. Well weren't they, Madeline thought, after everything we've been through together?

They avoided talking about the case and focused on understanding more about each other. Scott learned more about Madeline's life and more about Raven's Nest. She learned more about Scott and about the great state of Texas. Turns out, she might just want to visit there. Sometime.

When they returned to the mansion, it was late, and both were slightly tipsy from the wine. Scott escorted her to the front door, holding her hand. She unlocked the door and turned to say goodnight. Scott pulled her close and said, "You know, Maddie, I've been wanting to kiss you since you gave me a room to bunk in that night."

Madeline responded archly, "Oh? I thought you did kiss me......Scott."

He put his mouth on hers and kissed her long and slow. Her heart escalated till she nearly went into an old fashioned swoon.

They parted. "Not like that I didn't," Scott said softly.

They bid each other a reluctant good night.

Madeline began reading her mother's diaries. She was still reluctant to know what the diaries held, but she realized that in order to put demons to rest she had to know everything she could about Eleanor and Clay.

In many ways it was more than she had bargained for. The adoption she knew about. The circumstances, she did not. As she read the passages about Clay, her heart broke. She loved her father and now to know that he was, in fact, her actual father, it was nearly more than Madeline could bear. The diary also gave the name of her mother. Madeline was stunned.

As she continued to read, the affair was revealed between Eleanor and Greg. The murder trials wouldn't begin for probably a year, and the media details concerning the part Eleanor and Greg's relationship had played in the events had been vague. In the diaries was the truth, the details there for her to read. It became painfully obvious to Madeline that you can never know the inner workings of the relationships of others. No matter how close you are. Her parents had made mistakes and paid a very heavy price.

It surprised Madeline that the detective had not enlightened her about the triangle that was Eleanor, Greg and Helen. Scott had kept secrets it seemed. No doubt to protect her.

The most frightening and heart rending revelation was the circumstances surrounding the death of her brother, Michael.

Madeline carried intense guilt for years about having left Michael alone by the pool, even if it was for less than five minutes. She had heard the phone ring and raced down the steps to the extension that sat on a patio table, outside the kitchen door. When she answered the person hung up. By the time she was back up the hillside, Michael was floating face down in the pool.

Eleanor wrote in a cool and detached way about the fact that she was hidden, outside the fenced and hedged enclosure that surrounded the pool near the top of the hill above the house. She used her mobile phone to ring the house number. Eleanor secretly watched as Madeline sternly told Michael to stay in his chair then flew down the steps. Eleanor then calmly walked into the pool area and pushed Michael in the water and held him under. Afterward, she walked back out of the enclosure and down one of the wildlife paths that led down the hill through the woodland toward the road where she had left her car. She sat, shaking, screaming and sobbing until she heard the sound of sirens. Eleanor then wiped her face and pulled up the winding drive to face the disaster of her son's accidental death.

She wrote that in no way was she excusing her behavior, but she wanted to attempt to explain. It was the only way to release the boy from his suffering. During this irrational period she believed that she had gone insane. What else could account for her actions? She felt that if the boy was gone, the evidence of her mistakes and awfulness would disappear. Perhaps whatever maddening curse had befallen the family would be over.

In later entries, it was apparent that Eleanor finally came to her senses and realized the insanity, the horror, the selfishness of her choices. She had always intended to tell Madeline the truth. She was terrified at how it would change Madeline's feelings toward her. Guilt and sorrow never left her, even though she tried to undo the damage by dedicating the rest of her life to helping others. There was virtually no extent to which she wouldn't go for friends or family.

Eleanor considered suicide. Entries in the diaries showed that the only reason that suicide never happened was because she saw what it had done to Ben Highwater and didn't want that to happen to Madeline. When she was diagnosed with cancer, she thought it had to be her payment, her penance. She welcomed it. But, it never alleviated the overwhelming guilt.

Madeline continued with the diaries, reading when she felt emotionally strong enough. But the truth about Michael and her father left her grief stricken. After those passages, it was a few weeks before she was able to begin again. How long would it take to read them all? It would take, she decided, just as long as it takes.

Once Madeline began reading the diaries she realized that she had to wait before seeing any more of Scott Cooper. She was enormously attracted to him and wanted to explore a relationship. However, what she had learned about her family had left Madeline on a frazzled, miserable edge of sorrow. She had to have time to sort out her feelings and grieve for Michael and her father all over again. She told Scott truthfully that if he was willing to give her some time, time to sort things out, that she might just go with him to visit Texas. Sometime.

Made in the USA
San Bernardino, CA
21 May 2018